Praise for *The Gathering Table*

"A tender, touching story filled wi[th] [unforgettable char]acters who will sweep you away on a journey of hope, second chances, and new beginnings. As a master chef combines herbs and spices to delight the taste buds, Kathryn Springer skillfully blends multiple story lines to create a rich, satisfying read."
—Irene Hannon, three-time RITA® Award winner and author of the bestselling Hope Harbor series

"Heartwarmingly tender, wise and witty, with prose as lush and delicious as chocolate ganache... I loved it!"
—Linda Goodnight, *New York Times* bestselling author of *The Rain Sparrow*

"In *The Gathering Table*, author Kathryn Springer does what every reader would hope. She delivers a delicious, warm story with the very finest ingredients—unforgettable characters, an imaginative tale but completely real at the same time, and 'plated' beautifully, with elegant simplicity and reason to keep tasting to the very last nibble. Kathryn is a masterful storyteller and this may just be her best yet."
—Cynthia Ruchti, author of *Afraid of the Light*

"In *The Gathering Table*, Kathryn Springer invites us to a setting we'd like to call home and a cast of flawed but endearing characters we'd love to chat (or scrapbook) with. As in all of her novels, Kathryn's hero and heroine take readers on a rollercoaster journey of hope-giving transformation... A story to learn from as well as to savor."
—Becky Melby, author of *Candles in the Rain*

"*The Gathering Table* by Kathryn Springer is one of her best!... With flowing prose that draws you into this wonderful backyard-picnic of a story, Kathryn hands us a feast with small town quirks and values, served up with a side of winsomeness. I loved it!"
—*New York Times* bestselling author Lenora Worth

The Gathering Table

KATHRYN SPRINGER

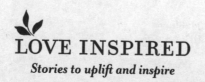

LOVE INSPIRED

Stories to uplift and inspire

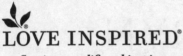

LOVE INSPIRED®

Stories to uplift and inspire

Recycling programs for this product may not exist in your area.

ISBN-13: 978-1-335-40188-5

The Gathering Table

This edition published by arrangement with Harlequin Books S.A.

For questions and comments about the quality of this book, please contact us at CustomerService@Harlequin.com.

Love Inspired
22 Adelaide St. West, 40th Floor
Toronto, Ontario M5H 4E3, Canada
www.Harlequin.com

Printed in U.S.A.

To all the women who've invited me to the table and
taught me that true hospitality is saying "You are welcome here."

O taste and see that the Lord is good.

—*Psalm* 34:8

The Gathering Table

Chapter One

"You have arrived at your destination."

Carson, the invisible navigator inside Jessica Keaton's cell phone, delivered the announcement in a crisp British accent that never failed to make her smile.

Until today.

Today Jess wanted to toss him...it...out the window.

Because a destination was something a person *chose*. Winsome Lake, Wisconsin, was a desperation. The kind of place you ended up when you had no choice at all.

"1525 Woodwind Lane is on your left."

Either Jess had imagined the hint of frosty disapproval that had crept into Carson's tone, or a week of sleepless nights was making her feel a little wonky.

"I heard you the first time," Jess muttered. Even though talking back to her GPS definitely added weight to the wonky theory.

She tapped the brake. Just once, not quite ready to commit, but hard enough to trigger a low rumble underneath her feet that signified an ominous disturbance in the Buick's rusty tectonic plates.

Oh. No.

Jess had forgotten how temperamental the car could be.

She cranked the wheel as a plume of charcoal-gray smoke erupted from the tailpipe. The tire grazed the curb, and the unexpected turbulence started a chain reaction that Jess was powerless to control. Two suitcases in the back seat collided with a thump, and the cardboard box balanced on top of them began to sway. In the rearview mirror, Jess watched the strip of packing tape holding the flaps together give way. A Burberry scarf, a gift to herself last Christmas, bobbed to the surface and spilled over the side, almost as if it had been waiting for an opportunity to escape.

Jess wasn't so fortunate. Her chance to escape was thwarted when the Buick released a dramatic shudder and went still.

She'd forgotten about the car's ability to play dead, too.

"1525 Woodwind Lane," Carson intoned. His polite, British way of saying, "What are you waiting for, Yank?"

Jess ended the conversation with one swipe of a finger against the screen and abandoned the Buick only because she could pretend—for at least a few minutes—that it didn't belong to her.

The smoke had dissipated and there seemed to be no witnesses to Jess's less-than-perfect landing, so she took a quick inventory of her surroundings. The neighborhood looked old but well cared for, the houses uniform in size and shape. Painted in an array of watercolor pastels, they lined the street like a tidy row of French macarons.

Jess's gaze locked on one the color of vanilla buttercream. The top tier was almost completely hidden behind a veil of English ivy. It flowed around the base of the stone chimney and fanned out over the roof, unraveling into a fringe of emerald green that covered the top of the mullioned windows in a jaunty half wink. A tangle of sweet pea, larkspur and blue delphinium peacefully comingled in the drift of lavender that hemmed the foundation.

The whole effect was sweet. Charming.

If you were Snow White.

Jess's vision blurred.

An image of soaring glass walls and miles of black slate flashed through her mind. Clean lines. Sleek surfaces. Anything green, shorn and sculpted into works of modern art.

You can still change your mind.

Jess shut down the inner voice and the tears that banked behind her eyes.

Because she couldn't change the fact that she had nowhere else to go. And a car Jess didn't trust to make it to the nearest service station, let alone the county line.

"Hello?"

Jess whirled around, unaware that while she'd been staring at the house, a small group of women had stopped on the sidewalk to stare at *her*, their expressions ranging from disbelief to blatant curiosity.

The shortest of the three took a step forward. She reminded Jess of Cinderella's fairy godmother. An iron-gray bob framed a face as round as a pumpkin, a smile carved in every line. The hem of the woman's voluminous denim sundress ended where the tops of her cherry-red Keds began.

"Are you Jessie?" she ventured. "The young woman Elaine hired to help around the house?"

I'm a chef, Jess wanted to shout, if only to remind herself. She managed a jerky nod instead. "Yes. And it's Jessica," she corrected. "Jessica Keaton."

She might have lost her reputation and her career and

the keys to the Audi, but she'd worked too hard to let go of her name.

The fairy godmother exchanged a quick look with the others and then silently passed the verbal torch to the next one in line.

The two women appeared close in age, Jess guessed early-to midsixties, but a sleek helmet of copper hair accentuated every angle and plane of her companion's exotic features. Spandex workout clothes did the same for her statuesque frame. When she extended a hand, Jess half expected her to strike a warrior pose.

"Nita." The brisk catch and release matched the woman's tone. "Elaine isn't here. We think she might have had a relapse."

Elaine. As in Elaine Haviland? The woman who'd offered Jess a place to live and a steady paycheck?

"I just spoke with Ms. Haviland a few days ago." Jess struggled to make sense of the words. "What do you mean...a relapse?"

"From the stroke, I imagine." The third member of the mismatched trio joined the conversation. In khaki cargo shorts and an oversize T-shirt with an equally oversize photo of a French bulldog silkscreened on the front, she was still the most ordinary-looking one in the bunch.

"We don't know any details. My cousin's best friend's aunt is a patient at the rehab center and she told me that whatever happened caused quite a stir in the wing." The woman's voice picked up steam as she rolled on. "I called a few hours ago, but Vanessa, she's the social worker, was in a meeting and the receptionist wouldn't tell me a thing. Those Hippo laws, you know. Pain in the neck if you ask me."

Jess might have laughed if the diet soda and energy bar

she'd eaten for breakfast hadn't started burning holes through the lining of her stomach.

Elaine Haviland hadn't mentioned anything about a stroke when she'd interviewed Jess over the phone the week before. All she'd said was that she needed some temporary live-in help to cook meals and do some light housekeeping.

Jess could handle both, of course, but the word *temporary* had sealed the deal.

"Elaine was looking so forward to coming home today," the fairy godmother murmured.

And Jess had been looking forward to *having* one.

Now what was she supposed to do?

"Call Sunrise Rehab," Nita, warrior princess, commanded, almost as if she'd read Jess's mind. "Ask for Vanessa Richards. If Elaine isn't able to speak again, she'll be your go-between."

Isn't able to speak. Again?

A dozen thoughts collided in Jess's head but she refused to let them throw her off balance. *Stay focused.* That was what Jess's instructor at culinary school had taught her. The advice had served Jess well in life and in Gwyneth Donovan's kitchen.

"Thanks." Jess shaped a polite smile. She'd have to find a place to fire up her laptop and start checking the help wanted ads again. "Is there a coffee shop in town?"

The woman wearing the bulldog shirt snorted, which Jess took as a no.

"*Peg.*" The fairy godmother pursed her lips. And then she stepped right into Jess's personal space. Pressed a key into her hand. "You don't need a coffee shop. I've known Elaine for twenty-five years. She wouldn't want you standing on the curb while you're waiting to get things straightened out."

Jess doubted there was anything *to* straighten out. If Elaine Haviland wasn't coming home, she didn't need Jess's help.

"Merri is right." Nita pointed to the house. "Go inside. Make the call."

The other women hummed in agreement, making it three against one.

At the moment the only thing Jess found remotely tempting about the suggestion was the possibility they'd leave her alone if she agreed.

"Thanks." Jess stuck to the safest response.

Nita consulted her watch. "I have to go." The abrupt announcement set her friends in motion.

Merri, an appropriate name for the fairy godmother, Jess thought, cast a smile over her shoulder. "Everything will work out...Jessica. You'll see."

A week ago Jess would have believed her.

Gwyneth Donovan's annual, by-invitation-only Fourth of July bash had exceeded her expectations. And Jess's, too. The guests raved about the food, demanded to know when Jess was going to share her talent with the rest of the world.

Soon, she'd wanted to say.

And then, a few hours later, her world had fallen apart.

Jess's hands fisted at her sides and she felt the edges of the key dig into her palm. She winced and loosened her grip before it made an imprint as deep as the image of Ian Holden's expression when he reached for her...

A car rolled past, but the driver appeared more interested in Jess than the road.

One of the many reasons she avoided small towns. Everyone knew who belonged...and who didn't.

Jess waited until the vehicle rounded the corner before she followed the cobblestone path to Elaine Haviland's front porch. A pair of wicker chairs rocked in the breeze, but two things stopped Jess from setting up camp there while she considered her next step.

The lack of privacy and the need for a bathroom.

She pulled in a breath, fit the key in the lock and gave it a turn. The door opened into a tunnel of wallpaper roses. A straw hat crowned the top of an old-fashioned coatrack, and an eclectic collection of jackets dangled from its spindly arms.

A mental picture of Elaine Haviland began to form in Jess's head. She followed the hand-hooked rug, a faded yellow brick road, down the corridor and turned right into the living room.

Jess expected dark paneling, crocheted doilies and dusty knickknacks. The baby grand piano that took up half the space stopped her in her tracks. The furnishings, out of deference to the piano, were minimal. Not a porcelain figurine in sight. A small sofa and chair shrouded in ivory muslin curved around the brick fireplace like a smile.

And just when Jess was beginning to think that first impressions weren't always accurate, she stepped into the kitchen.

It was tiny. Lilliputian. The butcher-block island smaller than the cutting board she'd used in Gwyneth's kitchen. The walls were the color of lemon meringue, the cabinets white with ceramic knobs and light blue trim.

And the stove...

Jess steeled herself and looked at the burners.

Electric.

Of course it was.

Jess's cell phone began to vibrate inside her purse and she sifted through the contents to find it.

She'd ignored an incoming call from an unknown number on the drive to Winsome Lake, assuming it was a scammer hoping to siphon her credit card information. But based on the new information she'd just been given, Jess took a risk and answered it this time.

"Hello." She flavored the greeting with just the right amount of "don't mess with me" spice. The same tone she used when she was buying fresh whitefish from the Corbin brothers.

"Is this Jessie Keaton?"

"Jessica," Jess corrected automatically.

"My name is Vanessa Richards and I'm a social worker at Sunrise Rehabilitation Center. I'm calling on behalf of Elaine Haviland…she said you planned to arrive sometime today."

Jess's fingers tightened around the phone. "I'm already here."

"Wonderful. This latest setback hasn't been easy on Elaine, but she'll be relieved I was able to get in touch with you."

"I'm sorry, Ms. Richards." Jess used the laminate—*laminate*—counter as a brace. "I don't know anything about a setback. Or a…a stroke. All I know is that Elaine Haviland offered me a job, this is the start date I was given and no one is here."

In spite of Jess's best efforts, the last word frayed a little at the edges.

"Well, I think we should take a few steps back, then."

Jess had no idea what the social worker looked like, but she'd chosen the right profession. Every word the woman spoke exuded warmth and comfort. The vocal equivalent of chocolate lava cake.

"Elaine has been with us at Sunrise since the beginning of June. There are several benchmarks a person needs to reach before we are comfortable sending them home. Elaine isn't quite ready to be on her own yet, but we'd reached a compromise. If she hired someone to help around the house and continued with her physical therapy, I would support her decision to leave the center.

"Yesterday afternoon Elaine fell and fractured several ribs.

She's in a lot of pain at the moment, so we agreed it was in her best interest that she remain here a little while longer. Pneumonia is always a concern after a fall like this, and her body will need time to heal."

Jess's heart plummeted. "How much longer?"

"I can't say for certain. It varies from patient to patient, but Elaine will call you as soon as she's able," Vanessa promised. "In the meantime, there's a guest room upstairs and plenty to do while you wait."

"She wants me to stay?" Jess must have misunderstood. "Here? In her house?"

"Of course." Vanessa chuckled. "Elaine said, and this is a direct quote, 'to make yourself at home.'"

Home.

Jess didn't even know what the word meant. But a place to regroup…alone. It almost balanced out the electric stove.

Almost.

"If you have any questions, feel free to call me," Vanessa said. "Elaine's cell was damaged when she fell, so I don't mind passing messages back and forth for a while if necessary."

"I… Thank you."

"I'm happy to help," the social worker said. "Everyone at Sunrise has grown quite fond of Elaine during her stay, and she mentioned how fortunate she was to find you."

The irony left a bitter taste in Jess's mouth.

Gwyneth had said the same thing…two hours before she'd told Jess to pack up her things and get out.

Chapter Two

Jess ended the call, closed her eyes and silently recited her barre instructor's favorite mantra.

Take a breath. You've got this.

When she opened her eyes again, Jess found herself staring into the kind of formal dining room she'd thought would be extinct by now. But it was the floorplan, not the outdated decor, that kick-started the diet-soda-energy-bar roller coaster again.

In Gwyneth Donovan's house, a quarter mile of travertine separated the kitchen from the main living space. Jess's employer entertained frequently but didn't embrace the modern trend of friends chopping vegetables together over a predinner drink. Nor did she want to hear the clang of pots and pans on the evenings she spent alone.

Gwyneth had business associates, a few close friends and a well-paid staff dedicated to making her life easier. Jess was under no illusions about which group she fell into.

As Gwyneth's personal chef, she'd been given a generous budget to work with, a vehicle to drive and a private suite overlooking the tennis court.

An arrangement that suited Jess just fine.

She'd seen the complaints from former classmates whose employers expected them to provide the food and the entertainment. Unlike the contestants vying for attention on those popular cooking shows, Jess didn't want an audience in the kitchen. But here, sandwiched between Elaine Haviland's dining and living rooms, she'd constantly be on display.

It suddenly occurred to Jess that the social worker hadn't mentioned anything about the meals she was expected to prepare. Were there dietary restrictions for people who'd suffered a stroke?

Would she have to *puree* everything?

The thought propelled Jess to the nearest exit's two doors, one she assumed led to the basement and the other, fresh air.

Jess chose door number two.

She pulled in a startled breath, the kind that would have earned a collective look of disapproval from the members of her barre class. The baby grand piano had been a surprise. This...this was a shock to the senses.

A wooden privacy fence, weathered to a dull silver by the changing seasons, didn't look strong enough to contain the mass planting of flowers and herbs that had taken control of the backyard.

Basil. Rosemary. Roses. Lemon verbena. Poppies.

The clash of colors and fragrances reminded Jess of the potager gardens she'd admired during a virtual culinary tour of France. Only this one was untamed, rebellious, flourishing in spite of its obvious neglect.

Jess stepped off the patio into a bed of creeping thyme. Following the stone pavers turned into a game of hopscotch.

A leap over a spiky mound of hens and chicks. A quick side-step past the rosebush.

She bent down, plucked a purple viola and popped it into her mouth. The burst of sweetness unlocked a memory of the garden party Gwyneth had hosted for the top tier of her elite clientele two summers ago.

Jess had overheard one of the guests complain it wasn't fair that Gwyneth kept such a talented chef all to herself. Gwyneth had dismissed the comment with an airy laugh, but it had taken root in Jess's heart. The moment her dreams had dared to outgrow Gwyneth's kitchen.

"I prefer a good burger myself, but whatever floats your boat."

Jess's head snapped up.

A man had materialized out of nowhere. Close to thirty, Jess guessed. Clean-cut. Slim with an athletic build and broad shoulders; traits she would have admired until a few days ago. Until Ian. Now he was merely a six-foot-tall obstacle between her and the house.

"I thought I heard someone back here." He waded toward her through an ankle-deep patch of lemon balm.

Jess remained mute; the viola lodged halfway down her throat.

Her silence didn't seem to make the guy uncomfortable, though. He stopped a few feet away from her. "Sorry if I startled you. I was expecting to see Elaine. I've been taking care of her yard the past few months."

"Really?" Jess's voice had returned, seasoned with sarcasm.

That didn't make him uncomfortable, either.

"The *front* yard." He waved his hand over a clump of flowers, and a dozen bees rose like miniature drones from the blossoms and took flight. "Elaine told me not to worry about all this. She probably knew I wouldn't be able to tell the difference between a weed and a flower."

"Or an herb." Jess eyed the mangled stems of lemon balm he'd left in his wake.

No wonder Elaine Haviland had decided her garden had a better chance of surviving on its own.

"Are you from Sunrise?" He cocked his head and a swatch of sable-brown hair slipped over his forehead. He swiped it back into place with the casual hand of someone used to the interruption. "I'd offered to bring Elaine home today, but she said the social worker was taking care of the arrangements."

"No." The guy obviously wasn't going away, but that didn't mean Jess couldn't. She began to inch toward the door. "Ms. Haviland hired me."

His gaze swept over Jess, pausing to linger on her open-toe Manolo Blahnik pumps almost as if he knew the shoes had set her back a month's pay. Understanding...no, *shock*... flashed in his eyes.

Blue eyes.

Jess wished she hadn't noticed what color they were, but it would have been like trying to ignore a perfect summer sky.

"*You're* the one who's going to help Elaine around the house?"

Did everyone in Winsome Lake know why she was there? Jess silently counted to five. Ten. "That's right."

"What time do you think she'll be home? I've been holding on to something of hers and I'm going out of town today, so I'd like to drop it off before I leave."

Jess couldn't see a way around the truth. "Elaine—" it felt strange to call someone she'd never met by her first name "—had a setback. According to the social worker, she has to stay at the rehab center a little longer."

"How much longer?" For a guy who mowed the lawn, he looked genuinely concerned.

Apparently, the staff members at Sunrise Rehab weren't the only ones who were fond of Elaine Haviland.

"I'm not sure."

"But..." He silently connected the dots. "What about you? Are you still planning to move in?"

Take a breath...

"Yes."

"I guess that officially makes us neighbors, then." He smiled. "Nick Silva. I live at the end of the street. The only house that isn't the color of an Easter egg, by the way."

Jess was tempted to smile back, but something told her it would only encourage him to linger.

Not that Nick needed encouragement. He extended his hand. "And you are..."

"Jessica Keaton." Jess recreated Nita Warrior Princess's brisk handshake.

The rosebush tried to hinder Jess's final quickstep to the patio, but she made it. Nick followed, Chuck Taylor high-tops trampling violas left and right.

"Does that Buick out front belong to you?"

Without thinking, Jess shook her head. As far as she was concerned, it wasn't a lie. The Buick belonged to Jessie Keaton, an eighteen-year-old escapee from a small town much like Winsome Lake. The car had aided and abetted her flight to freedom a decade ago until it eventually made its way to an outbuilding on the Donovan estate. Safely locked away. Like everything else in Jess's past.

But as much as she wished a tow truck would haul the thing to the nearest scrapyard, Jess doubted a vehicle was part of her new benefit package.

"I...it's temporary," she amended.

"Well, it's leaking oil, so I'd give the rental company a heads-up." Nick had drawn the wrong conclusion, but Jess didn't correct him.

"Thanks." The word was quickly becoming her default. A polite benediction that signaled the end of the conversation. She hoped.

Another head tilt. The swatch of hair tumbled over Nick's forehead again, like water seeking low ground. "Do you need help with anything? I noticed luggage in the back seat."

"No." Jess tried to soften the word with a smile. "I've got it."

She didn't want Nick Silva to see the wadded-up tissues on the passenger seat. Or the greasy fast food wrapper stuffed in the console, further evidence of how far Chef Jessica Keaton had fallen.

Fortunately, there was no sign of Nick when Jess scraped up the courage to venture outside again. But he'd been right about the Buick. A pool of liquid, dark and embarrassing, stained the road between the front tires.

At least Nick hadn't known that two small suitcases and three plastic storage bins filled with cookbooks and some personal belongings made up the sum total of Jess's worldly possessions.

Other than the wardrobe she'd built paycheck by paycheck over the past five years and the leather knife case that protected the tools of her trade, everything else had belonged to her employer.

Jess hadn't minded. Her job came with perks that extended beyond access to a media room, Olympic-size swimming pool and acres of walking paths.

Own It, the chain of exclusive clothing boutiques Gwyneth owned, had expanded beyond the Midwest. Jess's employer was stylish and business-savvy and successful. Respected by her peers and the community.

And Jess, who'd never had a mentor or role model, paid attention. She read the books Gwyneth discussed with her friends over cocktails. Shopped the sale racks at the stores her employer frequented. Learned about setting goals and achieving them.

On the Donovan estate, Jess had done more than create innovative cuisine. She'd created a whole new Jessica. A whole new *life*.

A life that had changed in the wink of an eye.

Stupid.

Jess should have suspected Ian Holden had more on his mind when he'd wandered into the kitchen during Gwyneth's party, but he'd been so complimentary. So sincere. Ian's restaurant was booked out months in advance, and he wanted to open another one. Asked what Jess's plans were for the future.

Then he'd destroyed it. One minute, Jess's dream of owning her own restaurant seemed to be within reach and then Ian—handsome, successful, *married* Ian—was reaching for her.

While Jess was locked in his arms, her mind and body frozen with shock, Crystal Holden, Ian's wife, walked in. Gwyneth had been a step behind her baby sister.

Ian had had a script prepared, almost as if he'd recited the lines on previous occasions, painting himself the victim. Which left Jess with only one role to play.

Gwyneth hadn't even asked for Jess's side of the story. She'd fired her on the spot, as if the past five years didn't count for anything.

As if *Jess* didn't count.

Jess reached for the Burberry scarf, folded it and carefully returned it to the box before trudging back to the house.

Vanessa Richards had mentioned the upstairs guest room during their phone conversation, so Jess hiked to the second floor.

The stairwell opened into a wide landing at the top of the stairs. Three doors, each one painted a different color.

It was a little too *Alice in Wonderland* for Jess, but she toed open the daffodil-yellow one and peeked inside, unsure of what she would find.

A cumulous cloud of white goose down engulfed the iron bed frame. An old wingback chair with a deep, comfortable lap and arms wide enough to balance a cup of coffee took up one corner of the room.

There were no personal possessions on the nightstand, no clothing in the closet, so Jess figured she was in the right place.

She set the box on the floor and went back to retrieve her suitcases.

On the return trip Jess heard a rap on the back door. She contemplated ignoring it, but whoever it was obviously knew there was someone inside because the next rap sounded a little more forceful.

"Hey." Nick had returned.

"Sorry." Jess greeted him through the screen door. "I'm unpacking..."

Instead of taking the hint, Nick held up a canvas tote bag that he erroneously deemed more important than the suitcase Jess was about to carry up the stairs. "This will only take a second."

Time's up, Jess wanted to say as she opened the door.

"Here you go." Nick set the bag down on the floor. "And

thanks. Being away from home…it's been tough on the old girl."

Jess frowned.

Old girl? It didn't seem like a very respectful way to refer to his neighbor.

"I'll…" Jess stopped. Because the tote had *moved*. "Is there something alive in there?"

"Uh-huh. Elaine's cat. I was the only one stup—" Nick paused "—who offered to keep an eye on her after Elaine's stroke. She's been with me ever since."

"But…what am I supposed to do with it? I've never had a cat."

"Technically, you still don't have one," Nick pointed out. "She belongs to Elaine."

A disturbing noise, one that reminded Jess of a dentist's drill, began to rise from the depths of the crate. A jolt of panic swept through her.

"Can't you keep it a little longer?"

Nick shook his head. "Trust me when I say that Violent will be much happier in her own home."

"Her name is *Violent*?"

"Did I say *Violent*?" Nick's chuckle was drowned out by the indignant yowl that pierced the air. "It's *Violet*. You know. Like the little purple flower?"

A set of claws that looked more dangerous than Jess's chef's knife poked through the holes in the mesh door, and she jumped backward.

"Seriously, Nick." Jess wasn't above pleading now. "You can't leave it…her…with me! I don't know anything about cats."

But he was halfway to the door already, the coward.

"You'll be fine. Just remember that Violet doesn't like to be held…or country music."

The screen door snapped shut and Jess knelt down. The claws retracted and the yowling abruptly stopped.

Surrender? Or an ambush?

There was only one way to find out.

Jess unzipped the door a few inches. And then a few inches more. Scooted backward and waited to see what would happen.

Nothing.

"Violet?"

A furry cannonball shot from the carrier, barely clearing the top of Jess's suitcase before it disappeared into the living room. Jess tried to keep up, but the animal clearly knew its way around the house. It skidded across the piano bench and ended up underneath the coffee table, only to emerge a few seconds later with a new destination in mind.

Jess followed, not sure what kind of damage a cat nicknamed Violent—yes, she knew Nick hadn't made a mistake—could cause if left unattended.

She jogged into the kitchen and looked around. There was no sign of the animal, but Jess could feel its beady eyes watching her.

She looked around. And up. And there it was. Perched on top of the cabinets, peering at her through a screen of faux ivy like a mountain lion sizing up its prey.

"Violet... I don't think it's safe for you to be up there." And Jess didn't exactly feel safe on the floor, either.

"Come on, kitty."

Violet retreated deeper into the silk foliage.

"Look." Jess parked her hands on her hips. "I know you're not happy I'm here. *I'm* not happy I'm here. But I promise it won't be for very long, okay?"

The cat's ears flattened, a sign it wasn't impressed by Jess's version of a pep talk.

Jess had heard reverse psychology worked on kids. Maybe it could be applied to animals, as well.

"Fine. No problem. I have other things to deal with." Like the kitchen. And what she'd been given to work with.

A quick inventory of the cupboards and pantry revealed what Jess had already suspected. Not very much.

She opened the fridge, a coffin-shaped relic from another era, and groaned. The shelves were completely bare. A bottle of ketchup and ranch dressing wobbled like bowling pins in the door. A more thorough investigation of the produce bins led to the discovery of a wedge of aged cheddar.

Jess's stomach rumbled.

She grabbed a knife from the drawer, dull, of course, and hacked off a slice.

Something soft and furry brushed against Jess's ankle. She squealed. The cheese slipped between her fingers and fell on the floor.

It disappeared, along with a puff of smoke-gray fur.

Jess didn't give chase this time.

A cat that didn't like to be held, hated country music and turned to cheese for comfort.

Maybe she and her new roommate would get along, after all.

Chapter Three

Two and a half months ago Elaine Haviland couldn't walk, dress herself or write her name.

Now she couldn't breathe.

The meds had started to work their magic. Taking the edge off the pain. Coaxing her to fall asleep.

Elaine fought against it. She wasn't going to give in and close her eyes. Not until she heard from Vanessa.

Staring up at the popcorn ceiling, she slowly filled her lungs with air. The nurse had warned her that shallow breathing could lead to pneumonia, and pneumonia was a complication she didn't need right now.

Tears backfilled Elaine's eyes and clogged her throat, even though she wasn't a crier by nature. It was a good thing, too, because when she'd broken down shortly after the stroke, it felt like she'd been waterboarded by her own mucus.

The door opened a crack and Vanessa Richards, social worker, cheerleader, drill sergeant and occasional late-night smuggler of chocolate chip ice cream, poked her head into the room.

"Elaine?"

"I'm awake." Elaine tried to sit up and the meds instantly lost ground. She sank against the mattress, shocked at how three hairline fractures had the power to strip away six weeks of progress.

"Hold on." Vanessa breezed into the room. Monday was her day off, so she'd traded business casual for her favorite Harley Davidson T-shirt and skinny jeans. "Your ribs are broken and I'm trying to work off the piece of raspberry cheesecake I ate last night, so how about I come to you?"

Elaine discovered that smiling hurt, too. "Just this once."

"That's the attitude that brought you this far...and will get you out of here before you know it." Vanessa hooked one leather boot around a chair, yanked it closer to Elaine's bed and sat down. "I got in touch with Jessica Keaton a little while ago."

Thank You, Lord.

"Is she on her way to Winsome Lake?"

Vanessa shook her head. "Already at your house. I explained the situation and told her that you won't be released today as planned."

Released.

Elaine knew Vanessa didn't mean it that way, but the word still conjured up images of a cage. Not Sunrise Rehab, of the faux potted plants, watercolor landscapes and soothing color scheme, of course. No. Elaine had become a prisoner in her own body.

The stroke had forced her to relearn all the things she'd taken for granted. Simple, everyday things like tying her shoes. Washing her hair. After four weeks in the hospital and a grueling month and a half of therapy, Elaine had finally conquered the PT's checklist.

It was her own stupidity that had landed her back in bed.

Elaine had taken an impulsive detour past the windows overlooking the courtyard after the church service on Sunday morning. A victory lap, roughly the same distance between her front door and the mailbox at home, to celebrate her upcoming freedom. She would have made it, too, if Sarah Peterson's birthday banner, handmade by her five-year-old twin grandsons, hadn't fallen off the door and landed in the middle of the hallway.

Elaine momentarily forgot her cane was meant to be used for balance, not as a tool for retrieving items on the floor. She'd ended up flat on her back, staring into the metal eye of the overhead sprinkler on the ceiling. The rest of the day had been a blur. A ride in the ambulance. X-rays. A revolving door of doctors and nurses.

Twenty-four hours spent hoping, praying, she wouldn't have to come up with a whole new plan.

Elaine's eyelids fluttered, a sign the meds were winning again. She shifted her weight, leaned into the pain, using it as leverage to stay awake. "What did Jessie say?"

"It's Jessica. She'll correct you if you get it wrong." Vanessa cocked one ebony brow. "And she said she didn't know anything about a stroke."

"That's because I didn't tell her." Elaine ignored a stab of guilt. "I didn't want her to think I needed a nurse. I need someone who can open a can of tomato soup. Vacuum the stairs. Fold towels."

"You didn't want to scare her away."

"Right." Now it was Elaine's turn to raise an eyebrow. "Did you?"

"I don't think so." Amusement backlit Vanessa's eyes. "I

repeated everything you said. Told Jessica there were plenty of things to do until you got home, but…" The social worker paused and Elaine braced herself for the bad news. "She seemed surprised you wanted her to stay. And, to be honest, I'm a little surprised, too."

"According to Jessica's résumé, she graduated from culinary school and worked for a catering company and a restaurant with a name I can't even pronounce."

"Exactly. She's a trained chef, not a live-in cook," Vanessa pointed out. "I saw her résumé, too, and the past five years are a great big blank. Did you ask about that during the interview?"

The only question Elaine had asked Jessica Keaton was if she could start on Monday.

"I did some checking and there are several agencies in your area that could provide live-in help," Vanessa went on. "You have time to find someone else if you're not comfortable with a stranger living in your home. Maybe your friends could recommend someone?"

Nita, Merri and Peg, the neighborhood trio Elaine had affectionately dubbed "the Scrappy Ladies" shortly after she'd moved to Winsome Lake, had taken turns watering her philodendron and checking on the house. They'd already visited twice, even though Sunrise Rehab was over an hour's drive from Winsome Lake. Nick Silva, who lived down the street, was taking care of Violet and the yard.

"No." The word sounded thick. "They've done enough."

"Okay, okay." Vanessa raised her hands in surrender. "I see that look of determination."

Elaine smiled and felt it slip sideways.

Not determination.

Desperation.

If Elaine had wanted someone from the area, she would

have contacted Pastor Newman at Lakeside Community instead of placing a help wanted ad in a newspaper that reached beyond the handful of subscribers in Winsome Lake.

Vanessa didn't understand she'd hired Jessica Keaton *because* she was a stranger.

Because there were parts of your life you couldn't share with anyone.

Not even your closest friends.

Chapter Four

Nick Silva felt bad.

Not because he'd finally rid his home of the feline scourge that had shredded his recliner and sent Bucket, his normally fearless shepherd mix, into hiding every day for the past two and a half months.

And not because he knew that Jessica Keaton's shoes cost more than the tires on his pickup truck. Information that, unfortunately, dredged up unpleasant memories of Whitney Blake, a big-city girl he'd dated his senior year of college. Nick had been head over heels by the time she'd accepted his invitation to visit Winsome Lake after classes ended for the summer.

Whitney had spent a week working on her tan and charming his family. Then she'd burst out laughing when Nick asked if she could see Winsome Lake becoming her permanent home. And if that hadn't been enough to douse the flames of any future relationship, Whitney told him she'd already accepted a job with a marketing firm in Chicago.

Nick acknowledged it was for the best. Whitney wouldn't have lasted more than a few months in a town without a coffee shop or high-end clothing store.

And that was why he felt bad for Elaine.

Because he had a feeling the woman she'd hired to help around the house wouldn't make it a week.

An image of Jessica Keaton instantly downloaded from Nick's memory.

Wheat-blond hair pulled back in a sleek ponytail, eyes the color of clover. Her sleeveless, form-fitting dress accentuated sun-kissed skin and slender curves, but would have earned a stamp of approval from Nick's mom, who'd always told his sisters that clothing should flatter, not flaunt.

Still, Jessica looked as out of place in Winsome Lake as a goldfish in a trout pond.

Even without the expensive shoes and Gucci handbag— yeah, Nick knew what one of those looked like, too—the woman's attitude revealed more than the labels on her outfit.

She was aloof. Almost...suspicious.

Although, if Nick was honest, he could probably take some of the blame for that. When he'd discovered her in Elaine's backyard, she'd looked as tense as a freshman on tryout day. But when Jessica had admitted she'd be staying at the house until Elaine returned, something in her eyes had him uneasy.

A shadow that told Nick she didn't *want* to be there.

So why was she?

And what was Elaine going to do when the woman she was depending on for help packed up her things and took off once she realized the locals referred to Winsome Lake as "the town that time forgot"?

"Hey!" A scrawny, sunburned boy landed in front of Nick

with a thump, yanking his thoughts back in line. A face still bearing traces of ketchup from lunch at a fast-food drive-through grinned up at him. "Are you going to help us set up the tent?"

"Sure." Nick glanced at the passenger van. The doors hung open, the now abandoned vehicle stranded in a sea of sleeping bags and backpacks.

"Where's Pastor Eric?" Nick's gaze swung to the squirming tangle of bodies rolling around on the patch of ground that separated their designated camping site from the others.

"Looking for the first-aid kit. Brady needs an ice pack."

No need to ask why. Ice packs were as necessary as air freshener when it came to sixth-grade boys.

"Come on. We'll round up the rest of the gang and get started."

The smile expanded. "Thanks, Coach."

It didn't matter the kid wasn't old enough to play on one of Nick's teams. Everyone in Winsome Lake, from the bank tellers to the guys who fixed potholes in the street, called Nick by the title. Most of the time it was kind of flattering. But there were those moments when Nick would have welcomed a little anonymity. He'd returned to his hometown after college, and everyone who'd watched him grow up had no qualms about sharing their opinion on everything from Nick's coaching style to his dating life. He loved his job, but even at the ripe old age of thirty, drinking coffee with the same people who'd once graded his papers still felt a little surreal.

A howl pierced the air and propelled Nick forward.

A boy clutching a football had extricated himself from the pack. A dozen hands reached for him, but the combination of bare skin, sweat and sunscreen made their quarry as slippery as a greased pig at the county fair. He only managed to make it several yards before disappearing again.

Nick fished the whistle out of his pocket, a highly effective tool, he'd found, for deflating a churning ball of testosterone.

Why had he volunteered to act as chaperone for the middle school youth group again?

Oh, yeah. For the same reason he'd offered to transfer Jessica Keaton's luggage from her car to the house.

Because in Winsome Lake, people looked out for each other.

But Nick couldn't shake the feeling that kind of attention would only give Jessica Keaton one more reason to leave.

Chapter Five

While hauling her belongings upstairs, Jess had created a mental to-do list. A triage based on order of importance, and Hide The Buick was now at the top of the list.

From the guest bedroom window, she'd spotted a lopsided garage on the other side of the fence. The buttercream paint matched the siding on the house, so she assumed they were a pair.

Jess grabbed her keys and slipped out the front door again.

The Buick sputtered back to life, hacking and coughing in a bid for sympathy that Jess ignored. Without Carson the Navigator's input, she found a narrow alley that cut a swath behind the houses on Woodwind Lane and a thick stand of trees. Jess parked in front of the garage, hopped out of the car and peeked in the window. A small compact already occupied the space, but the neighbors' overgrown hedges created a leafy private cubicle, and the gravel pad would soak up any motor oil leakage like butter on a biscuit. A win–win as far as Jess was concerned.

The sound of a car turning down the alley propelled Jess into motion. Not wanting to draw any more attention to herself than she already had, she made a beeline toward the wooden gate that opened into Elaine's backyard.

Something crunched underneath Jess's shoe. She glanced down and winced. A dirt-encrusted resin sign that proclaimed Life Began in a Garden now lay flat on the ground. Jess propped it against the stake that had been holding it in place and kept to the paving stone path again, gathering sprigs of rosemary and chives along the way.

Elaine Haviland's refrigerator might be empty, but the pantry had yielded all the ingredients Jess needed to make a loaf of flatbread.

She'd lived on the stuff in culinary school. The ingredients were inexpensive and simple. Flour. Salt. Water. But combining those ingredients and ending up with *bread*? Magic every time.

The screen door snapped shut behind Jess as she made her way to the kitchen. She buried her nose in the bouquet of herbs and inhaled. Jess would take these over roses any day…

"You're smiling. It's good news about Elaine, then?"

The lilting voice flash-froze Jess in place.

She hadn't realized she was smiling. Or that the three women she'd met on the sidewalk earlier that morning would invade Elaine's kitchen in the few minutes Jess had been gone.

"I… No." Jess stumbled over the words. "According to the social worker, she has to stay there a little longer."

"What happened? Was it another stroke?" Nita stepped in front of the other women protectively, offering herself as a human shield to absorb the impact of Jess's answer.

"She fell and cracked some ribs." Jess tried to remember what else Vanessa Richards had told her. "She's in a lot of pain so they don't want to release her yet. That's the only information I can give you right now..." Jess let her voice trail off, hoping they would take the hint.

No one moved.

So Jess did.

She gave the herbs a quick rinse, set them on the cutting board and removed her chef's knife from its leather swaddling. Some of her fellow culinary students had given theirs a name, but as far as Jess was concerned, the knife wasn't a puppy or a pet goldfish. It was a tool she used to achieve success.

The women pressed closer for a better look.

"Kind of a skimpy-looking salad," the one called Peg observed. "No wonder you're so skin—"

"We cleaned out Elaine's fridge weeks ago," Merri interjected quickly. "Thought you might need a few things to tide you over until you can get to the grocery store."

For the first time, Jess noticed the hodgepodge of foil-covered containers on the counter behind them.

"You didn't have to do that." Jess meant it. She wasn't a stray cat that had turned up at the door.

"It was no trouble at all," Merri said. "Neighbors take care of each other around here."

Elaine was their neighbor. Jess was the live-in help, and perfectly capable of feeding herself. She'd been doing it since she was a child.

Nita's watch chirped twice. Barely audible above the hum of the refrigerator, but it might as well have been an alarm the way the other women reacted.

Nita didn't say a word this time but Peg and Merri pivoted toward the door and fell into line like participants in a fire drill.

Jess managed to intercept Merri in the living room. "Wait. I'll give you back your key."

"Oh, you keep it. There's another one behind the pot of geraniums on the porch." Merri smiled and followed her friends out the door.

Good to know.

Jess deposited the foil-covered offerings into the fridge and watched the women out the kitchen window.

The moment they were out of sight, Jess slipped out to the porch and located the geraniums.

Then she took the key.

Jess came awake with a start.

The last thing she remembered was curling up on the couch with a piece of flatbread and channel surfing until she found an old sitcom with a set that resembled Elaine Haviland's living room.

Now the television cast eerie shadows on the wall and Violet, who'd made off with the stolen cheese and gone into hiding all day, was walking around the sofa pillow, her claws stitching an outline of Jess's profile.

At—Jess squinted at the grandfather clock in the corner of the room—two in the morning.

She didn't know anything about cats, but something told her the nocturnal visit wasn't a change in attitude. It was payback.

"Go on." Jess gave Violet a nudge and in response, felt the flick of a tail against her cheek.

Jess sat up and the cat immediately plopped down in the center of the pillow, expanding to fill the space where Jess's head had been.

"Fine. I'll take the guest room and you can have the couch."

The tips of Violet's ears twitched in acknowledgment. As if that had been her plan all along.

Jess took a detour into the kitchen for a glass of water. The scent of the flatbread she'd made that afternoon still lingered in the air. Too bad there weren't any leftovers. Her stomach growled, reminding Jess that she hadn't planned ahead.

Reminding her that her new normal didn't feel normal at all.

Because Jess *always* planned ahead.

She opened the fridge more out of habit than anticipation and spotted the mystery gifts that Elaine's neighbors had left for her.

Jess's stomach whined again. She grabbed the first container and peeled back a corner of the foil. A laugh tumbled out, catching her by surprise.

Tucked inside was a plastic clamshell filled with chunks of iceberg lettuce, wilted carrot shavings, two wrinkled cherry tomatoes and a sprinkling of shredded cheese.

Whoever provided the salad obviously hadn't wanted anyone to know it came from—Jess read the name printed on the label—Dan's Hometown Market and Deli.

Ha. If this is what the deli produced, Dan was having delusions of grandeur.

She moved on to the second container and found the main entrée, penne encased in marinara cement.

Jess's stomach clenched, but this time it wasn't hunger. She set the penne aside and opened the last one.

The scent of vanilla washed over her.

Nestled inside was a perfect wedge of pie, its only adornment a tidy pleat of golden-brown crust.

Custard? Sour cream?

Jess picked up the container for a better look and then gave in to temptation. She plowed a furrow through the filling with her finger and let the flavors dance on her tongue.

Butterscotch.

Jess didn't get much of an opportunity to bake. Gwyneth was strict about her sugar intake. But this...

She slid her fingers under the pie and lifted it from the container, didn't even bother to reach for the plastic fork that formed a crossbeam on top of the salad. With the entire piece plated in the palm of her hand, Jess finished it in *sixty* seconds and moved on to another course.

Salad. Because lettuce absorbed both guilt and ranch dressing. And at two in the morning, even stale croutons tasted good.

By now Jess was seated on the floor, the last container balanced on her knees, fork in hand.

The pasta wasn't visually appealing but it would carry her through until she made a grocery run.

Jess hadn't known that first bite would transport her back in time, too.

She was alone in another kitchen, eating cold ravioli she'd found in the refrigerator, wishing her parents would come home. And that she was tall enough to reach the microwave.

Based on experience, Jess had known the first wish wouldn't come true. It never did.

But the microwave...

Jess had pushed a chair across the floor, set the bowl inside the microwave and started pressing buttons until a whirring noise started.

Through the little window, she could see the sauce rise over the top of the bowl. Heard the spit and sputter before it erupted like a volcano Jess had seen on a documentary in science class.

She'd opened the door and grabbed the bowl. A cloud of steam had hit her square in the face. Jess lost her balance and fell off the chair and the bowl had slipped from her hands. It rolled across the floor, spattering the worn linoleum red, turning the kitchen into a crime scene.

Jess had picked herself up off the floor and cleaned up the mess she'd made, salvaging what she could.

And here she was, at twenty-eight, sitting on the kitchen floor in the middle of the night, eating a bowl of over-cooked pasta.

Only this time Jess wasn't sure if there was anything left to salvage.

Chapter Six

Ordinarily, Jess woke to the rhythmic swish of the underground sprinkler system that kept the grounds around the Donovan estate lush and green.

This morning it was…music.

Piano music.

Jess groaned.

All she wanted to do was burrow under the covers and try to catch up on the sleep she'd missed during the night, but unless Violet had skills that Jess didn't know about, someone had broken into the house. Again.

She rolled off the bed and made her way downstairs, clutching her phone in one hand just in case she had to dial 911, tugging her tank top over her hips with the other. When Jess reached the bottom stair, she saw Violet stretched out on the top of the piano, meticulously cleaning her whiskers with a lick and swipe of one front paw.

Jess's pulse evened out a little when she realized the intruder providing the background music for the cat's morning grooming session was a rail-thin teenage girl.

"Hey."

At the sound of Jess's voice, the girl practically levitated off the bench before vaulting to her feet in a twisting motion that brought them face-to-face.

"What——" Hazel eyes outlined in what looked like permanent marker widened underneath a jagged frond of carbon-black hair. "Who are you?"

Wasn't that the question Jess should be asking? But she stuck to the now-familiar script.

"Elaine…"

"She's dead, isn't she?"

"No." Jess blanched. There was no time to wonder why the girl's mind automatically took that dark path. Not when she was already stuffing sheets of music into a backpack on the floor.

"There were some…complications…and Elaine can't come home yet, that's all," Jess explained. "I'm… I'll be staying here to help out for a while."

A pause in the frantic shuffling. "You're the cleaning lady?"

As if Jess needed yet another abbreviated summary of her job description. "I'm Jessica Keaton."

Some of the color that had leached out of the girl's face returned. "Sorry," she mumbled. "I didn't know anyone was here." She shook the backpack until the contents settled and would have slunk away if Jess hadn't blocked her path.

She had a few questions of her own.

"Wait a second…how did you get inside?"

"The key by the back door."

How many keys did Elaine Haviland have squirreled away?

And why even bother when everyone in town seemed to know where they were hidden?

"Are you related to Elaine?"

"She lets me use her piano to practice." The girl's eyes lit on everything but Jess.

"At seven in the morning?"

A shrug. "Whenever."

Whenever.

Not what Jess wanted to hear, but if Elaine had given the girl permission to use the piano, it wasn't as if Jess could tell her to leave.

"Look…" She waited until the girl's gaze completed another circuit of the room.

"Sienna," she muttered.

Sienna. Unusual, but for some reason the name seemed to fit.

"You don't have to leave, okay?" Jess needed caffeine to dissolve the fog of a sleepless night. "Keep doing what you're doing. I'll be in the kitchen making coffee."

"Ms. Haviland drinks tea, not coffee."

Jess gave herself a swift mental kick for saying no when Elaine Haviland had asked if she had any questions during their phone interview. She retreated to the kitchen anyway and discovered that Sienna had been telling the truth.

No coffee. No coffee*pot.*

At the Donovan estate, Gwyneth would be on her way to work already, powered by a kale smoothie, while Jess camped out by the French press, prepping for the evening meal or working on a menu for a poolside brunch or weeknight dinner party.

She opened a small wooden box next to the spice rack and found a cache of tea.

Caffeine was caffeine, right? And given her options, Jess

had no choice but to try and guess how many packages of Earl Grey it took to make something that could reasonably pass for a cup of French roast.

The answer, Jess concluded a few minutes later, was none.

She'd hoped that, given the opportunity, Sienna would sneak out of the house as quietly as she'd come in. But the ripple of the piano keys, as soft as the morning breeze stirring the garden chimes, told Jess otherwise.

She tossed the tea bags into the wastebasket underneath the sink and peeked into the living room. The girl had reclaimed her spot on the bench and Violet the top of the piano.

Music accompanied Jess up the stairs as she retreated to the second floor to get dressed. The light on the bathroom ceiling flickered when Jess turned on the shower, creating a strobe-like effect that went along with the gold fixtures and seafoam-green tile.

The day before, Jess had been too preoccupied to pay attention to her surroundings. Now she noticed a floral bathrobe with a tissue peeking out of the pocket hanging on the hook behind the door.

Jess went to move a tube of moisturizer to make room for her toothbrush on the back of the sink and saw the cap sitting next to it.

A shiver sowed goose bumps up and down Jess's arms.

Had Elaine been standing here, in the midst of her ordinary routine, planning for the day ahead, when she'd had the stroke?

Life, interrupted.

Jess knew how it felt.

She left the moisturizer undisturbed and set her makeup bag on the floor instead.

Jess felt more like an intruder here than she had in Gwyneth's home. At least there, the boundaries had been clear. The terms of Jess's employment spelled out in a contract, not a five-minute phone interview.

At the time, she'd been relieved Elaine Haviland hadn't asked a lot of questions. It saved Jess from having to provide some key details about her employment history.

She hadn't realized that worked both ways. Elaine had left out a few key details of her own.

Maybe the woman had been afraid if she was honest about the stroke, Jess would refuse the position.

And she probably would have been right.

Jess stepped into the shower and gasped. Two minutes ago the water had turned the tiny space into a steam room. Now it was the temperature of an April rain.

She washed her hair in record time, grabbed a towel off the bar and realized she'd left her clothes in the guest room. Opening the door a crack, Jess heard the concert still going on in the living room and made a break for it.

She hadn't unpacked yet, although a survey of the tiny closet had revealed a row of empty hangers. Even after finding out that she wouldn't be homeless after all, unpacking had felt too…permanent.

Through a vent in the floor, the music changed from a lighthearted ruffle of the keys to a somber march. A tune that corresponded perfectly with Jess's mood as she unzipped her suitcase and surveyed the contents.

Gwyneth had expected her staff to look professional at all times, so Jess wore the traditional loose-fitting checkered pants and double-breasted white coat during the day. If anyone thought it strange that a chef preparing food in a private home wasn't dressed more casually, they never said a word. Jess didn't, either. The uniform was practical, comfortable. But more than that, she'd *earned* the right to wear it.

High-waisted linen pants and a white cotton tee from

Own It's summer collection was probably overkill, too, but working for Gwyneth had taught Jess that the clothing she wore when she *wasn't* working also made a statement. On more than one occasion, she'd overheard Gwyneth tell a colleague that if you wanted customers to put their confidence in you, then you had to project it yourself. And, of course, her clothing line was one of the ways to accomplish that.

But even if Elaine Haviland were there, Jess doubted her new employer would care what she wore in the kitchen.

Out of habit, Jess gathered her hair into a low ponytail, slipped on her shoes and padded downstairs.

The music had stopped but Sienna was still there. Shoulders stiff, hands frozen on the keys, staring at the swirl of notes on the sheet of music in front of her.

Jess resisted the urge to clap her hands and jolt the girl out of her trance.

She cleared her throat instead, which proved to be just as effective. Sienna's hands came down hard on the keys, striking a discordant note that sent Violet diving under the coffee table.

Why are you still here?

That was what Jess wanted to ask. What came out of her mouth was, "How long do you usually practice?"

Another shrug.

Okaaay.

"I'm going to run to the grocery store and pick up a few things. I'll be back in about an hour."

Sienna's head jerked in a nod.

The girl brought a whole new meaning to the term *body language.*

Jess didn't bother to ask Sienna to lock the door when she left. Not when half the population of Winsome Lake already had access to the house.

She tucked a market bag into her purse and stepped outside. The sun flirted with her behind a wispy veil of clouds and the breeze carried a hint of perfume, but Jess was on a mission, not a leisurely stroll through the neighborhood.

By the time she reached the stop sign on the corner, three people she'd never seen before in her life had smiled and waved at her. A woman jogging with her dog. The elderly man drinking a cup of coffee on his front porch. The driver of the recycling truck as he circled the block.

Jess couldn't remember the last time she'd felt so…exposed.

And then her subconscious helpfully uploaded a memory of Ms. Wainright, Jess's third grade teacher, standing next to her in the school cafeteria.

Did you forget your lunch again, Jessie?

When Jess had nodded, Ms. Wainright decided to use her empty tray as a teachable moment and addressed the entire table.

Does anyone have anything they're willing to share?

The next sixty seconds taught Jess a lesson she'd never forgotten. She could still hear the scrape of the chairs against worn linoleum. See the pile of cast off food piling up on the tray in front of her. Half a peanut butter sandwich. A damp square of processed cheese. The mountain of carrot and celery sticks because no one liked them anyway.

Jess had wanted to sweep everything into the enormous trash can stationed outside the kitchen door. Instead, she'd eaten it all.

The next day and every day after that, Jess had made her own lunch and brought it to school.

A horn beeped, jolting her back to the present. Jess's first thought was that her unexpected trip down memory lane had caused her to veer outside the crosswalk. Until the horn-honker smiled and waved.

She ducked her head and crossed the street, inwardly chiding herself for thinking the Buick would have drawn people's attention.

If Winsome Lake was the proverbial small-town fishbowl, the Donovan estate had been a microcosm. Jess knew the names of the other employees but they didn't socialize during the workday or their off-duty hours. Everyone employed by Gwyneth was a cog in the well-oiled machine that kept her life running smoothly.

Shortly after Jess was hired, one of the groundskeepers had mentioned that Gwyneth bought the estate with her first million and promptly gutted the entire house. All the antiques were sold. Every room stripped and modernized. A pool replaced the flower gardens, and the stable was demolished to make room for a tennis court.

Judging from the man's tone, he'd considered all that change a bad thing. It had made Jess respect her new employer even more. Gwyneth was confident. Successful. A woman who knew what she wanted and didn't let anything stand in her way.

Not even the truth.

Jess pushed the thought away and kept her gaze fixed in front of her. It didn't do any good to dwell on the past.

But that was easier said than done when every step Jess took down Winsome Lake's quaint little main street stirred up memories of a life she'd spent the past ten years trying to forget.

Chapter Seven

"One more deep breath, Elaine. And...hold." Dr. Kim moved the stethoscope a quarter inch to the left. "Good."

No. It wasn't.

The brackets that appeared between the physician's brows destroyed the fragile hope that Elaine would be leaving anytime soon.

Dr. Kim's next words confirmed it. "I'm going to order another set of pictures and take a look at your lungs this time."

Which meant Dr. Kim was concerned about pneumonia.

Lord...

Elaine's silent appeal balled up in her throat, but it was the best she could do at the moment. At this point in her life, Elaine might not know what to pray, but she knew it only made things worse if she *stopped*.

"What about therapy?" Yes. It was a test. But Elaine had to know.

Dr. Kim smiled. "Soon."

The vague response, no doubt meant to comfort, had the opposite effect.

For weeks Elaine had dreaded her therapy sessions. The only thing that had kept her going was knowing that she was moving forward.

Now she was losing ground, and not just physically. Discouragement lurked in the shadows, waiting for an opportunity to strike.

Maybe it was Elaine's imagination, but over the past twenty-four hours, she could *feel* the weakness invading her limbs. Stealing her strength little by little, like waves whittling away at the shoreline.

"I'll submit this order to X-ray and someone will be down to collect you before lunch. Plenty of time for a shower and hair wash," Dr. Kim continued cheerfully.

Over the doctor's shoulder, Elaine saw Leah, the thirteen-year-old CNA who worked the morning shift, hovering in the doorway. Okay…maybe that wasn't fair. Leah was probably fifteen. Fine. Twenty-five.

Oh, you are in a mood today.

Although Elaine had been known to agree with, argue her case, or sometimes push back, when it came to that inner voice, today she maintained a stubborn silence.

BF, Before the Fall, Elaine had reached the milestone of showering independently. Grab bars, a nonskid shower mat, they'd become her friends.

At the age of fifty-five, Elaine already had the dubious distinction of being the youngest stroke victim at Sunrise. And now she would have to be supervised and scrubbed down like a toddler again.

"I'd rather skip the shower and just get dressed." Elaine

heard the faint slur in her voice, like a person who'd had one too many gin and tonics, and hoped Dr. Kim hadn't noticed.

"That's fine." The physician nodded in agreement, not realizing she'd failed another test.

In a rehab center that encouraged patients to perform as many of their "normal" activities as possible, it didn't bode well that Dr. Kim was willing to humor her.

The moment she left, Leah skipped into the room and opened the wardrobe. She extracted one of the shirts that Nita had dropped off a few days after Elaine had been transferred to Sunrise. Dolman sleeves, no buttons and roomy enough to fit one of the linebackers on Nick's football team.

"How about this one?"

Because it wasn't Leah's fault that Elaine had fallen and cracked her ribs, or that she was in less than a cheerful mood, she fibbed. "Fine."

Leah opened the drapes, refilled Elaine's water pitcher and moved the call button within reach. "Let me know if you need anything else."

Elaine nodded.

What she needed was *home.*

In other words, Elaine needed divine intervention.

"Knock, knock."

Really, Lord? Not what I had in mind.

Flat on her back, limp as a piece of overcooked spaghetti, the last person Elaine wanted to see was the poster child for robust good health and vitality.

She closed her eyes as footsteps approached the bed.

"I ran into Leah in the hall. She said you were awake."

"She was wrong," Elaine said without opening her eyes.

A low, masculine chuckle rumbled through the room.

"I brought ice cream."

"Chaplains shouldn't break the rules."

"*Retired* chaplain. And Sunrise allows emotional support animals so I brought Moose Tracks."

Elaine's lips twitched. But refusing to give in felt a little liberating after two days of being treated like she was made of glass by Perky Leah and Sunrise Rehab's uber-efficient staff.

The scrape of a chair told Elaine that her visitor planned to stay awhile.

Elaine shouldn't have been surprised. Matthew Jeffries had been flouting convention since the day they'd met.

The first time Elaine had met the man, it was shortly after she'd arrived at Sunrise. She'd been slumped in her wheelchair, exhausted from rehab and waiting for an aide to take her back to her room, when Matthew appeared. He'd asked for her room number and then proceeded to wheel her down the hallway. Elaine assumed he was a new employee until he stopped outside her door and she'd noticed he wasn't wearing a navy blue polo and khakis like the rest of the staff.

"You're…" Like the wooden blocks the therapist had set out on the table during Elaine's therapy session, the words were there, but she couldn't grab the ones she needed and put them into a neat little row.

"In trouble, I know," Matthew had said. "Vanessa Richards is coming down the hall. Tell her this was your idea."

The request, followed by an audacious wink at Elaine, set the tone for their relationship.

And as it turned out, Vanessa hadn't been the least bit upset about the hallway abduction. Not only was Matthew Jeffries a retired military chaplain who visited the veterans in rehab every Friday morning, he also belonged to the same motorcycle club as the social worker.

But for some inexplicable reason, Matthew had started to drop by Elaine's room even though she a) wasn't a veteran, and b) wasn't very good company.

The second one had thrown Elaine off balance almost as much as the stroke.

She'd known her body would need time to reboot. She hadn't expected she would want to be left alone during the process.

After years of self-imposed exile, Elaine had deliberately moved to a small town where the houses were sown in tight rows, the neighbors' porches practically extensions of her own.

She encouraged the Scrappy Ladies' Thursday morning get-togethers around her dining room table. Loved the impromptu conversations by the mailbox or the stop sign at the corner.

On Woodwind Lane, Elaine had found her people. They were quirky and sweet and sometimes as irritating as a mosquito in a dark room, but then, so was she. Giving them access to her home, to her life, made both of those things more interesting.

When the paramedics had wheeled Elaine down the sidewalk to the ambulance, she could see her terror reflected in her friends' eyes as they'd gathered around her but hadn't been able to assure them that everything would be fine.

Sometimes Elaine had a hard time reassuring herself.

She'd thought she lived out her faith, held tight to God's hand, but there were days she wanted to stomp her foot and tell PT that she *wasn't going to try again.* Days she didn't want to be nice to Perky Leah. Days it took more effort to control her attitude than her fine motor skills.

Inevitably, those were the days Matthew showed up.

Making Elaine laugh when she didn't feel like laughing. Bullying her into playing some silly card game and calling it therapy. If she got salty, Matthew didn't look concerned and make a notation in a notebook. Most of the time, he got salty right back.

"Just so you know, I'm not going anywhere." The chair creaked underneath Matthew's weight. "Pretending you're asleep while we talk is fine with me. I get to eat the ice cream."

And there was a perfect example.

Elaine sighed and surrendered. Found herself staring into a pair of whiskey-colored eyes.

Vanessa had casually mentioned that Matthew Jeffries had turned fifty-six a few weeks ago, but he was one of those genetically blessed males whose looks only improved with age. Tall and fit with broad shoulders and a narrow waist. Close-cropped, light brown hair laced with a few distinguished strands of silver. He could have played the leading role in any action movie.

Over twenty-five years and two thousand miles away from Hollywood, and Elaine still noticed these things.

Matthew must have ridden his Harley to the rehab center because he wore jeans, a long-sleeved T-shirt and sturdy black boots. Elaine would have thought a man who lived in an area of the state where the whitetail deer outnumbered the people, and the roads were walled-in on both sides with trees, would choose a different mode of transportation, but no.

The summer sun had tinted Matthew's skin bronze, while Elaine, who'd been inside for months, was so pale she practically glowed in the dark.

"If you don't stop spending all your free time at the tanning booth, people are going to talk."

Matthew grinned. "And Leah claimed you didn't seem like yourself today."

"You aren't supposed to be discussing my case with the staff."

"I'm not supposed to do a lot of things." Matthew flashed another very un-chaplain-like grin, if there was such a thing, and peeled the lid off a single-serving cup of ice cream.

"That's it? Vanessa brings half a pint."

"It's pushing eighty degrees today. I didn't want to bring Moose Tracks soup."

"I don't know. I'd probably do better with a straw." And to prove it, Elaine heard that oh-so-frustrating slur in her voice again.

Matthew's grin slipped a little.

If you tell me you're sorry, you're going to be wearing that ice cream, buddy.

He handed her the spoon instead. No half-truths or denials. No bumper sticker platitudes. In that one, unspoken gesture was everything Elaine needed to hear. She could do this.

She dipped the spoon into the container, tunneling straight to the core of fudge. The ice cream melted on her tongue. Made her feel normal for the first time since she'd fallen.

"Do you want me to get you out of here?"

Elaine's eyes lifted to his face and she realized he was serious. In fact, Matthew looked like someone who not only knew how to carry out a mission like that, but had also successfully completed one or two prior to the offer.

"Tempting." He might be shocked if he knew how much. "But no. I can't go home until I'm one hundred percent better or I'll scare Jessica Keaton away."

"Who is Jessica Keaton?"

Elaine paused midbite to lift an eyebrow. "Vanessa didn't tell you?"

"Contrary to what you might think, we don't talk about you all the time." Matthew's wink made Elaine's chest feel a little tighter. "And no, I don't know anything about Jessica."

"I hired her to help with cooking and some housework

when I came home. I fell the day before she arrived." The spoon suddenly felt as heavy as a hammer in Elaine's hand. "I didn't mention that I'd had a stroke, though."

"Why not?"

"She didn't ask?" Unlike Vanessa, Matthew didn't appear startled by her confession.

"What makes you think she'd leave?" He gently slipped the spoon out of Elaine's hand, used it to mine another vein of decadent fudge and brought it to her lips.

Elaine didn't have the strength to protest. The pain medication was wearing off again, and it felt like someone had fired up a chainsaw in her chest.

"Jessica is a chef, not a home health care provider. The cracked ribs put me at risk for pneumonia, so Dr. Kim thinks I should stay here, where they can keep an eye on me."

"Pneumonia."

"Your sources aren't keeping up."

Instead of the teasing comeback she'd been expecting, Matthew's lips tightened almost imperceptibly.

Elaine shook her head when he offered the spoon again. Yet another reason for Jessica Keaton to leave. She'd be cooking for someone with no appetite.

"I'm looking at more therapy after my ribs heal." The words rolled out before Elaine could stop them. No one in the PT department had said anything, but she'd discovered over the past few months that her body always told the truth.

Matthew nodded slowly. "If this Jessica leaves, what happens then?"

"I'd have to hire someone else."

Someone who wouldn't question why Elaine kept the door to her office locked. Why she was talking on the phone with someone who'd been in the news the day before, or at her computer half the night, battling writer's block.

Someone temporary, who would pack up their things and move on, taking Elaine's secrets with them.

"Based on my *sources*—" the familiar gleam stole back into Matthew's eyes again "—you have a lot of friends who'd be willing to help out after you get home." He set the ice cream cup on the table. "But let me guess. You don't want to burden them."

"Everyone has things going on in their lives," Elaine said carefully. "It doesn't seem fair to add more to their plates. Would you?"

"Let's just say I've learned that it's hard to discern sometimes if I'm trying to make things easier for people who want to help or is it easier on my pride?"

"Me, too," she acknowledged softly. "Sometimes."

"You're admitting we have something in common." Matthew reached out and pressed the call button on Elaine's bedside table to summon the nurse.

"Busted," she whispered.

"I've walked a few miles in those ugly white compression socks, too."

And if that statement wasn't shocking enough, Matthew reached out and took Elaine's hand.

"We have something else in common, Elaine. We both know that God is bigger than this."

Elaine nodded, unable to speak. But that was okay; Matthew bowed his head and did it for her.

"Lord… Elaine's stroke, the fall, none of it was a surprise to You. But You're a loving Father who wants us to cast our cares on You. And to be honest, we're feeling a little overwhelmed right now. We hold on to Your promises for healing, trusting that You know what that looks like. Amen."

Amen.

Elaine's lips formed the word and she felt her eyelids start to drift closed.

"Hold on a few more seconds. The nurse should be coming in soon with your pain meds."

Matthew's footsteps began to fade, and Elaine struggled to sit up before he reached the door.

"Matthew?"

He turned around and for the first time, Elaine found herself wishing that he could see her in clothes with buttons. Her hair the way she used to wear it, before a simple braid had become an impossible feat. The glow from an afternoon in the garden in her cheeks.

"Thanks...for coming."

"I'll see you tomorrow."

"Tomorrow is Wednesday. You don't visit on Wednesdays."

Matthew smiled. A smile that told Elaine he didn't care about any of those things. A smile that made her feel more like a woman and less like a patient.

"I do now."

Chapter Eight

The produce section of Dan's Hometown Market and Deli was a narrow median separating the deli from the bakery. Jess paused next to a cardboard bin filled with green bananas and surveyed her options. On her left, a display lined with loaves of bread, cake doughnuts and Long Johns the size of seat cushions. On the right, a refrigerated case filled with grab-and-go salads and subs.

"Can I help you find something?" A woman wearing a hair net and a pink polo, the name *Gloria* appliqued on the stained front pocket, appeared at Jess's elbow.

How about a grocery store?

Jess bit back the words and pressed out a smile instead. "No…thank you. I'm just browsing."

When a wrinkle appeared in the woman's forehead, Jess realized it was what someone would say if they were shopping for a pair of shoes. She glanced at Jess's empty basket and seemed to come to a decision.

"If you like sourdough, I just pulled some from the oven. We only make it once a week and it sells out by noon."

"I love it." Jess followed the woman until she disappeared behind a fortress made of glass and chrome, its walls reinforced with smoked hams and blocks of cheese.

Jess rose up on her tiptoes and peered over the top. Rounds of crusty bread decorated the center island, golden-brown polka dots that released a heady fragrance into the air.

The woman gave one of the loaves a quick thump and smiled. "How many?"

On a table behind her, Jess's gaze landed on a mason jar, the opening bound with cheesecloth and a rubber band. "You use your own starter?"

From the look on Gloria's face, Jess might as well have asked if she moonlighted as a bank robber. Color deepened the magenta stripes on her cheeks. She looked around furtively, combing the area for potential witnesses.

"I'm not using the stuff they ship in," she muttered. "Not for this. I bring in my own starter from home." Her voice dropped another notch. "It's not a certified kitchen, though, so if anyone spills the beans..."

Gloria's gaze swept over Jess, as if realizing for the first time that she wasn't a local. Translation: someone who could potentially spill the beans.

"I won't say a word...if you sell me a cup of the starter, too."

Gloria's eyes widened. And then she winked. "Coming right up."

Ten minutes later Jess had filled her basket with staples and made her way to the checkout. The teenage boy who'd watched her risk frostbite searching for free-range organic chickens among a case filled with counterfeits handed Jess a piece of paper after he bagged the groceries.

She glanced down and saw a phone number scrawled between its tattered corners.

"I…" How to let the kid down gently? "I'm actually not going to be in town very long."

Color burned in his cheeks and ignited a fire in both earlobes. "It's my neighbor's number. I heard you asking about cage-free eggs and his chickens run all over the place. Four dollars a dozen but you have to collect them from the coop yourself. He's got a bad knee."

Jess handed back the piece of paper. "Then I guess I'll need the address, too."

He scrawled something else on the paper and tucked it between the olive oil and balsamic vinegar in Jess's market bag.

Her *thank you* produced another blush and an eye roll from the cashier.

Walking away, Jess could hear the rise and fall of a whispered conversation.

You know Anthony has a waiting list a mile long for those eggs.

Ms. Haviland…ride to the doctor a few times.

What has that got to do with anything?

Jess heard the words *hired her to help* before the doors closed and sealed off the rest of the conversation.

She was starting to wonder if her photograph was hanging on the wall at the post office, with her job description printed underneath.

Jess retraced her steps back to Woodwind Lane and let herself into the house. There was no sign of Sienna or Violet.

Jess didn't bother to stifle her sigh of relief.

Sunlight spilled through the kitchen window and puddled on the floor, turning the room into a sauna.

She hadn't even thought about whether a house this old would have central air. A quick glance at the thermostat confirmed the fact that it didn't.

A breeze stirred the valance above the window, a shy request to come inside. But the sound of lawn mowers and cars cruising down the street would have made their way in, too, and Jess preferred to work in silence. No background music. No podcasts. Just the sound of her knife against the cutting board and the soft tick of the clock marking time on the wall.

She unpacked the market bag, transferring the jar of sourdough starter to its new home next to the spice rack as carefully as if it were the Holy Grail.

Five minutes later she stood in the center of the kitchen, soul-deep in uncertainty.

For the first time in years, Jess had no idea what to do.

There was no menu. No plan.

No one to cook *for.*

Jess took a restless lap around the butcher-block island, looking for inspiration, but felt as empty as Elaine Haviland's refrigerator.

After leaving Gwyneth's house, Jess had applied for two separate positions as a private chef and never received a response. In spite of her experience, she hadn't even been granted an interview. It became clear to Jess that when Gwyneth had told Jess she was "done," it hadn't only been a reference to her job at the estate, but her career, as well.

Jess could have looked for something beyond the sphere of Gwyneth's influence. She'd worked in restaurant kitchens and for a catering company after culinary school. But Jess had quickly realized that even if she left the Donovan estate off her work history, there would still be a five-year gap to explain to a future employer.

Jess paused to straighten a faded tea towel hanging on the oven door and a message appeared, embroidered inside a frame of curlicues and flowers.

Taste and See.

She traced the words with the tip of her finger. A memory coaxed the barest of smiles.

Fridays with Chef Tomas.

The first four days of the week, the culinary school instructor terrified everyone in class. A bear of a man whose toque almost grazed the ceiling, he prowled around the test kitchen, correcting mistakes and barking out orders, tasting spoon in hand.

Chef Tomas didn't bother memorizing his students' names. If he wanted someone's attention he bellowed out the number on their station.

The first time he'd called on Jess, she'd almost had a heart attack.

"Number Five! I believe it is time for a pop quiz. Would you do us the honor of answering the first question?"

Jess, who sensed there was only one acceptable response, had nodded.

The entire class pressed closer, spiking the temperature in the kitchen several degrees.

Chef Tomas handed Jess a tasting spoon and gestured toward a shallow bowl on the counter. "What do you see, Number Five?"

Jess looked down at the mixture and almost breathed a sigh of relief. "A vinaigrette."

"That is correct. But we have other senses, yes? Now close your eyes and tell us what you taste."

Jess's confidence had evaporated as quickly as a drop of water in a hot skillet. She dipped the spoon into the mixture and closed her eyes. A pungent aroma stung her nose before the spoon touched her lips.

"Vinegar."

"What else?"

"Lemon." Jess tried to separate the flavors. "Garlic. Olive

oil." Something subtle, elusive, teased her taste buds. Tried to draw her into a game of culinary hide-and-seek. Jess named the ingredient vying for center stage instead. "Tarragon."

"Keep going."

Jess's eyes popped open. She saw Chef's glower and closed them again.

And then...there it was. But fear of looking foolish momentarily outweighed her fear of failure. "That's all."

"No! It is not! What else do you taste?" he'd persisted.

"O-oak?"

Silence. And then...three measured claps.

When Jess gathered the courage to open her eyes, Chef was smiling.

"Number Five is correct. The vinegar was aged in wooden barrels." His eyes crinkled at the corners. "It is like a marriage, yes? A few simple ingredients. A boy and a girl meet. They fall in love. They marry. But *time*." Chef had almost hummed the word. "It adds a flavor of its own."

After that, Friday became Jess's favorite day of the week. And Chef Tomas, her favorite instructor. On the day of their final exam, he'd passed out recipe cards to everyone in class and Jess felt her heart sink.

The card was blank.

"You have two hours," Tomas had announced. "The market down the street will be closing soon, so I suggest you move quickly."

"Chef?" One of the older students finally, bravely, raised his hand. "What are we supposed to make?"

Jess had felt the same panic boiling in her stomach, until Chef caught her eye. Winked.

"You are chefs, yes? Make something you love to eat."

With Chef Tomas's voice echoing in her head, Jess reached for the loaf of sourdough.

After another scavenger hunt through the kitchen, Jess finally located Elaine's toaster crouched behind an ancient mixer in the cabinet next to the sink.

The snap of a car door caught her attention and she peeked out the window just in time to see Nick Silva's lean frame unfold from the cab of the black pickup parked along the curb.

Her heart thumped against her rib cage.

Why had he come back?

Jess tracked Nick's movements as he walked up the sidewalk. Just before he reached the porch, he veered off course and followed the narrow path that led to the garden.

The toaster suddenly disrupted Jess's surveillance. It came to life with the cheerful pop of a jack-in-the-box and presented her with a coal-black piece of toast.

As an encore, Jess watched a curl of smoke drift toward the ceiling.

She growled under her breath.

Only the suspicion that Nick knew the hiding place of yet another key prevented Jess from ignoring the knock at the back door. She yanked the plug from the outlet on the wall and went to answer it.

"Hey." Nick's grin reached through the screen and did funny things to Jess's equilibrium.

A shadow of stubble darkened the angular jaw while a dark green T-shirt half-tucked into worn jeans accentuated the blue in his eyes. It wasn't fair the whole rumpled-outdoorsman look worked for him.

"Elaine isn't home yet."

"I know."

Jess didn't ask how. The fact that everyone she'd come into contact with knew that Jess was working for Elaine was an indication that the small-town grapevine was as healthy as the one weighing down the fence in the backyard.

Reluctantly, Jess opened the door.

Nick stepped inside and kept walking, leaving Jess with no choice but to trail along behind him as he made his way to the kitchen. He walked straight to the sink and opened the window a few more inches.

"It's pretty warm in here." Nick tossed a smile over his shoulder. "I keep telling Elaine she should put in central air, but she says she prefers the real stuff."

Jess was relieved he hadn't caught the whiff of failure in the air. But she doubted Nick had made a special trip over to talk about the house. She linked her hands together at her waist, battling the urge to fidget. "Was there something you needed?"

"Actually, I stopped over to ask you that question."

"I'm fine."

The response would have satisfied most people. But Jess had only met Nick Silva once and already knew he didn't qualify as *most people.*

"I thought you might need a general layout of the town. Post Office. Grocery store—"

"I already went to the grocery store," Jess interjected before Nick could offer his services as tour guide. "And based on what I saw on the way there, I doubt a person could get lost in Winsome Lake."

"That's probably true."

Some of the warmth left the kitchen and Jess had a feeling it wasn't because of the open window. Nick, apparently, was as loyal to Winsome Lake as he was to the people who lived in his neighborhood.

Elaine Haviland probably felt the same way.

As much as Jess wanted to be left alone, it suddenly occurred to her that her job could be in jeopardy if Nick told

Elaine that her new employee had a less than glowing opinion of their beloved hometown.

"I'll be over sometime this weekend to mow, then." Nick
started for the door. Five minutes ago Jess would have happily escorted him there. Now she blocked his path.

"Wait…" Jess fished the piece of paper out of her pocket.
"Maybe you could tell me where Birch Street is?"

Nick scanned the address and a slow smile drew up the
corners of his lips. "I can do better than that. I'm actually on
my way over there right now. I'll show you."

Chapter Nine

The next thing Jess knew, she was standing on the sidewalk, watching Nick toss what looked like an entire display of camping equipment, sans tent, into the back seat of the truck.

"Hold on." He brushed some crumbs onto the pavement and grinned. "Graham crackers. Where there's a campfire, there has to be s'mores."

Nick jogged around to the driver's side and Jess surreptitiously removed a tiny shard of graham cracker wedged in her seat cushion before climbing into the cab.

The driver's door snapped shut, sealing them inside.

Suddenly, Jess was questioning her impulsive field trip with Nick.

If only the thought of eggs from a coop instead of a carton hadn't momentarily outweighed her common sense.

Nick made a U-turn in the street and sunlight flooded the cab. Spots danced in front of Jess's eyes.

She'd left common sense *and* her sunglasses behind.

Jess flipped the visor down and something that resembled a cellophane wrapper fell out. She automatically reached out to catch it. Tried—and failed—to muffle a shriek.

"Snakeskin." Nick's hand shot out. In one single yet efficient motion, opened the window and let the breeze carry the thing away. "Sorry about that. Sixth grade boys think stuff like that is hilarious."

The dimple that flashed in Nick's cheek told Jess that guys his age did, too.

"You have kids?" The question slipped out before Jess could stop it.

"More than I want to claim sometimes."

Jess refused to let the dimple reel her in. She hadn't noticed a wedding ring on Nick's finger, but that didn't mean anything. Her dad hadn't worn one, either.

"Two hundred and eighty-seven, not counting the ones who skip my classes on a regular basis."

"You're a teacher?" For some odd reason, Jess had pictured Nick in another type of career. Landscaping or construction maybe.

"Middle and high school PE. I also coach a few sports."
Ah.

Now the man's Jedi reflexes made sense.

Jess had grown up in a town that marked the four seasons by the high school sports schedule, not the changing weather. If she'd been one of the school's star athletes, things might have gone differently. Maybe people would have seen her as something other than "that Keaton girl."

For some reason an image of Sienna popped into Jess's head.

"What?"

Jess blinked. "What...*what?*"

"You looked like you were about to say something."

And Jess thought Nick had been looking at the road. But now that he'd brought it up...

"A girl showed up at the house this morning," Jess said slowly. "Sienna?"

"Sienna Bloom." Nick nodded and the swatch of hair dipped over his eye.

"You know her?"

"I know she doesn't like PE," Nick said wryly. "I see her more in the hallway than I do my class."

Jess couldn't blame Sienna. Teams were just another word for cliques. And with mirrors everywhere, a high school girl's self-esteem was practically forged in the gym locker room.

"She claimed Elaine lets her practice on the piano." Jess left out the part about the teen showing up at 7:00 a.m. "But I'm not sure how Elaine would feel about her coming over when no one is there."

"Elaine wouldn't mind. She has kind of an open-door policy when it comes to the neighborhood."

Jess had noticed. But even if Elaine Haviland didn't mind, Jess wasn't sure it was okay with *her*.

Nick turned another corner and the thermos stuffed in the side compartment of Jess's door began to rattle. The row of Craftsman-style houses with their aprons of crisp green grass disappeared as Woodwind Lane descended into a series of twists and turns that reminded Jess of a vintage roller coaster. When the truck reached the bottom of the hill, a flash of sapphire caught Jess's eyes.

"There's a lake."

Nick slid her a sideways glance. "The town founders wouldn't lie about something like that."

Winsome Lake. Of course. Jess felt a little silly, but it wasn't like she'd pulled up the town on Google Earth before she'd accepted the position. All she'd cared about was its distance from the Donovan estate in Lake Geneva.

"It's a no-wake lake," Nick explained, as if Jess knew what the term meant. "Fishing is pretty decent, though." He swerved to avoid a pothole. "This part of the town was built first, so the houses are a bit more rustic."

Almost on cue, he turned down a gravel road. At the end of it, Jess spotted a one-story log cabin with a high roofline and wide, wraparound porch.

Now that they'd arrived, Jess was questioning her decision again. There was no sign in the yard, nothing that advertised eggs for sale.

"Are you sure it's okay if we drop in without an appointment?"

Nick scrubbed a hand across his mouth, and Jess got the feeling he was trying to hide a smile. "No appointments necessary. Promise."

Jess opened the door and hopped down. A combination of pine and wood smoke seasoned the air. The cabin was mere steps from the lake and Jess, who was used to swimming in water treated with chlorine, resisted an unexpected urge to kick off her shoes and wiggle her toes in the sand.

The front door suddenly swung open and a gray-and-brown rocket cleared the steps leading up to the porch and hurtled toward her.

In the dust churning up from the gravel, Jess caught a glimpse of pointed ears, a bushy tail and paws the size of dessert plates.

She was about to dive back into the truck when the dog veered from its collision course. Nick, walking several yards away from Jess, bore the brunt of the impact.

"Hey, Bucket." Laughing, he wrapped one arm around

the dog's neck and knuckled the top of its shaggy head. "You smell like dead fish."

The animal danced at Nick's feet, as if he'd just been paid a compliment.

An elderly man with a mane of silver hair stepped onto the porch and waved at Nick. Using the railing as a brace, he took the steps at a much slower pace than his dog.

Nick abandoned Jess and loped toward him, closing the distance between them in just a few strides. The man grasped Nick's hand and drew him into a hug.

"I was beginning to wonder what happened to you." His gaze swung to Jess and he smiled. "Now I can see you have a good excuse."

Heat flared in Jess's cheeks. The last thing she wanted to do was provide more grist for the town's rumor mill.

It wasn't exactly comforting to see a hint of red rising under the collar of Nick's T-shirt. The same thought must have occurred to him, too.

"I'm Jessica Keaton," Jess said when Nick didn't seem inclined to break the awkward silence.

"It's nice to meet you, Jessica." The elderly man stuck out a hand as brown and gnarled as the pair of oak trees that bowed over the shoreline. "Anthony Silva."

Silva?

Jess's gaze bounced between the men and this time, she saw similarities in the shape of the jawline and sky-blue eyes.

At her unspoken question, Nick nodded. "My grandpa."

"When he wants to claim me." Anthony smiled, and Jess instantly saw another thing the two men had in common.

Charm.

"Jessica is interested in buying some eggs," Nick said.

Anthony's shaggy brows shot up into his hairline. "Today?"

Nick nodded. "Do you think you can come up with a dozen?"

"I'm sure I can." Laughter danced in Anthony's eyes, although Jess had no idea why. "Let's walk around back and say hello to the girls. See what we can find."

Nick, Jess noticed, cut back his stride, matching his pace to the older man as they walked around the cabin. A yard of sorts had been carved out of the trees and Jess was surprised to see a ten-foot-tall circle of fence surrounding what looked to be a single tree.

"A Wolf River apple." Anthony had caught her staring. "The people who owned the original homestead planted it. My wife, Jenny, babied that tree and managed to coax a bushel of fruit from it every year. The deer got to it once but I put up the fence and won that particular war."

Jess couldn't help but notice he'd spoken of his wife in the past tense. And when he stopped a few feet from the fence, his expression almost wistful, Jess wondered if it was memories he was counting and not the number of tiny green apples on the tree.

"Can you whistle?"

It took a moment for Jess to realize that Anthony was speaking to her.

"Yes." At least she thought she could. It had to be like riding a bicycle, right?

"Make it a good one. Persephone is way past her expiration date for the average chicken and I think she's starting to go deaf."

"I…" Jess realized she had Nick's full attention now. With everyone—even the dog—watching her expectantly, she pursed her lips and blew the first four notes of the song that Sienna had played on the piano until it had become the background music stuck in Jess's head.

A flock of chickens in various shapes and sizes emerged from a shed at the edge of the yard. Jess recognized the larger ones as Rhode Island reds, but there were other breeds she'd never seen before. Tiny powder puffs with feathered legs and feet, they resembled bunnies more than birds.

In less than twenty seconds, Jess was surrounded. One of the bolder ones began to peck at her shoe.

Anthony dipped his hand in his shirt pocket and scattered kernels of corn on the ground. "This will keep them entertained while I check the coop for eggs."

Jess remembered what the teenage boy at the grocery store had said about a bad knee. The chicken coop appeared to be weather-tight, but the entire structure listed slightly to one side, and three narrow wooden planks leading to the entrance barely looked strong enough to hold Persephone, let alone a grown man.

"I'll do it," Jess offered. "It looks like fun."

"That depends on your definition, I guess." Anthony chuckled. "The basket's hanging on a nail by the door. Watch your head, though." He wagged a finger at her. "The ceiling is kind of low."

Jess smiled. "I will."

Chapter Ten

Nick wasn't prepared for Jessica's smile.

It came without warning, as unexpected and dazzling as a shooting star.

He was still caught in the afterglow when she disappeared into the coop, holding the basket in front of her like a shield.

"Care for a glass of rhubarb cider to cool off, Nicholas?"

Grandpop was the picture of innocence, but Nick felt a telltale burn in his cheeks. "Sure."

Once they were inside the house, though, Anthony made no move to open the refrigerator. He crossed his arms over his chest and stared Nick down.

"So…" His grandpa released the word into the air, leaving Nick to fill in the blank.

"I would have picked up Bucket sooner, but I had to wait at the church until all the kids got picked up by their parents."

Anthony's low huff told Nick that wasn't the information

he'd been seeking. "It explains why you're late, but not why you didn't mention you had a new friend."

Nick groaned. "Et tu, Grandpop? I thought you were one of the few people in Winsome Lake who doesn't care about my love life."

"I care that you're happy." Anthony's eyes twinkled. "So does the woman whose eggs you just gave away."

And that woman would be his mom. Nick winced inwardly. No doubt he'd hear about it later.

"I am happy. Ask Bucket." The dog had been Nick's roommate and running partner for seven years. He was also the reason Nick didn't need a vacuum cleaner, so there you go. The perfect arrangement.

Anthony glanced out the window. "At the moment your dog is trying to figure out if his head will fit inside the rain gutter, so you see why I'd be hesitant to take his word for it," he said drily. "And I'm not so old that I don't know when someone is trying to change the subject."

"I didn't mention Jessica because we just met. Elaine Haviland hired her to help around the house."

"How is Elaine?" Anthony's brows dipped together. "I heard she'd had another stroke."

"Not a stroke. A fall," Nick corrected him. "She cracked some ribs and the rehab facility wants her to stay a little longer."

Anthony's expression clouded over, and Nick knew he was remembering Grandma Jenny's rapid decline after she'd slipped on a patch of ice and broken a hip. No one had thought it strange when she complained of leg pain, but three days after she was released from the hospital, she'd died of a blood clot. Her passing left a hole in the family that, four years later, still hadn't healed.

"Keaton. Is that what she said?" Anthony tipped his head. "I don't recognize the name."

"Jessica isn't a local."

"Where are her people?"

Oh, Grandpop.

A rush of affection flowed through Nick. Anthony Silva had lived in Winsome Lake all his life. His son, Nick's father, two daughters, and multiple grandchildren lived within a twenty-mile radius of the city limits.

The Silva family was a veritable patchwork quilt when it came to careers and interests, but faith in God and each other held them all together. Even when the death of someone they'd loved had stretched the fabric thin.

"I'm not sure where she's from." But based on the disparaging comment Jessica had made about Winsome Lake in Elaine's kitchen, Nick doubted she'd lived in a small town. "She hasn't said much about herself."

Actually…nothing, now that Nick thought about it.

On the drive over, Jessica had let him go on about what he did for a living, but she hadn't reciprocated. Hadn't mentioned where she'd lived or how she'd ended up taking a job in Winsome Lake.

"Jessica is staying at Elaine's?" Anthony asked.

Nick nodded slowly. "Yes…"

"What's the matter?" Anthony must have seen something on Nick's face because his own eyes darkened with concern. "You don't think Jessica is going to get along with Elaine?"

Nick couldn't imagine anyone not liking Elaine Haviland. "No."

"Then what is it?"

In his mind's eye, Nick saw a charred piece of bread sticking out of the toaster.

"I'm not sure she can cook."

Chapter Eleven

A smudge of something that looked like dirt but could have been something a little more...*organic*...darkened the hem of Jess's pants.

She was too engrossed in her treasure hunt to care.

Every egg—and they ranged in color from a deep walnut-brown to sea glass–blue—that went into the basket had Jess's mind whirling with possibilities.

She spotted a freckled egg half-hidden in the nesting box. Wiped away a piece of straw stuck to the shell and tucked it into the basket.

A Nick-shaped shadow fell across the plank floor and blotted out the sun. "How's it going in there?"

"Fine." Jess straightened, keeping a protective hold on the basket as she turned toward him. "I found ten."

"Not bad." Nick grabbed Bucket's collar before he could join Jess inside the shed. "Grandpop had a few in the fridge from yesterday to make an even dozen."

Just the way Nick said the name, with a mixture of affection and respect, told Jess the two men were close.

The pinch of envy surprised her.

Grandparents had never been part of Jess's life. Her father had been estranged from the Keaton family before Jess was born. Her maternal grandparents, who'd moved to Arizona when Jess was in preschool, didn't approve of the way her parents lived so the tension simmering in the air whenever they got together made the visits as short as they were rare.

Jess ducked her head to avoid one of the low beams Nick had warned her about and stepped out into the sunshine again. She wrinkled her nose. The breeze off the lake couldn't hide the fact that she still smelled like a chicken coop.

Anthony Silva was waiting in the yard. "Thought you might want to take some maple syrup home. Friends of mine out in the county have their own sugar shack." He held up a mason jar filled with amber liquid and added two more eggs, one olive green, the other a dusty rose, to Jess's collection. "Don't worry about the basket. Nick can bring it back."

"Thank you, Mr. Silva." Jess started to unzip her purse, but Anthony was shaking his head.

"Tony," he said. "And consider the eggs a welcome-to-the-neighborhood gift."

"But—"

"Never argue with a retired attorney," Nick murmured.

Two against one. Jess had no choice but to give in.

"Now, I have an appointment with my fishing pole, so I better get going before someone parks their boat in my favorite spot." Anthony wrapped one thin arm around Nick's shoulders. "Coffee on Saturday?"

Nick smiled. "I'll be here."

Jess followed Nick down the driveway, careful not to jostle

the basket. She opened the passenger-side door of the truck, but the dog got there first and leaped inside.

"Hey!"

"Sorry." Nick chuckled. "That's his spot."

"His… This is *your* dog?" Jess had assumed he belonged to Anthony.

"Uh-huh." Nick's voice cut to a whisper. "Although he thinks he picked *me*." Nick reached out a hand and ruffled the dog's shaggy back. "Sorry, Bucket. It's the back seat for you this time, bud."

The dog obeyed, but that didn't prevent Jess from keeping a wary eye on him when she reclaimed her seat.

Nick jogged around to the other side and climbed in.

Bucket leaned forward, rested his head on the seat between them, doggy breath wafting in Jess's ear.

Nick started the truck and rolled all the windows down.

Because of the dog? Or because Jess smelled like a chicken coop?

She didn't want to ask.

"You like dogs?" Nick waved at the driver of another pickup that cruised past before backing onto the street.

Jess shrugged. "I've never had one."

"I grew up with them. After I moved back to town, I thought it would be nice to have a running partner. One that didn't complain if it was too hot or too cold." Nick smiled. "Marty, one of my assistant coaches, volunteered at the county shelter and mentioned a litter of puppies had come in. I drove out on the weekend to take a look.

"This guy was in the kennel next door." Nick reached back and gave the dog's moist nose a pat. "He'd been picked up as a stray and no one had claimed him. No one seemed to be interested in adopting him, either. When I asked if I could take him for a walk, the staff person on duty actually tried to talk me out of it.

"You don't want this one, Coach." Nick's husky alto deepened to a baritone. *"Look at those paws. He's going to be huge when he grows into them. And to tell you the truth, well, he's kind of a...a buckethead."*

Bucket flopped back down on the seat and heaved a sigh.

Jess refused to believe the dog had actually been following Nick's story.

"He must have been right or you wouldn't have named him Bucket," she pointed out.

"He was right about the paws." Nick grinned. "Buckets aren't always empty, though, you know. And just because something looks a little neglected doesn't mean there isn't good stuff inside."

Jess's grip on the basket tightened.

What did Nick know about neglect? The attractive, popular high school football star turned athletic coach? Guys like him were uncrowned royalty in a small town like Winsome Lake.

Unlike Jess, Nick didn't have to earn people's respect. It had practically been a birthright.

She was relieved when the truck rolled to a stop in front of Elaine's house.

Nick was already out of the truck and jogging around to open Jess's door before she could reach for the handle. He held out his hand and a smile like summer lightning crackled in his eyes when Jess reluctantly handed him the basket of eggs.

"Thanks." She jumped down. "Hang on a second and I'll bring you the basket."

"Don't worry about it now." Nick plucked a piece of straw

from one of the eggs and let it drift to the ground. "I'll be back in a day or two."

For some reason the words ignited a rush of panic.

"Now that I'm staying there... I was thinking that I could mow the grass." The thought hadn't occurred to Jess until now, but she ran with it. "You assumed Elaine would be home by now, and I'm sure you have other things to do."

Nick crossed his arms and shifted his weight onto one foot, studying her the way Jess assumed he studied players on an opposing team.

"Elaine hired you, but I have a job, too. I promised her I would take care of things around the house until she got back."

"The lawn," Jess clarified.

Nick smiled. "I believe I said whatever needs taking care of."

Before Jess could point out that she wasn't a dandelion or a leaky pipe, Nick was driving away.

Violet greeted Jess at the door with an expression that could only be described as reproachful.

Although how a small face covered with fur could have an expression at all was a mystery to Jess.

She kicked off her shoes and saw a feather stuck to one of the soles. She shook it off and caught a whiff of chicken coop.

Maybe that was what had drawn Violet out of hiding. Jess smelled like lunch...

Lunch.

Jess's head tilted toward the ceiling and she groaned.

She hadn't checked the little ceramic dish in the laundry room since she'd filled it the night before.

How often did cats eat, anyway?

She could imagine having to tell Elaine Haviland that

her cat had gotten tired of the staff's incompetence and run away from home.

"Are you hungry? Is that it?"

Violet turned and stalked down the hallway, tail lifted like a conductor's baton, bringing order to the house again.

Jess took that as a yes.

She set the basket of eggs on the counter and walked over to inspect Violet's dish.

It wasn't empty, but the three stray kibbles scattered in the bottom of the dish didn't do anything to alleviate Jess's guilt. She added more cat food, refilled Violet's water dish and carried the eggs over to the sink.

A feeling of accomplishment stole over Jess, knowing she'd collected them herself.

Gwyneth had insisted on quality ingredients, so Jess had connected with a few small business owners in the outlying area who sold organic meat and produce to upscale restaurants and a few select individuals. Gwyneth Donovan, of course, being one of the latter. Everything was delivered right to the door once a week, including the eggs. Their shells were always a uniform brown. Straw, dirt and feather free.

Jess set the basket on the counter and searched the cupboards for a bowl to put them in.

Elaine's kitchen wasn't well stocked even for the average home cook. In fact, Jess had started to wonder if the woman cooked for herself at all. She'd found a skillet here, a saucepan there, the Dutch oven high on a shelf in the pantry.

She opened one of the lower cabinets and spotted a mishmash of serving bowls hiding behind a stand-up mixer that looked as old as Jess's Buick. The largest bowl was chipped, breaking the chain of forget-me-nots painted around the rim, but looked to be the right size.

Jess transferred the eggs from basket to bowl, opened the

fridge and felt her mouth drop open, too. Next to the plate she'd set on the lower rack before leaving on her impulsive road trip with Nick was a bundle of fresh spinach, the stems tied together with a thin piece of twine.

That was it. When Jess received her first paycheck...*if* she received a paycheck...she was changing all the locks.

She closed the door with a little more force than necessary and noticed the three storage containers were missing. Which narrowed the list of possible intruders from the entire population of Winsome Lake down to three.

Jess had been hoping when the women claimed their containers again, she'd find out which one of them had made the pie. Based on first impressions, Jess had a hunch it was Nita. Pie crust was one of those things that looked simple enough but required precision. Nita, whose life seemed to be guided by her watch, looked like that sort of person.

She toasted another slice of sourdough, a beautiful golden brown this time, topped it with a fried egg and a paper-thin slice of Swiss cheese, and made a quick salad out of the spinach, a handful of cherry tomatoes and a splash of olive oil.

Then, juggling a glass of iced tea and her second attempt at lunch, Jess let herself out the back door. Instead of settling on the brick step, she wandered farther into the garden.

The afternoon sun was high overhead and some of the herbs were slumped over, dozing in the heat, while the flowers tipped their faces up to the sun.

"Watch out f-for bees."

The plate in Jess's hand tilted at the unexpected sound of a voice. One of the cherry tomatoes rolled over the side and was instantly swallowed up in a sea of chocolate mint.

A head had popped up on the other side of the fence. A teenage boy, with lively brown eyes and a shock of hair the same deep auburn as Anthony Silva's Rhode Island reds.

"Thank you," Jess said. "I guess I forgot the bees like flowers, too."

"They s-sting, you know." The warning was accompanied by an engaging smile. "My name is C-Christopher Benjamin Gardner. What's yours?"

"Jessica."

Christopher looked at the plate in Jess's hand and made a face. "You like t-tomatoes?"

Jess nodded. "Don't you?"

Christopher pressed both hands over his mouth and swung his head from side to side.

"I'll take that as a no." Jess laughed.

"B-but I like pizza with mushrooms. And h-hamburgers."

Ah. The staples of every kid's diet. She didn't point out that tomatoes were a key ingredient in marinara sauce, though. "So do I."

Jess heard the snick of a door opening and her neighbor looked over his shoulder.

"I better go. I f-forgot to tell my mom I was going outside." The grin disappeared and he looked every inch the disgruntled teenager now. "B-because I have Down syndrome, she treats me like a little boy. B-but I'm almost a man. I'll be seventeen in October."

"I think most moms—" Jess, not having had a mother that fell into that category, was totally guessing here "—think of their sons as boys no matter how old they are."

Christopher tipped his head. "You're n-nice...like Miss Elaine. She's sick and I've been praying every d-day for her. Now you're here."

It was obvious he thought the two were somehow connected.

Jess had been many things. Culinary student. Caterer. Personal chef. And now she could add housekeeper and cook to the list.

But one thing Jess knew for sure.

She'd never been the answer to anyone's prayer.

Chapter Twelve

"I come bearing gifts."

On Wednesday, Vanessa poked her head into Elaine's room and held up a small paper sack.

Elaine worked up a smile and motioned to her to come in.

The pillow behind Elaine shifted when she fumbled for the remote. The first set of X-rays had looked good, but even with the bed set at a ninety-degree angle to discourage fluid from building up in her lungs, Elaine's ribs still protested whenever she tried to move. She pressed the power button, and Fred Astaire and Ginger Rogers vanished from the screen.

"Chocolate chip or raspberry cheesecake?"

"Better." Vanessa strode into the room, every inch the social worker in a sleeveless navy shirtdress and conservative heels.

"My discharge papers?" It was the only thing Elaine could

think of that trumped ice cream at eight o'clock in the morning.

"No." Vanessa pulled a chair closer and set the paper sack on the bed. "But it is the next best thing to freedom."

"Okaay." Elaine tunneled through the layers of tissue paper and pulled out a cell phone. *"Vanessa."*

"I had it fixed." Vanessa grinned. "Your link to the outside world is restored."

Elaine turned the phone over. "And a new case."

"It has a little more pizazz, don't you agree?"

"Definitely more pizazz." Elaine ran the tip of her finger over the gold-and-pink rhinestones encrusted on the back. "I don't know what to say. Thank you."

"I know this latest setback has been hard." Vanessa reached out and squeezed Elaine's hand. "You might not be feeling up to a long chat with your friends yet, but you can always check your email or play Candy Crush."

Just the thought of scrolling through the messages clogging her in-box drained some of Elaine's energy. At least she'd been between writing projects when she'd had the stroke.

Well, with the exception of one. Although technically, it didn't qualify as a project until Elaine said yes.

The door opened and Kristina, one of the aides, peeked inside. She spotted the social worker at Elaine's bedside and drew back. "I can come back with the breakfast tray in a little while."

"No, no. I have to get back to my office." Vanessa stood up and pushed the chair back in place. "I'll be in meetings all day, but I plan to talk to Dr. Kim and PT about your goals first thing tomorrow."

Goals, plural. Elaine only had one. Home.

"Thank you again, Vanessa." She held up the phone.

"Running errands for patients isn't part of your job description and I know how busy you are."

"I may have outsourced this one to a private party," Vanessa confessed.

Elaine saw laughter, not guilt, in Vanessa's eyes, so it was easy to guess who'd been her partner in crime. But Matthew hadn't said a word when he'd stopped by her room the day before.

"Did he pick out the case, too?"

"Of course not." Vanessa tossed a smile over her shoulder as she walked to the door. "But if your ringtone is different, I'm not the one to blame."

"He changed my ringtone? Can he do that?"

"I guess you'll have to wait for a call to find out."

The door closed, and Elaine sank back against the pillows.

Kristina set the tray down on Elaine's bedside table. "How are you today, Ms. Haviland?"

"I have my cell phone back."

"That's good." The girl's shy smile reminded Elaine of Sienna Bloom.

Another reason Elaine was anxious to get home. Sienna's music scholarship depended on how well she performed at the summer recital. And how well she performed was in direct proportion to how often she practiced.

Elaine had tried to call Sienna a few days before she'd fallen. She'd wanted to let her know that she was coming home soon and planned to attend the recital, but an automated voice had announced the phone was out of service.

The last time that had happened, Sienna's father had thrown it against the wall after he discovered the phone company had added a late charge onto the monthly bill. He'd blamed Sienna's mother. She, in turn, had blamed him. The couple had separated a year ago. And while their marriage vows hadn't been able to keep them together, mutual hostility did. Sienna's parents continued to circle the edges of each other's lives like boxers in a ring, forcing their only child to be an unwilling spectator in the Fight of the Month Club.

Sienna hadn't confided in Elaine, though. It had taken months of collecting tiny snippets of conversation and putting the pieces together to get a clearer picture of the girl's life.

"Do you need any help, Ms. Haviland?" Kristina's soft voice intruded on her thoughts. She'd unwrapped the utensils and moved them around the tray like chess pieces. Spoon next to the hot cereal. Fork lower left corner. Butter knife beyond Elaine's reach on the opposite end of the tray.

"No, thank you. I've got it, Kristina." Elaine waited until the aide had left the room before she bowed her head.

Thank You, Lord, for a new day, for this food and for all the gifts Your hands provide.

Elaine opened her eyes and took a quick inventory of the breakfast tray. The contents generally told Elaine more about her progress than the weekly physical therapy report.

Applesauce. Yogurt. Cranberry juice. The ramekin of diced pears, one rung up the dietary ladder, gave her a glimmer of hope.

The dietician must have had a huddle with the respiratory therapist and Dr. Kim. Elaine had checked the little box next to French toast but the main entrée looked suspiciously like oatmeal.

The first thing Elaine was going to do when she got home was eat something that wasn't ground up into tiny pieces or had the consistency of glue.

Someone in the kitchen had tucked a sugar packet next to the bowl, but the coordination required to open it would take more time than Elaine was willing to commit to the task, so she reached for the yogurt instead.

She'd just started on the pears when the opening notes of the *Rocky* theme burst from her phone.

Elaine laughed and the pain in her ribs roared back to life, but she reached for the phone, anyway.

"Hello?"

"Elaine? Finally!"

It took a split second for Elaine to match a name to the voice. "Hilary?"

"Of course it's Hilary! I've been trying to get in touch with you for days. I thought you'd died."

Elaine, who should have been shocked by the morbid pronouncement, found herself smiling instead.

Hilary Cordelle had no filter. Whatever thought popped into her literary agent's head came out of her mouth. Plus, it would never occur to Hilary that someone might be ignoring her on purpose.

"I had a...setback. I'm still at the rehab center."

"That's terrible." The silence on the other end of the line told Elaine that Hilary was absorbing the information and what it meant for both of them. "I hope it wasn't another stroke."

"It was a fall. I cracked some ribs and my phone, which is why I haven't returned your calls. In fact, I just got it back about fifteen minutes ago."

"Then you haven't seen the contract I emailed to you?"

The contract?

Elaine closed her eyes. "Hilary...the last time we spoke, I told you that I was still thinking about it."

"I know, but that was months ago. I assumed you would have made a decision by now. The publisher already has a tentative release date."

Elaine was starting to regret the moment of weakness that had prompted her to even consider the project.

"What's your hesitation?" Hilary asked. "Whatever it is, I'll help you figure it out."

Elaine looked down at the splotch of yogurt on the terry-cloth bib Kristina had fastened around her neck.

The right side of her body still felt weak. Her fingers tingled and her speech had a tendency to slur when she was tired. What other people considered normal activities—walking across the room, getting dressed—required all of Elaine's concentration.

But Hilary, who ran on espresso and five hours of sleep, didn't understand that healing involved more than the body. It was a joint effort of heart and soul and mind.

In all fairness, though, Elaine hadn't known that, either, before the stroke.

"Once I get my strength back, the doctor will want me to go through another round of therapy before I go home," Elaine said slowly. "But at this point, I'm not even sure when that will be."

"I can talk to the publisher about pushing the deadline out another month or two, but they want to see your signature on the dotted line."

"I have a deadline?"

"It's in the contract. The contract with a very generous advance on royalties, I might add."

Elaine's head began to throb, joining in a sympathetic duet with her ribs.

As a ghostwriter, deadlines didn't bother her. They came with the package, as did major rewrites and last-minute changes from a demanding clientele that expected her to turn an idea that had popped into their heads while showering or sipping cocktails on the beach into a bestseller.

"The book will be amazing," Hilary said. "That's why I signed with you in the first place."

Elaine wanted to think that after three decades of working together, Hilary wasn't hinting that Elaine still owed the literary agent something for jump-starting her career, but she knew better.

And she still wanted to say no. To the contract, the deadline, the advance on royalties. Everything. But an inner nudge, the one Elaine had learned to trust, the one that had prevented her from turning down the project the first time Hilary contacted her, said *wait*.

"I'll let you know soon."

"How soon?"

"Give me a week."

"You're the one who doesn't believe in coincidence." Hilary switched tactics. "Maybe there's a reason this opportunity came when it did. If you don't tell Libby Tucker's story, someone else will. And no one knows her as well as you do."

Elaine closed her eyes.

If only that wasn't true.

Chapter Thirteen

Jess was wrist-deep in parsley when she heard the front door rattle.

She wiped off her hands on a towel on her way through the living room, rounded the corner into the hallway and almost bumped into Merri. A paisley bag large enough to hold a week's worth of clothing sat on the floor at her feet.

"Good morning, Jessica!"

Jess was sure she'd locked the door, but before she could question how Merri had gotten inside, Peg trudged in, balancing an oversize canvas bag on one hip and a dog that looked like a cross between a fox and a monkey on the other.

"Hello, Jessica. Beautiful day, isn't it?"

"Um…"

"You haven't been introduced to Bosco yet, have you?"

"No." But Jess was pretty sure she'd seen that face on the front of Peg's shirt the first time they'd met.

Jess took a step backward, but the dog still managed to

swipe its wet tongue against her arm when Peg trundled past her. Merri fell into step behind her friend, leaving Jess no choice but to follow the strange caravan all the way to the dining room.

The chunky candle in the center of the table was swept aside. Merri reached into the paisley bag and pulled out a smaller version in the same fabric. Inside that one, a shoebox secured with rubber bands, and a dented cookie tin.

What. Was. *Happening?*

Jess kneaded her fingers against her temples. "Is all this for Elaine?"

Peg shook her head. The tiny gold dog bones dangling from her earrings danced as she deposited both canvas tote bag and French bulldog on the floor. "It's Thursday."

Merri must have seen the confusion on Jess's face because she smiled.

"We get together here every Thursday. Elaine is the only one with a big enough table."

"A big enough table for…" Out of the corner of her eye, Jess saw a flash of gray. Violet, who'd been lurking in the shadows like the paparazzi since Jess had started cooking, suddenly decided to make her presence known. When the cat spotted Bosco, her tail doubled in size, the fur on her back turning into a ridge of cactus-like spikes.

"Ah…" Jess strangled on her next breath and leaped to intervene, but Bosco was quicker. He dove behind Peg, giving Jess a chance to sweep Violet into her arms.

The cat's indignant meow reminded Jess that she didn't like to be held. Jess released her quickly in the direction of the kitchen again.

"I didn't know Violet was here," Peg said.

"Nick dropped her off the day I arrived."

Merri and Peg exchanged a quick look that Jess couldn't quite interpret.

"You've met Nick, then?" Merri pried open the cookie tin and it instantly birthed three more.

"Yes."

The women exchanged another look. One that Jess had no trouble understanding this time.

"Everyone loves Nick," Merri said. "He's a sweetheart. Hardworking. Great with kids."

"And he's single," Peg added.

"Why?"

Peg looked a little taken aback by Jess's question, but Merri smiled serenely.

"Because he hasn't met someone who makes him want to be married, of course," she said.

"Bosco likes him." Peg started to empty her tote bag, too. "Nick adopted a dog from the shelter."

Jess was *not* going to admit she'd met Bucket, too. And because she was losing control of both the house and the conversation, she tried to guide it down another path.

"I'm sorry Violet scared your dog. She doesn't usually come out during the day."

"Violet *is* a bit…unique." Peg whispered the last word, as if she was afraid the cat was eavesdropping on their conversation. "Isn't she, Bosco?"

Bosco didn't answer. He'd shuffled away and was circling the philodendron in a way that made Jess nervous.

"Did you start without me?" Nita strode in, the strap of an insulated cooler bag looped over one shoulder, dragging a carry-on size suitcase behind her like a loose tailpipe.

"What's going on?" Jess asked bluntly.

Three pairs of eyes swung in her direction.

"It's Thursday," Peg said again.

Jess knew it was Thursday. She also knew they needed a table. What no one had told her was why.

Or more important, for how long?

"We scrapbook on Thursdays," Nita said matter-of-factly.

"Scrapbook?" Jess knew what it was, of course. She'd just never actually met someone who *did* it.

Merri bobbed her head. "We talked about it for years, but Elaine was the one who told us to stop talking and start doing."

"Elaine isn't home yet," Jess felt the need to point out.

"Oh, she never scrapbooks with us." Nita unzipped the cooler bag and pulled out a package of frosted sugar cookies imprisoned in a see-through plastic box, casting serious doubt on Jess's theory about the pie baker's identity.

"Elaine claims she's a terrible photographer," Merri added.

It suddenly occurred to Jess she hadn't noticed any family photographs taking up space on the walls or the end tables in the living room. No pictures of Elaine herself, either, standing on the beach or in her garden. But then again, Jess didn't have any, either. If she did take the occasional photo, the subject was food, not people.

Nita consulted her watch. "I have two hours and Chrissy's fifth birthday photos to organize."

Merri and Peg each claimed a chair, showing Jess who really had control of the room.

Her hands rolled into fists at her sides. She'd pictured this morning going differently in her mind. Maybe people didn't talk when they scrapbooked...

"Jessica met Nick," Peg told Nita.

And she was out of there.

Jess retreated to the kitchen, where she had an unobstructed view of the women sitting at the table and they, in turn, had an unobstructed view of her. Unless she was standing at the sink.

She turned on the faucet, patted cold water on her cheeks.

"It's going to be a warm one again today, isn't it?" Merri bustled in and made a beeline for the narrow closet that housed the broom and dustpan; opened the door and withdrew a coffeepot that Jess hadn't known was there.

Merri caught Jess staring.

"Elaine doesn't like coffee, but she lets me keep this here for emergencies. Help yourself if you'd like a cup. There are cookies, too." Merri cast a bright smile over her shoulder as she swept some of Jess's cooking utensils aside to make room on the counter.

Yes, to coffee. The cookies? A definite no.

Merri pressed the button on the coffeepot and glided away. Jess took a deep breath and reached for her knife again.

Focus, Jess. Pretend you're back in culinary school and Chef Tomas is singing opera to see if you can handle the chaos of the kitchen.

She finished the parsley and started on the chives she'd discovered growing by the back door.

Gwyneth was sensitive to dairy so it had been years since Jess had made a frittata.

She tossed a few tablespoons of butter in the pan, took the eggs out of the refrigerator and started cracking them into a clean bowl. No wonder Anthony Silva's eggs were in high demand. The yolks were large and beautifully round, the deep orange of a harvest moon.

Over the sizzle of the butter, the coffeepot began to sputter and gurgle.

In order to maintain some sort of boundary, Jess didn't wait for the women to descend on the kitchen.

She poked her head in the doorway. Blinked. The table

had become the foundation for mountains of photographs and decorative paper. In the valleys between were jars filled with buttons and beads and gadgets Jess didn't recognize.

"The coffee is done. Who would like a cup?"

Three heads remained bent. Three hands shot into the air. Okay, then.

Jess backed into the kitchen, poured three cups of coffee and converted a wooden cutting board into a serving tray. She pivoted toward the door and almost tripped over Bosco. The hopeful gleam in his marble-black eyes made Jess shake her head.

"Oh, no. Out you go. I work alone in the kitchen."

The dog cut a zigzag path behind her, nose pressed to the linoleum, vacuuming up bits of parsley that had drifted over the side of the butcher-block island.

Jess set a cup near each woman's elbow, careful not to trigger an avalanche. The cookies were still sealed inside their cellophane cocoon. The women were so engrossed in their project, no one had touched them yet.

Jess would have happily snuck away, but Merri sang out a thank-you a split second before Jess crossed the metal strip that separated the dining room and the kitchen.

And then Peg's head lifted, her glue stick suspended in midair, making escape impossible.

"Whatever you're making smells delicious," she said.

"It's just a frittata."

Peg's head tipped to one side. "A what?"

"A frittata. It's an egg dish."

"Oh! Like a quiche."

"A quiche is a quiche," Nita said without looking up.

"A lot of the ingredients are the same, but a frittata isn't baked in a shell, like a pie," Jess explained.

"If it's eggs, why not just scramble them?" Peg asked. "It's a lot easier."

Jess silently matched the salad from Dan's Hometown Market and Deli to its owner.

"It is easier, but the texture is different. Almost like custard, if you do it right," she said.

"My mom made a quiche every Easter," Merri said. "She'd let me whisk the eggs and sprinkle the cheese on top right before it went into the oven. I remember my twin brothers would always fight over the last piece." A mischievous smile broke out across her face and chased the years away. "Mom would give it to me, though, because I was the only one not making a fuss."

"Merri," Nita said, studying one of her photographs, "never makes a fuss."

"Would you like to see them? My brothers?" Merri didn't wait for an answer. She shuffled through a stack of photographs with the speed of a blackjack dealer and handed one to Jess.

"Michael and Mitch. Everyone in our neighborhood called them the M&Ms because no one could tell them apart."

Two little boys wearing matching baseball caps grinned at Jess. On the step between them, a slender girl a few years older with honey-blond hair and Merri's dove-gray eyes.

"I found boxes of photos after Mom passed away last year and decided to make albums for the boys. We were so impatient when Mom would make us pose for a picture, but I'm glad she did. It's like reliving my childhood all over again."

Jess suppressed a shudder. She was glad there wasn't a shoebox filled with photographs that would document hers.

"Excuse me," she murmured. "I have to check on something."

Jess retreated to the kitchen and their chatter resumed, providing the background noise while she went back to work.

An hour later the frittata came out of the oven, embedded with herbs, the edges a glorious golden brown, exactly the way Jess imagined it would be.

She cut a slice—heard the unmistakable sound of cookies being freed from their plastic cocoon—and cut a few more. With the cast-iron skillet swaddled in kitchen towels, Jess carried it into the dining room and set it on the buffet.

Conversation and movement halted when all eyes turned toward Jess. Suddenly, she felt as nervous as a culinary student on exam day again.

"I thought you might like to try the frittata."

"We aren't going to eat your breakfast," Nita said, but Peg and Merri were already on their feet.

Jess handed out forks, stepped back and felt a moment of panic when she watched them take the first bite.

Peg's eyes rounded. "Amazing," she mumbled. "Nita, you have to taste this."

Nita glanced at her watch for permission before she rose from the table and joined them.

Merri's eyes drifted closed on the second bite. "Delicious. I can't say for sure, but I have a feeling this isn't *just* a frittata."

Peg leaned closer to Jessica. "It's a secret family recipe, isn't it?" she whispered.

Jess almost laughed.

In a roundabout way, she supposed her family's secrets had had something to do with it. Her parents had left Jess to fend for herself so often, she'd had no choice but to learn how to turn simple ingredients into a meal.

Eventually, cooking began to nourish Jess's soul as well as her body. The long evenings and the weekends that she spent alone were spent in the kitchen. And when Jess was old enough to take over the grocery shopping, she'd started experimenting with different spices and seasonings.

Something she'd done to survive had turned into her passion. And that passion had led to freedom. Freedom to be judged by her accomplishments and not her last name.

"I didn't follow one," Jess said. "It's eggs and fresh herbs and the spinach someone left in the refrigerator."

She waited for that someone to confess, but the women were already trudging back to the table.

"There's plenty," she told them. "Feel free to have another piece."

"Aren't you going to join us?" Merri asked.

But Jess, who was already on her way into the kitchen, pretended not to hear.

Making the food didn't make her part of their group.

Less than a minute after Jess heard Nita's watch chirp out a reminder that two hours had gone by, Peg trotted into the kitchen, waving a piece of frittata in the air as bait.

"Bosco!" She looked around the room. "That sneaky pup. He was sleeping under the table a minute ago. Did you see which way he went?"

"No." Jess hadn't seen the dog since she'd banished him from the kitchen. "But there's nothing he can get into…"

Except the dish of cat food Jess had moved to the back hall so it wouldn't be in her way.

Who knew what would happen if cat and dog met face-to-face without a referee?

"I'll find him." Jess rounded the corner and spotted Bosco planted in front of the screen door, tail thumping the floor.

A wide-eyed Sienna Bloom stood on the other side.

Jess shooed Bosco away and reached for the handle, but

Sienna was already backing down the steps. Jess opened the door a crack so the dog couldn't escape.

"Sienna? Did you want to practice?"

"I..." The girl glanced at Bosco, who tried to feint past Jess and make a break for the garden. "No."

If the backpack she'd been wearing the other day wasn't slung over her shoulder, Jess might have believed her.

"Why..." She was talking to the flowers. Sienna had already disappeared around the corner of the house.

"Was that the Bloom girl?"

Jess glanced over her shoulder.

Nita, Merri and Peg were clustered together in the hallway behind her. Nita looked more grim than usual and even Merri's perpetual smile had disappeared.

The Bloom girl.

Jess had a sinking feeling why Sienna had left.

Chapter Fourteen

After the women packed up their supplies and went home, Jess cleaned up the kitchen and kept going. Elaine's house looked immaculate, but Jess had been hired to do more than cook.

She stumbled upon Violet's hideout with the vacuum cleaner, following the trail of light gray fur down a short hallway behind the living room. At the end of it was a built-in bookcase and another door, this one avocado green.

Two pointed ears inside a basket on the top shelf of the bookcase retracted at the approach of the vacuum. Jess let it idle a moment while she reached out to open the door. Stepped into a modern home office straight from the pages of a magazine.

A cherrywood desk shaped like a horseshoe faced the backyard. Sheer muslin curtains covered the window, allowing the sunlight free access while blocking the view of anyone in the garden who might want to look in. A crème-colored area rug with a pile as soft as whipped cream covered the hardwood floor.

Jess abandoned the vacuum, drawn to a print on the wall.

She recognized the artist. Gwyneth had several Deidre Simmons originals in her media room. This one had to be a reproduction, of course, but the wide brushstrokes of yellow and purple and crimson didn't match the subdued decor in the rest of the house.

There were no photographs on the walls, but everything in the room seemed more personal. Open shelves on the opposite wall showcased an eclectic collection of possessions. A handful of beach glass in a shallow ceramic dish. A piece of driftwood.

Dark-eyed children carved into the arms and lap of a Navajo storyteller's doll. Everywhere Jess looked, she saw mementoes gathered by a woman who'd traveled beyond Woodwind Lane.

She turned her attention to the desk again.

No one had mentioned that Elaine still worked for a living, but papers and books were strewn around the computer on the desk.

Jess picked up a china cup. The tea bag was petrified on a napkin. The contents had evaporated, leaving behind a pale brown ring, further evidence that Elaine had been in the middle of some kind of project before the stroke.

The familiar combination of guilt and unease, reminding Jess she didn't belong here, swirled in her stomach again. But Elaine had hired her to clean the house...

Jess pulled the wastebasket out from under the desk and dropped the tea bag and napkin inside.

The papers scattered across the desk looked like they'd been ripped in half through the middle and down the center while a few were completely intact.

The name Libby Tucker was written across the cover of a spiral-bound notebook embellished with hearts and flowers.

Jess started to gather some of the loose pages into a pile. Some of them were dated and some included simple sketches, but every entry was written in the same flowing script.

She bent down to pick up a piece of paper that had fallen on the floor. The penmanship matched the others, but there were no hearts and no flowers. Nothing but the logo and name of an inexpensive hotel printed at the top.

A girl should get some kind of warning before her life falls apart.

The words jumped off the page and grabbed Jess by the throat.

Mama said the Tucker girls always land on their feet, but she never told me what to do after that. I can't go back and I don't know how to start over. So I ran.

The door creaked, and the guilt that slammed through Jess didn't completely subside when Violet wandered into the room. She trotted past Jess, tail sweeping the air in an elegant princess wave, and launched herself onto the velvet cushion of the armless chair by the window.

Jess added the page to the mountain of loose papers.

She didn't know who Libby Tucker was or how Elaine Haviland had ended up with a diary someone had tried to destroy, but she wasn't being paid to read them. Still, it didn't stop Jess from wondering about a girl that she felt an odd sort of kinship with.

She wondered where Libby was now.

Had she started over? Or was she still running?

★ ★ ★

Jess was discovering there was a direct correlation between cats and sleep deprivation.

Violet seemed to take delight in substituting for an alarm clock.

"You nap during the day," Jess muttered. "Those of us who *can't* should be able to decide when we want to get up in the morning."

Violet continued to stare at her. But at least she wasn't puncturing tiny holes in Jess's pillowcase this time.

Jess rolled over and closed her eyes. Bolted upright in bed.

"I forgot to check your dish again."

The cat jumped down and stalked toward the door.

"I'm up. I'm up." Jess's guilty conscience had her reaching for a pair of cotton leggings. She yanked a sweatshirt over her head and shuffled down the stairs.

Out of the corner of her eye, Jess saw something move in the shadows and veered into the living room.

She spotted Violet immediately. Cradled in Sienna Bloom's arms.

And the girl looked like she'd logged about as many hours of sleep as Jess had during the night.

"It can't be seven o'clock already." Jess looked at the window for obvious signs of daylight. If there was any at all, it wasn't strong enough to breach the heavy drapes.

Sienna shrugged and gathered Violet closer. *Violet.* The cat that didn't like to be held.

It was too early in the morning to solve mysteries like this.

Sienna's backpack sagged against the piano bench. Jess admired the girl's dedication, but...

The crocheted afghan snagged her attention. The day before, it had been neatly draped over the back of the sofa. Now it unfurled like a runaway ball of yarn from one end to the other. And one of the pillows that bookended the corners had shifted position, too.

Jess felt her stomach contract.

Had Sienna *slept* here during the night?

Their eyes met for a split second and then Sienna's gaze dropped to her feet. Her *bare* feet. And Jess saw the telltale color flare in her cheeks.

The question was no longer if she'd slept on the sofa. It was why.

Memories Jess thought she'd put on lockdown began to leak out. Sleepless nights. The times she'd wanted to avoid going home. The only difference between her and Sienna was that Sienna had found somewhere else to go.

"Look..." Jess released a slow breath. "I don't mind if you practice. I'm going to start the coffee."

Relief shimmered in Sienna's eyes. Jess wasn't sure if it was because she'd given her permission to stay or because she hadn't asked any questions.

The moment Jess was alone in the kitchen, she rubbed her eyes and squinted at the clock on the stove.

Did Sienna's parents know where she was at 6:00 a.m. on a Friday morning?

Did they *care*?

Jess dumped an extra scoop of coffee grounds into the filter and stabbed the power button until it turned green.

Maybe she was wrong about Sienna. Maybe the girl was the neighborhood troublemaker and deserved every suspicious look cast her way. Maybe she was surly, not shy...

And maybe the music flooding the house wasn't an outlet for every emotion Sienna was afraid to express with words.

The way cooking had been for Jess at that age.

Jess checked Violet's dish and found an acceptable level of

kibbles. While the coffee brewed, she went back upstairs to brush her teeth and get dressed.

The music continued, welling up through the vents on the floor and sending out invisible pulses that rattled the painting on the bedroom wall.

Jess had a flashback of herself at seventeen, chopping vegetables in the middle of the night to block out her parents' brandy-infused argument. And her pain.

Some people ate their feelings. Jess chopped and diced and shredded hers.

She pushed the memory aside and went back downstairs.

Sienna's hands were a blur on the keyboard, her shoulders loose, so caught up in the song that she didn't realize Jess was standing a few feet behind her.

The music swelled, drowning out the gurgle of the coffeepot. Drowning out the knock on the front door.

"Hello in the house!"

Before Jess had time to connect a face to the voice, Merri breezed into the living room.

The music faltered and stopped on a high-pitched note that coincided with the deer-in-the-headlights look Sienna directed at Jess.

Merri's gaze bounced from Jess to Sienna and then back again. She didn't look at all surprised to see the teenager sitting at the piano.

"I was out for my morning walk and look what I found." The familiar lilt in Merri's voice, her smile, expanded to include both of them. She crossed the room and presented Jess with a plastic container filled with blueberries. They were smaller than the ones in the produce section of Dan's Hometown Market. A dusky blue-violet and beaded with dew.

"You picked these?" Jess asked.

"They grow along the road by the lake." Merri turned

toward Sienna, who still looked ready to bolt. "Elaine mentioned you have a recital this summer."

Sienna's eyes went wide. "She...she did?"

Merri nodded. "Your senior solo, I believe she said. Elaine was hoping you were still practicing while she's away."

And then Sienna did move. She swung her legs over the bench and faced Merri.

"How is she doing? Is she going to be okay?"

Those were the most words Jess had heard Sienna say.

"Yes, but it hasn't been easy. The stroke affected her right side and she's had to relearn how to do a lot of the things you and I take for granted," Merri said. "But Elaine is a strong woman, and we're all praying for a full recovery. She'll be home before you know it."

Doubt flashed in Sienna's eyes, but Jess couldn't tell what had triggered it. Merri's belief in prayer or a full recovery.

Maybe it was both.

"I'll put these berries in another container so you can have this one back." Jess steered Merri into the kitchen. "I hope you don't mind that I'm using some of your coffee."

Merri laughed. "Not at all! You did feed us yesterday. So delicious. I still can't believe you didn't follow a recipe. Oh! That's right. I almost forgot." Merri dipped her hand into the pocket of her dress. "This was the recipe I told you about yesterday. For my mother's quiche?" She handed Jess an index card. "I thought you might like to make it sometime."

Make it? Jess could barely read it. The ingredients had been written by hand in pencil, the letters smudged and pressed so tightly together they looked more like hieroglyphics. The last two lines of the directions were hidden underneath a grease stain that stretched from corner to corner.

"I'll take a screenshot so you can have it back," Jess said.

"No, no. You keep it. I'm not much of a cook. Mom tried

to teach me, but I was more interested in other things. His name was Don, by the way." Merri's smile turned pensive. "Mom said I was the artistic one, so she put me in charge of the relish tray at family gatherings. But if I'd paid more attention, maybe I could have made the quiche this year instead of reservations for brunch."

Jess took a closer look at the card. Someone had edited the recipe, crossing out the word *ham* with a decisive black line and writing *bacon* above it.

"Did your mom ever say where the recipe came from?"

"Probably Grandma Danner. She was a wonderful cook. I'm the weak link."

Sienna's playing, which had resumed but became more subdued after Merri's arrival, began to increase in both volume and intensity.

"She's very good," Merri murmured.

Jess silently agreed. There was a confidence in Sienna's playing that seemed at odds with the girl's inability to look people in the eye.

"None of us have seen Sienna for weeks. Elaine mentioned a music scholarship will be awarded at the summer recital, so I'm glad she came back. When she left in such a hurry yesterday, I was afraid we'd scared her away for good."

Given the cloud of disapproval that had settled over the hallway the day before, the relief in Merri's eyes was confusing.

"Does Sienna live in the neighborhood?" Jess asked.

"Sometimes."

Sometimes?

Jess wasn't sure how to interpret that, either.

Merri looked like she was about to say something else, but the tempo changed abruptly, the storm subsiding to a gentle rain.

"I think I'll sneak out the back door," she said. "I haven't visited Elaine's garden at all this summer. After our scrapbook meetings, we would laze away a whole afternoon back there, drinking iced tea."

Images of overgrown flower beds and herbs that had conquered their paving stone borders skipped through Jess's mind.

"I don't think it looks the same," Jess warned her. "It's kind of…wild."

"Then it's exactly the same." Merri smiled. "Elaine always said that was the beauty of it."

Chapter Fifteen

After Merri left, Jess's gaze shifted from the blueberries to the mason jar filled with the maple syrup Anthony had given her.

Her stomach rumbled in approval, as if she'd just solved a complex math equation.

Blueberries plus maple syrup equals...pancakes!

She retrieved the eggs from the fridge and opened the pantry. Searched through the cupboard drawers for a set of measuring cups and finally found them behind a stack of pot holders.

Once the ingredients were collected, Jess got to work. It was a new experience, cooking against a backdrop of classical music, especially when she also heard every mistake and huff of frustration.

Jess had been guilty of both those things in culinary school.

She found herself smiling as she whisked the eggs and buttermilk together.

Jess poured circles of pancake batter into the skillet, sprinkled blueberries on top and waited for the bubbles to form.

She hadn't made pancakes for years, but they'd been a staple of her diet while growing up. The trifecta of comfort food. Inexpensive ingredients, filling and easy to prepare.

When the music paused, Jess poked her head into the living room. She couldn't help but notice the pillow had been straightened and the blanket draped over the back of the sofa again.

"Sienna?"

The girl's shoulders twitched before she slowly turned around to face Jess.

"I made breakfast," Jess announced.

And then she went back to the kitchen, letting the aroma of warm maple syrup and buttermilk pancakes weave their magic.

Silence swelled in the living room.

Jess filled a plate and drizzled ribbons of maple syrup over the stack. And just when she was beginning to wonder if Sienna hadn't sneaked out of the house as quietly as she'd come in, she appeared in the doorway.

Jess reached for another plate. "Milk? Coffee?"

Sienna nodded.

Jess poured another cup and added a splash of milk. Picked up her cutting board turned serving tray and carried it into the dining room.

Sienna followed and slid into a chair on the opposite side of the table.

Jess's only experience with teenagers was having been one herself once. And even then, it hadn't felt like she'd had anything in common with her classmates. The snippets of conversations Jess overheard in the cafeteria centered around whatever new drama had unfolded between first and fifth period, boys and weekend plans.

Having parents who spent more time at the corner bar than they did at work or at home created all the drama that Jess could handle. Not to mention it also had a significant effect on the other two.

Everyone in Jess's hometown knew Ray and Tracie Keaton were as volatile and unstable as nitroglycerin. Invitations to slumber parties and birthday celebrations had started to taper off by the fourth grade. And since that was also about the time Jess realized she didn't want anyone to know how much time she spent alone anyway, she'd turned her attention toward other things. Like a future. A life that she made instead of the one she'd been born into.

Something told Jess the girl sitting across the table from her was doing the same thing. Only Sienna escaped into her music, not the kitchen.

"How long have you been playing the piano?"

"A while." Sienna, who'd turned her stack of pancakes into a grid of neat little squares, finally took a bite. The tension in her shoulders eased, and Jess nudged the pitcher of maple syrup closer to her plate.

"Thanks." Sienna was way more generous with syrup than she was with words.

Jess watched half the girl's pancakes disappear by the time she'd finished slathering hers with butter. "Merri mentioned a recital?"

Her mouth full of pancake, Sienna made a sound that sounded like an affirmative.

"When is it?"

"A week from Tuesday."

Jess didn't know anything about music, but in culinary

school, she'd spent hours perfecting a single dish for instructors like Chef Tomas to grade.

"How often are you supposed to be practicing?"

Sienna's gaze dropped to her plate again. She chased a blueberry around the plate with her fork until it bogged down in the syrup and became easier to spear. "Every day."

"And your teacher doesn't have a piano you can practice on?"

Sienna stopped eating.

"Ms. Grant goes on a long trip every summer. She'll be back for the recital and expects us to practice on our own." Sienna set her fork down. "But I'll figure something out."

Because she thought Jess was about to cancel her practice sessions, too. Because, like Jess at that age, she'd learned to deal with things on her own.

"I don't know when Elaine is coming back," Jess said slowly. "But I'll be spending a lot of time in the kitchen, not the living room, so we won't get in each other's way."

"You don't mind if I practice every day?"

"No." The disbelief on Sienna's face turned the pancake Jess had just eaten into a hard lump. "But I can't promise that I won't interrupt you once in a while if I need a guinea pig."

"A guinea pig...like trying something you make?"

"Exactly."

"I guess I can handle that."

Jess slid another pancake onto Sienna's plate. "And I guess I can handle Mozart."

The first smile Jess had seen skimmed across Sienna's face. "That was Chopin."

Jess smiled back.

Sienna ate three more pancakes and returned to the piano, Jess to kitchen cleanup.

Between the frittata and the pancakes, there were only two eggs left in the bowl.

She'd have to pay Anthony Silva another visit.

Chapter Sixteen

The heavens declare the glory of God.

The verse Nick had memorized in Sunday school when he was a kid played out in real time whenever he watched the sun come up over the lake.

It started out slow, the way a lot of good things did. A brushstroke of pink in the seam between water and sky that began to expand over the horizon. Turned the charcoal silhouettes of the trees to green and polished the silver finish off the lake until it turned a pale blue.

The only thing that detracted from the view was the old fishing lodge turned supper club that Nick had, in a moment of nostalgia, weakness or insanity—or a combination of the three—decided to purchase and restore to its original glory.

The one-room cabins scattered along the shoreline had fallen down years ago, but the main building was still intact. Barely.

When Nick was a kid, the lodge had been one of the most

popular gathering spots in the area. Even tourists who typically bypassed Winsome Lake made a point to stop and eat there. On Friday nights it was standing room only for a traditional northern Wisconsin fish fry. The dining room had hosted countless Silva family birthdays, anniversaries and milestones on the outdoor patio.

After the original owner passed away, a couple Nick no longer remembered had snapped it up. But they'd regarded people as customers, not family, and it had closed when Nick was a junior in high school. For years the building remained vacant until someone decided to turn it into a private residence. Nick had heard a rumor the owner had closed the place up and moved to a state with a warmer climate. A decision he'd neglected to tell the bank.

The foreclosure dragged on, and long before a local realty sign appeared in the yard, the lodge was showing obvious signs of decay.

Anthony lived a quarter mile down the road, so every time Nick drove past the lodge, it stirred up memories.

In late October, on his way to a football game, something had prompted Nick to turn down the driveway. The dock he'd fished from while his parents sipped drinks on the patio was half-submerged underwater. A branch had broken off one of the towering red pines and taken out a corner of the roof on its way down. Leaves clogged the gutters and a coat of pollen had tinted the windows the pale green of an algae bloom.

From a distance, the lodge looked neglected. Up close, it looked like something only a bulldozer could fix.

The locals knew what it would cost to fix it up and what taxes on the water would be. Vacationers weren't interested in a lake that wasn't large enough to accommodate jet skis and motorboats, their favorite water toys.

But Nick had always seen potential. It was what made him a good coach. A good teacher. The ability not to change something, but to coax out things that were already there.

He took another long pull from his travel mug and almost sprayed the entire mouthful on the windshield when something thumped on the driver's-side window.

Leo Mulvaney, Winsome Lake's former principal turned part-time Realtor, stood on the other side, wearing his post-retirement uniform of white V-neck T-shirt, faded overalls and perpetual grin.

Nick reluctantly dragged his gaze away from the lake and hopped down from the cab. Bucket, who'd been snoozing in the passenger seat, landed with a thud beside him. The moment all four paws hit the ground, he shot toward the lake to chase minnows in the shallow water.

Nick let him go. Bucket had a lot of energy. And like the parent of a rambunctious toddler, Nick was fine with any harmless activity that ended with a long nap in the afternoon.

"You're up pretty early."

Leo shrugged. "I'm heading out to see the kids and saw your truck parked down here. Thought I'd stop by and see what you've done. It's looking good."

"Uh-huh." Nick grinned. "You're only saying that because you found someone gullible enough to take the place off your hands."

Leo clapped his hand on Nick's shoulder, a habit carried over from years of hallway pep talks and predetention lectures.

"Someone with vision," he corrected. "Once it's fixed up, you'll be able to sell it and tackle another one."

"This is my one-hit wonder."

Nick already worked fifty-plus hours a week during the school year. And in spite of what those popular home makeover shows wanted people to believe, flipping houses took more than sixty minutes.

With all the time and money Nick was putting into repairs, he'd be happy if he broke even on the place.

"I'm surprised you haven't recruited the football team to help you out," Leo said. "Give them each a sledgehammer and call it training."

"Not a bad idea." Nick downed the last swallow of coffee. "Want to take a look around inside?"

"My daughter is expecting me for lunch so I better get on the road," Leo said. "But I'll be checking on you. Making sure you stay on task."

Nick wrestled down a smile.

In his mind's eye, he saw a younger version of the man, necktie askew, cruising up and down the aisles during study hall, saying the exact same thing.

After Leo drove away, Nick checked on Bucket one more time and went inside the lodge.

The first thing he'd done after signing the paperwork was replace the screens on all the windows, but the scent of mildew and neglect had become embedded in the walls.

He propped the door open with a two-by-four to let the fresh air in. Surveyed the construction zone. Nick found it helped when he approached the project the way he coached a football game. Picture the end goal and then break it down play by play.

The lodge was one large open room with a panoramic view of the water, a decent-size kitchen off the back and two tiny bathrooms at the end of a narrow hall.

Leo had mentioned the previous owner tried to convert the lodge into a single-family home, but Nick didn't know what that meant until his first walk-through.

The bar, a section of a hundred-year-old white pine that

had been sliced in half and sanded until the surface was satin smooth, was missing. Nick had found it by the boathouse after the snow melted, next to a lean-to filled with rotting firewood.

The bathrooms were gutted and random holes in the walls exposed outdated wiring and pipes. Nick had a hunch the owner had moved from room to room until he'd decided the easiest thing to do was leave town and make it someone else's problem.

Which, in a way, made Nick's job easier.

At least he knew what he'd gotten himself into.

He planned to take one room at a time, starting with what had once been the dining room, and then turning the two bathrooms into one. Other than a few cosmetic upgrades and new appliances, the kitchen wouldn't need a lot of attention. There was a spacious, second-story loft that needed flooring and a fresh coat of paint, but Nick hoped to have the place ready to put on the market before the first snowfall.

The lodge wouldn't look the same on the inside, but at least another family would have the opportunity to make memories there again.

Nick grabbed his safety glasses and picked up a sledgehammer.

Leo's idea to enlist the team wasn't a bad one, but Nick wasn't ready to supervise and let someone else have all the fun.

The sun moved from window to window, playing hide-and-seek with the dust motes in the air.

Nick's cell phone began a duet with the music blaring from the ancient AM/FM radio he'd found in a cabinet. He glanced at the number on the screen and then at his watch. Winced. It must be later than he'd thought.

"Hey, Grandpop."

"Where are you?"

"At the lodge." Nick pinned the phone between his ear and his shoulder and made a quick chalk line on the wall.

"You on your way over soon?"

"Yup. Sorry. I lost track of time. I'll be there in fifteen."

"No hurry," Anthony said gruffly. "Just wanted to let you know the coffee's on."

The coffee, Nick knew, had been on since five o'clock. Anthony had always been an early riser and now that they had a standing midmorning coffee date every Saturday, Nick suspected the hours in between stretched long.

He washed up and put his tools away before stepping outside to whistle for Bucket. A loud but enthusiastic splash preceded the dog's return. Bucket streaked toward the truck, leaving streams of water and sand in his wake.

What would Jessica think if she had to share the truck with the dog now?

The real question, an inner voice mocked Nick, *is what makes you think Jessica Keaton is ever going to ride in your truck again?*

Nick shook the thought away and opened the door.

"Back seat," he ordered, ignoring the side shade Bucket cast his way.

He stopped at the road to wait for a car to pass and the driver's expression, the same one Nick saw on people's faces when the Winsome Lake Wildcats were losing a game, summed up what everyone else in Winsome Lake was probably thinking about his purchase.

Nick turned down Anthony's driveway, but his grandpa wasn't sitting on the porch swing, waiting for Nick to arrive. Nick let Bucket out and the dog instantly spotted the chickens looking for bugs under the spirea bush.

They scattered at the sight of Bucket, a choreographed exodus of squawking and loose feathers that was strictly for show. In five minutes they'd be back, sedately pecking the gravel around the dog's massive paws.

The door squeaked when Nick pushed it open and he added fixing it to his growing to-do list.

Usually, the cabin smelled like buttered popcorn and Ben-Gay, both part of Grandpop's evening routine. Today the air smelled like cinnamon.

Like… Grandma Jenny was here.

Nick's throat tightened a little.

"Grandpop?"

"In the kitchen."

Nick rounded the corner and the world as he knew it tilted a little.

Anthony sat at the table. That, in itself, wasn't unusual. What was unusual was that the table was set. With dishes. And not just any dishes. The ones his grandmother had broken out on major holidays. Nick hadn't seen them in so long, he'd assumed Anthony had passed them on to one of his aunts or cousins.

"Sit down, Nicholas, before it gets cold." Anthony waved at the foil-covered centerpiece.

Nick sat. "What's that?"

"A thank-you." His grandpa smiled. "Your new friend dropped it off."

Nick didn't have any…*oh.* "Jessica? She was here?"

"Uh-huh. Showed up at the door a little while ago and we chatted for a bit." Anthony peeled off the foil, and Nick's stomach rolled over and begged. "She remembered we were having coffee together this morning and dropped it off with the egg basket."

Nick reached for the serving knife and Anthony coughed.

Oops. Right.

He sneaked one quick look at the pan before bowing his head.

"Lord, thank You for this beautiful day. Thank You for this food and the hands that prepared it. Amen."

"Amen," Nick echoed, still not quite believing the hands that had prepared it belonged to Jessica.

"She used some of the maple syrup I gave her for the icing." Anthony cut a generous piece and slid it onto Nick's plate. "I told her that if she kept baking like this, I'd cancel my other customers and give her all my eggs."

"And start a mutiny."

Anthony helped himself to a piece and sampled the icing. Smacked his lips. "I'd be willing to take that risk."

Nick had eaten coffee cake before, of course. Along with donuts from Dan's Market, it was standard fare in the teacher's lounge. But it had never looked like this...

Or tasted like it, either.

The cake practically melted in Nick's mouth and yet exploded with maple and cinnamon and flavors he didn't recognize.

Nick took another bite and heard himself moan.

Across the table, Anthony's eyes twinkled. "So does this mean an apology is in order?"

Nick scraped his plate clean and was reaching for another piece. "I'm sorry I was late."

"Not to me. To Jessica." Across the table, Anthony was grinning. "It appears you were wrong, Nicholas. The young woman does know how to cook."

Okay. Grandpop could be right.

But it didn't mean Nick was wrong about how long Jessica was going to stay in Winsome Lake.

Chapter Seventeen

Having a link to the outside world, Elaine decided, was both a blessing and an affliction.

She'd already dumped two dozen emails directly into the trash folder based solely on their subject line and was about to delete three more when a new message from Hilary popped up in her in-box.

IE CONTRACT...

"Aren't you supposed to take Saturdays off, Hilary?" Elaine muttered.

She'd told the literary agent a week. So technically, Elaine still had time to decide whether to dive headfirst into the world she'd left behind in California or remain blissfully content in the one she'd traded it for.

"What do You want me to do, God?" Elaine didn't expect an answer. She'd been asking the question a lot. After the initial nudge to wait, the Lord had remained silent on the matter.

She looked out the window overlooking the courtyard and saw a sparrow land on the edge of the hanging feeder. It picked up a seed, tipped its head at Elaine and flew away.

She laughed.

"I was hoping if I hung around long enough, I would hear that sound."

Until Matthew wandered into the room, Elaine hadn't realized she'd been waiting for something else.

Him.

Another complication she hadn't been prepared for.

For a woman who liked to keep things simple, Elaine never knew what to expect when it came to Matthew Jeffries. He fit in with his surroundings like a chameleon. Retired military chaplain. Amateur stand-up comedian. Vice president of the True North motorcycle club.

Elaine had seen Matthew passing out snacks in the cafeteria and leading a men's Bible study in the courtyard.

At Sunrise Rehab, he was "all things to all people."

She just hadn't figured out what he was to *her.*

Today Matthew wore a conservative charcoal-gray suit that would have looked somber if it hadn't been for the flamingo-pink necktie and matching pocket square.

"You look a little overdressed for the Harley."

"Wedding." Matthew grinned. "We had to work around the groom's therapy schedule."

"The ceremony is here?"

Matthew bypassed the empty bed and walked over to the window, where Elaine had set up camp in the tiny space between the built-in wardrobe and the television. "Courtyard. Three o'clock."

"And you're officiating?"

"Best man. Hence the disguise." Matthew patted the tic. "The bride said burgundy. What do you think? Am I close?"

Elaine smiled. "Close enough."

Matthew moved closer to the window and scanned the courtyard. "You're a tough audience, Elaine Haviland. It obviously wasn't my rapier wit that made you laugh. What am I looking for? A man likes to know what he's up against."

"God."

Matthew whistled. "I'm out."

Elaine laughed again. In the past forty-eight hours, the pain had finally begun to subside. A pocket of glowing embers instead of a raging brushfire in her chest.

"And a sparrow."

"You couldn't have led with that?"

The sparkle in Matthew's amber eyes cut a giant swath through Elaine's defenses.

"I've been dealing with…something…and then I looked outside and saw a sparrow. It wasn't the answer I wanted, but it was a good reminder that what I need to do is trust."

Matthew nodded. Not a polite I-think-they-upped-your-pain-meds kind of nod. The kind of nod that said he'd gotten reminders like that, as well.

"I showed up, too," he said unexpectedly.

"Meaning?"

"Meaning…maybe the sparrow was a reminder, but you're supposed to talk to me." There wasn't a hint of a tease in Matthew's voice or his eyes now.

Maybe she was.

But living with her secrets had become as comfortable, familiar, as the house on Woodwind Lane.

"You have a wedding."

"In two hours." Matthew flipped the empty chair around and straddled it. Rested his arms on the worn leather back.

Elaine's eyes narrowed. "You were good at your job, weren't you?"

"I never considered it a job, but yes. I also learned to recognize when someone is stalling."

"I'm not stalling. I...don't know where to start."

"You just did." Matthew's smile calmed some of the butterflies in Elaine's stomach, but she still felt as nervous as an alcoholic at her first AA meeting.

My name is Elaine Haviland...

"I'm a ghostwriter. That's what I do." She glanced at Matthew. "Questions?"

His smile expanded and coaxed a dimple Elaine had never seen before out of hiding. "Not yet."

Well. That was new.

Early on in her career, Elaine had discovered that people were intrigued by what she did for a living. Just saying the name inevitably preceded a barrage of questions.

Elaine had been evasive, which of course only ramped up the element of mystery. And Elaine didn't *want* to be mysterious. Mysterious drew attention. Led to more questions she didn't want to answer.

What did she write? Who did she write for? Did she know any famous athletes? Actors? Country music stars?

Questions that would have undermined the *ghost* part of Elaine's job description and rendered the nondisclosure agreement in her contract null and void.

When Elaine moved to Winsome Lake, transplants were as rare as sunshine in January, so it was natural that people would wonder about her. At that point in her career, though, Elaine had learned to describe herself as a freelance writer. It was vague and lacked the veneer of glamour that piqued curiosity. No one had asked for details, so Elaine hadn't offered any. It helped that she worked late at night, leaving her days blissfully ordinary.

Elaine loved ordinary. It had its highs and lows, but the rhythm was fairly easy to follow.

The contract Hilary wanted her to sign would take her back to a world where everyone jostled for the spotlight. Elaine had never fit in there and was in no hurry to go back.

"Hilary, my agent, is encouraging me to take on a project I'm not sure I'm ready for yet," she said slowly.

"Not ready because…"

Elaine felt a little glow inside that Matthew didn't automatically assume her hesitation was due to the physical side effects from the stroke.

"Well, things aren't working at one hundred percent yet." She held up her right hand and wiggled her fingers as proof. Her thumb and index finger stubbornly refused to join in. "But there's a contract sitting in my in-box now and I have to make a decision soon."

Now Matthew frowned. "It can't wait a while? You don't even know when you'll be going home yet for sure."

"I know. But Hilary has already been waiting for my answer. She contacted me with a book idea last spring and I told her I'd think about it. Three days later I had a stroke. I had no idea she'd already pitched it to a publisher. They're on board and want me to sign a contract.

"Most of the books I've worked on are memoirs and autobiographies. People whose names are in the opening credits of movies, the backs of jerseys, and they want to see it on the cover of a book, too. They just don't have time to write one, which is where I come in." Elaine paused, choosing her words with care. "Hilary takes care of the business end of things, but I have to work with the author during the writing process. Sometimes it means research. Conducting interviews. Sometimes meeting...people...face-to-face."

Matthew remained silent but Elaine could see the wheels turning in his mind. "So...the challenge is the project itself."

She nodded.

"You can trust me," Matthew said. "But if you're bound by confidentiality—"

"No. Not yet, anyway." Elaine did trust him. Right now the only thing that held Elaine captive was a reluctance to open the door to her past. "Have you heard of Libby Tucker?"

"Doesn't ring a bell."

"She was the teenage star of a family-friendly television show in the eighties. A very short-lived show called *Life with Libby Tucker.* The series wasn't picked up for syndication, so you won't even see an episode if you turn on the TV in the middle of the night," Elaine told him. "I won't go into all the gory details, but Libby was involved in a scandal that destroyed her reputation. The network pulled the plug in the middle of the season and that was the end of her career."

"And now Libby wants to tell her side of the story?" Matthew guessed.

"Hilary does. Celebrity tell-alls are always a hot commodity but Libby's story is—" Elaine searched for the right word "—unique. I told Hilary I would think about it, but everyone is getting anxious." And she felt anxious at the *thought* of signing on the dotted line.

"If you turn it down, won't they find someone else? It doesn't have to be you, does it?"

"Hilary is convinced I should do it because someone who was there at the time would be able to fill in the blanks."

Matthew couldn't quite hide his surprise. "You knew Libby Tucker?"

"A lifetime ago," Elaine said.

"Based on your tone, I'm guessing you weren't close friends."

Fragments of the past came together and formed an image of Libby in her mind. Blond curls. Big brown eyes. The wholesome girl-next-door smile.

The ambition. The drama. The lies.

"Libby Tucker didn't have friends. She had fans. At least for a while, anyway. She disappeared after the scandal broke and no one has seen her since."

"Disappeared? People can't just disappear these days."

"These days," Elaine agreed. "But this was way before cell phones and the internet. It wasn't as difficult as you'd think back then. Especially for someone who had the money and the means to start over again."

"So finding Libby…finding out where she went, what she's doing now, would sell books."

"A lot of them," Elaine confirmed. "That's another reason Hilary wants me to write the book. I have…access…to inside information about Libby."

"What kind of information?"

"She left behind her diary. And…" Elaine hesitated, not sure how much to tell him, but Matthew, being Matthew, figured it out.

"You know where she is."

He *was* good.

"Yes." Elaine's stomach twisted. "But Libby is a part of my life I'd rather forget. I closed that door a long time ago and I don't know if I'm ready to open it again. Or…" Elaine paused to release a slow breath. "If I even *want* to. That's why I've been asking God for wisdom. When we're new in Christ, aren't we supposed to put the past behind us?"

Matthew leaned forward, his hands resting loosely on his knees. "Yes…and no."

Why did Elaine know he was going to say that?

"When I was a chaplain, my job was mainly to listen. But some of the guys were so torn up emotionally and physically, they didn't just need to share their stories, they needed to hear mine, too. I didn't like to go back there, either. The past was a pretty dark place. But my past was their *present*. They needed to know there was hope. That they could come out on the other side."

"You're saying it isn't about me?"

Matthew smiled.

"I'm saying that Libby Tucker's story may have the power to change someone else's."

Chapter Eighteen

"I don't know where she is, either."

On Sunday morning Jess found Violet sitting on top of the piano, waiting for Sienna to make an appearance.

That made two of them.

Jess had nothing to go on other than her gut instincts, a rumpled afghan and Merri's cryptic comment about the girl's home life, but the sight of the vacant piano bench propelled Jess toward the window again.

When Sienna had told Jess that she was supposed to practice every day, Jess assumed that included weekends. There was no questioning Sienna's commitment, so something—or someone—had caused her to be a no-show two days in a row.

Jess wasn't naive. She knew there were things that pancakes couldn't fix.

Not everyone grew up in a family like Nick's.

When Anthony had invited her into his cabin the day before, the number of photographs crowding the paneled walls rivaled that of the ones in the boxes and bags that Merri, Peg and Nita had unloaded onto the dining room table. Vacations. Holidays. Birthday parties. Weddings. No matter what the event, there never seemed to be less than a dozen members of the Silva family smiling for the camera at any given time.

Jess's gaze had gravitated toward photographs of Nick, but she'd refused to let it linger there. She'd yanked it back in line, just like she did her thoughts whenever they drifted in that direction.

So, yes. Nick was attractive. Really attractive. There was no arguing with genetics. But if even half of what Merri and Peg had said about him was true, no doubt the single women outnumbered the fans at every football game. Single women who planned to *stay* in his hometown.

Unlike Jess.

Winsome Lake was a place to figure out her next step. And her job, though temporary, at least gave Jess access to a kitchen. It was one of life's strange contradictions. Cooking required focus and yet at the same time it cleared her head.

Maybe—Jess glanced at the empty piano bench again— because she controlled the outcome.

She opened the refrigerator door to grab the milk and pulled out the eggs instead.

Nine this time.

Persephone, Anthony had told Jess while helping her search for eggs, had been slacking off in the heat.

Until now Jess had thought of eggs in terms of recipes. But after an hour with Anthony, she knew the names and personalities of the chickens who laid them, too.

She'd also discovered something else.

A calendar tacked to a bulletin board on the wall in Anthony's kitchen. Inside every square, written in permanent marker, was the name of someone who made a special trip to Birch Street for eggs.

On the day Nick had offered to drive Jess there, a woman named Rebecca had gone home empty-handed.

When Jess had asked Anthony about it, he'd waved away her concern. "Oh, don't worry about that. Rebecca is my daughter-in-law and Nicholas knows she has more eggs than she knows what to do with."

Nicholas, Jess had thought darkly, knew a lot of things he didn't bother to share. Like the fact that the man whose eggs were in such high demand was a close relative. He had to have known his own mother was the recipient of the Friday eggs, but for some reason he'd neglected to mention that, too.

Jess cracked an egg against the side of the bowl with a little more force than was necessary and released it into the bowl.

The tiny piece of shell suspended in the egg white was his fault, too.

"*Nick.*"

Jess grabbed the wooden spoon and started chasing it around the bowl.

"Did I hear my name?"

Jess turned and the spoon slipped from her fingers. It bounced across the floor, shedding drops of egg white all the way to the refrigerator.

"Stop sneaking up on me!"

"Sorry." The half smile on Nick's face belied his apology. "I knocked and heard my name..." He strode into the room and disappeared into the pantry. Returned a split second later with a roll of paper towels, proof that he was more familiar with Elaine's kitchen than Jess was.

Before Jess could react, Nick was on his haunches, cleaning up the mess.

"I can do that." Jess tried to intervene, but her efforts,

which involved wrestling the paper towel from his hand, were gently rebuffed.

"There was a rule growing up in the Silva house. If you make a mess, you clean it up."

Well, that was a lot different than at Jess's house. She'd finally given up cleaning up the messes her parents had made. Of their lives. Hers.

Nick tossed the damp toweling in the wastebasket—he knew where that was, too—and rinsed off his hands in the sink.

He'd mentioned mowing the grass the last time they'd spoken, but the crisp white button-down and gray cargo pants Nick wore weren't the standard uniform for yardwork.

Jess started whisking again, keeping one eye on Nick as he took a slow lap around the kitchen. He paused in front of the stove, lifted a corner of the towel covering the loaf of sourdough bread she'd baked earlier that morning, and snagged the heel. Before Jess could protest, he'd dragged it through the stick of butter she'd left on the counter and popped it into his mouth.

"How is it?"

"I have two words. One more?"

Jess bit the inside of her cheek to keep from smiling. Nick was way too appealing. He was also trespassing. But the guy had just complimented her first attempt at making sourdough from her own starter and she *was* a chef.

He helped himself to another slice and wandered over to the island. "What are you making?"

"Mayo."

"What's wrong with the stuff in a jar?"

"Um…it's from a jar? Mayonnaise takes less than ten minutes to make. Are you here to mow the grass? Or did Dan's Market run out of free samples?"

Nick grinned. "I'm on my way to church, actually, but I wanted to drop something off for you."

"The last time you said that I ended up with a cat who wakes me up before the crack of dawn every morning."

"No cats this time. Promise." The warmth in Nick's blue-sky eyes made Jess want to believe that some people actually kept them.

"Nick…"

"Five minutes. Meet me on the back patio. And bring a fork."

A fork?

Oh, he totally wasn't playing fair.

Jess put the mayo in the fridge, swiped the dishrag over the island and stepped outside.

Nick was already reclining on the bottom step, his long legs stretched out in front of him. Jess sat down next to him and held up her fork.

"Fine." He laughed. "You held up your part of the bargain, I'll hold up mine."

Nick's part of the bargain turned out to be a wedge of dark chocolate cake. Three moist, glorious layers divided by ribbons of chocolate buttercream.

It didn't look anything like the ones Jess had seen in the deli case at Dan's Hometown Market.

"Is this a bribe?"

"It's a thank-you for a thank-you." Nick shoulder-bumped her. "And someday we're going to have a conversation about your trust issues."

Jess had no idea what he was talking about. And no, they weren't.

"The coffee cake you dropped off at Grandpop's yesterday?" Nick jogged her memory. "There's a potluck after church today, but no one will say anything about a piece missing. I always have to taste test it first."

Jess would think about Nick the Churchgoer and Potluck Attendee later. Right now Nick the Baker took precedence.

"*You* made this?"

"Hey, don't look so surprised. I have some kitchen skills. Okay…not many. Two, to be exact."

Jess turned her fork sideways, snipped off the corner, and took a tentative bite. Tentative because Nick had tracked the fork's entire journey from the plate to Jess's lips.

And then she forgot he was there.

People talked about "death by chocolate," but the real danger when baking a cake like this was that it looked better than it tasted. While Jess's taste buds swooned, her mind began to separate the ingredients. Two kinds of chocolate, which kept it from being boring. A hint of something…

"Cinnamon."

Jess must have said the word out loud because Nick's mouth dropped open. "How did you know that?"

Jess shrugged. She'd already taken another bite and it wasn't polite to talk with your mouth full.

"It's my grandma Jenny's recipe," Nick went on. "Every time someone in my family had a birthday, they requested her chocolate cake. We all begged her for the recipe, too, but she claimed she never wrote it down.

"After she passed away, some of us tried to duplicate it, but it didn't taste the same. The general consensus in the family is that I got the closest when I figured out that she'd added cinnamon."

"It's the best chocolate cake I've ever tasted."

Jess was telling the truth, but Nick didn't look as pleased by the compliment as she would have expected.

"Thanks. But I can tell there's still something missing.

The texture isn't quite the same." Nick's gaze cut away from Jess and paused to linger on one of the rosebushes. "I always threatened to follow her around the kitchen and take notes while she was making one, but…" A shrug finished the sentence, but Jess filled in the blank.

He never did.

"Even if you'd taken notes, I'm not sure the cake would turn out the same," Jess said cautiously. "Home cooks are notorious for tweaking things as they go along. When they make something over and over again, like your grandma did, they follow their instincts more than a recipe."

Nick turned to face her again. "You're telling me I shouldn't feel guilty."

"I'm telling you that it doesn't matter who makes it or if it doesn't quite taste the same. It will always be your grandma Jenny's chocolate cake because…because it's one of the things that keeps her memory alive."

Nick was silent for a moment. "You're right. I never thought of it that way."

Because he'd never met Chef Tomas.

Food brings people together. Weddings. Funerals. First dates. You tell stories. You look each other in the eye.

But what if there were stories you didn't want to share?

This time Jess was the one who looked away.

"What about you?" Nick asked. "Are you one of those home cooks who follows her instincts?" Fortunately for Jess, he didn't wait for an answer. "Because there are rumors going around about a frittata that I'm really bummed I missed out on."

"It's a glorified omelet," Jess said. "Things must be pretty slow if that's what people are gossiping about."

Nick frowned. "I wouldn't call it gossip. More like singing your praises."

"I grew up in a small town. I know..." Jess stopped before she said too much. She started to rise to her feet, but Nick caught her wrist. Gently pulled her back down. The space between them narrowed and the warmth of his touch lingered on her skin even after he let go.

"I don't think you do," Nick said. "Your being here...it means something."

It means I got fired for something I didn't do, Jess wanted to shout. *It means that everything I worked so hard to achieve is gone. It means my dream of owning a restaurant is going to stay a dream.*

"Did you know that Merri was the one who found Elaine?" Nick continued, unaware of the storm raging inside Jess's head. "She was on her morning walk and noticed the kitchen curtains were closed. It seemed strange to her, because Elaine is an early riser and it was going on eight o'clock.

"When Elaine didn't answer the door, Merri found the extra key and went inside. Elaine had collapsed on the kitchen floor. She was conscious, but she couldn't talk. Couldn't move. Merri called the rescue squad and stayed with Elaine until it got here.

"Elaine was in the ICU for several days until they could get her stabilized. The doctors couldn't tell right away how much damage the stroke had caused." A shadow passed through Nick's eyes. "After that, it was straight to rehab. Everyone in the neighborhood pitches in to do what they can, but they miss Elaine. They're frustrated she's so far away. Now they see lights on when they walk past. The house isn't silent when they come over. Your being here...it gives them hope. It means Elaine is coming home."

Jess's fingers knotted together in her lap.

Her? A symbol of hope?

That ranked right up there with being an answer to prayer.

"Elaine hired me to cook," Jess said stiffly. "So that's what I've been doing."

"Anyone who makes mayo from scratch would cook whether they were paid to do it or not." Nick cocked his head and Jess found herself watching for that swatch of hair to rebel. "You *enjoy* it. And you want people to enjoy what you make, which is why you're cooking for the neighbors, and lonely widowers and piano students."

He knew about the pancakes, too?

"You want to know what else I think?"

"Hey, Nick!"

Jess was spared from having to answer the question when a familiar face popped into view.

And his timing couldn't have been more perfect.

"Christopher." Nick hopped to his feet and loped across the yard. Two palms connected over the fence in an enthusiastic high five and then Christopher waved at Jess.

"Hi, J-Jessica!"

Jess waved back and walked over to join them.

"I see you two have already met."

"Jessica is h-helping Miss Elaine," Christopher said. "Where's B-Bucket?"

"I left him at home. Unfortunately, Pastor Eric won't allow dogs in church. Yet." Nick grinned. "So what you been up to this summer? I haven't seen you around."

Christopher's expression changed. He shrugged. "Not much."

Nick must have heard the faint rumble of discontent in the boy's voice that Jess did because he took a step closer to the fence.

"I'm hoping you'll be team manager again this year."

"My m-mom doesn't want me to. She doesn't want me to do anything until after my surgery."

"That's scheduled for November, right?"

"November f-fifteenth. I told Dr. Stuart the t-team needs me, though, and he s-said it would be okay."

"That's a tough one." Nick raked his hand through his hair. "Moms usually have the final say over stuff like that, bud. But the team needs people cheering for us in the bleachers. That's an important job, too."

"It's not a-as much fun, though." Christopher looked at Jessica and his engaging grin surfaced again. "Nick is the best football coach in the w-world. Go Wildcats!" He held up his hand for another high five.

Nick grinned back and slapped Christopher's palm again.

"Paid endorsement?" Jess murmured under her breath.

He laughed. "Only if chocolate cake counts as currency."

"Cake always counts."

Christopher's gaze swiveled toward the house and he waved at someone. "I'm okay, Mom. I'm t-talking to Coach Nick and Jessica."

A few moments later another familiar face appeared at the fence.

Jess struggled to hide her shock.

The mother that Christopher claimed treated him like a boy the first time they'd met...the one who'd said no to team manager...was Nita.

Jess knew the woman lived on Woodwind Lane, but she'd had no idea they were next-door neighbors.

"Good morning, Jessica. Nick." Nita's voice was as crisp as the sheets hanging on her clothesline. "Christopher, we have to leave for church in a few minutes. Did you brush your teeth yet?"

"No." The word rolled out with a sigh.

"Better get to it." Nita consulted her watch. "We don't

want to be late." She looked at Nick. "Are you going to the potluck today?"

"That's her way of asking if I made a chocolate cake," he whispered to Jess.

Nita gave him a look. "And I'm still waiting for an answer."

"Yes." Nick winked at Jess. "Minus one piece."

Nita didn't say anything, but Jess had a sinking feel it wouldn't be long before her friends heard about the chocolate cake...and the wink.

Chapter Nineteen

When Jess came downstairs to make coffee on Monday morning, she discovered a wicker basket filled with fresh produce on the counter and Sienna sound asleep on the couch.

Vegetables Jess knew what to do with, so she dealt with those first.

She carried the basket over to the sink and rinsed off three beautifully misshapen heirloom tomatoes, the skins deep burgundy with streaks of gold, and a bundle of French radishes with the leafy green stems still attached.

Violet trotted into the room and began to weave figure eights between Jess's ankles. The display of affection didn't fool Jess. The cat's appearances, more frequent and of a longer duration now, tended to coincide with the times Jess was working in the kitchen.

"I'm going to replace you with a dog," Jess told her. "A dog that barks when people break into the house while other people are asleep."

Violet ignored the threat and sauntered down the hallway to check out her food dish.

While the coffee brewed, Jess took the eggs out of the fridge.

She blamed Persephone for her new obsession.

Chefs were a little like artists in that they gravitated toward a certain medium. When Jess worked for Gwyneth, the menu was based on her employer's likes and dislikes, so Jess hadn't had the time or opportunity to play with flavors and ingredients.

She'd loved her work, but meeting Gwyneth's exacting standards had created a different kind of stress. For the first time in five years, the kitchen had become Jess's playground. She was having fun.

Jess peeled two ripe avocados, smashed them in a bowl with some sea salt, and cracked two of the eggs into separate bowls before adding them to the water simmering in the skillet.

Sienna appeared in the doorway while Jess was standing guard over the toaster to avoid another burnt sacrifice.

Their eyes met over the butcher-block island. The pillow had left a hashtag mark on Sienna's cheek, and her hair stuck up in all directions like the quills on a porcupine.

"Poached eggs on avocado toast. You can top off my cup, too."

Jess pointed to the coffeepot while she searched the drawer for a slotted spoon.

Sienna slinked past her, surreptitiously smoothing wrinkles from the hull of the Millennium Falcon on the front of her T-shirt.

The toast popped up and from the way Sienna jumped, Jess would have thought someone had fired a shotgun in the house.

Dread pooled in Jess's stomach.

This landed so far outside her job description, she had no idea what to do.

She'd planned to have her coffee on the back patio. The golden sunshine pouring into the kitchen promised another beautiful day, but the fence wasn't tall enough to guarantee privacy or muffle a conversation.

If Sienna was willing to talk at all.

Jess smeared avocado on the toast and topped each slice with a poached egg and a dash of ground pepper. She carried the plates into the dining room. Sienna trailed behind with the coffee and set the cups down before taking a seat.

The tension radiating from the opposite side of the table was thicker than béchamel sauce.

When Sienna turned her fork into a scalpel and began to dissect the poached egg, piece by piece, Jess was forced to intervene.

"Sienna…"

"I know." The girl's fork clattered against her plate. "I'm sorry. I… I won't do it again." The words tumbled out in a rush. "It was early, and I didn't want to wake you up."

"How early?"

Sienna speared a piece of egg and shoved it into her mouth instead of answering the question.

"How early?" Jess repeated. "Five? Six?"

Sienna looked down at her plate again, but Jess waited her out. There were only so many seconds a person needed to chew and swallow between bites.

"One."

Only a few hours after Jess had gone upstairs to bed.

She had no idea if this had happened before. If Elaine Haviland knew there were times Sienna spent the night on her couch.

Now it was Jess's turn to stall.

She took a bracing sip of coffee and watched Sienna peel the crust off her toast and banish it to the side of the plate.

At that moment the girl looked about seven years old instead of seventeen.

Jess waded cautiously back into the conversation. "You didn't practice over the weekend."

Sienna's gaze lifted. The wary look in her eyes told Jess she hadn't been expecting a change in topic. "No."

"Do you have a summer job?"

"I was at my mom's," Sienna mumbled. "Her volleyball team needed a sub for the tournament."

Jess's past rose like a specter in her mind.

The bar her parents frequented had taken over the vacant lot behind the alley and turned it into a sand volleyball court every summer. Jess knew it wasn't always the case, but a *tournament* became an excuse for a weekend-long drinking party.

"I take it you don't like volleyball?" Jess kept her tone neutral.

"I'm terrible at it. Mom says the only way I'll get better is if I keep playing."

"I would think that applies to the piano, too."

"Mom…she thinks music is a waste of time. My grandma was the one who paid for my lessons. She let me play her piano whenever I stayed with her. Gran…" Sienna's voice hitched. "She said I was a natural."

"Your grandma doesn't live in Winsome Lake anymore?"

Sienna shook her head. "She died a few years ago. We moved into her house, but my dad said the piano took up too much room. He sold it to Ms. Haviland."

Two losses that had cast permanent shadows in Sienna's eyes.

"How did Elaine know you played?"

"My grandma and Ms. Haviland were friends. She must have told Ms. Haviland about my lessons, because she called me after she bought the piano. Said I could practice on it whenever I wanted to."

Does Sienna live in the neighborhood?

Sometimes.

Jess's conversation with Merri popped up in her memory again. "You live on Woodwind Lane?"

It took Sienna a moment to answer, and Jess could practically hear the doors and windows slam shut, the walls sliding back into place.

"When I'm with my dad. He got the house after my parents split up. He works third shift, though, so he's not around much." Sienna began to chop up the egg into even smaller pieces. "My mom isn't, either, now that she has a new boyfriend."

A warning light began to blink in Jess's head. "You don't like him?"

"Cal is okay." Sienna picked at a streak of turquoise nail polish on her thumb. "But he moved some of his stuff into our apartment and he...he hangs around when Mom goes to work."

"Sienna." The warning light was a full-blown beacon now. "Cal...he doesn't say or do anything that makes you uncomfortable, does he?"

A heartbeat of silence sucked the oxygen from the room and left Jess feeling light-headed.

"I'm fine," Sienna mumbled.

I'm fine.

It was the same thing Jess had told Ms. Sutton, her sophomore English teacher, when she'd asked if everything was okay at home.

Ms. Sutton had caught her sleeping in class for the second

day in a row. When the bell rang, she'd intercepted Jess on the way to the door and told her that she wanted to see her after school. Jess would have preferred detention to a one-on-one meeting.

She'd thought about faking a stomachache after lunch and skipping the rest of her classes, but someone as smart as Ms. Sutton would see right through that. It would only be delaying the inevitable.

Ms. Sutton had been sitting at the table in the back of the room, not behind her desk, when Jess shuffled into her classroom. The two bottles of root beer and chocolate cupcakes left over from some celebration in the teacher's lounge, meant to put Jess at ease, had the opposite effect. Jess had nibbled on the cupcake to be polite, but when she'd swallowed, it had welded with the lump of panic forming in her throat.

"You're a good student, Jessie. You always turn in your homework on time and you're prepared for my tests. It isn't like you to fall asleep in class."

"I stayed up late watching TV." Jess had forced herself to look Ms. Sutton in the eye.

"Do your parents know that?"

The question dangled in the air like a lifeline.

For years Jess had wanted someone, anyone, to notice her. To ask how she was doing.

Jess didn't know how things worked, but she knew parents were supposed to take care of their children. All she'd had to say was that her parents were the ones who woke her up when they stumbled in after the bar closed, angry at each other or the person one stool over who'd offended them.

But what if it backfired?

When it came to home, Jess knew what she was dealing with. Her parents were consistent in their inconsistencies. But who knew what doors the truth would open? The name

Keaton was already well-known in the community. Would it become a file in a social worker's bulging caseload?

Or even worse, what if no one believed her and Jess got her mom and dad in trouble? Staying under the radar was safer than having them unleash their tempers on her.

"Jessie, please. I can't help you if you don't tell me what's going on," Ms. Sutton had said.

"I don't need help."

If Ms. Sutton had continued to press her for information, if Jess had seen doubt, not pity, in the teacher's eyes, she might have changed her mind.

After she'd left the school, Jess cut through the park and followed the crumbling spine of the old railroad tracks, every step strengthening her own resolve. By the time she got home, she'd made a decision.

She'd be successful someday. Jessica Keaton would be a famous chef and people would have to wait months for a reservation to taste her cooking and no one would ever feel sorry for her again.

"I have to practice." The scrape of Sienna's chair against the floor yanked Jess back to reality. "Thanks for breakfast."

"Sienna…"

"I'm fine," Sienna said again. She scooted backward toward the door, her eyes seeking Jess's. "Really."

Jess wanted to believe her. Wanted to believe she really was okay.

But it sounded a lot like the one Sienna was trying to convince was herself.

Jess could relate to that, too.

Chapter Twenty

Elaine knew she'd parked her wheelchair outside the OT room, but when her session was over, it was nowhere in sight.

Matthew, wearing faded jeans and a Hawaiian shirt louder than the music blaring from the courtyard, stood in its place.

"Ready for the luau?"

"I didn't sign up for it." Elaine hadn't joined any of Sunrise's group activities over the past six weeks. And because a luau created images of hula dancing and limbo sticks, she was pretty sure she wouldn't fit in with the rest of the group.

"I doubt anyone is checking names off a list." Matthew's eyes sparkled. "There's kabobs and grilled pineapple ice cream and you need a little time outdoors in the sun. Leah said you've only left your room for therapy the past couple days."

That was because Elaine's ribs were finally beginning to heal. She trusted the therapists more than her own judgment. The last thing she wanted to do was fall down and delay going home again.

"I can't go. Someone stole my wheelchair."

"But they brought you this instead." Matthew reached for the wooden cane propped against the wall. The one Elaine hadn't noticed until now.

It was hand-carved from a sturdy piece of wood, the outer surface sanded satin smooth.

"I talked to therapy about the upgrade and got the okay," Matthew said. "The rubber bottom will prevent it from slipping."

Elaine barely heard him. She was too busy studying the tiny, intricate vines and wildflowers etched into the marbled wood.

"You made this?"

"It's kind of a hobby. A friend gave one to me when I completed therapy and I decided to keep the tradition going."

It wasn't the first time Matthew had alluded to being in rehab, but he'd never told her why. Elaine guessed it had something to do with the role Matthew played at Sunrise, spending time with military veterans. It was also a good reminder whenever Elaine found herself thinking about him. Chaplains, even retired ones, were there to provide encouragement to the residents. And that was what she was. A resident.

"Thank you." Elaine took a tentative step forward, testing her balance. "It's beautiful."

"You probably want to show it off," Matthew said. "Mmm. Where could you go where there's a lot of people? Some music and food..."

"Fine." Elaine laughed. "For a little while."

He accompanied her down the hall and opened the door that led to the courtyard. The activities director had outdone herself for the midsummer party. Crepe-paper lanterns hung from the trees and a trio of smiling CNAs were handing out colorful silk leis.

Matthew chose a table partially in the sun and pulled out a chair for Elaine.

Leah bounced across the lawn with two leis. She dropped a necklace fashioned from pink hibiscus blossoms over Elaine's head. Matthew got the other. "I'm going to lead the hula in a few minutes, but I'll get you some lemonade!"

"I know this makes me sound like an old lady, but I wish I had half that girl's energy," Elaine whispered.

"Then I'm an old man, because I was thinking the same thing." Matthew leaned back in the chair. "They really went all out, didn't they?"

Elaine picked up a starfish.

Matthew, who noticed everything, caught her smile.

"I think I just saw a good memory," Matthew said. "Have you spent time on the beach?"

"Just once."

"It must have made quite an impression."

"Matt?" A man shuffled up to their table. The sun was shining, but his expression was shadowed as if there were an invisible cloud above his ahead. "Got a minute?"

Matthew glanced at Elaine, and she nodded.

"I'll be back in a few minutes," he murmured.

When they walked away, Elaine turned the starfish over in her hand and smiled again.

It was a good memory.

And it hadn't just made an impression. It had changed her life.

Samantha O'Dell was the kind of person Elaine would have normally walked past without a second glance. In shorts and a daffodil-yellow tunic with a gigantic starfish on the front, she looked like every tourist Elaine had seen browsing in the hotel gift shop or lounging around the pool.

But on a deserted stretch of beach on Christmas morning, the woman was impossible to ignore. And it wasn't because she sat cross-legged on the sand, feeding pieces of driftwood and skeins of seagrass to a campfire that broke more than a few rules, hotel and otherwise.

It was because she didn't look like a rule-breaking type of person at all.

Still, the sight of her triggered a rush of annoyance. Elaine had picked this time, this place, for a reason. No one was supposed to be on the beach, alone, on a major holiday. They should be sleeping in. Or eating a breakfast buffet with Santa and his elves.

It hadn't occurred to Elaine the same thing could be said about her.

She thrust her hands into the pockets of her linen jacket and surged ahead, bare feet leaving angry imprints in the sand, pretending she didn't see the only other human being for half a mile.

When Elaine was even with the campfire, curiosity got the better of her and she glanced over at the woman.

She couldn't have been more than forty, but her hairstyle, a conservative blunt cut, and the glasses perched on the end of her nose aged her another decade. A disposable cup balanced precariously on her knee teetered a little as she poked at the fire with a stick.

The wind changed directions suddenly and carried a cloud of smoke in Elaine's direction.

Two things happened at once.

The thin leather strap on one of Elaine's Birkenstocks broke and she stumbled as her foot slipped out. While she was balancing awkwardly on one leg like a flamingo, trying to assess the damage, the woman looked up.

Elaine had been expecting an apology for the smoke. Maybe a Merry Christmas. Those could be handled with a polite nod as she walked away.

"I don't believe in coincidences. Do you?"

That threw her.

So Elaine said the first words that popped into her head. Something she never did.

"I don't know what I believe."

The woman tossed another piece of driftwood into the fire. "I've been there."

Elaine didn't know why she didn't kick off the other sandal and keep walking. But the crackle of the wood and the warm ocean breeze wrapped around Elaine and drew her closer to the fire.

"Sit down." The woman pointed her stick at a depression in the sand on the opposite side of the fire.

Elaine balked at the outer perimeter, a circle of mismatched stones. "I don't want to intrude."

"I don't believe in coincidences, remember?"

Elaine wasn't sure what that had to do with anything, but she lowered herself to the ground.

"I'm Samantha O'Dell. Sammy to my grandpa and Sam to everyone else." A bright smile. "Including the ones who like to watch the sun rise over the ocean."

"Elaine." No point in telling a stranger that one sunrise looked exactly like another. She'd been walking the beach to avoid the hotel staff's manufactured holiday cheer. The families in the dining room, dressed in scarlet and green.

"It's nice to meet you." Sam pushed her fingers through the sand and came up empty. "I'm running out of wood. Pick some grass from that clump beside you and toss it in."

Elaine looked around. It suddenly occurred to her that accepting Samantha O'Dell's invitation to join the campfire made her a coconspirator in the eyes of hotel security.

"Did you start the fire?"

"Well, I'm usually better at it, but in my defense, look what I have to work with." Sam's eyes twinkled behind the heavy plastic frames. "Someone will come along eventually and tell me to put it out, but big decisions require a long conversation with God, a campfire and a cup of Earl Grey."

"I've never tried any of those."

Elaine had no idea why she continued to blurt out personal information to a total stranger, but Sam merely nodded.

"I'd say it's about time, then." She unscrewed the cap on the thermos and poured the contents into the little plaid cup. Handed it to Elaine. "It pairs well with the ocean."

Elaine smiled. There was something different about Sam O'Dell. She sipped the tea, expecting it to taste bitter, but a hint of sweetness danced on her tongue. "It's good."

"I add honey from my grandparents' beehive."

"Where do you live? Mayberry?"

Sam laughed. "Close enough. Winsome Lake, Wisconsin. Population 3,045."

"That is small."

"One café, a librarian who calls you when you have an overdue book and neighbors that keep an eye on each other."

Elaine felt a stab of envy. "You must like it there."

"I love it." Sam sighed. "But I want to leave. That's the big decision part. I'm forty years old and I want to go to Africa."

"Like...on a safari?"

Sam laughed. "No, but that sounds like fun. I've been supporting a mission school for years and there's an opening for an administrative assistant. I'm the secretary at the church I attend, so it would be a perfect fit."

No wonder Samantha O'Dell had long conversations with God. She worked for Him.

"Then why is it a big decision?"

"Because I was born and raised in Winsome. The best part, though, is that my three best friends live on Woodwind Lane, too." Sam paused. "That's why I'm here. We host a round-robin for the neighborhood at Christmas every year, and the girls know me so well, they'd be able to tell something was up. The one and only time I tried to keep a secret from them, they held me captive in our tree fort until I finally confessed that I had a crush on Andy Blankenship. I was thirteen at the time, by the way, and Andy already had his driver's license." Mischief danced in Sam's eyes. "Grounds for a scandal in my neighborhood."

Elaine almost smiled.

"You don't think they'd support your decision to leave?"

"Of course they would," Sam said instantly. "I've wanted to go there since we were kids, but I never thought I'd get the chance. You'd think a dream would be something you'd grab on to with both hands when it was finally in reach, wouldn't you? But in order to do that, you have to let go of something, too, and I don't know if I can leave them. So here I am, trying to figure it out. This time I had to fly to an island so they wouldn't suspect anything, though."

Elaine took another sip of tea. Farther down the beach, a child's laughter mingled with the shriek of seagulls. Someone would notice the smoke and wander over to investigate. They wouldn't be alone much longer. Funny how Elaine had wanted to avoid the woman and her campfire, and now she was reluctant to leave them both.

"They'll call me later today, after the round-robin, to make sure I opened the presents they smuggled into my suitcase."

Her friends had sent presents.

Elaine had bought herself a Chanel clutch at a boutique the day before. A souvenir to take her mind off the holiday, not to celebrate it.

"I can see why it's a difficult decision." She reached for another piece of driftwood, but Sam shook her head.

"Not that one. It's a little bird."

Elaine looked at the driftwood more closely. It did look like one of the shorebirds who left tiny footprints chain-stitched in the sand. She traced the curve of the wing with the tip of her finger before setting it down again.

"Do you think God will tell you what to do before you get back?" Elaine hoped she sounded curious rather than skeptical.

"Oh, this is the closing arguments. I have a list of reasons why I can't leave but I know God will take care of things. He always does. My cousin has already hinted that he'd like to buy my house..." Sam's voice trailed off.

"But?"

"Rex wouldn't be a good fit for the neighborhood. He's thirty years old and still plays in a garage band." Sam's forehead puckered. "I know the minute the paperwork is signed Rex's buddies will turn my flower garden into their personal parking stalls. The last time Rex was over, he suggested the front porch would look better if it was converted into a deck.

"I know I shouldn't be sentimental about a house, but it's been in the family a long time. My grandparents gave it to my parents as a wedding gift and then I moved in after they retired to Phoenix." Sam chuckled. "I'm rambling, aren't I?"

"I'll buy it," Elaine said. "Your house, I mean."

"Buy..." Sam choked on the word. "Why would you buy my house?"

"I work from home. I can live anywhere. I've been traveling a lot and I'm kind of tired of it…and this probably sounds crazy." It sounded crazy to Elaine. Crazy. Impulsive. And *right*.

"Yes. It does. You don't know anything about the house… or Winsome Lake." Sam wasn't laughing, though. And she wasn't discreetly collecting her things. She leaned forward, her gaze focused on Elaine, the posture of someone who wanted to hear more. "Why would you want to live there?"

"It sounds nice."

Sam's brows lifted, disappearing inside the neat hedge of brown bangs. *Not good enough*, those bangs said.

"Some people run away from home," Elaine said slowly. "I think I've been running around, hoping I'd find one." Something she hadn't realized until now. "I'd like a garden. And a porch with a rocking chair."

And friends. People who fussed over you and loved you and didn't mind when you fussed over them and loved them back.

Sam was still staring at her. Only now she was staring in a way that made Elaine wish her answer to Sam's question would have been, "Because I can afford it." Which was also the truth and, maybe, what she should have led with. "I suppose that sounds crazy, too."

"I told you that I don't believe in coincidences. The minute I saw you, I knew why God had led me out here this morning. I thought you might need some encouragement. I had no idea it was for both of us."

"I don't know God like you do."

Sam poured the last of the Earl Grey into Elaine's cup and smiled.

"I can't think of a better time than Christmas morning to introduce you."

★ ★ ★

"Hey." Matthew's voice intruded softly on Elaine's thoughts. "Are you okay?"

Elaine realized she was still holding the starfish. She looked up at Matthew and blinked. His features still looked a little fuzzy so she did it again. The fuzz disappeared but the world tilted a bit.

"I guess I'm not used to the sun."

"I'll get you a glass of water."

"No. I'm fine. I'll have some more lemonade." Elaine reached for the glass and knocked it over. A wave of sticky yellow liquid washed over the seashells and spread out over the table.

Lord. Please. No.

Matthew's chair flipped over backward as he rose to his feet and caught her.

Which was strange, because Elaine hadn't realized she was falling.

Chapter Twenty-One

"Hello in the house!"

Merri's lilting voice preceded the muffled thump in the front hallway.

Jess wiped her hands on the towel looped over the handle of the oven and walked into the living room. Sienna's fingers stilled on the keyboard and she shot Jess a panicked look.

"Hello?" Jess hadn't realized it would sound like a question. The days had been funneling together, but she was pretty sure it was Wednesday.

Merri rounded the corner, weighted down with enough bags to fill the cargo hold of a small airplane. "Don't stop because of me." She smiled at Sienna. "I could hear you from the sidewalk. I recognize the song but not the composer. It's one of the famous ones, isn't it?"

Sienna glanced at the open window and then at Merri. "Yes. Chopin."

Since it was twice the amount of words Sienna had spoken to Jess, she considered that progress. When she'd discovered Sienna at the piano at 7:00 a.m., all she'd gotten was a mumbled hello.

"Chopin." Merri rolled the name around in her mouth and smiled as if she'd tasted something sweet. "I'm sure he'd be proud of you."

Instead of brightening at the compliment, Sienna's shoulders dropped a notch. And the dark smudges under the girl's eyes weren't from runaway eyeliner. Sienna had the look of someone who would break into a thousand pieces from a careless word or gesture.

Jess felt another stab of concern. She'd taken a discreet sweep of the living room when she'd come downstairs. Sienna's backpack had been open on the coffee table. Some of the contents had spilled out but there were no telltale signs she'd spent the night on the couch again.

Jess had a feeling that didn't mean things were better at home. It only meant that Sienna was trying to avoid her, too.

"Oh!" Merri clapped her hands. "Do you know 'Ode to Joy'? It's one of my favorites—"

"Merri." Jess dove into the conversation before Sienna could bolt. "Did you change the day of your scrapbook meeting?"

"Oh, no." Merri chuckled. "We're still planning to meet tomorrow. But my brother and his wife are stopping to see me on their way to Duluth in a few weeks, so I'd like to have his album finished by the time they get here."

Why didn't anyone bother to mention these things?

The front door opened again and Violet, who'd staked her claim on top of the piano, leaped to the floor, her tail doubled in size. A split second later, Bosco trotted into the living room. Peg was a step behind, pulling her wheeled case. She spotted Sienna and did a double take.

Please please please don't say anything, Jess silently begged.

Peg, of course, didn't hear her. And Jess wasn't convinced it wouldn't have mattered if she had.

"I played the oboe when I was in high school." She stopped next to the piano and peered down at Sienna. "Hated it. The silly reed kept getting hung up on my braces. You were a smart girl to choose the piano. Smart." Peg adjusted the bag over her shoulder and trundled into the kitchen.

Jess heard more thumping as bags hit the floor. "Oh, good! You made coffee."

"That's my cue to get to work." Merri flapped a hand at Bosco, who'd been eyeing the plastic bag filled with trail mix peeking out of Sienna's backpack, and followed her friend.

Jess stepped closer to the piano.

"They'll be working at the dining room table," she murmured. "You don't have to cut your practice time short."

"Like it even matters," Sienna muttered.

Now Jess understood why there'd been more silence than music. She'd had bad days in the kitchen, too. Days she'd burned the main course and her fingers, been chastised by instructors and the mocking voices inside her head that said she was going to fail.

"I'll let you and Chopin work it out." Jess reached for the trail mix and set it on the bench beside her. "Pick out the chocolate chips if you get really frustrated. It'll help."

Jess thought she saw a smile flicker on Sienna's lips, but it came and went so quickly, she could have imagined it.

Peg and Merri hadn't migrated into the dining room yet. Merri was putting something in the freezer, and Peg was staring at the bundles of herbs clipped to the curtain rod.

"What are you doing with these?"

"I'm not sure yet." Jess wove through the maze of bins and bags. "That's why I decided to dry some of them." The thyme and the lemon balm in particular seemed to have tripled in size overnight, so Jess had tried to come up with new ways to incorporate them into her recipes. She was thinking crepes. Or popovers.

Peg pointed to the lemon balm. "Elaine puts that in our iced tea."

Merri looked up and smiled. "She'd be glad you're putting it to good use."

You give them hope that Elaine is coming home again.

Jess hadn't taken Nick's words seriously, but they circled through her mind again while she watched Merri help herself to a cup of coffee.

How had it happened that she'd landed in the one house on Woodwind Lane that everyone treated like a second home?

"We better get started." Merri picked up one of the bags, and Jess helped them transfer the rest to the dining room.

"Will Nita be coming over, too?" Jess asked.

Merri and Peg exchanged a quick look.

"Nita was having some…issues…when I called her this morning, so she wasn't sure," Merri finally said.

Peg muttered something under her breath and began to line up tiny plastic containers on the table.

Jess walked back into the kitchen and almost tripped over Bosco. Lying on his back in a puddle of sunshine, the dog looked like a black velvet footstool turned upside down with his short little legs sticking up in the air.

Jess started on the rest of the herbs she'd picked, rinsing off the dirt and patting them dry with a paper towel.

Popovers it was. Thyme and flat-leaf parsley and grated parmesan.

She'd just pulled the flour from the pantry when someone rapped at the back door.

"We're here," Nita announced before Jess could get there to open it.

Nita had one tote bag and Christopher in tow. He gave Jess a halfhearted wave, but balked in the kitchen doorway.

"I c-can stay home by myself."

A we-talked-about-this sigh slipped between Nita's lips. "The plumber has to fix the pipes in the bathroom this morning."

"I can h-help him. I can hand him the tools."

"That's very nice of you, but the plumber doesn't need help," Nita said evenly.

"You can s-set the alarm," Christopher said. "I'll be okay for t-two hours."

The watch on Nita's wrist that dictated her comings and goings suddenly made sense to Jess. Those intermittent beeps weren't meant to keep her on schedule. They kept her connected to her son.

Peg and Merri entered the kitchen and flanked Nita's side as if summoned by a silent SOS.

"Hey, Chrissy." Peg held Bosco up in front of Christopher and waved the dog's front paw. "You can sit next to me. I need some stars cut out with the paper punch. You like to do that."

Chrissy?

Jess tried not to wince. It was an affectionate nickname that should have been packed away with childhood keepsakes like a rattle or first pair of shoes.

"Or," Jess heard herself say, "you can be my sous-chef."

Four pairs of eyes swung toward Jess. In the living room, Chopin lapsed into silence.

Christopher looked intrigued. "What's that?"

"A sous-chef assists the executive chef in the kitchen.

They're—" Jess tried to think of a description that would appeal to a teenage boy "—second-in-command."

Nita, who never looked anything but perfectly composed, nibbled on her lower lip. "Are you sure, Jessica? Christopher likes sorting through photos, too."

Jess had never had a sous-chef before, but from the expression on Christopher's face, it was clear he'd rather be in the kitchen than the dining room.

"I'm sure."

"Yes!" Christopher raised his arm.

Jess smiled and slapped her palm against his. "Come on. We'll round up an apron for you."

She felt, rather than heard, a collective exhale of relief. Nita still looked a little uncertain, but Merri and Peg linked their arms through their friend's and yanked her back into the dining room.

Christopher's forehead wrinkled and then he nodded. "What are we going to make?"

"Mmmm." Jess, who, five minutes ago, could smell the scent of freshly baked bread and see the steam escaping from a perfectly baked popover, mentally scratched that recipe and started over again. She didn't know how much experience Christopher had in the kitchen, but the margin of error when making popovers was a little high.

You are chefs, yes...

Chef Tomas's voice boomed in Jess's head.

"What do you like to eat?"

Christopher's entire face lit with a smile. "Pizza!"

"Pizza, it is."

Jess reached for the apron she'd seen hanging in the broom closet. It was the kind popular at craft fairs; the fabric tissue-paper thin, the hem appliquéd with yellow ducks and watering cans. Cute, but a flimsy barrier against heat, spills and stains.

She tied it around her waist and handed Christopher her bib chef's apron. A protective suit of armor in basic black. "Do you help your mom in the kitchen?"

"Sometimes." Christopher tugged the apron over his head. "Am I a s-sous-chef now?"

Jess looked him over. "Mmmm. There's something missing... I know what it is. Hold on a second. I'll be right back."

Christopher's mouth fell open when Jess returned a few minutes later with her toque.

"Is th-that hat for me?"

"It's called a toque. And yes, it is." Jess set the hat on his head. "One more very important thing before we get started. The executive chef—" she tapped her chest "—is in charge of the kitchen. When the chef gives an instruction, the sous-chef's response is always, 'Yes, Chef.'"

Christopher bobbed his head. "Okay, J–Jessica."

Jess gave him a look and his shoulders straightened. "I mean, yes, Chef!"

The conversation in the dining room and the music simultaneously stopped. Both resumed again when Jess laughed.

"*Now* you're ready."

She opened the pantry and found the ingredients they needed to make the dough. While Christopher was combining the flour and yeast, Jess measured out the olive oil and water.

"Stir this in and I'll look around and see what we have for toppings." Jess took out the block of fresh mozzarella she'd bought for a caprese salad and set it on the counter.

"How d–does this look?" Christopher asked.

Jess took a peek inside the bowl. "Great. While the dough

rests, we're going to cut up the onions and peppers," she told him.

"My m-mom does that part. Knives are d-dangerous."

"Only in the hands of someone who doesn't know how to use one." Jess unwrapped the leather case and took out her chef's knife. "And this one is very, *very* sharp," she warned. "But I'll show you how to do it the right way and you won't get cut."

Equal parts terror and delight shone in Christopher's eyes. "Yes, Chef."

Jess demonstrated on an onion before she let him pick up the knife.

"Curl these fingers under," she instructed. "You'll need them later."

Now Jess wasn't only hearing Chef Tomas in her head. She was repeating his favorite jokes, too.

Christopher snickered, but followed her instructions with an intensity that told Jess he was taking his job as sous-chef seriously.

"Great," she said. "It's not about speed, okay? I've been doing this a long time. The more you practice, the faster you'll get."

Uneven bits of onion began to collect on the cutting board.

Nita came into the kitchen under the guise of refilling her coffee cup and pulled up short when she saw Christopher standing at the butcher-block island, chopping away with Jess's knife.

"What…" The word tumbled out with a strangled gasp.

"Don't worry, Mom." Christopher didn't look up. "J-Jessica showed me how to do it the right way."

Nita's gaze traveled from the white toque that listed

slightly to the right on her son's head to the flour-smudged apron tied around his waist. And then it locked on Jess.

"Jessica." Nita's voice had evened out, but the turbulence in her eyes told Jess that her emotions hadn't caught up yet. "Could I talk to you for a minute?"

She didn't add the word *alone*, but Jess figured that was a given. She'd obviously broken some unspoken rule.

"Chris?"

Christopher stopped chopping and looked up at her; the slump of his shoulders told Jess he suspected what was coming next.

"The mushrooms need to be wiped off before you slice them," Jess said.

"Slice th-them?"

"That's your job."

Christopher grinned. "Okay, J-Jessica! I mean, yes, Chef!"

With Sienna on one side of the kitchen and Merri and Peg on the other, the only place left for a private conversation was Elaine's garden.

Nita followed Jess outside. When the screen door snapped shut behind them, Jess expected to get hit with the full force of a mother's wrath.

The tears welling up in Nita's eyes sent Jess's heart plummeting to her feet.

"I'm sorry, Nita. I should have asked you before I let Christopher use my knife."

"That's not..." Nita swallowed hard and started over.

"I've been so worried about Chris's surgery that all I've been saying is no. He's so good about everything, but I know he gets frustrated. You...you reminded me that he needs to hear yes sometimes."

Relief turned Jess's knees to liquid and she leaned against

the metal railing for support. "Christopher is doing great. I wouldn't have let him get hurt."

"I know." Nita blinked to disperse the tears and one cut a crooked path down her cheek. She dashed it away. "And I'm the first one to admit I can be a little overprotective…"

The clatter of metal against porcelain disrupted the melodic flow of Sienna's solo.

Panic flared in Nita's eyes and she lunged toward the door, but Jess got there first.

"I've got this."

Nita looked as if she was going to argue but then a smile lifted the corners of her lips.

"Yes, Chef."

Chapter Twenty-Two

Jess hip-checked the screen door and carried another pizza outside.

The bistro table she'd seen by the garage had been relocated to the patio. A mason jar filled with roses, lipstick-pink with white piping at the edges, added a touch of sweetness to the air.

"Number three." Jess set the pie down between Sienna and Christopher. "Mushroom and onion."

The women had staked their claim at the table, the teens on the bottom step. Bosco camped out in the space between, waiting for the crumbs to fall.

Christopher shook his finger at Sienna. "I t-told you there would be enough."

Jess hadn't had to convince Sienna to stay for lunch. Christopher insisted everyone in the house try their pizza and that included the girl playing the piano. A moment after it registered that her sous-chef had disappeared, Christopher had re-entered the kitchen, leading a wide-eyed Sienna by the hand.

Jess reached across the table and grabbed the almost empty pitcher of iced tea. "I'll fill this up again."

When she returned a few minutes later, a bright blue soccer chair had sprouted from the ground between Merri and Peg.

"This is for you," Merri sang out.

"You should reap the benefit of all your hard work, too," Peg chimed in.

"I'll eat later." Jess set the pitcher down and would have backpedaled toward the step, but Peg had already set an extra plate on the table and Nita was pouring a glass of tea.

Leaving Jess with no choice but to join them at the table. Peg slid the plate closer and offered her a slice.

Jess felt off balance, but she couldn't blame it on the wobbly legged chair.

On the evenings Gwyneth dined at home alone, Jess would prepare and serve the meal. She would start the initial cleanup while Gwyneth ate and then collect the empty dishes forty-five minutes later. After that Jess would either warm up a plate of leftovers and take them back to her room or eat while jotting notes for the following day's menu.

When Gwyneth hosted an event, Jess prepared and served the food, but it would never have occurred to her to invite Jess to mingle with the guests.

But now, wedged between Peg and Merri, Jess felt like a stationary target for questions she didn't want to answer.

"This is so good." Merri peeled a mushroom off the top of her slice and popped it into her mouth. "Ten times better than The Cozy Corner's."

"Is that a café?" Jess didn't remember seeing one on Main Street.

"It was," Nita said. "The place shut down about three years ago."

"Four," Merri said softly. "A month after Don passed."

Nita and Peg shifted in their chairs, making room for memories.

"That's right." Peg rested her cheek on the slope of Merri's shoulder. "Frank still misses their Wednesday morning breakfast meetings."

Merri smiled. "If you asked our husbands why it took three hours to drink a cup of coffee, they'd say they were—"

"Solving the world's problems one plate of biscuits and gravy at a time."

The women's voices merged together in a gruff duet.

"If Frank hadn't liked my pie better, I wouldn't have seen him all day." Peg chuckled. "Everyone knows I can't cook, so I had to keep baking to keep him at home."

The women traveled as a set, so Jess hadn't thought about husbands. Out of the corner of her eye, she saw Nita rub the bare finger on her left hand, almost as if she was soothing a phantom pain.

Jess's gaze strayed to Christopher, who'd wheedled Sienna into playing a game of rock, paper, scissors. Sienna was giggling almost uncontrollably, her usual reticence no match against the innocent competition and Christopher's contagious grin.

Nita was looking at them, too. Pride and fear clashed in her eyes.

Was it always a daily battle between the two? Jess wondered. And what happened if the fear won?

"What was your restaurant like, Jessica?"

Jess's head swiveled toward Merri. She should have expected questions. The average home cook didn't have a toque lying around.

"I didn't work at a restaurant. I was employed as a personal chef."

"Oh." Peg nodded in understanding. "For people who aren't able to cook for themselves. Like Elaine."

For people who didn't *have* to. Like Gwyneth.

"It sounds easier than working at a restaurant," Nita said. "Cooking for one."

Jess couldn't begin to explain the differences between the Donovan estate and Woodwind Lane any more than she could explain the difference in her duties.

She wasn't even sure she could call what she'd been doing the past few days *cooking*. It felt more like she was struggling again to find the elusive ingredient so everything else would make sense.

What do you taste, Number Five?

Failure…

"I w-want to work in a restaurant." Christopher had tuned in to the conversation between matches. "Jessica says I'm a g-good sous-chef, Mom."

Nita's expression softened. "I wish Winsome Lake still had one."

Jess saw a lot of wishes in her eyes.

"I do, too. Every time Bosco and I walk past the café, he pulls at the leash." Peg tossed a tiny piece of crust to the dog. Bosco, in a move that defied both his weight and the laws of gravity, caught it in midair. "He remembers the pancakes."

Merri released a dreamy sigh. "Everyone remembers the pancakes."

Jess didn't mind the change in topic. Reminiscing about their past meant they weren't asking questions about hers.

"I suppose in a town this size it's hard to keep a restaurant going," Jess ventured.

"There were plenty of customers," Nita said. "Brenda

Goodwin's parents turned the place over to her when they retired, but she was a better cook than a businesswoman. The café went under a year after she took over. I heard rumors someone was thinking about opening it up again, but an insurance company swooped in and bought the building and that was that."

"There's a bar and grill next to the hardware store, but it's not the same." Merri picked up her napkin and waved it in front of her face like a fan. "Everything on the menu is deep fried. Even the dill pickles."

Nita's watch chirped and she glanced down at it. "The plumber needs my signature on the receipt."

"What time is it?" Peg squinted up at the sun. It had shifted position while they ate and was shining directly over the garden.

"Two o'clock."

"Oh my." Peg vaulted to her feet. "My hubby will be home at five and I still have to make biscuits for the strawberry shortcake I promised him."

Jess had an epiphany.

"You made the butterscotch pie."

"Mmm-hmm. It's one of Frank's favorites." Peg brushed the crumbs off her shirt and Bosco trotted over to vacuum them up.

"When Peg was fifteen, she caught Frank stealing one of the chocolate chip cookies she'd entered in the county fair and figured he had a sweet tooth," Merri added. "She used that information to lure him in at the next church potluck."

"Turtle brownies," Peg said without a touch of remorse or regret. "And it worked. Mom said she was glad when Frank proposed because she was tired of spending half her grocery budget on flour and sugar."

County fairs. Church potlucks. High school sweethearts.

Friends who completed each other's sentences and each other's lives.

None of these things had been ingredients in Jess's life.

In culinary school, everything was a competition. The need to stand out, to bring something unique to the table, didn't exactly foster a feeling of comradery among the students.

And a sweetheart?

That hadn't happened, either. Jess's career had demanded all her time and energy.

"Do we have to l-leave?" Christopher noticed the sudden flurry of activity around the table.

"Yes." Nita watered a rosebush with what remained of her iced tea and set the empty glass on her plate. "I'm sure Jessica wants to spend the rest of this gorgeous afternoon outside."

Actually, Jess planned to spend it in the kitchen. Images of the popovers she'd planned to make before Christopher and Nita's arrival were still dancing in her head.

When Jess walked into the kitchen, Merri was already at the sink, rinsing off plates. Sienna deposited her dishes on the counter and slipped back into the living room.

"I'll send the leftovers home with whoever wants them," Jess announced. "Right after I find the tin foil."

"Second drawer on the right..." Merri whirled around, water cascading from her fingertips onto Jess's spotless floor.

"Merri!" Nita barked. "What on earth are—?"

"Shush."

Nita, who was the kind of person one didn't shush, shushed.

"'Ode to Joy.'" A smile broke out across Merri's face and she bustled away, leaving a trail of iridescent soap bubbles dancing in the air.

"Oh, I love that one, too." Peg swept Bosco into her arms and trotted after her.

"Come on, M-Mom." Christopher grabbed Nita's hand and towed her toward the door.

Jess snagged a piece of tomato off the plate and joined the mass exodus to the living room.

She could barely see Sienna through the wall of bodies clustered around the piano.

Jess winced.

Poor Sienna. She probably thought she'd be providing background music for the clean-up crew. She wasn't expecting an audience that swayed and tapped their feet and hummed along.

Applause rocked the tiny living room when the song ended.

Sienna slowly turned around. Her cheeks were on fire, but she halfheartedly returned Christopher's high five.

"That was wonderful, Sienna," Nita said.

"Is that the solo you're going to play at the recital?" Peg asked.

Sienna licked her lips. "No."

"She's playing Chopin," Merri said. "But you could win with this one. I've been praying Elaine will be well enough to attend your recital."

"It doesn't matter," Sienna muttered. "I'm not going to be there."

Jess waited until everyone had left before she confronted Sienna.

"What is this about skipping the recital?"

Sienna's lips formed a tight seal, but Jess wasn't going to let her off the hook this time.

"Merri mentioned something about a scholarship being awarded to one of the seniors. Was that true?"

Sienna's chin tipped almost imperceptibly.

Jess took it as a yes.

"Then what's wrong? Is it because you don't feel prepared?"

"It's not the solo. I didn't know..." Sienna stopped, and Jess tamped down her frustration. Getting the girl to say more than a few words at a time was like pumping a dry well.

"Know what?"

"That the recital was such a big deal, okay? Ms. Grant, my piano teacher, sent an email to all her students. She's going to announce the winner of the scholarship after the recital, and a reporter from the newspaper will be there.

"Some of the girls said they already made appointments to get their hair and nails done." Sienna wadded the hem of her T-shirt. "And Ms. Grant wants us to get dressed up..."

Jess tried to keep her mental footings now that the floodgates had opened.

"You've got the solo down." Jess waited until Sienna looked her in the eye. "I can help with the dress."

There were two hanging in Jess's closet. A polka dot midi she'd worn while serving the guests at one of Gwyneth's garden parties and the simple black sheath Jess had bought after culinary school, the building block of a wardrobe limited by budget and closet space.

Sienna bit her lip. Jess waited.

Finally, she heard a whispered, "Okay."

Okay.

Jess released the breath she hadn't realized she'd been holding.

"I'll see you tomorrow morning?"

Sienna didn't answer. She closed the fallboard with the tenderness of a child putting her favorite doll to bed and picked up her backpack. Slung it over her shoulder and glanced back at Jess when she reached the door.

"They won't come, you know."

Sienna slipped out, but Jess knew who she was talking about.

Just like she knew that a mani-pedi, a new dress, or even a prestigious scholarship couldn't fill two empty chairs.

Or the hole in your heart where a family should be.

Jess walked into the kitchen just as her cell phone started to ring. She picked it up and saw a familiar number flashing on the screen.

"Hello?"

"Jessica? This is Vanessa Richards. I'm afraid I have some bad news."

Chapter Twenty-Three

"Bucket! Get back..."

Here.

The dog streaked past Nick like a quarterback going for a touchdown. Eyes fixed on the goal, deaf to the roar of the crowd.

Or, in this case, his owner.

Bucket, Nick had discovered, was an extrovert. If he spotted a potential playmate—red squirrel, jogger, dragonfly—he felt obligated to deliver a personal invitation to join in whatever game he'd been playing.

Nick couldn't see Bucket's newest target, so he dropped the board he'd been sanding and sprinted across the yard. *His* goal to stop the dog before he reached the road.

"Bucket! You..." *Are so going to get an extra rawhide chew today, buddy.*

Because Jessica stood at the end of the driveway, held captive by Nick's wonderful, intelligent pup, who was preventing his quarry's escape by performing impressive figure eights around her feet.

Nick jogged up to them. He'd run the same distance in a lot less time, but suddenly it hurt to breathe.

Jessica was wearing shorts and a gauzy top with cutouts that bared her shoulders. Instead of the sedate ponytail she seemed to favor, her hair fell in loose waves around her face.

"Sorry." Nick looped his fingers through Bucket's collar and made him sit. "He got away from me."

"That seems to happen a lot." Jess was smiling at Bucket when she said it, though, which Nick took as a good sign.

"You're out and about pretty early…" He suddenly noticed the market bag in her hand and connected the dots. "You're out of eggs already?"

"Almost." Her smile faded. "And I needed to get out of the house for a while."

The stab of disappointment that slid between Nick's ribs and caused a hitch in his breathing took him by surprise. He wasn't sure why. Jessica had already stuck it out longer than he'd thought she would.

He wanted to ask if something had happened, but the shadow in her eyes warned him not to push.

"You wouldn't be using those eggs for a coffee cake, would you?" Nick strove to keep his tone light.

"I haven't decided." Jessica lifted her chin. "And just for the record, my name is officially on the egg list now."

Nick had the Silva family hotline to thank for that. It surpassed the town grapevine for speed and efficiency. Once Grandpop had mentioned Jessica and the coffeecake, Nick's mom and his aunts suddenly decided they had a surplus of eggs and scratched their names off the list. Nick wanted to think it was out of kindness to the new kid in town, but he knew that other, less-than-altruistic forces were at work.

Matchmaking forces.

What they didn't realize was that Jessica, the unsuspecting victim in their diabolical plot to graft another branch on the Silva family tree, didn't completely trust him.

Nick couldn't understand why. He was a coach, not a player. He'd never made a move on her. Kept his eyes and thoughts in line.

Nick had hoped the chocolate cake would be a bridge to greater communication, but even now Jessica was maintaining the cautious distance of a quarterback trying to avoid a sack.

Bucket bumped Nick's kneecap and added a bark for good measure. A reminder that Nick wasn't holding up his part of the conversation. If the dog fancied himself Nick's wingman, he wasn't very subtle.

"I stopped over at Grandpop's a little while ago. He's got the smoker going today, so he camps out in a lawn chair in the back."

Jessica's gaze strayed from Nick to the lodge, and her eyes widened as she took in the sight.

Nick could only imagine what she was thinking. He supposed that someone who'd never seen the building in its original glory would have a hard time getting past the weathered shake siding and the scabs of moss on the roof.

"I bought this place last winter and I've been fixing it up to sell."

"Wow."

"Yeah." Nick brushed at the sawdust clinging to his jeans. "That seems to be the general consensus around here, my family included." He was probably going to crash and burn but took a risk anyway. "Do you want the ten-minute tour?"

When Jessica nodded, Nick had to clench his teeth to prevent his jaw from hitting the ground.

"I'm hoping to get it on the market this fall." Nick released Bucket. Instead of taking off, the dog walked sedately at Jessica's side.

That's right. Best foot forward, bud.

"You flip houses in your spare time?"

"House, singular," Nick corrected. "Renovation is a full-time job and I already have two of those."

A breeze skipped across the surface of the lake and set the rowboat tied to the dock into motion. The boat had been one of the things Nick had found on the property after the snow began to melt and he put it to good use several times a week.

He glanced at Jessica's footwear. Open-toed sandals that revealed ten toenails coated with pale pink shellac. "There are nails on the floor, so be careful where you step."

Jessica followed Nick inside the lodge. She stopped just inside the door and drew in a quick breath. Nick wasn't sure if she thought he was a genius or the dumbest guy that ever lived.

He couldn't fault her for that. Depending on the day, he wondered the same thing.

She spun a slow circle, taking everything in. Sunlight gilded the knotty-pine walls and stenciled intricate patterns on the floor.

"What was this place?" Her voice dropped to a library whisper.

"When Grandpop was a kid, it was a fishing lodge that catered to wealthy businessmen who rode the train up from Chicago on the weekends." Nick could have devoted the next hour to a history lesson, but he'd promised a ten-minute tour. "It sold after the railroad shut down, and the Whitman family turned it into a supper club. That's how I remember it. We'd come here for special occasions.

"You're standing in the middle of the dining room right

now." Nick walked to the window overlooking the lake. "Mom and Dad would sit right there—" he pointed to the corner of the crumbling stone patio "—while my sisters and I played tag around the pine trees. The hostess would ring a bell when a table was ready. One ring for table one. Two for table two. You get the idea. If Grandma Jenny made the reservation, she always booked table ten just because she loved the sound."

Nick had searched everywhere for that bell. A member of the Whitman family could have claimed it before the sale or it might be collecting dust in an antiques store somewhere.

Jessica paused midspin and turned to look at him. "Why did it close down?"

"It was a family-run business that ran out of family." Nick shrugged. "After that the place passed from owner to owner like a stray dog." He glanced down at Bucket. "No offense, buddy.

"The last guy who lived here bought it as a vacation home. He converted this space into a living room because of the view. There are two rooms and a full bath upstairs, but it'll be a while before I get up there."

Jessica was picking her way through the debris field to get to the fireplace. "What about this?"

Nick hesitated. He'd done a little research and found out the stones had been gleaned from the property when the lodge was being built, but the estimate he'd gotten from a local mason to restore the fireplace would take a sizeable chunk of his budget. Nick's aunts, die-hard HGTV fans, insisted he tear the whole thing out and put in something more modern, but Nick wanted to follow his gut, not a trend.

He realized Jessica was still waiting for an answer. The safe one was, "I haven't decided yet."

Jessica tipped her head and a river of wheat-blond hair flowed over her bare shoulder. "I think you have."

It was a little disconcerting, knowing she could already read him that easily. Especially when Nick was having the hardest time trying to figure *her* out.

"Maybe. Okay…yes. It's going to be hard to match the stone and I'm sure whoever buys the place would rather have a gas insert, but it's part of the building's history. And…"

Now he was really going to sound sentimental. "Mine."

"Have you thought about living here?"

Nick had. But no one, not even the members of his own family, had asked that question.

"For about a minute," he admitted. "Restoring it feels right, but I'm happy on Woodwind Lane. I grew up there and my parents wanted some land outside of town, so I bought the house after the school board offered me the job. This place…" He ran his hand over the dust coating the windowsill. "It's meant for someone else."

Nick couldn't believe he'd said that out loud.

He waited for Jessica to laugh, but she'd walked across the room and was tracing the edges of a gaping hole in the wall that resembled an open wound.

"The bar was there," Nick said. "I found it in the drop box."

Jessica glanced over her shoulder, a question in her eyes.

"Sorry. While the guy was starting the remodel, he took out everything he didn't want and tossed it behind the boathouse. I call it the drop box even though I'm pretty sure it was going to be a giant bonfire when he was done.

"I managed to salvage a few things, but the lodge is the priority right now. I'll hire some of my players for a final cleanup when it's finished." Nick followed a path through the maze of two-by-fours scattered on the floor. "What do you want to see next? The second floor or the kitchen?"

Jessica didn't hesitate. "Kitchen."

"Kitchen it is." Nick resisted the urge to take her hand and guide her through the obstacle course of tools and lumber.

-"It hasn't changed much since the place was a supper club," he warned her. "I don't think the guy who lived here even used it. I'll have to replace the appliances and pull that thing out." He pointed to the stainless-steel eyesore in the center of the kitchen.

"The prep station," Jessica murmured.

"Right." Nick bent down to discreetly check the live trap in the cabinet underneath the sink. Most of the mice had moved out when spring arrived, but there were still a few of the furry squatters who preferred the kitchen cabinets to a home in the woods.

"Nick..."

The tension in Jessica's voice drove Nick to his feet. She was pointing a shaky finger at the ancient cooktop.

Nick was about to scan the burners, searching for a cone-shaped head with beady little eyes, when Jessica reached for the cast-iron skillet he'd been using as a catch-all for rusty screws and nails.

"Whoa. Careful. Don't drop that thing." Nick shook away disturbing images of blood and broken toes.

"This *thing*—" Jessica was scooping out nails and dumping them on the counter "—is a Griswold thirteen."

"A Griswhat?"

"Griswold. That's the brand name." She turned the skillet over, traced the imprint of what looked like a cross on the back with the tip of her finger.

"It probably got lost in the shuffle after the supper club closed," Nick said. "I found it in the drop box, too."

"Someone threw it away?" Jessica hugged the skillet against her chest like she was protecting a small child.

"I'm going to go out on a limb here and guess there's something special about it?"

"It's a *thirteen*. Griswold didn't produce very many because people were superstitious about the number. The demand wasn't high, so they stopped making them."

"And rare equals valuable."

"To collectors," Jessica murmured. "To a chef..." The sentence trailed off.

But based on the look of excitement on Jessica's face, the sparkle in her eyes, it wasn't that hard to figure out which one she was.

A dozen thoughts ricocheted through Nick's mind, but only one broke free.

"It's yours."

Nick's words barely registered as Jess scraped away some rust on the handle.

She couldn't believe someone had actually tossed the skillet into the trash. Or—she resisted the urge to cast a dark look at Nick—used it to collect the flotsam and jetsam from a construction zone.

"Do you see how smooth the surface is? The iron is thinner than other brands, which makes it lighter. But that's also why it cooks so evenly. And this ridge on the bottom? It's a smoke ring—"

"Jess."

She looked up. Nick was staring at her with a strange expression on his face. Because he thought *she* was strange.

Of course Nick wouldn't be interested in cookware.

"Sorry. I got a little carried away." Jess patted the bottom of the skillet. "What did you say?"

"I said it's yours. You can have it."

Jess laughed. And then realized he was serious. "Nick. Collectors pay two or three thousand dollars, minimum, for skillets like this. You could put the money back into building materials for the house."

"I could. But I also think things should be used, not displayed." Nick held her gaze. "And I'm guessing you'd be using it, right?"

Jess didn't know why she hesitated telling him that she was a chef. It wasn't like she was revealing a superpower. But admitting it would lead to more questions. Like how she'd ended up as a glorified housekeeper in Winsome Lake.

A question even Jess didn't know the answer to.

"Yes. But I can't accept it as a gift." The words tumbled out in a rush. "You have to let me pay for it."

"Fine," Nick said without hesitation. "The cost is dinner."

"Dinner?" Jess's heart broke free from its moorings and bumped against her rib cage.

"I'll be in charge of the main entrée and the sides, and you're in charge of dessert."

"You want to cook...together?" One hundred percent, undiluted panic rushed through Jess's veins.

She didn't share her kitchen with anyone. Well, Christopher. But he'd been an exception to the rule and Jess had taken on the role of teacher. Something told her that Nick wouldn't be shouting "yes, Chef" when Jess gave out an instruction.

"That's right." Laughter danced in Nick's eyes. "One authentic northern Wisconsin fish fry."

"What kind of fish are we talking about?" Jess asked cautiously. "Cod? Haddock?"

"Whatever I catch that morning." The laughter in Nick's blue eyes spilled over and lit up his face with a full-blown grin. "Remember when I said that I know how to make two things really well? One is Grandma Jenny's chocolate cake. The other is panfish.

"I'll keep the skillet safe until tomorrow night so you don't have to lug the thing home. After dinner you'll be granted full custody. It makes sense to meet here because this kitchen has more room than mine and Elaine's. And there will be less to explain if anything goes wrong."

Spending an entire evening trapped with Nick in a kitchen that made Elaine Haviland's look modern. Making a dessert instead of the entrée.

Jess couldn't begin to count how many things could go wrong.

"What do you say? I was the one who filled old Gris here with rusty nails, so I feel there are amends to be made."

What should Jess say?

No.

What *did* she say?

"All right. But don't you dare put this skillet in the dishwasher."

Chapter Twenty-Four

Nita, Merri and Peg had commandeered the dining room table again. Only this time there wasn't a photograph or paper punch in sight.

Jess could think of only one reason the three women weren't scrapbooking, talking or drinking the pot of coffee she'd made before leaving the house.

They'd already heard about Elaine.

Jess put the eggs in the fridge and washed her hands, not sure whether she should start cooking or join the somber group.

The decision was taken away from Jess when Nita called out, "Jessica? Can you come in here when you have a minute? We'd like to talk to you."

Jess poured herself a cup of coffee and carried it into the dining room. She glanced at Merri as she slid into an empty chair, but for once, the older woman's expression was impossible to read.

"We're concerned about Sienna," Nita said without preamble.

"Sienna?" Jess echoed.

"Is she going to drop out of the recital?"

"I don't think so. She was practicing this morning when I left for Anthony's."

And ended up at Nick's...

Jess shook the thought away. The man was more distracting than the pie cloaked in tin foil on the buffet.

"Thank you, Lord." Merri directed the words at the ceiling and Nita looked at Peg.

"Tell Jessica what you heard."

That sounded ominous.

"I went to the Sassy Scissors to get my hair cut yesterday. It was getting so long I couldn't see my earrings anymore." Peg reached up to finger the tiny gold dog biscuits dangling from her lobes. "Yvonne White was there, too, getting her *roots* touched up even though I have the yearbook photo to prove she wasn't a blonde until our senior year..."

Nita's meaningful cough nudged Peg back on track.

"We ended up sitting next to each other under the dryers and she mentioned her granddaughter was going to be in a music recital next week. Sienna's recital," Peg added, just in case Jess wasn't keeping up. "Anyway, she went on and on about the open house she's hosting afterward."

She stopped to take a breath, and Jess waded cautiously into the space. "And?"

"And from the way Yvonne talked, it sounds like all the families are planning something special. It's a tradition."

Now Jess understood.

If Sienna's parents weren't planning to attend their daughter's recital, chances were slim either one of them cared about a tradition.

When Jess graduated from culinary school, all the students were given two guest tickets for the ceremony and the gala that followed. Jess doubted her parents would come. They'd been upset when she'd chosen culinary school over a full-time position at the lumberyard, where her dad had *put in a good word for her.*

But part of her had longed for them to be there. To cheer when she received her certificate. Sample some of the food she'd learned to prepare.

Jess had agonized over the decision for a week before she'd finally dropped an invitation and the tickets in the mail.

A week after graduation Jess's mother had called to let her know they were coming. When Jess told her they'd missed it, it somehow became Jess's fault. Why hadn't she called to remind them? And why did she go to school to learn to cook anyway? Couldn't she follow a recipe?

The next time Jess had seen her parents, they'd shown up at her door without an invitation. The visit hadn't gone well and they'd rarely spoken after that...

"We'll help," Nita was saying. "Christopher and I can pull weeds in the garden and tidy it up. Merri is the creative one, so she'll take care of the decorations."

All Jess heard was *the garden.*

"You want to have it *here*?" Even to her own ears, Jess's voice sounded a little shrill. ·

Merri bobbed her head. "We were hoping you could make the food. Nothing too fancy. Maybe some of those little finger sandwiches. Something sweet."

"And I can make a pan of brownies or a sheet cake," Peg offered.

"There's a stampede at the church potlucks for Peg's brownies," Merri said.

"That's because I frost them. It's like having two desserts instead of one."

Jess massaged her temples.

"What's the matter?" Nita asked bluntly. "You don't think it's a good idea?"

At the moment the idea ranked right up there with spending an evening in the kitchen with Nick.

"Sienna doesn't seem like the kind of person who enjoys the spotlight," Jess said carefully. "And if she isn't awarded the scholarship, she might prefer to be alone that night."

"When you want to be alone is when you need your people the most," Merri said softly.

Not people. *Your* people.

Sienna had been dodging Elaine's neighbors half the summer, afraid they might judge her. Someone running away drew attention to themselves, but Sienna had made a mistake in assuming no one would take the time or effort to pursue her.

For the second time that day, Jess found herself up against forces stronger than she was: the determined looks on the faces of the women gathered around the table, and the unexpected generosity of a man with sky-blue eyes.

"The recital is at four o'clock," Jess said slowly. "The reception would have to be later in the evening."

Peg's chuckle sounded more like a snort. "I guarantee the neighbors won't complain about the noise."

"And Elaine would love the idea of doing something special for Sienna," Merri added.

Elaine.

Jess had been wrong. The fact that no one had mentioned Elaine's recent trip to the hospital meant they hadn't heard about it yet. Vanessa had been given permission to contact Jess if there was a change in her situation, but Jess had a feeling Elaine would want to put her friends' minds at ease, too...

"Jessica?" Nita prompted.

"Vanessa Richards called after you left yesterday," Jess said. "Elaine is in the hospital again. She had a high fever, but the doctor thinks it's a virus, not an infection. They'll be running some more tests just to be sure, but Vanessa thinks Elaine will be released today or tomorrow."

The room became as silent as a library as they processed how even a minor setback like this would affect their friend again. Merri reached out and squeezed Peg's hand.

"Thank you for telling us," Nita finally said.

Jess had single-handedly sucked the enthusiasm from the room and they were *thanking* her.

"So...a garden party," she said slowly. "I'm thinking tarragon chicken salad on miniature croissants. Macarons or petit fours. Or both."

Now Merri was squeezing Jess's hand. "That sounds lovely."

"Fancy, too," Peg said. "I think Sienna deserves a little fancy."

Jess did, too.

Her eyes started to burn. She stood up and backed toward the kitchen. "I made a quiche last night. Merri's recipe. Does anyone..."

Three hands shot up in the air.

On Friday Jess put together a menu, ironed the little black dress Sienna had chosen for the recital and lost hours of sleep trying to decide what kind of dessert paired well with an *authentic northern Wisconsin fish fry.*

If she was sure the Griswold wouldn't be repurposed as a

dog dish or boot scraper, Jess would have canceled her date with Nick.

No. Not a date. Dinner, she reminded herself for the umpteenth time that day.

A dinner she was going to be late for if she didn't step it up a little.

Jess slid her knife case into the market bag. Not because she'd be using it, but because it would feel like she was missing an appendage if she left it behind. She rolled up her apron, tucked it inside and checked to make sure the level of fish-shaped kibbles reached the Happy Kitty line on the dish Jess had found in the pet aisle of the grocery store the day before.

She walked out the back door and almost tripped over Christopher. He was kneeling at the edge of the patio, yanking out weeds between the paving stones.

He grinned up at her.

"You look p–pretty, Jessica."

"Thank you." Jess looked down at her white cotton tank and wraparound linen skirt.

She'd chosen the outfit because the lightweight fabric was comfortable in a hot kitchen. The silver bracelets stacked on Jess's wrist had been a last-minute addition she was currently rethinking. Jewelry posed a potential hazard in the kitchen, so chefs tended to avoid wearing any.

Which tipped an invisible arrow toward *date* instead of *dinner.*

Nita's head poked up behind the rosebush. The afternoon sun had turned her nose the same shade of red as her hair. She blotted the moisture from her forehead with the back of a gloved hand and left a smudge of dirt behind.

"What's the occasion?"

"No occasion." Jess smoothed the front of her skirt and the bracelets jingled a cheerful contradiction. Tattletales. "You should have told me you were working out here. I made a fresh pitcher of iced tea."

"We brought lemonade." Nita pointed to two insulated cups on the bistro table.

Christopher rocked back on his heels. The gloves he wore looked as thick as oven mitts. A rooster tail of russet hair poked through the hole in the back of his ball cap. "I p-picked all these weeds." He pointed to the overflowing wheelbarrow.

"You did a great job." Jess meant it.

What Nita had called *tidying up* had turned into an all-out war against anything that didn't belong in the backyard garden. The weeds sprouting between the cracks in the paving stones were gone. Herbs the size of small shrubs had been tamed by Nita's clippers, ready for transport to the kitchen.

"We'll be back tomorrow," Nita said. "The spirea by the corner of the garage could use a little trim, too."

"I can stick around if you need some more—"

"No." Nita cut Jess off with the same decisiveness she'd just used to deadhead a brown-eyed Susan. "We'll be going home to make supper in a little while anyway."

"All right." Jess started down the path, keeping the market bag in place with one hand, smothering the bracelets with the other.

"Jessica?"

Jess spun toward Nita, hoping she'd changed her mind.

Nita smiled instead.

"Say hello to Nick for us."

Chapter Twenty-Five

Nick wasn't sure Jess would show until Bucket's tail began to thump out a reggae beat against the floor.

"Stay."

His dog lifted a bushy eyebrow and trotted toward the door.

Nick followed, every nerve in his body shifting into hyperdrive. He didn't get this rattled before the first game of the season.

It's dinner.

Nick mentally addressed the nerves in what his family liked to call his "coaching" voice.

Part of your day for the past thirty years. Sometimes, there's even been a woman to share it with.

But never this one, the nerves retorted.

Nick had no comeback for that.

He opened the door before Jessica had a chance to knock, and temporarily lost the ability to speak.

She looked stunning, as usual. A white tank top skimmed the waist of a flowing, calf-length skirt embroidered with vines and multicolored flowers. Open-toed leather sandals showcased the raspberry polish on her toes.

And Nick's idea of casual Friday was jeans and a Wildcats T-shirt fresh from the laundry.

"Am I too early?" Jessica asked.

Because he was frozen in the doorway like a mannequin instead of inviting her inside.

"No." Nick's voice cracked in the middle of the word.

So smooth, Silva.

"Come on in." Nick stepped aside, and Jessica walked in, hugging the market bag close to her body with the trepidation of someone entering a dark alley.

She hadn't looked this tense during her tour of the lodge.

Nick's heart sank a little. Was Jessica regretting that she'd agreed to have dinner with him? Because he'd been looking forward to it all day.

Bucket, who didn't care that he wore a stained camouflage collar and smelled like minnows, bumped against Jessica's leg. A shameless bid for attention that worked, because she bent down and gave his ear a scratch.

"Hey, Bucket."

She'd warmed up his dog. Maybe some of that would spill over...

"Ready to get started?"

Or, maybe not.

"Sure. Follow me." Nick led the way to the kitchen. He'd turned his to-do list completely upside down. Instead of patching holes in the walls, he'd spent the majority of his day in the kitchen, dusting out cabinets, wiping down the stainless-steel until he could see his reflection, and scrub-

bing away years of neglect until the linoleum floor underneath it appeared.

Jessica didn't seem to notice. She made a beeline toward
the stove to check on her skillet.

Nick wasn't worried. He'd gone through half a dozen steel
wool pads to make the Griswold presentable again.

"I looked up the proper way to clean cast iron online."
Nick had also, out of curiosity, looked up the value of a Griswold thirteen. Jessica was right. Collectors paid big bucks
for that particular number, but Jess's reaction when Nick
had given it to her was...to quote a popular commercial...
priceless.

He saw an instant replay of that moment when Jessica
picked up the skillet and looked it over with the cautious delight of a child getting acquainted with a brand-new puppy.

No doubt about it. He'd give up custody again in a heartbeat.

"See? I took good care of the baby while you were gone,
sweetheart," he teased.

The barest of smiles tipped her lips, but Nick considered
it progress.

Jessica Keaton was a tough audience, but he'd never backed
away from a challenge.

"Where should I set up?" She set the skillet down on the
burner again, once again reminding Nick this was dinner,
not a date.

"Right there." He pointed to the stainless-steel monstros-
ity in the center of the kitchen that Jessica had called the prep
station. A Windex shower had improved its overall appearance, but some of the larger dents looked like they'd been
made with a baseball bat. "I'll need the counter next to the
burners."

Jessica set the market bag down. The piece of white cloth

folded neatly on the top turned out to be an apron. And it looked way more legit than the one he'd brought along.

Nick pulled it over his head anyway and heard a noise that sounded suspiciously like a snicker.

"What?" He ran his palm over the giant hamburger on the front. A metallic gold fork and knife, bright enough to blind anyone within a three-foot radius if the sunlight hit it just right, formed an X below the burger like a family crest. "Grill Master is an honor that few can achieve, you know."

Unless they were Bobby Flay. Or faithfully shopped the summer clearance sales like his older sister, Lydia, who'd given the obnoxious thing to Nick as a gag gift for his last birthday. Still, the apron did what it was supposed to do, and Nick liked to think of himself as a practical man.

"Uh-huh." Jessica reached into the bag again and removed a leather case that looked similar to the ones the professional chefs used on the cooking shows his mom watched.

Whoa.

Doubts suddenly stormed the field in Nick's head again.

After he'd moved back to Winsome, Nick reaped the benefit of being the youngest boy in the family and the bachelor coach of a school known for its bake sales and fundraising dinners.

There were more disposable pans of lasagna stacked in his freezer than gold blocks in Fort Knox.

In other words, if a person didn't count the protein shakes Nick drank for breakfast every morning, he didn't cook for himself more than a handful of times a week.

He'd bragged to Jessica that he made two things well. Chocolate cake and pan-fried perch.

But that was before he'd known the woman had skills. And—Nick looked at the knife case again—some serious tools to get the job done.

He'd tossed a metal spatula and a pair of tongs into a paper sack with the rest of the ingredients before he'd left his house and called it good.

Jessica pulled a small towel from the bag and looped it through the apron ties cinched around her slender waist. Next came a saucepan with a copper bottom.

It made Nick wonder what else she had stashed in there. A lamp? Houseplant? Full-length mirror?

"Did you really catch the fish this morning?"

Nick tore his gaze away from the tower Jessica was building out of storage containers.

"At dawn." He unwrapped a stick of butter, tossed it into the Griswold and turned the flame on low.

Come on. Make me look good, Thirteen.

"The perch were biting pretty good. I caught enough for tonight and I'll pass the rest on to my sister's family. She has three kids who eat her out of house and home during summer vacation."

Nick skirted around Jessica and took the filets out of the fridge. He was glad he'd done most of the prep work before she'd arrived. When Nick had suggested dinner in exchange for the skillet, he hadn't taken into consideration that they would be working in such close proximity. Or that he'd be distracted by bracelets that tinkled like wind chimes every time Jessica moved. And, even more inexplicable, an apron that covered her from chest to knees.

Maybe it was because of the faint stains on the pocket. The frayed edges on the ends of the bow perched on the curve of her hip.

Tiny imperfections that made Nick remember the other reason he'd suggested dinner. He wanted to get to know the woman who'd sat on Anthony's porch and learned the names and history of every chicken in the coop. Made blueberry pancakes for a teenage girl she didn't even know. Reached out to a teenage boy too many others shied away from because they were uncomfortable around him. Didn't know what to say.

Jessica was a study in contradictions. High-end wardrobe. A rusted-out car hiding like a fugitive in Elaine's garage. An aversion to small towns and yet she'd accepted a job in Winsome Lake.

If she wasn't going to talk about herself, Nick figured he'd try to speak her language.

And based on what he'd witnessed so far, that language was food.

Nick grabbed a quart of milk from the door of the fridge and almost bumped into Jessica when he turned around.

"What do you use for breading?" She started to inch closer, but Nick stepped in front of her.

"Oh, no. This—" he motioned to the counter by the stove "—is my dance space." He clasped Jessica's shoulders and turned her toward the prep station. "Your dance space."

Jessica rolled her eyes and walked away, a bit of a swirl in her skirt, but not before Nick saw her smile again.

A "this evening might be more fun than I thought" smile.

Nick didn't consider it progress.

He called it a win.

Jess set the carton of eggs on the prep station and sneaked another glance at Nick. He stood at the counter with his back to her, humming. The knot in his apron strings had already come undone and they dangled an inch from the floor like loose kite strings.

"No peeking," he said without turning around.

Laughter bubbled up inside Jess and no amount of vigorous whisking could completely dissolve it.

She moved on to the next step in the recipe. The one she was making up as she went along. She took one of the smaller knives from the case and began to scrape the inside of the vanilla bean she'd wheedled out of Gloria at Dan's Market that morning.

Tiny flecks drifted into the bowl. She separated a wooden spoon from the bouquet of utensils she'd brought along and stirred them into the egg and cream mixture.

A cabinet door opened and closed. The soles of Nick's tennis shoes squeaked against the floor. The hum of the refrigerator provided the background music and Jess felt her shoulders relax.

The scent of vanilla and chocolate was more soothing than a day at the spa.

Until she heard a muffled *"ouch."* Followed by, "Don't turn around."

"Are you okay?"

"Great. Almost ended up with another filet, though." Nick's low laugh added more texture to the sounds and scents that filled the room.

Jess, who'd seen more than her share of kitchen mishaps that ended with a trip to the emergency room, didn't believe him.

She abandoned her station. "Let me see."

"I'm fine. No blood."

Nick held up both flour-coated hands as proof and Jess's heart started to beat again.

She took a step forward, but Nick blocked her view of the stove and gave her a look.

"Right. Your dance space." Jess rolled her eyes. "But I need the oven."

"Isn't there one in your market bag?"

"Very funny."

"If it was, you'd be smiling…and there it is." Nick grinned. "Point for Nick."

The man was way too appealing for his own good. And for hers.

"It's minus two if you burn dinner." Jess nodded at the smoke rising from the skillet.

Nick didn't appear the least bit fazed by the threat.

"If it doesn't turn out, we can always make a pizza."

Something in his voice told Jess there was a reason he'd chosen pizza as an alternate menu item.

"And before your apron strings get tangled in a knot," Nick said, "the neighbors weren't talking about you."

"They weren't?"

"No. It was only one of them. I shot hoops with Christopher last night and he couldn't stop talking about the pizza party."

"It wasn't a party. Technically." Jess still wasn't sure what it was.

"It meant a lot to Chris. In fact, he seemed more excited about helping you in the kitchen again than he was when Nita agreed to let him be the Wildcats' manager this fall."

"She did?" Jess pictured Christopher pulling weeds in the garden under Nita's watchful eye, hat and gloves protecting him from the sun and bees and thorns. "How did you convince her?"

"I think you did."

"Me?"

"Nita said someone reminded her that it's important to say yes sometimes. I've known the Scrappy Ladies all my life and they're as protective of Chris as Nita, so I figured it was you."

"The Scrappy Ladies?"

"That's what Elaine calls them." Jess heard the smile in

Nick's voice. "Because they're into scrapbooking. But even if they didn't, I think the name would fit."

So did Jess. And it made her even more curious about the woman who'd hired her, too. Curious about the woman who hadn't replaced her ancient appliances but had a Deirdre Simmons hanging on her office wall.

"Have you known Elaine all your life?"

"She moved to Winsome when I was in elementary school," Nick said. "I remember it caused quite a stir in the neighborhood."

"Why is that?"

"Samantha O'Dell was supposed to sell her house to a family member. I can't remember which one, but she accepted a cash offer from a stranger instead. No one knew anything about Elaine, but after she moved in, it was like she'd lived on Woodwind Lane all her life. She's…"

Nick paused and Jess had to pitch her voice over the low grumble of the garbage disposal.

"She's what?"

"I was going to say she's *Elaine*. When you meet her, you'll know what I mean."

Jess still wasn't sure when that would be.

She hadn't heard from the social worker for several days and wasn't sure it was her place to call the rehab center and ask for an update. She'd decided that when it came to Elaine Haviland's condition, no news meant good news.

"You're doing a great job," Nick said. "Keep it up."

Jess was about to say thank you when she realized he was talking to her skillet.

Her skillet.

Jess was still blown away by Nick's generosity. She wanted to believe that dinner was the only thing Nick wanted in return, but the memory of Ian Holden's *offer* remained fresh in her mind.

She poured the custard mixture into separate ramekins and carried them over to the oven on the metal tray she'd brought over.

"Coming through." Jess bumped her hip against Nick's, slid the tray into the oven and took advantage of the moment to see what Nick was doing.

"Potato pancakes." Nick flipped three over in quick succession. They were beautiful. The edges a deep golden-brown and as delicate as lace. "Some people prefer fries or rye bread, but for me, it's not a true fish fry unless potato pancakes are involved. It takes more effort...but some things are worth it."

He wasn't looking at her when he said the words, but Jess felt the heat rise in her cheeks.

"Is there anything I can do to help?"

"There's a jar of applesauce in the fridge. Second shelf. Can you grab it while I make the tartar sauce?"

"Sure." Jess jumped at the opportunity. She opened the fridge and smiled. The mason jar sported a red-and-white checkered gingham cap.

She set the jar down on the counter and watched Nick plate the food with a calm efficiency that would have earned a nod of approval from Chef Tomas. He emptied the applesauce into a small serving bowl and put a generous scoop of tartar sauce on the side of each plate.

Jess expected Nick to pat himself on the back for a job well-done, but he braced his hands against the counter and sighed instead.

"Is something wrong?" Jess ventured.

"We're missing something."

"What?"

"A table." Nick almost groaned the words. "I was so focused on making the food, I didn't think about where we were going to eat it. There's a picnic table down the by water, but at this time of night, the mosquitoes would treat us like the main course. The rest of the place is a construction zone—"

"Then we'll eat in the kitchen."

"Um…still no table?"

"You don't need a table for a picnic. All you need is a blanket or a rug or something."

"I have something. Be back in a sec." Nick disappeared but unfortunately, not long enough for Jess to sneak a bite of potato pancake. "Beach towel." He held it up. "Wrinkled, but clean."

It must have been as old as Nick, too, because a faded image of a cartoon character stretched from top to bottom.

"Perfect," she said.

A strange expression crossed Nick's face, but Jess didn't take the time to dwell on it. Not when the steam rising from their plates was already beginning to subside.

She plucked the towel from Nick's hand and scoped out the cleanest spot on the floor. Bucket, who'd been sleeping in the hallway, started to army-crawl toward them, his nose in full twitch. Nick tossed the dog a rawhide bone and shooed him out of the kitchen.

Jess set the bowl of applesauce on the center of the makeshift picnic blanket while Nick tried to get comfortable on the floor. He finally ended up with his long legs stretched out at an angle, his back against the pantry door.

Jess settled on the opposite side and tucked her legs underneath her. Before she could pick up her fork, Nick caught and held her gaze.

"Would you mind if I ask a blessing?"

Jess shook her head.

"God, You are our provider. Our daily bread. Thank You for this food and for all the blessings Your hands provide. Amen."

Amen.

It wasn't the first time she'd heard people pray, but the simple words found an empty place inside her. Stirred up a different kind of hunger.

But God hadn't provided for her. From the time Jess was a child, she'd been on her own.

It was easy for someone like Nick to thank God for His blessings. He'd been showered with them. A close-knit family. A career he loved...

"Well? How does it taste?"

Jess speared a piece of fish and popped it into her mouth. In culinary school, she'd gotten used to having a small crowd of people staring at her, watching her reaction to that first bite.

But for reasons Jess didn't want to analyze too closely, she felt self-conscious when it was Nick.

"Delicious," she murmured. "Really delicious."

"Coming from someone who's an honest-to-goodness chef, that means a lot."

The spoonful of applesauce Jess had just swallowed felt like it took a detour into her lungs.

"Who told you I was a chef?" she asked between coughs.

"Ah, let's see. The Griswold? The scary set of knives on the counter? The apron that laughed at mine?" Nick grinned. "Even a former jock can put two and two together."

Jess reached for her napkin to hide a smile. "Aren't you still a jock?"

"Guilty," Nick said cheerfully. "And as long as we're going there, I have another confession to make."

He waited until Jess looked up again.

"I didn't think you could cook."

Chapter Twenty-Six

Jess stared at Nick in disbelief.

"You didn't think I could…"

"Cook," Nick supplied helpfully. "I blame it on the toast."

"The toast."

"Charred to a crisp? Smoking a little?"

It was all starting to come back to her now. Jess remembered Nick showing up unannounced while she was starting lunch. The sourdough bread that Elaine Haviland's toaster had incinerated and spit back out like a rejected sacrifice.

"I was…distracted." Thinking about him. But there was no way Jess was going to confess to *that*.

"But even if you hadn't hugged a cast-iron skillet—"

"I didn't…" Okay. Maybe she had. For a second or two.

"The coffee cake changed my mind," Nick finished.

Jess smiled and reached for her glass of water. "I'm not a baker, but it's fun to experiment sometimes."

"That was an experiment?" Nick laughed. "It's the reason I put you in charge of dessert."

"I know how to bake. I just didn't have a lot of opportunity until now."

"Did you work in a restaurant?"

The simple question tore through Jess like shrapnel, peeling back the scar tissue on old wounds and opening up some new ones.

"I was a personal chef."

"Wow." Nick blinked. "I didn't know that was a thing. Does that mean you cooked for one family?"

"Some personal chefs do." The breading Jess had thought was delicious five minutes ago tasted like sawdust now. "Gwyneth Donovan, the woman I worked for, didn't want to cook after a ten-hour workday."

"You dropped off meals every day?"

"I lived on the estate. I was also in charge of dinner parties and spur-of-the-moment weekend brunches, so it made sense."

"An estate," Nick repeated. "Where was that?"

"Lake Geneva. Gwyneth's main office was in Chicago so she could keep a close eye on her boutiques."

"My mom claims I was separating my sisters' stuffed animals into offensive and defensive lines when I was six years old. Did you have one of those little plastic ovens with the light bulb inside when you were a kid?"

"No, I started with a real oven. I didn't even know what a chef was. My parents…they weren't around much and I got tired of eating peanut butter crackers." Jess saw Nick's expression and shrugged. "Every town has that one family, right? The one that makes everyone else feel like they're doing okay. In Winsome Lake, I'm guessing it's Sienna's. Where I grew up, it was the Keatons."

As soon as the words slipped out of her mouth, Jess wanted to take them back.

She never talked about her childhood.

Nick's brows dipped together, and he slipped another pancake onto Jess's plate. "Looking at you, I have a hard time believing that, but I know kids can be hard on each other."

Hard on each other didn't begin to describe it. That was why Jess had spent the past ten years removing every vestige of the girl whose wardrobe consisted of whatever her mom could stuff into the "fill for five dollars" bag at the thrift store and who'd gone to bed hungry most nights.

Suddenly, it became important that Nick understand what girls like her, like Sienna, experienced when they weren't in class.

"When I was a junior, my class had a bake sale to raise money for the prom. I made cupcakes. Banana split, with real whipped cream and maraschino cherries." Jess had washed glasses for the bartender downstairs for a week to pay for the ingredients. "At the end of the day, I stopped by the cafeteria to see how many had sold." She paused, the memory of that day an ache that hadn't quite gone away. "They were in the trash can. Two guys from the football team saw me and said that no one wanted to catch fleas."

Jess could still hear their laughter. She'd wanted to show her classmates that she could contribute something of value. And then she'd remembered that in their eyes, she was worthless.

She avoided Nick's eyes and forced a smile.

"What I didn't know was that one of my teachers had bought one. She'd found out I made them and ordered three dozen for her daughter's birthday. She also told me I should go to culinary school and run my own business someday.

"I sold enough cupcakes to pay for my tuition the first year and received a scholarship for the next one. After graduation I worked at a catering company until Gwyneth stole me away."

"She *stole* you?"

"Gwyneth was a guest at a wedding reception and found out I'd made the hors d'oeuvres. She offered twice what I was making and told me I could start the next day."

When Nick's frown deepened, Jess rambled on, "And her kitchen. An induction range and a double convection oven. Marble countertops. A butcher-block island the length of this room. The week I started working at the estate, I actually drew a map so I could find everything faster. I was terrified of making a mistake."

"I make mistakes all the time," Nick said. "In front of a very large group of people. They're part of the process."

"Not according to Gwyneth Donovan. She was...is...very successful. She set goals and didn't let anything stop her from achieving them. She could be demanding, difficult to please, but it pushed me to do my best. I learned a lot working in her kitchen. It was...it was a dream job."

"Was it *your* dream?"

Jess wasn't prepared for that question.

"It was a path to get there," she heard herself say. "My dream has always been to have my own kitchen."

"You mean a restaurant?"

"I worked for Gwyneth for five years. Watching her scale walls and reach her goals made me think I could achieve mine."

"Is that why you left?"

Nick wished he could take back the question when Jess set her plate down and pushed to her feet. "I have to check on dessert."

Bucket, who'd been patiently lying in wait for leftovers, started to follow her, but Nick snagged his collar.

"Oh, no, you don't. Time to go outside and run off a little energy." He opened the back door and shooed Bucket outside. The temperature felt almost balmy for a Wisconsin evening in late July.

Bucket loped down to the water, but Nick followed at a more leisurely pace. The sun had melted into the lake and shadows were starting to collect in the pockets between the trees. Fireflies winked at him from the tall grass around the boathouse.

Children's voices and the smell of a campfire drifted in on the breeze. The frogs were starting to practice their scales for the evening symphony.

While Bucket splashed in the shallow water, Nick speared his hands in his pockets and kept one ear tuned to the sounds in the kitchen. Proof that Jess hadn't run out on him.

Nick had been trying to make conversation, get to know her better, not realizing his questions would strike a nerve. Or that her answers would reveal more than she wanted him to know.

Nick worked with kids. If he suspected one of them was being neglected or going to bed hungry, he did something about it. But he wasn't naive enough to believe that none of them fell through cracks in the system, either.

If Jess was one of them, she'd picked herself up and moved forward, become a chef.

My dream has always been to have my own kitchen.

Nick admired that. Understood goals and dreams.

But Jess had lived on an estate and now she was staying in Elaine's house. Maybe it wasn't a kitchen she needed.

Maybe it was a…home.

A shaft of light slipped over the yard and Nick turned around. Jess waved from the doorway.

Nick looked for Bucket. The dog had followed a school of minnows into the reeds. His tail slashed the air like a windshield wiper set on high, and water cascaded from his muzzle.

"It's the porch and a rawhide for you," he told the dog.

Bucket's ears lifted and Nick narrowly missed a minnow-scented shower when the dog made land again.

"I'll be right there." Nick toweled Bucket dry with a rag and closed him into the screened-in porch with the dog's favorite bedtime snack.

Jess was waiting for him at the door. She'd taken off her apron. Wisps of hair had escaped from her ponytail and the heat of the kitchen had kissed her cheeks pink but the tension in her shoulders told the walls were back in place again.

Nick spotted the beach towel folded into a neat square on the counter.

"What happened to our table?"

"I thought we'd have dessert on the patio." Jess picked up a tray, covered with a dish towel so Nick couldn't see what was underneath.

"The patio?" Nick's brain instantly downloaded an image of the old director's chair he'd rescued from the drop box. "I don't think it's very comfortable...but neither was the kitchen floor. Lead the way."

Jess carried the tray over to the stone half wall that separated the patio from the rest of the yard.

"You're a guinea pig." She folded the towel back and revealed two shallow ceramic dishes. "I've never made this before, but we're on a lake in the woods, so I thought of s'mores."

It didn't look like the s'mores Nick was used to eating.

"This looks amazing, Jess."

He'd never thought about presentation before. Whatever fit on the plate, fit on the plate. Whatever was left became seconds.

"Milk chocolate crème brûlée—I didn't have a kitchen torch, so it's a good thing the broiler worked—with toasted marshmallows and graham cracker crumbs."

"You made this? While I was frying fish?"

"It's one of those desserts that looks fussier than it is."

Jess handed him a fork.

Neither one of them broke the silence as the moon freed itself from the branches of the trees and rose over the lake.

Nick still had questions. A lot of them. But he'd already crossed a line. He didn't want to say anything that would send Jess running for cover again.

Like, for instance, *when can we do this again?*

Nick took his time, savoring every bite, every moment, wishing Jess had used a casserole dish instead of a ramekin because it would have made dessert and the evening last a little bit longer.

But the moment his spoon scraped the bottom of the dish, Jess rose to her feet. "I'll help you clean up."

Nick knew he should be polite and refuse the offer, but if it meant Jessica stayed a little longer...

"You wash. I'll dry."

They went back inside, and Jess slipped her apron back on, almost as if it were a shield. Nick turned the water on and out of the corner of his eye, saw Jess dip a spoon into the jar of applesauce and take a bite.

"I saw that."

"It's kind of addicting..." She paused. Pressed her fingers against her lips.

"Seed?" Nick guessed. "Grandma Jenny cut up all the apples by hand and a few would get past her."

"Your grandma made this?"

Nick nodded. "From the Wolf River apples. There aren't many jars left, but this was a special occasion... Are you okay? You aren't having an allergic reaction to something, are you?"

"Close your eyes."

Nick felt them get wider instead. "Close..."

"Your eyes."

He did. And felt the tip of the metal spoon against his lips.

"What do you taste?"

How was Nick supposed to focus on one of the senses when all five were competing for his attention? The scent of toasted marshmallow. The bracelets on Jess's wrist brushing against his arm. The rapid thump of his heart.

"Apples. Cinnamon." Nick opened his eyes a crack, saw Jess shake her head and obediently closed them again.

He'd helped his grandmother make her homemade applesauce at least a hundred times over the years and there weren't that many ingredients. Lemon juice. Water. A pinch of salt.

Nick had no idea what Jess wanted from him, but what he'd initially thought was a game had suddenly turned serious.

He felt the spoon touch his lips again.

"What do you taste, Nick?" Jess persisted.

"Chocolate cake."

Nick had no idea where that came from. He opened his eyes and Jess's face looked blurry; her smile distorted by the film of tears coating his eyes.

"It wasn't the cinnamon you tasted," Jess said softly. "Your grandma put applesauce in her chocolate cake. That's why you couldn't get the texture quite right. She probably added a few tablespoons to the batter without even thinking about it."

In his mind's eye, Nick saw the canning jar filled with applesauce on the bottom shelf of the fridge, within easy reach when hungry grandchildren or unexpected guests came over.

Nick had heard his mom teasing Grandma Jenny about it when they were elbow to elbow in the kitchen, filling serving bowls that would surround the Thanksgiving turkey in the center of the table like Saturn's rings.

Mom… I can't believe one tree produces enough fruit for all this applesauce. Or maybe it's like the widow's jar of oil. It never runs out.

Nick heard his grandma laugh. She'd leaned over and kissed his mom's floury cheek and she'd passed it down the line to Nick's aunts…

The fruit of one life.

And Nick was going to lose it. Right there in front of Jessica.

"Some people cry over spilled milk…" The laugh got stuck in his throat. "For me, I guess it's applesauce."

"It's okay." Jess's voice was soft. "Your grandma must have been a very special person."

So was she.

"Thanks." Nick framed Jess's face in his hands. He'd planned to kiss her forehead, but his head and his heart parted company and he kissed her lips instead.

Jess went completely still. Her hand flattened against his chest. Nick felt her mouth soften beneath his. Felt the warmth of her fingers as they curled into the fabric of his T-shirt. And then her hand fell away. She turned her head, breaking the connection.

Nick didn't know what to say. *Sorry* would be a lie. *Again* would have Jess running for the door. Silence seemed to be the best option.

Jess must have agreed, because she didn't say another word during cleanup. Or when Nick walked her to the door.

"Thanks, for coming over tonight," he murmured. "And for dessert."

Jess's cheeks turned pink, and Nick realized he shouldn't have added that last part.

"Good night." She slipped out the door.

Nick walked back to the kitchen on autopilot. The stainless steel gleamed; the countertops empty again. There were no reminders they'd had dinner together, but he saw Jess everywhere. Standing at the prep station, gliding across the room with the grace of a ballerina, sneaking a piece of pancake to Bucket when she thought he wasn't looking.

Nick closed his eyes.

What do you taste, Nick?

Nights like this. Laughter. Promises.

The future.

Chapter Twenty-Seven

"Are we late?" Peg marched into the kitchen with a foil-covered loaf pan in each hand. Merri was a step behind her, carrying a large cardboard box labeled *Christmas*.

Jess wasn't sure how to answer Peg because she hadn't been expecting them at all. At least not for a few hours, when Sienna's reception started.

"I left a basket of cherry tomatoes on the back porch," Merri said.

"It's bigger than the one Bosco sleeps in," Peg whispered.

Merri smiled. "The garden really took off this year."

"She says that every year." Peg gave Merri's arm an affectionate pat. "I could build an addition on the house with the loaves of zucchini bread I made over the weekend."

Now Jess knew what was in the loaf pans.

"Sorry we're late!" Nita strode into the kitchen, making Jess wonder if the three women had had the house under surveillance. She scanned the countertop, found an empty space next to the coffeepot and set down a paper grocery bag. "I know you have the menu planned, but in case we run out of food, it's always nice to have a Plan B."

Jess peeked into the bag. Nita's Plan B was a dozen of Dan's World-Famous Sugar Cookies encapsulated in a see-through tube, and a bag of pastel mints.

She could work with that. "Thanks, Nita."

"Peg and I are going to string up the lights," Merri said. "She drafted Frank to set up the tables and chairs."

"Christopher can help." Nita tossed her purse in the pantry. "I'm going to pull a few of those weeds that sneaked into the garden yesterday."

Jess saw Chris cast a longing look at the runner of wax paper that stretched from one end of the butcher-block island to the other.

"I could use an extra set of hands," she told Nita. "If it's okay with you."

The flash of relief—and gratitude—in Nita's eyes told Jess it was more than okay. She mouthed the words *thank you* behind his back as she headed for the door.

"I saw Nick when he was out for a run this morning and told him about the party," Merri said. "He said he'd stop over and make sure the yard looked good."

Nick.

Jess hadn't let herself think about him. It was a habit as dangerous as a dark chocolate truffle. Once you started, it was almost impossible to stop.

She hadn't seen him since Friday night. Saturday she'd bought a dozen eggs, as snowy white as the disposable carton they'd been packed in, from Dan's Market. Sunday she'd planned the menu for Sienna's reception and compiled a shopping list. Jess had discovered it was easier to keep Nick at arm's length when he was actually in the room with her.

When she was alone, he sneaked past her defenses and invaded her thoughts.

She'd given away more of herself than she'd intended. Her past. Her dreams.

She shouldn't have cooked with him.

Shouldn't have *kissed* him...

"What do you w-want me to do, Jess?"

And she was doing it again.

"You can brush some of that egg white wash on the violas, sprinkle them with sugar and put one on each of those petit fours."

Christopher eyed the tiny purple flowers dubiously, but grabbed his apron and set to work. "Sienna is going to be s-so surprised."

Jess hoped the girl showed up.

Sienna had been so nervous that morning, she'd taken laps around the piano instead of playing it. And she'd picked apart one of the croissants Jess had made until it looked like pieces of confetti on the plate.

"Stop over after the recital," Jess had told her. "I want to hear all about it."

Sienna had responded in her usual way—silence—which meant the evening could become a block party for the neighborhood instead of a reception to celebrate a senior solo.

"J-Jess?"

She finished piping whipped cream on one of the lemon tarts and glanced at the violas. "They look great."

"I'd do b-better if I had my hat."

"Ah." Jess hid a smile. "My bad. I'll be right back."

She went upstairs and opened the closet door. The toque was perched on a shelf above her chef's coat.

Memories crashed through her.

The last time she'd worn the uniform seemed like a lifetime ago.

Gwyneth hosted several elaborate parties over the year, but an invitation to her annual Fourth of July party was particularly coveted, the guest list curated from a small but exclusive list of fellow entrepreneurs.

Jess had spent weeks working on the menu, experimenting with different recipes during her free time, placing orders for ingredients that could be notoriously difficult to find.

The guests had raved about the food and insisted that Jess come outside and take a bow before the fireworks started.

Jess, still feeling the heady effects of the guests' enthusiastic applause, had been caught off guard when Ian Holden sauntered into the kitchen a few minutes later.

Memories began to rise and inwardly, Jess scrambled for safer ground.

She ran her fingers down the sleeve of the coat. Looked down at Elaine's apron, flecked with pink specks of raspberry jam.

She yanked it over her head and removed her coat and checkered pants from the hanger.

Jess stared at her reflection in the mirror a few minutes later, tightened the scarf around her hair and went back downstairs to control the things that she could.

"N-Nick is here!" Christopher announced.

Yes. Jess could see that.

He stood at the sink, filling a glass with water. Jess was used to seeing him in jeans, but today he looked every inch the high school football coach in black athletic shorts and a V-neck tee that drew attention to the tanned column of his throat. And with his hair damp from a recent shower, he looked as fresh as the proverbial daisy.

Unlike Jess, who'd opened every window on the first

floor and still felt like she was standing inside the oven instead of next to it.

Nick turned around and his eyes went wide.

Jess's fingers automatically went to the buttons on her coat. They were all fastened, so maybe she hadn't noticed a smudge of flour that inevitably ended up on her cheek.

"I came to see if you needed any help," Nick said slowly. "But it looks like you've got things covered."

"M-Mom says many hands make light work," Christopher said. "And now we have s-six."

"You're right." Jess couldn't argue with an old proverb or the math. Out of the corner of her eye, Jess saw Nick scoping out the tray of macarons. "But no sampling until we're done."

Both of the men in the kitchen heaved a disappointed sigh.

"I'm going to whip up the filling for the macarons. You two can slice cucumbers for the tea sandwiches."

Nick nodded. "Okie dokie."

Christopher leaned toward him. "When J-Jess tells you to do something, you have to say 'yes, Chef,'" he whispered.

"Is that so?" Nick's lips twitched.

Which made Jess think of other things his lips could do.

Which momentarily stripped away her ability to concentrate on petit fours and macarons and tarragon chicken salad.

Focus, Jess.

She grabbed her checklist off the counter and mentally added two more items.

Don't think about Nick.

Don't look at Nick.

Jess set to work on the buttercream. Raspberry lemonade, because it tasted like a summer day.

"Whoa, bud," Nick said behind her. "That's Jess's knife and it's pretty sharp. Maybe you should—"

"Let him show you how it's done?" Jess interrupted. "That's a great idea. Isn't it, Christopher?"

"J-Jess taught me how. I didn't cut myself."

Jess shot Nick a meaningful look over the island. He caught it and volleyed it back to her, raising his hands in mock complaint.

"You let him use your knife? You wouldn't let me use your knife."

And since teasing Nick was safer than thinking about Friday night and kisses as sweet as crème brûlée, Jess spiked back, "You're a prep cook. Chris is my sous-chef."

"But—"

"Yes, Chef," Christopher prompted under his breath.

"What happened to 'okay, Coach'? That's what I want to know."

"We're in the kitchen. N-not on the field," Christopher said.

Nick looked at Jessica, who nodded.

"What he said."

The laughter Nick was struggling to contain spilled into the tiny creases fanning out from his eyes. "Yes, Chef."

"I'll show y-you, Nick," Christopher offered. "T-tuck these fingers under. You'll need them later."

Jess smiled.

Christopher and Nick talked about the upcoming football season while they worked, and Jess crumbled the sugar cookies Nita had brought over and turned them into a crust for the lemon tarts.

"Mission accomplished." Nick appeared at her elbow a few minutes later. "Now what?"

Jess glanced at the clock. Quarter to four. The recital started in fifteen minutes.

Butterflies took wing in Jess's stomach and began to perform a lively ballet.

How was Sienna holding up? As much as Jess wanted to believe the girl's parents would be there to support their daughter, the chances of them agreeing to a temporary cease-fire were slim.

"Now we take a lemonade break. You both earned it."

"Did we earn a c-cookie, too?" Christopher looked at Jess hopefully.

"One. And I'll know if you take more, because I counted them." Jess pulled a pitcher of lemonade from the refrigerator and walked to the back door to find out if the Scrappy Ladies were ready for a break, too.

When she'd glanced out the screen door, all Jess could see was the tops of three straw hats moving through the garden.

Now the women stood in a circle, holding hands like children on a playground. Their heads were bowed, the brims of their hats touching.

"They're praying for Sienna."

Jess didn't jump at the sound of Nick's voice behind her. She wasn't sure if that was good or bad.

"You think God cares about piano recitals?" The words slipped out before Jess could stop them.

"I know He cares about Sienna. And that means whatever she's concerned about, He is, too."

Something inside Jess wanted to lean into the words. Wanted them to be true. But all her life, she'd been on her own. No one—not her family, not God—had intervened. Jess had always believed there was someone bigger out there. Someone who'd created lakes and stars. Crisp green apples and autumn leaves.

She just wasn't convinced she would ever meet with His approval.

Merri's lilting "Amen" signaled the end of the prayer. The smiles on their faces linked them together even as they stepped apart.

Peg saw Jess standing in the doorway and waved.

"I'll be right back." Jess slipped out the door and didn't look back at Nick.

"What do you think?" Peg asked. She'd left Bosco home this time, but his slightly distorted face grinned at Jess on the front of her T-shirt.

Jess couldn't believe the transformation that had taken place over the course of the afternoon.

At some point, while Jess was busy in the kitchen, every card table in the neighborhood had been dusted off and transported to Elaine's backyard. Each one wore a vintage tablecloth. The centerpieces were chunky white candles or mason jars filled with cut flowers. A garland of white lights decorated the wooden fence.

"It's…stunning."

Merri beamed. "Well, I'm going to scoot home and freshen up a little before the party starts."

"That's a good idea." Nita adjusted one of the vases. "Do you have things under control in the kitchen, Jess? Christopher can stay a little longer if you need him to."

"I can handle it from here."

"We'll be back at five," Peg said. "Frank saw the pound cake cooling on the table this morning and assumed it was for him. The only thing that stopped him from eating a piece was permission to crash the party."

Jess could only hope the additional tables and chairs didn't mean the rest of the neighborhood had been given last-minute invitations.

"I'll send Christopher home. And…thank you. The garden looks beautiful."

"Pulling weeds and setting up tables is the easy part," Nita said.

Before Jess could disagree, she was wrapped in Merri's arms, breathing in the scent of basil and roses and strawberry shampoo. "We couldn't have done this without you."

The women filed down the path, and Jess went back inside. Christopher was sitting cross-legged on the floor, petting Violet.

Nick was gone.

He was so gone.

When Merri told Nick about the reception for Sienna, he'd hoped it meant that Jess was starting to feel like she was part of the neighborhood.

Until she'd walked into the kitchen and reality smacked him upside the head with the force of a Griswold thirteen.

Jess's designer shoes, the stylish clothing—Nick understood now why those things were important to Jess. Gwyneth Donovan thought it was important to project a certain image and Jess had embraced the philosophy. Nick had felt a check in his gut when Jess was talking about her former boss, but it was clear Jess admired the woman's success.

No, it was the pristine white chef's coat and checkered pants that sent him reeling. A reminder that when Elaine no longer needed her help, Jess would move on.

Nick knew God had brought her to Winsome Lake for a reason.

But until now, he hadn't realized how much he wanted her to stay.

Chapter Twenty-Eight

"Here she comes."

Christopher's loud whisper galvanized everyone into action. While Nita shooed everyone into the garden, Jess went out to meet Sienna before she reached the front door.

The relief pouring through Jess made her legs a little wobbly. Based on the timeline Sienna had given her, the recital should have ended almost an hour ago.

"Sorry, I'm a little late," Sienna panted. "The photographer from the newspaper wanted to take a picture of me."

It took a moment for the words to register.

"You got the scholarship?" Jess breathed.

Sienna performed a little curtsey.

Jess grabbed the girl's hands and squeezed them. "Sienna, that's amazing! I knew Chopin would come through."

Sienna bit her lip. "I kind of changed my mind at the last minute. I played 'Ode to Joy' instead. Ms. Grant just about fell off her chair when I started playing my solo. But I don't know…it felt like the right thing to do."

"Come with me. I have something to show you." She led Sienna around the house to the garden before she had time to wonder why Jess had dressed up, too.

She unlatched the gate and let Sienna go first. The girl took a few tentative steps forward and then lurched to a stop. Her sharp inhale drowned out by a loud chorus.

"Surprise!"

Jess hoped it was a good one.

Sienna threw a panicked look at Jess. "What…"

"It's for you. They…we…thought all your hard work deserved a party."

Sienna looked around. Took in the twinkling white lights draped over the fence. The luminaries outlining the paving-stone walkway and the bouquets of flowers on the tables.

"Jessica is right." Merri swept up to them and took Sienna gently by the hand. "Tonight we're celebrating you."

Sienna looked at Jess helplessly, tears cresting in her eyes.

Christopher bounded up, his signature grin in place. "Are you hungry? I'm h-hungry. Jess wouldn't let us eat until you got here."

Sienna laughed. "I'm starving."

"That's my cue to bring out the food." Jess backed toward the house.

"I'll help," Nita said.

It didn't cross Jess's mind to politely turn down the offer.

"I cannot believe you did all this." Nita scanned the trays of food in disbelief. "You must have spent every waking hour in the kitchen for the past four days!"

Every waking hour and the ones when Jess probably should have been sleeping.

But it was worth it, seeing the expression on Sienna's face.

Jess tucked a few more macarons on a plate and followed Nita onto the patio. She'd just finished refilling the water pitchers a second time when a movement by the gate caught her eye.

A woman stood watching them. Tall and pretty, in her early- to midfifties, with short, silver-blond hair.

Jess couldn't remember seeing her in the neighborhood before. Someone who'd heard the commotion and decided to investigate?

She took a step toward the gate and heard Merri's excited cry behind her.

"Elaine!"

"Surprise." She smiled and opened her arms to the stampede of women who abandoned their chairs, almost bowling Jess over in their haste to reach her.

Jess tried to smile, too, as two thoughts collided in her mind.

The woman was Elaine Haviland.

And everything had changed.

Chapter Twenty-Nine

Nothing had changed.

Elaine soaked up the sound of her friends' laughter and the weeks of grueling therapy and sleepless nights fell away.

She'd hoped to attend Sienna's recital, but the formal discharge papers had taken a while to complete. Almost as long as it had taken Elaine to convince Vanessa that leaving before the home safety check didn't mean the virus that had sent her back to the hospital with an IV drip for three days had affected her common sense.

She hadn't expected to find the teenager—and half the neighborhood—in her backyard.

"You didn't know I was coming home," Elaine teased. "So I'm guessing Sienna is the guest of honor?"

Sienna ducked her head to hide a blush and nodded.

"We wanted to do something special," Merri said. "To celebrate the recital."

"I h-helped Jessica make the food," Christopher chimed in.

And that was when Elaine noticed the young woman standing in the background. She wore her blond hair pulled back into a neat twist at the nape of her neck and a chic polka-dot dress that looked as if it had been designed for a summer garden party.

Her eyes met Elaine's over the bistro table and then she glided toward her on heels that looked more suitable for a fashion runway than uneven garden stones.

"Ms. Haviland."

Elaine might not recognize the face, but she remembered the voice.

"Jessica?" Elaine said the name almost tentatively.

This is the person I hired, Lord? She looked a lot different on the phone.

Jessica extended her hand, a polite smile on her face. "It's nice to finally meet you."

Elaine felt the tremble in her fingers and tried not to wince.

So much for first impressions.

"You should have told us you were coming home," Nita scolded.

Elaine, who could count on one hand the number of times she'd seen Nita cry over the past twenty-five years, was shocked to see tears in her eyes.

"I'm sorry. I got out of the hospital yesterday and when Dr. Kim said the word *home*, I didn't think about anything but making it back in time for Sienna's recital."

"We've been praying ever since Jessica told us you were back in the hospital." Peg scanned Elaine from head to toe. "No wonder you're so thin. The food is terrible in those places. Sit down and have a macaron." She guided Elaine toward the card table.

"I'll get some water." Jessica took the pitcher off the table and disappeared into the house.

Elaine sat down and buried her nose in one of the roses on the table. Oh, she'd missed her garden. The familiar faces and the fragrance of friendship.

Merri's cherry-red Keds, the slight pucker between Nita's eyebrows, the way Peg's earrings jingled like the tag on Bosco's collar.

These were the women who'd seasoned her life with their laughter and their tears.

"Everything looks so beautiful," Elaine murmured. "And the refreshments…"

"Jess is a r-real chef," Christopher said. "She has a special knife and everything."

If Jessica Keaton had provided the food for Sienna's party, she'd already gone beyond the duties she'd been hired to do.

Elaine glanced at the house, but Jessica hadn't returned yet. She turned to Sienna. "How did it go tonight?"

Elaine, who'd expected a one-word response, was surprised when Sienna gave a moment-by-moment recap of the recital.

"You got the scholarship?" Elaine sent a silent thank-you heavenward.

"I can play it for you sometime," Sienna offered.

"I would love that." Elaine smiled. "So. What happens next?"

"Ms. Grant asked me to play for a fancy dinner the dean is hosting in a few weeks." Sienna looked excited rather than terrified by the opportunity.

Peg nudged a plate toward Elaine. "You better try one of these before Frank finishes them off."

Pastel-pink macarons and petit fours decorated with sugared flowers looked like miniature works of art. There were squares of lavender shortbread embossed with sprigs of rosemary. Delicate cucumber sandwiches and miniature croissants filled with chicken salad.

Elaine took a bite of one of the macarons and her taste buds, dormant after days of pain medication, came instantly back to life.

The creativity, the attention to detail, told Elaine more than Jessica's résumé did.

What it didn't tell her was why Jessica had answered her ad.

"It's nice to have you back." Merri reached across the table and squeezed Elaine's hand.

Elaine squeezed back and felt the tremble again. The day was catching up to her but she wasn't ready to let go. Not yet. She wanted to cup her hands around familiar faces and breathe in air scented by roses and lavender. Lean into the glow of the lights and the laughter.

Thank You, God. Thank You for all of these.

She looked at Sienna. "I think I'm ready to hear that solo now."

Peg frowned. "You look tired. Don't you want to put your feet up and settle in for the night?"

"I think I want to celebrate a little longer."

"You heard the lady," Merri said cheerfully.

Nita acquiesced but linked her arm through Elaine's, using her trim frame to shore up the right side of Elaine's body as they walked toward the house.

"It smells like a bakery in here," Elaine whispered. "Not that I'm complaining."

"Jessica spends a lot of time in the kitchen." Nita visibly shuddered. "She seems to like it, though."

Elaine allowed Nita to steer her into the living room and

over to the couch. She barely had time to adjust the pillow behind her back when Violet vaulted into her lap.

"Hey, you." Elaine gathered the cat closer and stroked her back. "Miss me?"

Violet reared up and bumped Elaine's chin. The tickle of whiskers, the familiar furry weight holding the afghan in place while Elaine watched TV, was another thing she'd missed.

Sienna sat down at the piano, her back straight, both hands resting on the keys. She leaned over and said something to Christopher that made the boy grin.

Now that the dust of her arrival had settled a bit, Elaine had time to study Sienna more closely.

She looked...older. More confident.

Sienna had always been a pretty girl, but now the heavy curtain of bangs that fell over her eyes had been trimmed back, the baggy clothes she tended to favor replaced by a simple but stylish little black dress.

Maybe Elaine's prayers were answered and Sienna's mother had had a change of heart. Finally stepped up and stepped back into her daughter's life.

Sienna nodded at Christopher.

He swept his arm out with the grace of a conductor, the cucumber sandwich pinched between his finger and thumb the wand. "Sienna Bloom playing Ludwig van Beethoven's 'Ode to Joy.'"

Merri's gasp was absorbed into the opening notes of the piece.

Elaine made a mental note to ask her about it later.

When the song was over, Sienna stood up and took a bow.

"That was beautiful, Sienna." Elaine had forgotten to speak slowly and her tongue forgot what it was supposed to do for a moment. The result was a thick slur that everyone in the room, even Peg, pretended they hadn't heard.

One of the many reasons why Elaine loved them.

Merri covered a delicate yawn. "I think I'm ready to say good-night."

"So are we." Peg included Frank with a look as subtle as Merri's yawn. He scooped up a handful of mints and reluctantly pushed to his feet.

"G-good night, Miss Elaine." Christopher loped over and bussed her cheek. "I'm glad you're h-home."

"Me, too, sweetie." The words were spaced evenly apart this time. "Me, too." Elaine stood up and wished she hadn't packed Matthew's cane away with the rest of the belongings Vanessa had promised to deliver the next day when she came to do the home safety check.

Her silly pride again.

Why was it so much easier to extend grace to other people than it was to herself?

Jessica appeared in the doorway, and Elaine realized she'd stayed in the kitchen while Sienna performed her solo.

"We'll help with the cleanup before we leave," Nita told her.

"I've got everything under control." A black bib apron covered Jessica's party dress now. The ties wrapped around her waist twice and ended in a neat little knot that sat on the curve of her hip.

Sienna drifted close enough for Elaine to catch her hand.

"Thank you for sharing your gift. And I hope you're going to keep practicing even though the recital is over. Mr. Gladstone played his harmonica in the activity room a few times a week, but it wasn't the same."

"I will." Sienna looked over at Jessica. "And I'll bring your dress back tomorrow."

"How about we trade?" Jessica suggested. "Unless polka dots aren't fancy enough for a concert with the dean?"

"Polka dots are great." Sienna flashed a smile that Elaine hadn't seen since Wanda Bloom had passed away.

"I'll bring Bosco by to say hello tomorrow." Peg stepped up and squeezed Elaine's hand. "He missed you, too."

Elaine smiled, not quite trusting her voice.

Jessica had lent Sienna a dress for the solo.

I'm sorry I doubted You, Lord.

"And I'll bring over some vegetables," Merri said. "I have more green beans than I know what to do with."

"You don't have to have a garden," Nita pointed out. "It's a lot of work for someone who doesn't like to cook."

"But it's perfect for someone like our Merri, who loves to give things away." Elaine winked at Nita, patted Merri's arm.

"I'd love some fresh tomatoes."

"Maybe Jessica will make you a frittata." Peg wrapped one arm around Elaine, careful not to squeeze. "It's like a quiche without a crust and it's delicious."

Nita's watch beeped twice, and Christopher's face lit up.

"My f-favorite show is starting. B-bye, Jessica. Bye, M-Miss Elaine."

Elaine would have followed them to the door, but Nita stopped her with a look. "We know our way out."

Elaine nodded. "See you tomorrow."

Nita turned to Jessica and smiled. "Do you mind if I take a few of those petit fours for the road?"

"I made up some boxes for everyone. Grab one before you go."

Jessica stood to one side, watching over the procession as they made their way to the door.

After the door closed, Elaine sank back onto the couch. Violet climbed back into her lap, but at the moment Elaine couldn't summon the strength to stroke the cat's fur. Pain flared in her ribs again and she had to concentrate on every breath.

She'd packed away her pain pills, too.

"Do you need anything, Ms. Haviland?" Jessica stood a few feet away, watching her with an expression Elaine couldn't quite identify.

The young woman was good at hiding her thoughts.

Like someone else you know.

Elaine shooed that pesky inner voice away.

"Yes. I need you to call me Elaine." Elaine wrestled down the pain and smiled. "You're probably exhausted from preparing all the food for Sienna's party. And I'm fine."

Jessica's lips parted as if she was going to say something else and then she nodded.

Elaine waited until she heard the creak of the top stair before she pressed the pillow over her face to muffle the moan she could no longer contain.

Vanessa would have revoked Elaine's ice cream privileges if she'd known about the stairs. Elaine had climbed them at least half a dozen times a day before the stroke, but now they looked as steep as the old fire tower located on the edge of town.

Elaine had assured Vanessa that her bungalow was small but it wasn't a death trap, so the social worker had agreed to postpone the home visit for a few days.

Violet rubbed against Elaine's foot.

"That's about as subtle as Merri's yawn," Elaine told her. "You know that, right?"

The cat trotted toward the kitchen, and Elaine levered herself off the couch. Being the caregiver instead of the person in need of care felt good for a change.

She braced one hand against the doorway leading into the

kitchen, and bile rose in her throat along with a memory she'd suppressed until now.

The last time Elaine was in this room, she'd been lying on the floor, crying out to God but unable to speak.

It had started out like any other morning. Violet, Elaine's alarm clock, woke her up at six and she'd gone downstairs to make a cup of tea.

Elaine remembered feeling a little light-headed and leaning against the island until the sensation passed. A few seconds later she was staring up at the ceiling. She'd tried to sit up, but none of her limbs would cooperate. Her body felt like it was encased in wax.

Elaine had fought against the panic rushing through her and limbs that refused to move. Her cell phone was out of reach, still plugged into the charger on her nightstand, so she'd cried out to God for help.

A few minutes later Elaine heard a knock on the door.

It had snowed during the night and Nita was always the first one to shovel the sidewalk in front of their houses. She was also a certified first responder. She'd taken the course after Christopher was born and renewed her certification every year.

But God had sent Merri instead.

Merri, who always left her cell phone at home. Merri, who got teary-eyed over greeting card commercials.

Merri, who'd found Elaine's phone and called 911 while holding Elaine's limp hand and didn't let go until the ambulance arrived.

Elaine suddenly felt light-headed all over again. Her heart was pounding in her ears and her breath was coming out in short little bursts.

You're all right.

You're home.

She inhaled slowly to steady her breathing and the scent of vanilla icing came with it.

So did the knowledge she'd been wrong that things hadn't changed.

Bunches of dried herbs were hanging from the curtain rod. The coffeepot that Merri brought out on Thursdays had taken up residence on the counter, and a cast-iron skillet sat on the burner.

Elaine took a halting step forward and her gaze dropped to the leather case in the center of the island. The block that held Elaine's steak knives had vanished, along with the set of empty canisters that collected dust on the counter.

Elaine was looking at someone else's kitchen.

"Ms. Haviland... Elaine?"

She turned around and saw Jessica framed in the doorway. She'd moved so quietly Elaine hadn't heard a single creak on the stairs. Her hair was loose around her shoulders and she'd exchanged the party dress for wide-legged palazzo pants and a batik cotton tee in peacock blues and greens.

Elaine smiled. "Did you need something?"

"No..." Jessica looked a little confused by the question and it occurred to Elaine she'd probably been wondering the same thing.

But this was as good a time as any to remind Jessica Keaton that she didn't need a nurse.

"I like what you've done to the place."

Color bloomed in Jessica's cheeks. "I'm sorry..."

"Please." Elaine cut her off with a laugh. "Don't apologize. It looks...inviting. Like someone who actually spends time in the kitchen lives here." She nodded at the leather case. "I'm guessing the knives that Christopher mentioned are in there?"

Jessica nodded her head and an awkward silence descended that neither of them were inclined to break.

Elaine took a play from Merri's book and faked a yawn. "I think I'm going to go to bed now. I'm still on Sunrise's schedule, and the CNAs tuck us into bed by nine."

She could tell by the expression on Jessica's face that she wasn't sure if Elaine was joking or telling the truth.

"I'll see you in the morning, then," Jessica murmured. "Is there a certain time you like to eat breakfast?"

What Elaine really wanted to do was sleep until Violet decided to wake her up and drink her first cup of tea in the garden.

But both of them had had their share of surprises that evening, so Elaine kept that to herself.

"Don't worry about breakfast." Elaine summoned a smile. "We can talk in the morning."

Jessica disappeared up the stairs and Elaine went back to the living room.

Violet was already curled up on the afghan.

"You have to share tonight." Elaine lay down on the sofa and pulled a corner of the blanket over her legs.

In the morning she'd have to figure out stairs and schedules. Make a decision on what to do about Jessica Keaton.

And Libby Tucker.

Chapter Thirty

Jess closed the bedroom door and walked over to the window. The same moon that had skipped diamonds across the surface of Winsome Lake when she'd been sitting with Nick on the patio Friday night refused to show itself now.

She realized she'd left her cell phone in the kitchen after she got ready for bed. It wasn't a big deal, except that lately she'd been setting the alarm for five to make breakfast for Sienna and she didn't want to wake up Elaine that early in the morning.

She'd tiptoed down the stairs, avoiding the ones that squeaked, and almost ran over the woman standing just inside the kitchen doorway.

Elaine had smiled, but Jess couldn't help but notice she looked a little pale. Had she been thinking about the stroke? Or having second thoughts about someone taking over her kitchen?

Jess was still having a hard time matching the Elaine Havi-

land she'd pictured in her head to the one she'd seen standing at the garden gate.

She'd expected the woman to be...older. Maybe even older
than the Scrappy Ladies, given the fact she'd suffered a stroke.

The biggest surprise, though, was that Elaine Haviland
didn't look like someone who needed live-in help.

Sure, she walked a little slower and her movements were
more deliberate, more methodical, than the other women.
Physically, Elaine Haviland was still regaining her strength
but there was nothing *feeble* about her. Anything she needed,
Nita, Merri and Peg could provide.

We can talk in the morning.

Jess took a restless lap around the room.

Why did the words have an ominous ring?

Jess had no idea why Elaine had placed that ad in the newspaper. Elaine had been gracious about the changes Jess had
made in the kitchen, but it didn't mean she wasn't regretting her decision now.

She listened for Elaine's footsteps on the stairs, but only
heard the now-familiar sounds of the house settling in for
the night.

Jess sank onto the edge of the bed and looked at her phone.

No missed calls. No new texts.

Maybe Nick was having regrets, too.

Otherwise, why hadn't he come back for Sienna's party?

*You didn't want to spend more time with him. Nick Silva is a
complication, remember?*

A complication who had a steady hand when applying sugared flowers to the tops of petit fours. And made her laugh.
And whose light kiss had made her toes curl.

Made her want more.

Jess flopped onto her back, trying to dislodge the memory, but knew it wouldn't matter. Nick had been showing up in her dreams.

And dreams were dangerous things.

Elaine pulled the pillow underneath her head and tried to get comfortable. The couch predated memory foam, but the cushions molded to the contours of her frame in a welcoming embrace. She reached out to give Violet another scratch under the chin and the cell phone on the coffee table hummed, signaling an incoming text.

Elaine winced.

She'd totally forgotten the promise she'd made to Vanessa to let her know when she was safe and sound in Winsome Lake.

Except the text wasn't from Vanessa.

Elaine's heart performed that strange little flip that had become more frequent after Matthew Jeffries kidnapped her in the hall outside physical therapy.

Excited about going home tomorrow?

Elaine sat up so quickly that Violet squawked in protest.

She hadn't seen or spoken to Matthew since the hospital had pumped her full of fluids and antibiotics for the weekend and then returned her to Sunrise. But Vanessa had oh so casually mentioned Matthew had committed to lead a commemorative ride to several veterans' cemeteries and wouldn't be meeting with his group at the rehab center for a few days.

Which had been fine, because Elaine wasn't sure how she would look him in the eye when the last time they'd been together, she'd fainted in the man's arms like the heroine in a Regency romance novel.

Should she wait until morning to respond? Or confess now and get it over with?

Elaine reached over and turned on the reading lamp. Violet, disgruntled by all this unnecessary moving and jiggling, jumped off the couch and went to find a more peaceful place to sleep.

I'm already here.

Elaine hit Send and waited. And waited.

Just when she was starting to get nervous, tiny bubbles appeared on the screen.

Does Vanessa know that?

Elaine grinned. She tucked the pillow behind her back and started the slow, one-finger hunt and peck again. The therapist should have added typing on miniature keyboards to her sessions.

Yes. But it involved a lot of promises and outright begging. I missed Sienna's recital but got home in time for her surprise party.

The bubbles appeared right away, and Elaine chewed on her lower lip, waiting for the message to appear.

Did your friends know you were coming home? Or were you surprise number 2?

Surprise #2. Doc and PT signed my paperwork and I couldn't wait until tomorrow. Hired transport van to bring me home.

For the second time, Elaine waited in vain for those little bubbles to appear. Maybe Matthew had gotten distracted by another call. Fallen asleep...

I wanted to take you home.

The little heart flip turned into a series of somersaults that left her feeling short of breath.

Elaine read the words again. Tried to decipher what they meant.

Matthew knew she was going to be released sometime that week, but he hadn't said anything about driving her back to Winsome Lake.

You're reading too much into this, Elaine chided herself.

Matthew was being Matthew. He was kind. He had a servant's heart. He'd volunteered to take the veterans on a memorial ride, hadn't he? Matthew had probably offered to escort her home to save the transport driver the long trip.

Another text popped up. Elaine had been so distracted by the thoughts ping-ponging inside her head, she hadn't noticed the bubbles.

And no. Vanessa didn't put me up to it. I want to see where you live. Meet the Scrappy Ladies and Violet. Turn you into a coffee drinker.

Elaine covered the screen with her hand. Which was silly, because Matthew couldn't see her face or read her mind.

He'd made her laugh, been both confidant and prayer partner, but Elaine knew any relationship they had would die a natural death after she left the rehab center. She hadn't expected more.

Wasn't sure if she *wanted* more.

Elaine closed her eyes.

You always do this. You let people in, but it's always on your terms. There are places you cordon off. Places you won't let anyone in. Not even your closest friends.

Because she didn't want them to know *that* Elaine. Didn't want to be defined by her mistakes.

You must be tired. I'll let you get some sleep.

Matthew was giving her an out.

Elaine sank lower into the pillows and started typing. Hit Send before she could change her mind.

1525 Woodwind Lane.

The bubbles appeared immediately.

I'll see you soon.

How soon?

No bubbles. No reply.

But Elaine could see the crinkles around the corners of Matthew's eyes deepening to catch the overflow of his smile.

She could see a lot of things she would have thought impossible three months ago.

Chapter Thirty-One

Elaine woke to the sound of purring.

Violet was draped over the arm of the sofa, performing more morning ablutions.

For a split second Elaine thought she was dreaming. And then she remembered. She was home.

She reached out to pet Violet and the cat stopped licking her paws for a moment, accepting the interruption with the patient tolerance of an actress agreeing to pose for a selfie with a fan.

"Still the diva, I see," Elaine whispered.

She pushed herself into a sitting position and felt the muscles in her back rebel. Still, she felt more rested after spending one night on the sofa than she had during her entire stay at Sunrise.

Elaine glanced at the grandfather clock and hoped Jessica Keaton wasn't an early riser. She wanted to start her first day at home the right way. Talking to God over a cup of tea.

She got up slowly, tested her limbs to make sure they were all still working and went into the kitchen.

A ceramic bowl, forced into early retirement due to lack of use, had been recommissioned. Elaine lifted the corner of the flour sack dish towel and saw a half-risen mound of yeasty bread dough that hadn't been there when Elaine went to bed.

Either the Keebler elves were alive and well and living in Winsome Lake, or Jessica Keaton had been in the kitchen again.

It was probably too much to hope she hadn't noticed Elaine sleeping on the couch.

She opened the cabinet and reached for the tin of Earl Grey. Elaine thought she'd bought a new one before the stroke, but there were only two tea bags left.

She filled the kettle with water and carried it to the stove, her hand trembling underneath the familiar weight.

The simple act of brewing her own cup of tea was something Elaine would never take for granted again.

She watched the water turn amber as the tea bag sank to the bottom of the cup. Steam rose into the air and released the earthy scent of lavender and bergamot. While it steeped, Elaine slipped into the half bath, put on her robe and ran a brush through her hair.

There were still no sounds coming from upstairs, but something told Elaine that one of Jessica's superpowers was knowing when the dough was ready to be punched down before its second rising.

She picked up the teacup and padded down the hall to her office.

The garden was Elaine's favorite spot to spend time with her friends; the room tucked under the eaves, with God. It was too small to host a gathering, but the perfect size for ideas to take root and grow. And like a collage, it was beau-

tifully unorganized. An eclectic blend of things that fit together because they meant something to her. Memories of
the places she'd traveled. Touchstones that reminded her to
keep going when the past obscured her view.

A hint of lemon furniture polish hung in the air, and
Elaine stopped so suddenly, tea sloshed over the side of her
cup. The air emptied from her lungs in one short, painful
burst.

The day she'd had the stroke remained a little foggy, so
Elaine couldn't remember if she'd locked her office door.
What she did remember was that the tattered pieces of Libby's diary had been scattered across her desk, not stacked
in a neat pile on the corner. After that brief but memorable
conversation with Hilary in the spring, Elaine had started to
sort through them for the first time in years.

Had Jessica read them?

Or, and this would be even worse, seen the notes she'd
jotted down?

She felt exposed. Vulnerable. And not only because Jessica Keaton had ventured into a room even Elaine's closest
friends had never seen.

If she reacted this strongly to one person reading Libby's
diaries, how could she possibly include them in a book for
thousands of people to see?

Elaine set the cup down and gripped the edge of the desk.

And here she'd been worried about Jessica witnessing the
terry-cloth belt on her bathrobe coming undone because she
couldn't tie a decent knot. Struggling through simple tasks
like using a knife or tying her shoes.

She'd pay Jessica for the two weeks she'd vacuumed and
dusted the house. She'd be doing the young woman a favor,
really. Jessica's talents would be wasted on her. And after

last night, when she'd seen Elaine teetering in the doorway, maybe she'd welcome the opportunity to part company, too.

Okay, Lord. One decision down, one to go.

Elaine took a slow lap around the room, letting the familiar surroundings fill the nooks and crannies in her soul, the way her friends' laughter had the night before.

She paused in front of the driftwood bird sitting on the edge of the shelf.

You take it, Sam had said. *I want you to remember that God always knows what we need. And He knew we needed each other.*

Jess finished getting dressed and slipped out of the bathroom, trying to avoid the floorboards that creaked in case Elaine was still asleep.

When she'd spotted the lump on the sofa at four-thirty, Jess had assumed Sienna had snuck into the house. But then the lump had moved and the afghan slipped down, revealing strands of silver-blond hair, not black.

Jess didn't know why Elaine had spent the night on the couch. Or why she felt so guilty about it.

Elaine had told her not to worry about breakfast, but Jess had mixed together a sweet roll dough anyway, because she had a hunch a lot of people would be stopping by to visit Elaine.

And because she couldn't sleep.

Jess zigzagged down the stairs to get the dough ready for its second rise. Nothing looked out of place, but Jess took one look at the immaculate countertop and knew someone had been in the kitchen. She recognized the scent of Earl Grey lingering in the air.

Jess dared a look at the couch and saw Violet sprawled on the afghan, sharpening her whiskers into fine points, but there was no sign of Elaine.

Did she want to be left alone?

Should she be left alone?

For her own peace of mind, Jess needed to know Elaine wasn't lying on the floor, waiting for someone to find her.

Jess knew she wasn't upstairs. She looked out the windows overlooking the garden and the front porch and crossed both of them off the list. By process of elimination, that left blue door number two at the end of the hall.

But there was no opportunity to check on her employer and beat a hasty but quiet retreat. The door to the office was wide-open.

The floor squeaked, giving Jess's position away, and Elaine turned around.

If Jess wasn't sure whether or not she'd made the right decision to clean the office, the expression on Elaine's face told Jess everything she needed to know.

She didn't say anything, but it was clear to Jess that her new employer, unlike Gwyneth, was trying to come up with a cordial way of telling Jess she was fired.

A girl should get some kind of warning before her world falls apart.

"I'm sorry... I didn't mean to intrude, but you hired me to clean the house." Jess pulled in a breath and released it again. "I didn't realize this room was off-limits."

She should have. Simply because it looked so different from the rest of the house. Filled with things that Elaine, for whatever reason, didn't share with anyone else.

Elaine picked up the piece of driftwood Jess had dusted around. She hadn't realized it resembled a tiny bird until it was cradled in the nest of Elaine's palm.

"How did you see the ad?"

Jess was so busy mentally packing her things, Elaine's question didn't register for a moment. "The ad?"

"The one Vanessa put in the newspaper for me."

Jess licked her lips, not sure why this was relevant. "I was staying at a hotel. When I went down to breakfast in the morning, all the tables were taken except one. Whoever had been sitting there must have left the paper for someone else to read. There were people at the buffet, so I glanced at it while I waited for them to go through the line."

"A hotel," Elaine repeated.

"I'd...lost my apartment."

"Do you have ties to this area?"

Images of the Scrappy Ladies, of Anthony and Sienna, Christopher and Nick, toppled through her mind.

"No," Jess said softly.

"Vacationed here?"

Jess shook her head.

"A professional chef decides to answer an ad for a live-in cook and housekeeper in a town she's never visited before?"

Jess hadn't thought it strange at the time. All she'd been thinking was that she needed a job.

And now she'd have to start the process all over again.

She wouldn't beg, though. She'd tried to convince Gwyneth to change her mind and ended up feeling more humiliated when every attempt to tell her side of the story was firmly rejected.

Jess lifted her chin. "I needed a job."

"Because..."

"I was fired."

"Would you mind telling me why?"

"Yes."

And that was it. Elaine Haviland would realize she'd made a mistake and write a check that Jess could cash on her way out of town.

"I don't believe in coincidences, do you?" Elaine set the

driftwood bird back on the shelf. "You're an amazing cook, Jessica. How are you at putting puzzles together?"

The abrupt turn in the conversation felt Jess feeling off-kilter again.

"Puzzles?"

Elaine smiled. "Let's sit down and I'll explain. After that you can take some time to think it over and let me know if you want to stay."

Want to stay.

Like the decision would be up to Jess.

She started toward the armless chair in the corner, but Elaine shook her head. "It'll be easier if you're sitting at the desk."

Where the evidence that proved Jess guilty of trespassing was stacked in a neat corner.

"I'm a freelance writer," Elaine said. "I was approached about a new project right before the stroke, but as you probably noticed, it's going to be a challenge to include the diary entries in their present...ah...form. I could sort through the pieces, but the wires in my brain start to smoke when I read more than a few paragraphs." Elaine gave Jess a wry smile. "Even if I got them in the right order, I'd be calling 911 again and the EMTs would find me on the floor wrapped in a roll of scotch tape. I'm glad it's sandal weather because I still have a hard time tying my shoes."

The tight knot in Jess's chest began to loosen.

Gwyneth would have never admitted there was something she couldn't do, let alone find the humor in anything she considered a weakness. Physical, mental or emotional.

"I was going to turn down the project, but if you'll agree to put Libby Tucker's diary back together, I'll compensate you for the extra hours you put in. Wherever it fits in your day is fine with me. Once the diary is back together, we should be able to scan the pages into a file."

Jess's gaze drifted to the tattered pages again.

She wouldn't have to find another job. Another place to live. Wouldn't have to leave.

At least for a while.

Thank you, Libby Tucker. Whoever you are.

Chapter Thirty-Two

Grandpop was sitting on the porch when Nick pulled into the driveway.

Bucket spotted him, too, and began to tap-dance on the seat.

Nick tried to ignore a pinch of guilt.

"It hasn't been that long since we've seen him," he muttered.

Bucket whined and pressed his wet nose against the window. Confined to a small space, seventy pounds of enthusiasm funneled into his bushy tail. It knocked the rearview mirror sideways and sent the tree-shaped air freshener into a wild spin.

Nick ducked his head to avoid getting a tail in the face, but there was no escaping the odor of pine and dog that washed through the cab.

He pulled up to the cabin, unbuckled and opened the driver's-side door.

"Manners," Nick reminded the dog as he got out.

Bucket ignored him and tore up the front walkway as if he hadn't seen a human being other than his master for days.

Okay. Maybe because he hadn't.

But Nick had been busy. Busy with the construction project. Busy putting together a practice schedule before the school year started.

Busy keeping himself busy so he wouldn't think about Jess.

Grandpop stood up and waved a hello when Nick got out of the truck.

Bucket was already sprawled on his back when Nick reached the porch in a shameless bid for a belly rub. Grandpop complied and smiled at Nick.

"How is Elaine doing?"

Good morning, Grandpop. Nice to see you, too.

"I assume she's okay," Nick hedged. "I haven't stopped over there yet. I thought she might need some time to get settled in again."

Because Nick definitely needed some time to get his emotions in check before he saw Jess again.

Grandpop fished a biscuit out of his pocket and tossed it up in the air. Bucket performed a triple Axel worthy of a gold medal and swallowed it whole before trotting off to harass the chickens.

"I brought over the nail gun you asked for. Are you sure you don't want me to fix the loose board on the porch?"

"And ruin my fun?" Grandpop chuckled. "But there is something else you can do for me."

"Anything you need."

"I've got two dozen eggs taking up room in my refrigerator," he said. "Do you mind dropping them off?"

Anything except that.

"I planned on working at the lodge the rest of the day and

I have to turn the electricity off for a while, so the fridge will be down." Nick would make sure of it. "Another day might work out better."

"Uh-huh." Grandpop gave him The Look. The one that said he knew there was more to the story but wouldn't push. For now.

Nick took advantage of the reprieve and prodded a reluctant Bucket back inside the truck. Cranked up the radio in a futile attempt to drown out the thoughts rolling around in his head.

Thoughts of Jessica wearing a pristine white jacket, a dusting of flour on her cheek.

He turned down the driveway and hit the brake twenty yards in. A line of pickup trucks made it impossible to go any farther. In the distance, Nick could see giants roaming the property. Giants in Wildcats jerseys.

Bucket stuck his head out the window and barked a greeting that was swept up in the bass pulsing from a set of wireless speakers on the hood of the pickup parked in front of Nick's.

"Hey, Coach!" Delaney Albright, honor student, captain of the cheer squad and point guard for the girls' basketball team, waved to Nick from the open tailgate of a fire engine–red Ford.

He pivoted toward her. "Del?"

"It was Ben's idea." Delaney threw her steady boyfriend under the bus with a wide Julia Roberts grin. "They want you to finish the house so you can focus on them."

If the Wildcats' quarterback was in charge, it was a good thing Nick had arrived when he did. Hopefully, the guys hadn't ventured into the house and stumbled upon the tempting display of demolition tools yet.

Nick hadn't brought his whistle, so he improvised by using the same technique his mom had implemented when it was dinnertime and her children were scattered around the neighborhood. He put two fingers in his mouth and blew.

The team funneled together and charged toward Nick like a herd of sweaty teenage buffalos.

"Hey, Coach!" Ben, Nick's star quarterback, reached him first. "Mr. Mulvaney said you needed some help cleaning up the yard."

Apparently, both Nick's football team and his Realtor had a vested interest in his finishing the lodge on time.

"There's a lot of junk piled up in that shed, Coach," the running back chimed in. "Want us to start there? We can fill up the trucks and haul it away for you. Cheaper than renting a Dumpster."

"I appreciate it, guys." *Really* appreciated it. Because now he had a legitimate reason to delay the errand for Anthony.

"And girls," a feminine voice added.

The team parted like the Red Sea to make room for Delaney and two of her friends from the cheerleading squad.

"And girls," Nick echoed. "Okay. Move your trucks over there." He pointed to the grassy area by the property line. "Let's empty the drop box."

Half an hour later two of the trucks stuffed with old tires and the rusty skeletons of broken-down appliances rumbled down the driveway. Nick was helping load up the third when Ben and Marcus staggered toward him, their biceps straining under the weight of a ten-foot-long section of oak.

"This thing is heavier than Gil," Marcus panted, shooting a sideways grin at Nick's offensive lineman.

"Do you want this in the truck? Or should we chop it up for firewood?" Ben asked. Hope gleamed in his eyes in anticipation of using Nick's chainsaw.

Nick ran his hand down the polished surface of the lodge's old bar top. Dirt and debris filled the knotholes. The varnish protecting the wood had started to fleck off and there were a few deep gashes that Nick didn't remember seeing before. Other than that, it was in decent shape after spending several winters at the mercy of the elements.

Nick couldn't come up with a good reason to keep it. It wasn't as if a sawed-off tree would fit in his kitchen and he doubted any of his family members would have a place for it, either. But he couldn't imagine cutting the thing up and watching the pieces turn into ash...

"Coach?" Marcus prompted through gritted teeth.

"Sorry." Nick was probably going to regret this. "Just set it over by the patio and I'll figure out what to do with it later."

"Sure thing," Ben croaked.

A few more players sprinted over to help, and Nick watched them haul it away.

It seemed he was the only one questioning his decision to save half of a rough-hewn section of timber when they were surrounded by forest.

Nick offered ice cream bars in exchange for their labor, but the teens had already made plans to spend the rest of the afternoon at a popular swimming hole.

After the last truck disappeared in a cloud of dust, Nick cracked open a bottled water from the cooler and walked out to the patio to join Bucket, who'd claimed the only shady spot for his afternoon nap.

Nick contemplated going back inside, but without central air, the lodge felt like a sauna. And crowded with memories of the evening he'd spent with Jess.

"Got another one of those?" Anthony came around the corner of the building. "It's hotter than a chili pepper today."

"What are you doing here?" Nick realized how that sounded and rephrased the question. "Did you need another tool? I could have run back over."

"I haven't seen the place in a while," Anthony said mildly. "Wondered how things were coming along."

Uh-huh.

Nick knew the signs. Grandpop was checking up on him, too.

He reached into the cooler and grabbed another bottled water. Handed it to Anthony. "I've been working outside today. The team stopped over and helped clean up the yard."

Grandpop took a swig of water. "Because they know you'd do the same thing for them."

"And they want practice to start on time," Nick said with a laugh. "But I've decided only one remodel per lifetime."

"I'm still pretty good with a hammer," Grandpop said. "You don't have to go it alone."

"Said the man who won't let anyone touch his woodpile."

"I do my best thinking when I'm chopping wood."

"Then you understand."

Grandpop didn't answer. He was staring down at the dirt-encrusted slab of timber that Ben and Marc had set on a patch of dead grass near the patio.

"Is that the—"

"The original bar?" And proof that sentiment had won over common sense? "Yes." To both. "I'll probably end up hauling it away— Grandpop?" Nick leaped forward to steady Anthony. The man's thin frame had started to tremble like a leaf on an aspen tree.

"I'm fine." Grandpop's voice shook, too, as he tried to wrestle out of Nick's grip. "You can let go, Nicholas. I'm not going to keel over."

Nick wasn't so sure about that, but reluctantly obeyed. The moment Grandpop was free, he dropped to his knees on the patio.

Nick's heart stopped for three full beats before he realized that Grandpop's was still going strong. Strong enough to lift up the bar and point to a crisscross of white scar tissue in the bark.

"Look at this, Nicholas."

"I know. It's in rough shape…" Nick squatted down just in case Grandpop lost his balance, and peered at the underside of the bar. "Are those initials?"

"They sure are." Grandpop traced the pad of his thumb over the scratches in the wood.

Nick leaned closer.

A lopsided heart encircled the letters.

AS + JC. And then it dawned on him. His grandmother's maiden name was Callahan.

Nick's gaze cut to Grandpop and he saw the telltale moisture glistening in his eyes.

"*You* did this?"

"The one and only time I was guilty of vandalism." Grandpop pressed a hand against his heart. "Of course, I thought I was boldly declaring my undying love for the spunky redhaired girl who showed up at six o'clock every Friday night and sat at table number two. The hostess didn't see it that way, though. She added washing the dishes to my list of duties."

"You worked at the lodge?"

"Only the summer between my junior and senior year. I bussed tables and set up tables for special events. Your grandma was visiting her aunt Rose before she went to college.

"I tried to get her attention. She pretended to ignore me. And while all that was going on, we fell in love."

Nick could see where this was going. "Jessica…she isn't like Grandma Jenny. Grandma loved Winsome Lake."

"She did," Anthony agreed with a smile. "But not at first.

Winsome is the kind of place that has to grow on a person. Jenny had big plans and Winsome is a small town."

"Like Whitney."

"Whitney Blake and Jessica are *nothing* alike." Grandpop's bony elbow sank into Nick's side to push the point home. "I think you know that, Nicholas."

He did. Just like everyone in the family knew his grandparents' romance could have been the plot for one of those popular chick flick–type movies. But Nick had never heard of any bumps along their road to happiness until now.

But there were bumps and then there were roadblocks. Detours. No-trespassing signs…

"I appreciate what you're trying to do, but there's no reason for Jessica to stay."

"You care about her, don't you?"

Nick wanted to deny it, but he'd been taught to always tell the truth. "Yes."

"Then do what I did." Grandpop squeezed his shoulder. "Give her one."

Chapter Thirty-Three

Elaine should have known that Matthew would make an entrance.

Nita, Merri and Peg had already staked a claim in their usual spots at the table. Jess had left for Dan's Market with Christopher and a shopping list shortly after the women arrived.

Elaine was sipping her tea, sifting through photographs of Merri's brothers, when her first Thursday morning at home was disrupted by an ominous growl.

Peg cocked her head toward the sound and frowned. "I hope the Petersons didn't give in and let their son buy that motorcycle he's been begging them for. Bosco hides under the bed when Frank runs his leaf blower."

"Probably someone from out of town taking a shortcut to the lake," Nita said without looking up. "They'll keep going."

"Did you hear that, baby?" Peg crooned to Bosco, who'd

already dived underneath the table. "That bad motorcycle is going to keep right on going."

The growl rose in volume and intensity and the china teacups in the hutch above the buffet began to rattle.

Right along with Elaine's pulse.

He wouldn't...

After forty-eight hours of silence, Elaine had started to think that Matthew's last text had been one of those polite, well-meaning gestures, like the friend who sees you at the grocery store and claims they want to get together for coffee "sometime." But then you don't see them until the next high school reunion.

Elaine listened for the growl to fade as the bike swept down Woodwind Lane and spiraled toward the lake. Instead, the noise stopped so abruptly that even Peg looked concerned.

"Do you think it broke down?"

"Maybe it got stuck in the pothole I've been asking the city to fix," Nita said.

Or, Elaine fought the urge to join Bosco under the table, maybe it was *parked*. Outside her house.

"I'll be right back." She set the cup down on the plate. "You don't have to..."

The three women were already on their feet.

Elaine reached for the cane propped against the wall behind her. Not because she needed it for balance, but so she could clobber Matthew on the head with it.

Because even with a helmet concealing his features, there was no denying the man who'd invaded Elaine's neighborhood was the same one who'd been invading her thoughts every waking hour since she'd come home.

"I'll—" Elaine turned around in the doorway and bumped into Merri, who in turn bumped into Nita and Peg. Bosco was still nowhere in sight, but Violet had jumped up on the windowsill in the living room, curious what all the fuss was about.

"He must be lost," Nita muttered. "I can't imagine who he knows around here..."

"Nita, right?" Matthew had already pulled off his helmet and looped it through the handlebar. His hair was mussed and a grain of stubble shadowed his jaw, which made him look more like the villain of the story than the hero.

Until he grinned.

Nita's mouth opened but the only sound that came out was a noise that sounded like a cross between a gasp and a wheeze.

Elaine couldn't think of what to say, either, but it didn't matter, because Matthew's black leather boots were eating up the space between them and he was greeting her friends as if he'd known them all his life.

"I was hoping you'd all still be here." He extended his hand. "Merri?"

A beat of silence followed the question and then Merri nodded hesitantly. "Yes. Yes, I am."

Peg, who was extremely protective of Elaine and Bosco, wasn't as easily charmed by a stranger on a loud motorcycle.

"Who are you?" she demanded.

Matthew's gaze slid to Elaine. Laughter crackled in his eyes. "You've been home for two days, and you haven't mentioned me?"

"No." Peg answered the question for her. "She hasn't."

Over Matthew's shoulder, Elaine could see curtains moving in the front windows of the houses across the street. The mail carrier had paused on her route and was pretending to look for something in her bag.

"This is Matthew Jeffries," Elaine said. "Matthew is..."

They all leaned forward. So did Matthew.

"He... We met at Sunrise." It seemed like the safest response until Elaine figured it out.

Peg clucked her tongue. "I suppose you crashed that thing," she said, not quite ready to forgive him yet. She looked him up and down. "Everything looks good, though. Nothing out of place that I can see."

Another grin. "Thank you, Peg."

A car cruised past at a snail's pace, the driver hanging halfway out the window, gawking first at the Harley crouched beside the curb and then at Matthew.

Elaine had to get him off the street. But that meant inviting him into the house...

"Come inside out of the heat." Merri linked her arm through Matthew's. "You must be as hot as Jess's cast-iron skillet, dressed in all that black leather."

"I won't turn down a glass of water." Matthew's eyes met Elaine's over Merri's head and he winked. She volleyed a warning look in return, but the smile that lifted the corners of her lips proved that her emotions had gone rogue.

They filed through the front door and into the living room.

Matthew spotted Violet soaking up the sun and took an unsanctioned detour over to the window.

"Don't pick her up!" The chorus of voices, Elaine's included, didn't seem to faze him.

Violet's ears flattened and then she stretched out her neck, giving the stranger permission to move closer. Which, in Elaine's experience, could have been a trap, but in Matthew's case, meant she was offering him the chance to win her over.

Which, of course, he did.

Out of the corner of her eye, Elaine saw Merri and Nita nodding in approval.

"I don't want to interrupt your scrapbooking session."

Matthew looked at Peg. "But I'd like to meet Bosco, if he's here."

Peg beamed, not mentioning that her beloved dog was cowering under the table in a Harley-induced state of panic at the moment. "He is."

It appeared Matthew had officially won everyone over.

They filed through the kitchen, where the smell of the sweet rolls Jess had made for breakfast still lingered in the air.

"You look good," Matthew whispered in her ear.

"Jessica," Elaine said, trying to ignore the shiver that coasted down her spine. "I think I've gained five pounds already."

"Coffee?" Nita, who'd been leading the procession to the dining room, paused by the island. "Or a glass of Jess's mint tea?"

"She brews it herself from the herbs in Elaine's garden," Merri said.

"Tea would be great."

"I'll get it," Elaine offered quickly.

Her attempt to separate Matthew from the herd backfired. He was swept up in a tide of perfume and carried into the dining room.

Elaine wanted to bang her head against the cabinet door, but reached inside for another glass instead.

When she entered the dining room, Matthew was sitting at the head of the table, a tower of photos in front of him. When Elaine set the iced tea down at his elbow, she saw a five-by-seven of Bosco wearing an It's My First Birthday bib around his neck. Elaine had been at the party. She'd brought a chipmunk squeaky toy that looked like the one who taunted Bosco from the willow tree in their backyard for the occasion.

"I dog-sat a Frenchie for a friend last year. Smart critter.

Good-natured, too," Matthew added, earning Peg's undying loyalty.

Elaine sat down next to Merri and watched Matthew charm the rest of her friends. He wasn't used-car-salesman smooth, though. They were savvy, intuitive women. They would have seen through that right away.

He was the man Elaine had gotten to know over the past few weeks. Funny. Intelligent. Insightful.

And, she couldn't deny it, pretty easy on the eyes.

Nita's watch chirped and she glanced down at her wrist. "Christopher...he and Jess are leaving Dan's."

"The market," Elaine explained. "Jess wanted to buy tahini, but my guess is that no one will know what it is. Pasta is in the ethnic food aisle at Dan's."

"Christopher would rather go to the grocery store than the park now," Nita said. "We were there over an hour yesterday, talking to Phil in the meat department about the difference between flat iron and hanger steak. Phil claimed he had to take a phone call, but I know he Googled it."

"I didn't notice a grocery store, but I saw the park on my way through town," Matthew said.

"There's not much more to the town than that," Peg said affectionately. "But it's just the right size."

Merri turned to look at Matthew. "You didn't see the lake?"

The question sounded innocent enough, but Elaine knew better. Merri's bookshelves were filled with romance novels. This was a setup.

"Not yet," Matthew said.

"You *have* to see it," Peg chimed in. "It's beautiful on a day like today."

"I was hoping to get a tour of the neighborhood." Matthew leaned back in the chair, totally onto her friends' scheme and, judging from the laughter dancing in those whiskey-colored eyes, all in.

"I'd volunteer but my leathers are still at the dry cleaner," Elaine said.

A collective gasp told Elaine the women gathered around the table had no idea that Matthew's sole purpose in coming to Winsome Lake was to cause trouble.

His eyes twinkled. "I meant walking, if you feel up to it."

Elaine expected pushback, not smiles, from the women who'd fussed at her earlier that morning about climbing the stairs. Even Nita, who'd sworn off men after Christopher's father walked out on them, was bobbing her head.

"Elaine's therapist said she's supposed to be getting out for a walk every day," she told Matthew.

"I don't want to leave you alone—"

"Since when?" Nita snorted. "It's not like you're working on an album."

No. But she could start one…

"We'll be fine." Merri dismissed them with a wave of her hand. "Take your time."

The moment they were alone, Elaine bumped Matthew's leg with the tip of her cane.

"You had to pick a Thursday."

"I told you I wanted to meet your friends."

Elaine couldn't blame him for that. "They're great, aren't they?"

"They are," Matthew agreed. "I do have one question, though."

"Okay."

"Why are you living in someone else's house?"

And the question confused her. "Because…it's my house."

"Is it? Because there isn't anything in there that looks like the Elaine Haviland I know."

"You don't know me very well," Elaine murmured.

"I'd like to change that."

It was easier to deal with the house than Matthew's honesty.

"I bought the house from Samantha O'Dell when I moved to Winsome. It was already furnished, so I didn't feel the need to go out and buy something new."

"That explains the couch," Matthew said drily. "But not the wallpaper roses and the Brady Bunch carpeting."

"I had no idea that interior design was part of chaplain's training."

Matthew's lips twitched. "It wasn't." His hand cupped her elbow and he steered her around a deep crack in the sidewalk. "But I do have eyes. How long have you lived there?"

"Twenty-five years," Elaine admitted grudgingly.

"Are you in the Witness Protection Program?"

"Matt!" Elaine choked on a laugh. "Seriously?"

"It's the only thing that makes sense."

Elaine stopped so quickly she began to teeter. In the space between two heartbeats, Matthew's hand was on her arm, steadying her. But the words he'd said continued to ping-pong inside Elaine's head until they merged into a single thought.

He was right.

Elaine didn't care for the wallpaper roses or the painted doors or the couch, for that matter. The only thing in the entire living room she actually *liked* was a piano she couldn't play.

When Elaine had moved to Winsome Lake, she'd wanted to fit into the neighborhood so badly. She was afraid that any changes, no matter how small, would remind everyone on Woodwind Lane that she wasn't Samantha. She'd left the heavy drapes on the windows and called a repairman whenever the ancient refrigerator started making funny noises. Had the hardware store make up a batch of blue paint for touch-ups on the kitchen cabinets.

Elaine's office was the one room in the house she'd renovated, and no one but Jessica had ever seen it.

No wonder Matthew had teased her about being in Witness Protection. She'd been hiding in plain sight.

"I was kidding about the WITSEC thing," Matthew murmured. "But now I admit I'm getting a little worried."

Elaine realized she was standing in the middle of the sidewalk, watching the past twenty-five years pass before her eyes.

"Not Witness Protection," she said slowly. "The protection part, though…you might actually be onto something."

Matthew slanted a look at her. "The light fixture over the dining room table isn't bad."

"I replaced it five years ago because Peg needed better lighting. She never remembers to bring her reading glasses."

They were still on the sidewalk. Matthew's hand slid down Elaine's arm and his fingers wove through hers. Not to hold her up…to keep her close.

"Ready to go farther?"

Elaine knew Matthew was referring to their walk. She also knew that while he might point out things along the way, he would always let her set the pace. Maybe it was time to push herself a little.

"I think I am," Elaine said slowly. "When we get back to the house, there's something I want to show you."

"Intriguing. Sea foam–green tile? Macramé plant hanger?" Matthew smiled down at her.

Elaine loved his smile.

"My office."

Chapter Thirty-Four

Jess blew a strand of hair off her forehead and looked at the clock.

Peg, Nita and Merri had pounced on her the moment she'd walked through the door.

"You have to make lunch so he'll stay a little longer," Merri had said.

"He?" Jess echoed.

"Matthew Jeffries. The man who owns the motorcycle parked out front. He came to visit Elaine. They met at Sunrise."

Jess had noticed the sleek black Road King lounging next to the curb, overshadowing Peg and Frank's light blue Hyundai like the new kid on the first day of school.

"And he's here to see Elaine," Peg said as if that part of the story bore repeating.

"They went for a walk, but if you have something for

lunch when they get back, Elaine will have to invite him to stay."

"Does she *want* him to stay?" Jess asked cautiously.

"Of course she does." Merri folded her arms over her chest. "There were more sparks going off in the dining room than fireworks at the Fourth of July."

Jess looked at Nita.

"There was definitely something," she confirmed.

Jess hoped her role in the *something* wouldn't end up getting her fired.

"How long ago did they leave?"

Peg and Merri looked at Nita, who consulted her watch.

"Ten minutes ago," she guessed. "Give or take a few minutes."

If they were walking, Elaine would tire easily.

Which meant that Jess had about half an hour to whip up something for lunch. Give or take a few minutes.

"Lunch for two it is." Jess pointed to the pantry. "Grab an apron, Christopher. I'm going to need your help."

"Yes, Chef!" He snapped to attention as Jess pulled a bag of free-range chicken breasts from the grocery bag and set to work.

"We'll pack up and get out of your way," Nita said.

Peg scooped up Bosco. "But we want to hear all the details later."

"You want me to cook *and* eavesdrop?"

Merri beamed at her. "Of course, sweetie. It's called multitasking."

Jess heard Elaine before she saw her.

The breeze caught the sound of her laughter outside the window and swirled it through the air like dandelion seeds.

Jess had heard Elaine laugh before, but the texture was lighter this time. More carefree.

"They're b-back," Christopher said.

"Okay. You know what to do." Jess would have preferred a little more time, but everything except the dessert was ready. "I'll plate the chicken and vegetables."

Merri had brought over a bag of fairy tale eggplant, a beautiful shade of lavender with streaks of vanilla cream. Jess had cut it into pieces, tossed it in olive oil and shoved it in the oven while Christopher took control of the mallet and happily pounded out the chicken breasts.

Now he galloped through the living room and intercepted them at the front door.

"Hello. I'm Christopher B-Benjamin Gardner," Jess heard him say. "Lunch is b-being served in the garden today."

Jess grinned. He'd been practicing the last line but she hadn't told him to recite it in the lofty tone of a high-end restaurant's maître d'.

She put the plates on a tray along with two linen napkins she'd found in the drawer of the buffet and stepped outside.

Christopher stood at attention beside the couple seated at the bistro table. His apron was gone, but somewhere between the kitchen and the front door, he'd planted Jess's toque on his head.

Jess's gaze fell on Elaine first. Her cheeks were flushed from the walk, but nothing in Elaine's expression indicated Jess was going to be fired for following orders from the Scrappy Ladies instead of waiting on hers.

"Matthew, this is Jessica Keaton," Elaine said. "I don't know what I would have done without her the past few days."

Jess flushed at the compliment.

"It's nice to meet you, Jessica."

Now she understood why the Scrappy Ladies had orchestrated an intimate lunch for two. Matthew was close to Elaine's age with kind eyes and Harrison Ford good looks that complemented the motorcycle parked out front.

"It's nice to meet you, too." Jess set the plates down in front of them and filled their glasses with sparkling water.

"Can I start the d-dessert now, Chef?" Christopher asked in a loud whisper.

Jess nodded, and he bounded toward the house.

"I can already tell you that I might not have room for dessert," Elaine murmured.

"I will." Matthew smiled up at Jess. "I don't know how you pulled this together while we were gone, but everything looks delicious."

"Chicken Dijon goes together fairly quickly," Jess said. "And it helps when you have fresh herbs right outside the door."

Elaine remained silent. When she picked up her fork almost tentatively, Jess instantly recognized her mistake. The chicken breast was thin but Elaine still needed both hands to cut it.

Jess wished a crack in the patio would open up and swallow her whole.

Why hadn't she chosen something easier to manage with one hand? Turned Merri's vegetables into a nice gazpacho instead?

"Wow. Amazing. You have to taste this." Matthew reached out, snipped off the corner of Elaine's filet and held it up to her lips without a hint of awkwardness or embarrassment.

While Elaine was chewing, he deftly cut up the rest and then turned the knife on his own.

No wonder Matthew Jeffries had won over the Scrappy Ladies.

"I'll leave you alone to enjoy your lunch." Jess backed away from the table.

"You and Christopher should join us," Elaine said.

"Thank you, but it was Say Cheese Day at Dan's and we ate enough samples at the deli to tide us over until supper," Jess said.

Neither one of them, she noticed, tried to change her mind. In fact, Jess wasn't sure they even realized she'd gone back inside the house.

Christopher was already lining a glass bowl with the chunks of leftover pound cake when Jess walked into the kitchen.

"Do you think M–Miss Elaine is going to get married?" he asked.

"Whoa there, bud." Jess laughed. "I'm not sure this even counts as a date."

"They're eating t-together and they're laughing," Christopher said. "That's a date, J-Jessica."

If only she'd known that the night she'd gone over to Nick's.

Jess still hadn't talked to him. She hadn't even seen him in the neighborhood since Elaine had come home. It was possible Nick was giving Elaine some space, but Jess had a feeling he was avoiding *her*. She'd sensed a subtle change while he was helping with Sienna's party, but Jess assumed that, like her, he'd been focused on the preparations. It wasn't until later she realized that while Nick had teased and joked with Christopher, he'd barely spoken to her.

She shouldn't have said anything about her past.

Now whenever Nick looked at her, he'd remember their conversation and see the girl who'd taught herself to cook so she could eat, not the one who'd become a chef.

"I'm d-done with this part," Christopher said. "What's next, Chef?"

"The fun part."

Jess whipped the cream and layered it with the pound cake and a pint of blackberries she'd bought at a farmer's market stand in the park on the way home. Trifle had saved Jess on more than one occasion in the past. It was one of those simple yet elegant desserts that looked like it had taken an entire day to make.

"I need some recon, Christopher. Are they finished with the main entrée?"

The teen loped over to the screen door and returned a few seconds later with a thumbs-up.

"C-can I carry it out?"

Jess nodded. "That would be great. I'll be right behind you with the coffee."

Elaine and Matthew looked up when the screen door opened.

It might have been Jess's imagination, but their chairs looked closer together.

"The food was amazing, Jessica," Matthew said. "I've eaten at restaurants all over the country and I've never tasted a sauce like this."

"The secret is Elaine's lemon thyme."

"I have lemon thyme?" Elaine looked around the garden. "Where is it?"

Matthew grinned. "Let me guess. You didn't plant this garden."

"No...but I've been keeping it alive," Elaine shot back. "That has to count for something."

"It does, as long as you're enjoying it, too."

"They're t-teasing each other," Christopher told Jess. "People on d-dates do that, too."

Jess tried not to smile. "Plates, Chris," she said under her breath.

He whistled while he collected the dishes, and Jess set the trifle in the center of the table.

Matthew turned his attention to dessert. "We should have started with this."

"It's called a t–trifle," Christopher said. "Jessica says that means p-party in a bowl."

Matthew laughed. "I can see why." He handed the serving spoon to Elaine. "I'll let you do the honors."

Jess barely knew the man, but she really liked Matthew Jeffries.

She paused a few feet away, waiting for them to take that first bite.

"I want this for supper." Elaine's eyes drifted closed. "And breakfast tomorrow morning."

"J-Jessica is going to have a restaurant someday," Christopher announced. "It's her b-big dream, isn't it?"

He looked at Jess for confirmation, a wide smile on his face.

Jess tried to smile back.

Now she understood where Nita's struggle came from.

How could you tell someone like Christopher, someone sweet and optimistic and joyful, that sometimes dreams, small or big, just didn't come true at all?

Chapter Thirty-Five

It's my birthday. I am 13 today! Officially A TEENAGER!! While Mama was washing her hair in the bathroom at the truck stop, the lady behind the counter asked where we were going. I told her that I wasn't sure. All Mama says is that we'll know when we get there. The lady said that sounds like quite an adventure and she gave me this diary! She said I should keep it in my backpack and write down all my wishes and hopes and secrets on the way.

So here goes!

I wish that Mama will drive all the way to California so I can see the ocean.

I hope I get some new clothes for my birthday so the kids at my new school won't laugh at me.

My secret is that I'm not going to tell anyone, not even Mama, that I have a diary.

★ ★ ★

Jess smoothed a piece of tape between two pieces of paper and connected a broken row of hearts and flowers.

It had taken three hours of sifting through the torn paper trail until she'd pieced together the first page of the diary.

Jess knew nothing about Libby Tucker's life from birth to twelve, but a wish, a hope and a secret told Jess they had a lot in common.

The overhead light flickered, keeping time with the rumble of thunder outside. A flash of lightning illuminated the garden. Stretched out on the floor, surrounded by paper, Jess caught a glimpse of the crab apple tree by the garage. Embraced by the storm, its branches twisted in a wild dance.

Jess hoped the noise wouldn't wake up Elaine. Vanessa Richards had spent several hours at the house that afternoon, pointing out the potential danger in seemingly benign household items like footstools and throw rugs. She'd glared at the stairs, then at Elaine and pulled out her phone to order a hospital bed for the first floor until a handrail could be installed.

It was Jess who came up with a solution that appeased both Elaine and the social worker. A sleeper sofa would fit in Elaine's office and give her more privacy than a hospital bed tucked in a corner of the living room.

Jess had already decided she'd work on Libby's diary in the evenings, so having the office double as a bedroom wouldn't pose too much of a challenge.

While Vanessa was comparing the ratio of outlets to nightlights, Jess pulled up the website of a local furniture store and found two in stock. She'd held up her phone and Elaine pointed to the one covered in turquoise leather. The manager promised it would be the first delivery on Monday morning, which sentenced Elaine to two more nights on the living room couch.

She never complained about any of the changes, but by the time Vanessa left, Elaine had looked exhausted.

Jess made cream of broccoli soup for supper and set it on the coffee table, next to Elaine's cell phone and the TV remote.

The rain started an hour after Jess closed herself in the office, surrounded by the jagged pieces of Libby Tucker's life.

The last time she'd checked on Elaine, shortly before nine, her employer was sound asleep, the bowl on the coffee table scraped clean.

The light flickered again and Jess checked the time on her phone. Almost midnight.

A shard of lightning ripped open the sky as Jess picked up another piece of paper. The boom that followed rattled the entire house, but it was the loud, feminine shriek that pushed Jess to her feet.

She tore down the hallway, her journey guided by the soft glow of the brand-new night-lights, and fumbled for the switch on the wall of the living room.

Light flooded the room and Jess's gaze immediately went to her employer. Elaine was on the floor, wedged between the couch and the coffee table.

Sienna was kneeling next to her. She was soaking wet, her clothing plastered against her body like a second skin. Her eyes locked with Jess's.

"I'm sorry!" she wailed. "I didn't know she was here!"

Elaine was already trying to sit up when Jess rushed over. She slid her arm around Elaine's waist and heard her suck in a ragged breath.

Her ribs…

"Sienna, let's give Elaine some room, okay?"

The girl was shaking so hard they were all getting wet. "I didn't know she was here," she said again.

"Run upstairs and get some dry clothes from my closet," Jess directed.

Sienna whirled around and dashed away, shedding a trail of water on the carpet behind her.

"I'm fine, Jessica." Elaine used Jess's arm for support and eased back onto the couch. "I'm not so sure about Sienna, though. When she pulled the afghan off the couch, I don't think she was expecting to see someone underneath it."

Jess mentally smacked herself.

The past few days had been so hectic, it hadn't occurred to her that Elaine wasn't the only one sleeping in the living room.

"Elaine..."

"Later," Elaine murmured. "You should check on her."

Jess made her way upstairs and knocked on the door. It opened a few seconds later. Sienna had found a pair of yoga pants and a clean T-shirt, but with her dripping hair and wide eyes, still looked as bedraggled and forlorn as a stray kitten.

"I can't go down there," she moaned.

"Elaine is okay. You startled her, that's all." Jess tucked her arm through Sienna's. The shudder that rocked through the girl almost threw both of them off balance. "Come downstairs. You'll see."

Sienna reluctantly accompanied her down the stairs, but kept a death grip on Jess's arm.

Elaine sat on the couch with the afghan draped around her shoulders and Violet purring in her lap.

"I'm sorry," Sienna whispered.

"Don't apologize," Elaine said. "The storm would have woken me up anyway."

On cue, thunder shook the house again.

"This reminds me of a scene from *The Sound of Music*." Elaine smiled. "I feel like I should clutch a pillow against my chest and break into song."

Jess had never seen the movie, but Sienna must have. Because, wonder of wonders, she returned Elaine's smile with a tentative one of her own.

Some of the tension holding Jess's heart in a vise loosened its grip.

"I'll warm up some soup."

Jess backed into the kitchen, relieved that Elaine was home and Sienna had someone to confide in again.

While the soup was heating, she cut a few slices of sourdough bread and arranged them on a plate. Jess opened the fridge to get the butter and saw the leftover trifle. She sank a serving spoon into the center of the dessert and added the bowl to the tray.

Sienna was sitting at the piano when Jess carried the tray into the living room. There was no music. Sienna's eyes were closed, her fingertips brushing across the surface of each key as if she were reading Braille.

Okay.

They'd start with the trifle.

Elaine tucked the afghan around Sienna's shoulders, put her finger against her lips in a silent warning to Violet to behave herself and reached for her cane.

Jess was at the counter, cleaning up from the impromptu feast she'd served in the living room. Her movements reminded Elaine of Sienna at the piano. Silent. Focused. Her concentration, by accident or design, keeping the rest of the world at arm's length.

"She's asleep."

The tap of Elaine's cane against the floor should have

warned Jess she wasn't alone, but a few seconds passed before she turned around. The turbulence in her eyes reminded Elaine of Sienna, too.

She leaned against the island, ignoring the flare of pain in her rib cage.

"I'm sorry..."

They stopped, stared at each other as the apologies tangled in the air.

Jess waited for Elaine to go first.

"I should have told you about Sienna." Elaine wasn't quite sure what Jess's reaction would be, but shock hadn't been on the list of possibilities.

"I was about to say the same thing," Jess said.

All right. Now Elaine was shocked. "She's shown up in the middle of the night since you came here?"

Jess hesitated. "A few times," she hedged.

A few times.

Elaine obviously slept more deeply than Jess. The one time she'd discovered Sienna sleeping on the couch, the girl had told Elaine she'd taken a break from practicing and drifted off for a few minutes. Elaine had wondered at the time if it was true, but didn't want to press her.

"When you were heating up the soup, Sienna said that she and her mom got into an argument tonight."

Jess's expression darkened. "Did she say why?"

"Desiree put in for third shift and Sienna doesn't want her to. Desiree told her that she'd make more money and accused Sienna of being selfish." Elaine sighed. "The apartment complex they live in can get a little rowdy. Maybe Sienna is nervous about being alone at night."

"Or maybe she's afraid she won't be," Jess said tightly. "Sienna said Cal has been spending a lot of time there."

"Who is Cal?"

"Her mother's boyfriend." She frowned. "Sienna didn't tell you about him?"

"No," Elaine admitted. "I'm hearing all of this for the first time. I could tell that Sienna was having a hard time after her parents separated, but she wouldn't talk about it. What did you do to get her to open up to you?"

"Nothing," Jess said slowly. "She was here early in the morning, so I made her blueberry pancakes for breakfast. And avocado toast. That was a failure, though, because Sienna doesn't like crusts and runny yolks."

"Pancakes." Elaine remembered offering Sienna a glass of orange juice once.

Why hadn't it occurred to her that teenagers liked to eat?

"Sienna and Cal… I take it they don't get along?"

"He makes her feel…uncomfortable."

The tea Elaine had just swallowed backed up in her throat. *Lord.*

"She wouldn't tell me why, but I can read between the lines," Jess murmured. "Sienna is used to handling things on her own. She's afraid if she says anything about Cal, her life could get worse."

Something told Elaine that Jess was speaking from experience.

She could read between the lines, too.

"Why don't you go back to bed," Elaine suggested. "I'm going to have another cup of tea and watch the sun come up over the garden."

And lay all of this at God's feet.

Jess was already reaching for the kettle on the stove. She topped off Elaine's cup with a stream of hot water that raised the tepid brown liquid to the rim.

"I suppose there isn't any of that trifle left?"

"Sorry." A smile shimmered in Jess's eyes. "Sienna ate the

rest. But I set aside some petit fours in the freezer for a rainy day. It's after midnight, so I'd say this qualifies."

"So would I."

Jess took those out, too, and put them on a plate. "This is the appetizer. Pancakes at seven."

Elaine thought of all the times the Lord had brought Sienna's name to mind while she was in rehab. She'd prayed for Sienna's protection. For peace. Encouragement.

"Jess?"

Jess paused in the doorway and glanced over her shoulder.

"What you said about Sienna not having anyone she can count on? It's not entirely the truth." Elaine smiled. "She had you."

Chapter Thirty-Six

Nick could feel beads of sweat popping out on his forehead and wished he could blame the heat. But the storm that had rolled through town during the night had taken the balmy temperatures with it, leaving behind a cloudless sky and a breeze scented with rain and freshly cut grass.

He glanced at Elaine's kitchen window again. Nick had seen the silhouette of someone standing at the sink when he'd started up the lawn mower, but they hadn't waved or poked their head outside to say hello.

A dead giveaway the person had been Jess.

It was his fault things had gotten awkward. Nick had decided it was only a matter of time before Jess left Winsome, so he'd stepped back first to avoid getting hurt. But the truth was, not having any kind of relationship with her hurt even more.

Grandpop had told him to give Jess a reason to stay, but right now Nick needed something to rebuild the bridge he'd burned when he'd left without a word the day of Sienna's solo.

He dusted off the blades of grass sticking to his jeans, adrenaline sluicing through his veins as he strode up the walkway to the front door.

"Nick." It was Elaine who answered his knock on the door. "I was hoping you'd pop in for a few minutes. We can have a glass of iced tea in the garden. I can't wait to hear how you and Violet got along."

The cat stretched out on top of the piano was giving Nick the stink eye, which pretty much summed up their relationship. Well, that and the permanent scar on Bucket's nose.

There was no sign of Jess when Nick entered the kitchen, but she'd been baking again. A dozen buttermilk biscuits were cooling on the counter.

"Shortcake." Elaine had come up behind him. "Jess bought two pints of strawberries at the farmer's market yesterday morning. I have to be careful when I tell her what I missed during rehab or it suddenly appears on the counter."

"Tell her you missed s'mores crème brûlée," Nick said. "It's amazing."

Elaine tipped her head to one side. "I've heard Jess has been baking for the neighborhood, but no one mentioned that one."

Now he was blushing. "We...she..." And stammering. "Jess made dessert after our fish fry."

"And the fish fry was payment for my cast-iron skillet." Jess walked into the kitchen, and Nick's heart slammed against his rib cage. Now that Elaine was home, he half expected Jess would be wearing her chef's whites again. But today her hair was tied back with a red bandanna and she wore loose-fitting denim overalls over a plain white T-shirt.

Nick's gaze dropped to her bare feet and lingered a moment on the apple-red polish on her toes.

"So…" Elaine cleared her throat, reminding Nick they weren't alone. "I see you two have already met."

Met.

Kissed.

Color flared in Jess's cheeks, and Nick wondered if she was thinking the same thing.

"Nick and I were about to have a glass of iced tea in the garden, Jess," Elaine said. "Would you like to join us?"

Jess's expression said she'd rather consume raw chicken. "No. Thank you, though. I only took a break from…from straightening your office to see if you needed anything."

Elaine chuckled. "I'd say strawberry shortcake, but I'm sure there's an unwritten rule somewhere that you have to wait until lunch."

"It's fruit. No guilt." Jess's warm smile made Nick grateful that she and Elaine seemed to be getting along.

Grateful and a little envious.

She was having a difficult time looking *him* in the eye.

"I'll bring out a tray." Jess skirted around him, leaving the faint scent of lavender and vanilla in her wake.

"I think that's our cue to leave, Nicholas," Elaine said cheerfully.

Maybe. But Nick wasn't ready to give up yet.

He offered Elaine his arm, and they walked outside onto the patio. She moved slowly, both eyes fixed on the ground as if she was concentrating on every step, but Nick was a football coach and well acquainted with injuries. Her grip might lack strength, but determination overcame a lot of obstacles.

Once she was settled in a chair at the bistro table, Nick sat down on the opposite side.

"So..." Elaine leaned forward. "Have you made much progress?"

Nick choked on a breath, cast a quick look at the house. "Excuse me?"

"On the lodge. You'd just started the renovations when I landed in the hospital."

The lodge. Right.

"The old dining room is finished, and I should be starting on the upstairs rooms next week..." Nick was distracted by the snap of the screen door.

Jess emerged from the house, carrying the wooden cutting board she'd converted into a serving tray. Nick rose because it seemed like the polite thing to do. His knee bumped against the table and the jar of daisies in the center began to wobble.

"Sorry." Nick righted the vase before it tipped over and sent a river of water flowing over the side and onto Elaine's lap. The daisies continued to wag their heads at him, though, reminding Nick that he was supposed to be a super-focused, coordinated athlete.

And he was. Unless Jess was around.

Jess waited until Nick sat down again before she trusted him not to upend the contents on the tray.

"The shortcake looks delicious, Jess," Elaine said. "For some reason, my biscuits always look like hockey pucks."

Jess smiled.

Nick had noticed that Jess liked to watch people's reactions when they took that first bite of the food she'd prepared, but by the time he picked up his fork, she was already halfway to the door.

Before Nick lost his nerve, he called out, "Jess?"

She paused midstep and turned around, her expression wary.

"The team did some work at the lodge last week and I'd

like to thank them with a pizza party. I was hoping you'd cater it." Nick saw Jess's shoulders stiffen and plunged on. "I wouldn't expect you to do it for free, of course. Any evening this week would be great. Or a weekend. Whatever works best for you..."

Nick paused to take a breath. The ball was in Jess's court now. He expected her to pick it up and go home, especially when she started shaking her head.

"I won't have time. Elaine—"

"Wouldn't mind tagging along, actually."

Nick did a mental fist pump when his neighbor stepped from the sidelines and joined the conversation.

Jess, on the other hand, looked as tense as Bucket when Nick pulled up in front of the veterinary office. "But...the grocery shopping, the prep work, will take me away from other things."

"It would be good for me to get out a little and I'd love to see what Nick has accomplished while I was gone."

Was Nick imagining things, or was there a hint of laughter in Elaine's voice now?

"And I'm sure Christopher would love to show off his sous-chef skills for the team if you needed some help," she added.

Nick made a mental note to ask Elaine if she knew anything about football. Because he could sure use her gift of strategy when it came to running plays.

Jess nodded. "All right."

Reluctant, but at this point Nick would take it.

"You can use the kitchen at the lodge," he told her. "I'm going to set up a volleyball net for the guys, too." Buoyed by the thought of spending time with Jess again, he went for the gold. "What day should we plan on?"

"I'll check my calendar and get back to you."

Jess turned on her heel and disappeared inside the house. Nick blew out a sigh.

"Don't be discouraged, Coach." Elaine reached out and patted his hand. "Jessica's calendar is synced with mine for the time being and I happen to know we're free on Tuesday."

"There isn't a weed in that garden, Elaine Haviland. Why are you sitting on the ground?"

The fence cut Nita off at the shoulders, but Elaine could tell her friend's arms were crossed.

"You'd laugh."

"Maybe. But tell me anyway. After the morning I've had, I could use one."

"On hold with the insurance company?" Elaine knew Nita wrangled with them on a regular basis, but when it came to Christopher, she hung on with the tenacity of a bulldog.

"YouTube. Two hours spent watching someone make choux pastry."

"I'm watching a caterpillar spin a cocoon." Wrestling with God about the things she couldn't control. Like a teenage girl trying to plan for the future and a young woman who didn't want to talk about the past.

A smile softened the sharp angles and planes of Nita's face. "That sounds like a good way to pass a summer afternoon. I'll put these sheets on the line and join you."

She came around the fence a few minutes later and dropped to the ground beside Elaine. She leaned forward to inspect the tiny creature's progress.

"Do you think he's terrified of change, too?"

Nita, with her usual directness, voiced what Elaine had been thinking when she'd seen the caterpillar hanging upside down, attached to the underside of a leaf by one thin gossamer thread.

"Trust should come that naturally to all of us," Elaine murmured.

The caterpillar began to sway in the breeze created by Nita's sigh.

"Maybe it does, if you knew all along you were meant to be a butterfly."

"Christopher's surgery," Elaine guessed.

"I'm terrified. He's excited. He sees the doctors fixing the valve in his heart like the plumber fixed our broken pipe. He doesn't realize the risk of anesthesia or infection. He sees himself coming out of the surgery whole and happy. Stronger than he was before."

Elaine reached out and squeezed Nita's hand. "Chris has always had a strong faith."

"He knew you were coming home." Nita squeezed back. "I had my doubts about that, too."

"So did I."

"Change of subject before we both melt into a puddle on the ground." Nita checked her watch. "We have ten minutes before Chrissy realizes I'm gone and three months to cover. Where do you want me to start?"

"Cut to the last two weeks," Elaine said. "Nick stopped by this morning and asked Jessica if she would cater a pizza party for his team. She agreed, but I sensed some tension. Did they have a misunderstanding or something?"

Nita's lips twitched. "I'm not sure about the misunderstanding…but there's definitely a something."

"Don't tell me the three of you have been matchmaking while I was gone."

"Okay."

"Nita!"

"They're both single."

"There's usually a little more to it than that."

"Like fireworks?"

"Fireworks?" Elaine repeated. "I think I would have noticed fireworks."

Nita gave her a look. "I'm not so sure about that."

"What does that mean?"

"Do you really want me to explain?"

No. No, she didn't.

"Well, I hope Nick isn't going to get his heart broken, because I don't think Jessica plans on making Winsome Lake her permanent home." Elaine shooed away a bee hovering near the caterpillar. "I don't know anything about her. She doesn't talk about her family. Where she came from. Why she's here…"

"I remember saying the same thing to Merri about you."

"I loved this town before I saw it!" The words tumbled over each other, but Elaine was so stunned by Nita's statement she didn't care. "And the day I moved into Sam's house, I loved all of you."

"I know you did." Nita caught Elaine's gaze and held it. "But it took a while before you let us love you back."

Elaine wanted to deny it. But twenty-five years ago, she'd been as guarded as Jess. Her life in pieces, like Libby's diaries.

Nita's watch chirped.

"Five minutes," she said. "My turn to pick the topic."

Elaine was not comforted by the gleam in Nita's eyes. "I'm not talking about Matthew."

"Good. Because this is about Lance Holcomb. He asked me out."

Elaine's elbow buckled and she almost toppled over onto the paving stones. "Lance Holcomb? As in *married-to-Jeanne* Lance Holcomb?"

Nita gave her a look. "It was before he married Jeanne, of course. We'd been attending the same Bible study for years and out of the blue one Sunday, he pulled me aside after class and asked if I would have dinner with him."

Elaine did a quick calculation in her head. "Lance and Jeanne have been married for almost a decade and you're just telling me this now?"

"It didn't matter. I turned him down."

Elaine didn't understand why. Everyone liked Lance Holcomb. He was calm and steady, with roots in Winsome Lake as deep as his faith. He also had a younger brother with cerebral palsy, so Lance understood the unique challenges a loved one with disabilities faced.

"Go ahead and ask," Nita said. "We both know you want to."

"All right…why?"

"When Tom left, he told me that he wouldn't have stayed even if Chrissy was…normal. He said he wasn't attracted to me anymore. He said he wanted a woman who knew how to have fun and wasn't tired all the time. Someone who was softer. Not so outspoken."

It was a good thing Tom Gardner had moved to Arizona after the divorce or Elaine would have been tempted to pay the man a visit.

"It was easier for Tom to blame you than face his own weaknesses," Elaine said.

"It's hard to convince yourself of that when your husband walks out the door. When Lance asked me out, all I heard was Tom, telling me I wasn't enough. If he didn't stay, why would anyone else?"

Elaine flinched at the raw pain in Nita's eyes. "That's not true, Nita."

"I know. But when it's someone you trust…someone you care about…you believe the lie.

"Lance was so proud the day he announced he'd met

someone on one of those online dating sites. People thought
he was making a mistake, but I was envious of Jeanne. It had
to have been scary to put herself out there, but look how it
turned out."

Nita paused, waiting for Elaine to connect the dots.

"You think I should go out with Matthew if he asks."

"I don't know what's going on in that head of yours, but
I don't want you to make the same mistake I did. Fear wants
you to say no. But a God-yes, as Chrissy likes to call it, is
always worth the risk."

Chapter Thirty-Seven

"Hey, Ms. Keaton!" A teenage boy ambled into the kitchen. "We're almost out of ice!"

Jess pointed at the box freezer in the corner. "It's Jess. And help yourself."

"Thanks!" He grinned and raised his hand to give Christopher a fist bump. "Are you sure you don't want to play on my team? I could use someone who knows how to spike a ball."

"Can't," Christopher said. "Jess needs m-me."

Actually, Jess had more help than she knew what to do with. Elaine sat on a folding chair, creating a spiral pattern out of pepperoni on the pizza crusts Jess had rolled out. Sienna stood at the prep station with Christopher, chopping up onions and bell peppers from Merri's garden.

And then there was the revolving door between the kitchen and the stretch of lawn that had been converted into a sports field for the afternoon.

Nick had set coolers filled with soda and bottled water on the patio, but for some reason every member of his football team, their girlfriends and the occasional parent, wandered into the kitchen under the guise of needing something. Ice. A refill on Jess's homemade caramel corn. Extra napkins.

In fact, the only person who hadn't invaded the kitchen was the man hosting the event.

The teenager left with two bags of ice slung over each shoulder and Jess slanted a look at Elaine.

"If they want to know how you're doing, why don't they just ask?"

Elaine looked up. Smiled. "Because I'm not the one they're curious about."

"Who..." Jess's knife almost sheared off the top layer of skin on her knuckles as the truth reared up and smacked her in the forehead. "Not me?"

"You're the new kid in town."

Or the outsider who might lead their beloved coach astray.

Like a compass needle seeking true north, Jess couldn't prevent another quick glance out the window. This time, like the last nine hundred and ninety-nine, Nick was surrounded by teenagers jostling for his attention. And seeing the hero-worship on their faces, it was obvious he was one of those rare coaches who'd found the perfect balance between mentor and role model, teacher and friend.

He was pretty perfect in a lot of ways.

Which explained the dark-haired woman who'd crashed the event while Jess was in the hot kitchen, shredding mozzarella, and positioned herself at Nick's side.

"S-smoke, Chef."

Jess's nose registered the scent a split second before Christopher's announcement.

She yanked open the oven door and slid the pizza out. The

cheese was bubbling, the crust, thankfully, a deep golden brown.

"Chris...another pepperoni, onion and mushroom."

"Yes, Chef." Christopher grabbed a colander filled with mushrooms and loped over to the sink.

It was a challenge, having only one oven when making pizza for a group this size, but Jess hoped the snacks she'd made had put a dent in the team's hunger while they waited.

She cut the pie into squares and carried it out to the picnic table Nick had set up in a pocket of shade under the trees.

A boisterous cheer erupted from the teenagers playing volleyball. Only this time Jess realized it was directed at her.

Before she could set the pizza down, the stampede of large, sweaty males was heading directly toward her. For one crazy second Jess was tempted to toss the pizza in the air and run.

A piercing whistle stopped the teens in their tracks.

"Form a line." Nick jogged up, a metal whistle dangling from a nylon chain around his neck.

And Jess had thought the guy looked good in a tool belt.

"It looks delicious, Coach," one of the boys said. "Not like the ones you usually make."

"Those came from a freezer. This one was made by a chef." Nick winked at Jess and it had a domino effect. Grins and nudges were passed down the line until they reached the tall, dark-haired woman at the end. Tan and fit, she wore denim shorts and a T-shirt with the words WIN. REPEAT. on the front.

"Jessica...this is Colby Wendt." Nick made the introductions when she moved to the front of the line. "Colby's in charge of the cheer squad."

"It's nice to meet you, Jessica." Colby grinned. "And Ben is right. This pizza looks amazing. The squad could make a fortune selling slices at the concession stand."

The red-haired girl standing behind her gasped. "That's a great idea! We have a fundraiser coming up at the end of October. Can we order the pizzas from you? We'd need like... I don't know...twenty of them."

Jess could feel Nick's eyes on her.

For a moment she let a future unfold in her imagination. Crisp days. Cool autumn days. Cheering on the Wildcats from the bleachers on Friday nights. Long walks with Bucket. Continuing Grandma Jenny's legacy by restocking the Silva family pantries with jars of applesauce.

Kisses as sweet and addictive as chocolate cake.

Jess manufactured a smile for Colby. The woman who already had a place in Winsome Lake. In Nick's life.

"I'd love to help out, but I won't be here that long."

Still awake?

Matthew's text popped up on Elaine's cell phone while she was sitting in a dark kitchen, nibbling on a cold pizza crust.

Funny he should ask.

After helping out at the lodge all afternoon, Elaine should have fallen asleep the minute her head touched the pillow. Which might have happened if she'd actually gone to bed instead of raiding the fridge for leftovers.

Yes. You?

Elaine added the last part just to make him smile.

Haha. How was the party?

I had too much pizza and an idea that scares me more than the step machine in PT.

Elaine waited. Instead of bubbles, her cell began to ring.

She should have known he'd call. Matthew had told her that text messages were like the drive-through of conversation. Fine when you didn't have a lot of time, but the flip side was, you missed out on a lot, too.

Like peoples' expressions. The undercurrent of panic and elation he would no doubt hear in her voice.

Elaine answered before she changed her mind. "Hi."

"Hi." Matthew's husky alto came over the line. "What's going on?"

"I wish I knew." Elaine shifted on the stool and winced when it squeaked. She didn't want Jess coming downstairs to check on her so she slipped out of the kitchen and limped down the hall to her office, pizza crust and phone in hand.

"You changed your mind about the book?"

The book.

Elaine's gaze shifted to the papers stacked neatly on her desk. The last time she and Matthew had talked, she'd told him that Jess had agreed to help her with the project. Jess hadn't said much, but based on the growing pile of diary pages and the empty tape dispenser in the wastebasket, she'd been making some progress, too.

"It's not about the book this time. Did you ever have something pop into your head, something you never would have thought of on your own, but once it's there, it won't let go?"

"Not too long ago, as a matter of fact. But keep going."

"Nick Silva, the coach who hired Jess to cater the pizza party, started renovating an old supper club over the winter. There isn't a lot going on up here, as you can imagine, so the lodge became kind of a gathering place for the community. I went there at least once a week before it closed down.

"Nick has done an incredible job fixing it up. He's put in

a lot of updates, but remained true to the building's original charm."

"Is he going to live there?"

"Nick wants to put it on the market this fall. And... I want to buy it."

"*You* want to live there?"

"No. When I was working alongside Jess today, I saw a restaurant, not a home." Elaine sat down on the chair in the corner and tipped her head back. "This is the part where you try and talk some sense into me."

"You have plenty of sense already." She could hear the smile in Matthew's voice. "But I do have a few questions."

"You're doing better than I am, then," Elaine confessed. "I've been asking God dozens of them since I got home."

"I know you've been running your own business for years, but do you have any restaurant experience at all? Dishwasher? Line cook? Waitress?"

"None of the above. But Jess does. That's why I want to turn it over to her."

Silence.

Panic overrode the elation until Elaine remembered that this was Matthew's MO. He always took a few moments before he spoke, deliberately sifting out his own emotions or any form of judgment, allowing the grace he'd been extended to wash over his thoughts before he said them out loud.

"Jess is a talented chef," Matthew said slowly. "But does she *want* a restaurant?"

As intuitive as Matthew was, Elaine couldn't believe he'd missed the expression on Jess's face when Christopher had shared, in his words, her "big dream" that day in the garden.

But something had happened before Jess had answered Elaine's ad. Something that had stripped the hope from her eyes. In Elaine's experience, it occurred when your dream lay in pieces at your feet. Picking up the pieces was impossible, so you did the only thing you could do. You ran away.

Elaine had done the same thing twenty-five years ago.

"You should have seen Jess today. She *owned* that kitchen, Matt. She's a hard worker. She's focused and organized. She works well under pressure. And by pressure, I mean making pizza for an entire football team and fielding questions from everyone who waltzed into the kitchen to see if there was something going on between her and Nick."

"Coach Nick?"

"Right."

"*Is* there something going on?"

"I think there could be, if Jess stays. But that's not why I'd buy the lodge." Elaine could feel the *rightness* of the decision flow through her again.

Jess was hurting. Angry. Suspicious of people's motives.

Elaine had been there, too. It had kept her from staying in one place for very long. She'd written about other people's lives, hidden behind their names, afraid to show herself.

And then, on a beach one Christmas morning, God had called her name.

"A woman named Samantha O'Dell gave me a chance to start over," Elaine said. "Jess hasn't given me any details about how she ended up in Winsome Lake, but I think she needs a place to start over, too."

"A restaurant." Matthew repeated the word and Elaine wished she could see his face. See if the tiny, almost imperceptible dent had settled between his brows or if a smile kindled in his eyes. "Most people would offer their name as a reference. Help them find an apartment, you know. Jessica could agree and then in a few months, decide to move on."

Elaine had not only considered that possibility, but a whole truckload of other what-ifs besides.

"That's why I'm praying about it." Elaine walked over to the window. The moon cast a silver sheen on the leaves of the hydrangea that protected a brand-new chrysalis. "I know a lot of things could go wrong. But a God-yes...it's worth the risk."

"Did Samantha O'Dell teach you that?"

Elaine's gaze moved to Nita's house, where a football-shaped night-light glowed in the upper window.

For such is the kingdom of heaven.

"Someone even braver."

Chapter Thirty-Eight

After countless hours repairing the broken pieces of the window into Libby Tucker's soul, Jess knew why she'd torn up her diary.

Jess would have done the same thing. And then burned the evidence so no one could do what Elaine had asked her to do. Put them together so people could judge Libby all over again.

She ran her finger over the edges of the tape, smoothing them down. The words, written in pink ink, jumped from the page.

Daryl and Mama sat me down today and I thought for sure I was going to get another lecture about chewing on my hair or not smiling enough. Daryl says my smile alone is worth a million dollars, so Mama reminds me to do it a lot.

But it wasn't that. Daryl got me an audition for a new television show and he thinks I'm perfect for the part! They're look-

ing for someone who is fifteen or sixteen (I'll be sixteen in two weeks). A girl-next door type with blond hair (check) and brown eyes (double check) to play the lead role. The script says she grew up on a farm in Iowa but after her parents die in car accident (cliché!), she moves in with her rich aunt in New York City and goes to a private school. Maybe they'll film on location!

Mama came in when I was practicing my lines tonight and said the producer might ask me questions about myself so I won't be nervous. She's the one who's nervous because she doesn't want anyone to know why we left Kentucky.

I told her that and she got mad. Mama doesn't like it when I tell her things. She says my job is to keep my mouth shut and do whatever she and Daryl tell me to if I want to be a star.

I don't care about being a star. I just want to be someone else.

Mama says she's protecting me, but that's a lie, too. She's protecting herself. She's afraid...

The door swung open and the emotions Jess had been trying to contain bubbled over when Elaine stepped into the office. Her eyes widened. The last time she'd checked on Jess's progress, the papers scattered on the floor resembled an early snow.

Over the past week, they'd fallen into a rhythm of sorts. In the morning Jess made breakfast while Elaine did her therapy exercises and Sienna practiced the piano.

Desiree Bloom had agreed to let Sienna move in with her dad until freshman orientation, but Sienna still spent most of her time at Elaine's, pouring out her heart with every song, the same way Libby had in her diary. The Scrappy Ladies took turns keeping Elaine company in the afternoon, and Christopher helped Jess fine-tune some new recipes. In the evening Jess worked on the diaries until Elaine was ready for bed.

Nick had stopped over twice, once to mow the lawn and once to drop off a dozen eggs, but both times Jess had sought refuge in the office. It was self-preservation, not cowardice. The desire to spend time with Nick, talk to him, laugh with him, was strong. But Jess knew when she left, the ache in her heart would be more painful than the longing to be in his arms again.

Libby's diary had provided Jess with a much-needed distraction when she wasn't in the kitchen. What Jess hadn't anticipated was after hours of reconstructive surgery, she'd become fiercely protective of the teenage girl who'd framed her dreams with hearts and flowers. Whose charmed life had been built on secrets.

"How is it going?"

Elaine's simple question required a simple answer, but Jess's emotions, so close to the surface after what she'd just discovered, spilled over.

She waved a hand over the pages of the diary.

"Did you know Libby Tucker killed her father?"

The color drained from Elaine's face. She took several faltering steps forward, her grip tight on the wooden cane, and sank into the desk chair.

Jess regretted blurting out the words like that, but now that she'd opened that Pandora's box, there was no choice but to go forward.

"Right here." She held up the last entry she'd taped together. "Libby says her mom is afraid of what will happen if anyone finds out she killed her dad."

"She was eleven years old at the time," Elaine said quietly. "And Roy was her stepdad. Libby's biological father died when she was three.

"Roy and Arlene had a...volatile...relationship. When he was drinking, things could get ugly. Libby heard her mom scream one night and ran into the kitchen. Roy had Arlene by the throat and it didn't look like he was going to let go that time. Libby was terrified and went to get the pistol Roy kept in a drawer by the bed. Arlene had managed to struggle free by the time Libby got back, but Roy was already coming at her again. Libby gave the gun to her mom, thinking it would scare him into backing down. It didn't...so Arlene shot him."

Bile rose in Jess's throat. She remembered the times she'd been roused from the bed by her parents' fighting. They'd never laid a hand on Jess, but she'd lived with the fear their anger might eventually spill over onto her. "But if that's what happened... Libby didn't *kill* him."

"She gave the gun to her mom. In her mind she was just as guilty. The authorities decided it was self-defense but Arlene and Libby left the area shortly after that. They hopped from relative to relative until they wore out their welcome.

"Arlene didn't have a steady job or an education. All she had was a pretty daughter who charmed everyone she came into contact with. They were eating at a diner one day and the waitress told them a man at the counter had paid their bill. Arlene was never one to pass up an opportunity, so when she thanked him, she made sure she mentioned they didn't have very much. The man laughed and told her that Libby's smile alone was worth a million dollars.

"A few weeks later they were on their way to California. Libby starred in a few commercials, but her first big break came after they signed with an agent."

Daryl. The other person who'd benefited from Libby's million-dollar smile.

"I've pieced together almost the entire diary and Libby

never mentions it again," Jess said slowly. "You found all this out while you were doing research for the book?"

Elaine's gaze cut away from Jess for a moment and then dropped to the paper still clutched in her hand. "That was a secret Jolie Mayes was supposed to take to the grave."

"Jolie?"

"Libby's real name. Arlene had it legally changed before they moved to California. The producers thought it fit the sweet, wholesome character they wanted Libby to portray, so they decided to use it for the show." Elaine's smile tipped sideways. "But *Life with Libby Tucker* didn't turn out the way anyone planned."

"Libby must have decided to tear up the diary so no one would see it."

Elaine stared at Jess for a long moment, almost as if she was debating if what she was about to say fell outside the lines of her confidentiality clause.

"Arlene was the one who ripped it up, but she was too late. Someone already had," Elaine finally said. "Bryan Foster, Libby's costar, was twenty-two to her sixteen, but they cast him because he was prep-school handsome and could pass for a teenager. Bryan had been in the business since he was in diapers and he took Libby under his wing. When the show took off, they became the golden couple.

"Bryan stopped by the apartment one day to pick Libby up for a party. He saw the diary and looked through it while she was fixing her hair. Gave her an ultimatum. She had to pose for a private photo shoot or end up with her past splashed all over the tabloids."

Bryan's betrayal burned through Jess. At the beginning of Libby's career, she'd considered him a friend.

"Libby's popularity was based on her role as a sweet, wholesome girl next door," Elaine continued. "Parents loved her because she was a role model for their daughters. Libby was terrified it would end her career if people found out that her past didn't match the one on her press release. So... she agreed."

Jess felt sick to her stomach. "Bryan showed the photos to someone, didn't he?"

Elaine closed her eyes, almost as if she was trying to block out a memory.

"Bryan's fiancée found them a few days later and confronted him. He claimed Libby had given him the photos because she had a massive crush on him and wanted to break them up. The fiancée happened to be Libby's best friend so she felt justified in going public with the truth. Except the part about Bryan blackmailing Libby." The words carried an edge Jess had never heard in her employer's voice before. "He conveniently left that out."

Of course he had. Jess remembered the entry she'd read, written on a piece of hotel stationery.

"What about Arlene? Libby's agent... Daryl? Didn't they stand by her?"

"Daryl was Bryan's agent, too, and he was more marketable. Arlene...passed away a few days after the news got out."

"Passed away? How?"

"An accidental overdose of sleeping pills." A shadow skimmed through Elaine's eyes. "When word got out about the photos, Arlene couldn't handle the stress."

What about the stress on Libby?

Based on what Jess had read in Libby's diary, she'd loved Arlene even though the woman was more manager than mother.

"So Libby's life, her career, was over. Just like that."

"She thought it was," Elaine said. "Maybe you're thinking if Libby had been stronger, if she'd put her self-respect over saving her career, she wouldn't have let Bryan take those photos. That she shouldn't have left—"

"I know why she left." The sheaf of paper toppled over as Jess pushed to her feet. "She left because it didn't matter how hard she worked. It didn't matter that all she wanted was to do the work that she loved. She knew no one would believe her. She knew good things didn't happen to people like her—" Jess bit back the words and the metallic taste of blood filled her mouth. She pivoted toward the door.

She thought she heard Elaine call her name, but she didn't want to hear any more.

Libby's mistake was thinking she could put the past behind her and start over again.

Jessie Keaton had made that mistake, too.

Chapter Thirty-Nine

Elaine had just finished buttering a piece of toast with her left hand—note to PT, include this in therapy session—when she heard footsteps on the stairs. Quiet. Tentative.

The opposite of the way Jess had exited the office the night before. Elaine hadn't had time to absorb Jess's outburst when she'd dropped the page from the diary as if it was on fire before bolting from the room.

When Elaine had sought Jess out, the diary had been the last thing on her mind. But it was pure Libby Tucker, upsetting the balance in Elaine's life again.

She just hadn't expected the diary to upset Jess.

God, I still don't know what happened. Jess tries to hide it, but that girl is in a world of hurt.

Elaine had thought about following her, but instead of climbing the stairs, Elaine had dropped to her knees beside the desk and prayed instead. And she'd continued off and on during the night, until the sky turned from cobalt to a soft, watercolor blue.

Jess pulled up short in the doorway when she spotted Elaine.

"I... I'm sorry," she stammered. "I must have overslept."

She didn't look like she'd slept at all. Her hair fell loose around her shoulders instead of being confined in a neat little twist. Jess typically didn't wear her chef's coat in the kitchen during the day, but Elaine was used to seeing her in something other than the wrinkled tee and cotton leggings she'd probably worn to bed.

"What would you like for breakfast?" Jess stumbled into the kitchen. She slid an elastic band off her wrist and in one deft movement, used it to create a slightly crooked ponytail. "I was going to make a frittata today, but if you're hungry now, I can do a yogurt parfait with maple granola—"

"I already made breakfast." Elaine tempered her interruption with a smile. "For both of us."

Jess's gaze zeroed in on the two plates Elaine had set out. There was more butter smeared on the counter than the toast, but Elaine thought it wasn't half-bad for a first attempt.

"I'll make—"

"Coffee's done, too." Elaine hoped Jess didn't notice the grounds scattered all over the floor. "I'll heat up some water in the microwave for tea and then all we have to do is eat."

Jess was already turning on the faucet. It was impossible to read her expression now, but Elaine guessed she welcomed the idea of having breakfast together as much as she welcomed someone else planning the menu.

But Elaine had a plan, too. It was Thursday, so Sienna and the Scrappy Ladies would be arriving soon. She wanted time to talk to Jess and she wanted them to be alone.

Later, when the time was right, Elaine would call in the reinforcements.

Jess carried their plates into the dining room and made a second trip for the coffee and tea.

When she finally sat down, Elaine prayed for wisdom and a side helping of mercy and grace.

"Last night—"

"I shouldn't have left like I did," Jess interjected. "What you said about Libby... I wasn't expecting it."

Wasn't expecting it? Or because Jess had been afraid of what might spill out with all those other emotions?

"There are things about Libby you don't know, but she isn't the reason I came into the office to talk to you last night," Elaine said carefully, keeping her eyes trained on Jess's face and her heart tuned to God's voice. "When Nick stopped over yesterday, he told me his plans for the lodge."

Jess tried to keep her expression neutral, but the flicker of longing in her eyes told Elaine everything she needed to know and then some about her feelings for Elaine's neighbor.

Whatever had happened to Jess was getting in the way of a relationship with Nick, too.

"He's planning to sell this fall." Jess nibbled at a corner of the toast. Reached for the jar of blueberry jam she'd put on the table. "There's still a lot of work left to do, but I'm sure his team and his family will pitch in if he needs help. Grandpop, too."

Grandpop?

Elaine suppressed a smile.

The seeds Jess sowed had bloomed beyond the neighborhood.

"I hope so. Because Winsome Lake needs a restaurant."

"A restaurant?" Now she had Jess's full attention. "Someone wants to turn it into a restaurant?"

"I do." Elaine felt the *rightness* of it again. "But I'd be a silent partner only. I'd take care of the books and sign the checks, but you'd be in charge of everything else."

"Me?" Jess's lips shaped the word.

"A restaurant needs a chef." Elaine tried to read Jess's expression. If anything, she looked more wary than she had when they'd sat down. "Nick planned to convert the upstairs space into an office and extra storage, but at this point he said it would be easy to turn it into a small apartment instead. There's already a full bath up and you wouldn't need a kitchen because you'd have one downstairs."

Elaine had heard the echo of another "yes" when Nick had told her about the additional space, but she saw the struggle in Jess's eyes.

Elaine knew what it felt like to stand at the crossroad between the past and the future, where your biggest dream intersected with your greatest fear.

But Elaine had no idea what Jess was afraid of. Success? Failure?

"You barely know me," Jess said, her voice not quite even. "Why would you do this?"

Elaine smiled. "I know you're flexible. You proved that when you came here on your starting date and found an empty house. I know you work well under pressure because you didn't flinch when a dozen football players looked like they were about to mow you down. I also know you're a great chef because I've gained back all the weight I'd lost during rehab."

Elaine hadn't expected Jess to jump up and down, but she could see the walls sliding into place, the kind only God could get through.

"I know you'll need time to think it over," Elaine said. "And don't think that I'm kicking you out. Nick said the lodge will be ready by October, but I'll need your help until I finish therapy…and the book. It could be January—"

"Hello in the house!"

The front door opened. The pitter-patter of paws and Violet's abrupt departure from the sunny spot in the windowsill told Elaine that Peg had arrived.

Elaine had hoped she and Jess would have more time to talk, but Jess leaped to her feet almost as if she was grateful for the interruption.

By the time Elaine had extricated herself from the chair and collected her cane, Peg was in the kitchen, too.

"We're not scrapbooking today," she announced. "You'll see why when Merri gets here."

The screen door swung open and Merri came in, weighted down with grocery bags. "Christopher and Sienna have the rest."

Jess watched a rogue potato escape from the bag she'd set down and roll across the counter. "The rest?" she said cautiously.

"Honestly, Merri! Did you hold up a market stand?" Nita strode into the room, a cardboard box balanced on the narrow ledge of each hip. "This is double what you brought over last year."

"Rain and sunshine and good soil," Merri sang. "They make things grow."

Christopher trailed in behind Sienna, but neither one of the teens was holding bags. Sienna cradled a baby Hubbard squash while Christopher tried to balance the cord of sweet corn stacked in his arms.

"Stone soup day," Peg announced, surveying the bounty.

Jess looked even more confused. "Stone soup?"

"You've never had stone s-soup?" Christopher rounded

on Jess, his eyes wide with shock, and almost dumped the corncobs on the floor.

"I've never *heard* of it."

A grin broke out on Christopher's face. "We'll show you how to make it. You can b-be our sous-chef."

Was Elaine the only one who noticed the smile Jess gave him in return lacked its usual spark?

Nita put the boxes on the floor and surveyed the counter. "We're going to need a bigger Nesco."

"It will be fine. We'll cut things smaller." Merri opened a cabinet and pulled out the colander, humming under her breath.

"It's on a shelf at the bottom of the basement stairs," Elaine said. "Do I have a volunteer?"

"I don't like s-spiders," Christopher said. "And it smells f-funny down there."

"I'll get it." Jess darted toward the door leading to the basement.

Merri paused in the middle of pouring herself a cup of coffee and looked at Elaine. "We aren't interrupting your therapy, are we?"

"Are you kidding?" Elaine picked up a cherry tomato. "This *is* therapy."

Jess staggered into the kitchen a few minutes later, wearing a veil of cobwebs, her face pale.

"Jess?"

All sizes and shapes of hands reached out to steady her, but Jess dodged them all.

"I... You should start without me."

And then she was gone.

Merri's brows knit together in a concerned frown.

"We shouldn't have taken over her kitchen without asking," she said. "Jess always has a plan."

"If she does, I'm the one who messed it up," Elaine admitted.

Now she had the attention of everyone in the room.

"You didn't fire her, did you?" Peg asked. "Because we all know how independent you can be."

"No." The word rolled out with Elaine's sigh. "I think it was worse."

"What could be worse than that?" Nita demanded.

"I offered to buy her a restaurant."

Chapter Forty

Jess's phone, on silent, was still ringing when she stumbled out the door.

She felt the spike in her heart rate, keeping time with the name and number flashing on the screen.

For a split second, Jess was tempted to let the call go straight to voice mail.

But Gwyneth didn't leave messages.

If I'm trying to get in touch with you, it's important, she'd told her staff. *I hired you, not a machine, so unless you want to be replaced by one, I suggest you answer your phone when I call.*

Jess had never put that threat to the test. And even though Gwyneth was no longer her boss, the habit must have become embedded in Jess's internal hard drive, because she swiped her finger over the screen.

"Hello." Jess tried to keep her voice even, but some air escaped with it, putting a slight hitch in the middle.

"Jessica." Gwyneth, however, sounded exactly the same.

Crisp. Commanding. "There's been a change in your situation."

Jess simultaneously waved at the mail carrier and dodged a large crack in the sidewalk. "A change…"

What did that even mean?

"Crystal saw a text message on Ian's phone," Gwyneth continued briskly. "She confronted him and he admitted he was having an affair with one of the waitresses."

Jess reached the end of the sidewalk and kept going.

"How is Crystal doing?"

There was a brief silence and then, "She's better off without him."

That was Gwyneth's opinion, not an answer, but Jess let it go.

"Ian also admitted that he lied about you."

The breath emptied from Jess's lungs.

"Crystal got suspicious after she caught the two of you kissing. That's when she started going through his emails and text messages."

Jess's stomach heaved. Ian had used his strength and opportunity to take advantage of her. Their lips might have been touching, but there was no way anyone could call it a kiss.

Because of Nick, she knew the difference.

"What are you doing?" Gwyneth asked.

"Walking." A car waited while Jess crossed the street and she waved at the driver.

Gwyneth chuckled and the sound was so unexpected Jess almost dropped the phone. "Let me rephrase that. Did you find another position?"

"Yes."

No thanks to her.

Jess tamped down the resentment that curled in her belly.

"No matter. Is Monday too soon?"

Jess had been listening, but it still felt like she'd missed part of the conversation. "Too soon for what?"

"To come back to work."

No apology. No I'm-sorry-I-didn't-ask-for-your-side-of-the-story. Crystal, not Gwyneth, had had doubts about Ian. If she hadn't discovered the text, this conversation wouldn't be happening.

"But...didn't you replace me?"

"Of course." Gwyneth sounded surprised by the question. "There's a probationary period, so it won't be a problem."

Except for the person who'd left another job and apartment to work at the Donovan estate. But of course, Gwyneth didn't concern herself with that.

Jess swallowed. Hard.

"I'll need some time to think about it."

There was silence on the other end of the line and then Gwyneth said smoothly, "I realize it might be a little inconvenient to leave without giving notice, so you'll be getting a raise, of course. We can go over specifics when you get here."

Gwyneth thought Jess was playing hard-to-get when in reality, she could barely think.

"I'll call and let you know," Jess murmured.

As soon as the words were out of her mouth, she expected Gwyneth to hang up, ending both the call and any future arrangement with Jess.

"I know you'll make the right decision. You always said this was your dream job."

Her dream job.

Gwyneth's tone was light, almost teasing, but Jess knew there was a reason she'd used those particular words. What she didn't know was that Jess had another dream.

But Elaine Haviland did.

When comparing the offers Jess had received that morning, Elaine's was still the more shocking of the two.

Over the past two weeks, Jess had figured out why 1525 Woodwind Lane was the most popular gathering spot on the block. It wasn't because there was a large dining room table and a baby grand piano and a backyard garden made for conversation and gallons of iced tea.

Elaine, not her house, drew people in.

When Jess came downstairs, formulating an apology for her abrupt departure the night before, Elaine was already there, with toast and an offer Jess had no choice but to refuse.

Elaine might make a decent living as a freelance writer, but opening a restaurant in a town the size of Winsome Lake was definitely a risk.

And so was Jess.

What if she failed? What if something happened that she couldn't control? Everyone would rally around Elaine, the woman they knew and loved, but where would that leave Jess?

Looking for another job. Another place to live.

Only it would be worse this time. Because now Winsome Lake wasn't a destination or desperation. It felt like…home.

Something large and furry brushed against her leg and Jess stifled a shriek.

A familiar furry face grinned up at her.

Bucket.

Bucket.

Nick suddenly realized the dog was no longer splashing through the reeds, scaring the minnows into deeper water, or taunting the red squirrel that had made its home in the woodpile.

This was what happened when a guy was thinking about a green-eyed chef instead of his reno.

Only now the two had become woven together in Nick's mind.

If that wasn't God working behind the scenes, working things for good, he didn't know what was.

He prayed Jess would see it that way, too.

Had Elaine said anything yet?

He glanced out the window overlooking the patio to see if Bucket had settled down for an early nap, but the only thing taking up space in the strip of shade was a half-chewed rawhide bone.

Great. Nick hoped Bucket hadn't made an unsanctioned visit to Grandpop's cabin.

He strode over to the front door to widen the search for his recalcitrant pup.

"Buck…" The rest of the word disintegrated when Nick saw him prancing up the driveway at Jess's side.

One look at her face and Nick knew Elaine had made the offer. But she didn't look like someone who'd just found out her dream was finally within reach.

He held the door open, and Jess walked in without saying hello, another indication something was wrong.

Bucket must have sensed it, too, because he nudged her hand.

Jess reached down to pat the dog's head. When she straightened again, her entire body went rigid.

Nick realized she was staring at the bar.

He'd put it up at midnight, his mind whirling with possibilities that extended far beyond the lodge.

"It would make a great counter, wouldn't it? For…what do you call it…quick service?"

"Why did you put it back?"

"Come here." It was easier to show her. Nick reached for Jess's hand. Her entire body went rigid, as if he'd touched her in a game of frozen tag, but she didn't pull away so he tugged her toward the bar. "Do you see the initials scratched in the wood?"

Jess bent down and peered at the letters. Glanced up at Nick with a question in her eyes.

"AS and JC. Anthony Silva and Jenny Callahan."

"Your grandparents?"

"I was kicking myself for not getting rid of the bar when I had the chance and then Grandpop stopped over and saw it. He'd bussed tables here when he was a teenager and my grandma was visiting her aunt that summer. According to Grandpop, he carved their initials into the wood the first time they met.

"After the pizza party last week, I realized the lodge wasn't meant to be someone's weekend home. It should be a place where people can get together and share their stories and memories.

"I'd already made the decision to advertise the lodge as commercial use only. I thought it deserved another chance. And then Elaine called."

Any doubt that Jess had mixed feelings about Elaine's offer was strengthened by the panic Nick saw rising in her eyes.

"I can't accept help from Elaine. You've seen her house! She doesn't have enough money to replace the furniture in her living room." Jess wrapped her arms around her middle, fortifying the invisible barrier between them. "I don't want her to take a loan out for me."

"The town needs this. And... I think you do, too."

When Jess's eyes narrowed, Nick wished he hadn't added the last part.

"I'm not a charity case."

"A char…" Nick couldn't even finish the word. "Is that what you think this is about? You think Elaine feels *sorry* for you? You're a chef, Jess. A good one. Elaine is a smart lady. She knows that backing your restaurant is a good investment."

Sure, there was a lot to figure out. But owning her own restaurant was Jess's dream. She knew what would be involved in the day-to-day operations and she wasn't afraid of the commitment.

What *was* she afraid of?

Failure?

Not gonna happen. The entire town had mourned the demise of the Cozy Corner. People would pack the tables of a café with a stunning view of the water. Tourists, too, once word got out there was an executive chef in the kitchen.

"It's not that simple." Jess pivoted away from Nick, but at least she didn't storm out the door.

Just in case, though, he stepped in front of her.

"Then tell me what's complicated, and we'll figure it out."

Chapter Forty-One

We'll figure it out.

Jess wanted to lean in to the word. Lean on Nick.

But she knew what would happen when she told him the truth.

"Gwyneth Donovan called. She wants me to come back."

Jess watched the emotions skip across the surface of Nick's blue eyes. The sincerity changing to confusion and then wariness. "The woman you worked for before you came to Winsome?"

Jess nodded. The memory of her recent conversation with Gwyneth still felt a little surreal.

"I got the impression you didn't leave your last job on a good note," Nick said carefully.

"Gwyneth fired me. But she thought it was justified."

"Was it?"

"No."

Jess braced herself for more questions, but Nick only had one.

"Then you told her to take a hike, right?"

"I told her I would think about it."

"What is there to think about?" Nick demanded. "Even if Gwyneth hadn't fired you, you'd be working for someone else again. Your dream is to own your own restaurant."

Why had she told him that?

"Word travels through Gwyneth's circles like it does here. This is a chance to save my reputation. To prove—"

"You shouldn't have to prove anything," Nick interrupted. "Not to the people who probably raved about your skill in the kitchen, but didn't step up and hire you to work in theirs after you were fired. Or, at the very least, ask for your side of the story. Whatever happened, Gwyneth Donovan should be the one to set the record straight, whether you come back to work for her or not."

Nick must have seen the answer on her face because he muttered something under his breath that Jess didn't dare ask him to repeat.

"She won't, will she?" he guessed. "And this is your role model? The person who taught you about success?" Frustration sharpened the words to steel. "I guess it depends on your definition of the word, and ours must not be the same."

Jess flinched.

"You don't understand," she said. "You have everything. A close family. Friends. A career you love."

"You can have all those things, too. Here. Along with a lifetime supply of eggs, right after Grandpop and I build you a chicken coop. He says Persephone has taken a shine to you."

Tears scalded the backs of Jess's eyes.

Nick reached out and brushed a strand of hair from her face. His fingers lingered for a moment, a whisper-soft touch on the curve of her jaw. "Talk to me, Jess. Help me understand. Isn't this what you always wanted? A restaurant of your own?"

"Yes..."

Nick's hand dropped to his side. "But not in Winsome Lake."

"Nick—"

"Don't, Jess." Nick cut her off with a shake of his head. "I can see you already made up your mind. And it's okay if you'd rather live in a city and eventually cook for foodies and bloggers and get five-star reviews. Because you will. You're that good. I just want you to be sure you're leaving because it's what you want to do and not because you're afraid to stay."

The lump in Jess's throat doubled in size.

She wasn't afraid.

She was terrified.

Terrified of staying. Terrified of leaving.

Terrified that no matter what she chose, she would end up losing everything again.

Elaine heard the screen door open and close.

Her "Thank You, God" rolled out with a sigh a relief.

Jess had been gone for almost four hours.

Nita, Peg and Merri had stayed through the morning, washing, peeling and chopping vegetables. After Elaine told them about the lodge, the soft squeak of Christopher's tennis shoes as he trekked back and forth between the center island and the window, was the only sound in the kitchen. Sienna helped for a while before she'd finally retreated to the living room. Elaine hoped she was going to play for them until she heard footsteps in the front hallway and the click of the front door.

"Big decision," Peg had said after Sienna left. "It's not every day someone gives you a restaurant."

Merri and Nita had murmured in agreement.

No one asked how Elaine could *afford* one. Or why she was willing to turn it over to a young woman she'd just met.

But for the first time in twenty-five years, Elaine wished they had.

Jess appeared in the kitchen doorway.

Lord, give me eyes to see and ears to hear. Wisdom to know what to say.

Jess's quick glance at the mound of carrots on the counter gave Elaine the opening she'd just prayed for.

"I could use some help," she said. "It turns out I'm better with a butter knife than a vegetable peeler."

With a reluctance evident in her brief nod and measured steps, Jess claimed her space on the opposite side of the island. Carefully unwrapped her knife from its leather swaddling.

Elaine picked up a bunch of kale with matte green leaves that curled at the edges like the pages of an old book. It felt clumsy, tearing pieces from the spine, but safer than using a knife.

Jess picked up one of the carrots, her expression shielded behind a curtain of blond hair.

"We have a stone soup party every summer," Elaine told her. "Don, Merri's husband, was so proud of his vegetable garden. I don't know if you've seen it, but it takes up three-quarters of her backyard.

"After he passed away, Merri started to replant it. She'd weed and water and fertilize, just like Don did, but when it was ready for harvest, she'd give it all away. I'd get buckets of green beans and tomatoes and Nita would be up to her knees in zucchini. I finally suggested we throw everything in a pot and turn it into soup. We sit down together and have a bowl or two, then freeze the leftovers for the winter.

"There's no recipe. It tastes different every time, depending on what's ready at the time and what Nita finds in her pantry." Elaine smiled. "My contribution is the Nesco, salt and pepper and whatever herbs happen to be growing in the backyard."

There was no response, but Elaine could hear the emotions Jess was trying to suppress in every vibration of the knife against the butcher-block counter.

She lifted the lid on the Nesco and dumped a handful of kale inside. She couldn't force Jess to open up, but that didn't mean *she* couldn't.

"Jess, I made a mistake—"

"That's all right." Jess cut her off with the same swift efficiency with which she wielded the knife. "A restaurant is a huge commitment. I understand why you'd have second thoughts."

Elaine stared at Jess, a little stunned she'd made that leap when all Elaine was going to do was apologize for bringing up the restaurant over breakfast, when she knew they wouldn't have a lot of time to discuss it.

"I'm not having second thoughts about the restaurant, Jess," Elaine said. "Or about you."

"Why? You don't *know* me."

The knife had stilled, but the rattle in Jess's voice told Elaine the inner battle was only growing in intensity.

She drew in a silent breath and exhaled a prayer, asking for wisdom again.

"I know that I could barely get Sienna to look me in the eye when she came over to practice the piano, let alone have a conversation with her. And Christopher... Nita says he wants to work in a restaurant now. He's heard his classmates talk about their dreams for the future and now he has one, too."

Elaine paused, interrupted by a thought that sounded more like a divine whisper. "I *trust* you, Jess. Not only because you're a wonderful chef, but also because I hired you to cook for me and you *fed* the people I care about the most."

The knife clattered against the counter. "Until I offend someone or burn their steak and then you have to *choose.*"

Jess's teeth snapped together on the last word.

"Is that what happened before you came here?" Elaine asked cautiously.

Jess opened her mouth, and Elaine thought she was going to flatly refuse to talk about the five-year gap on her résumé again. But even if that was her original intent, the secret Jess had been keeping tumbled out instead.

"I was a personal chef for Gwyneth Donovan. The company I'd worked for catered a wedding reception Gwyneth attended and when she found out I'd made most of the food, she offered me a job even though I didn't have a lot of experience.

"A year after I started, my parents showed up. They claimed they were *out for a drive* even though my hometown was three hours away. Gwyneth came home from work and caught my dad in the wine cellar. He'd just opened a hundred-dollar bottle of cabernet. I'm not sure what Mom was doing at the time. Sunning herself by the pool or looking up how much the paintings would sell for on eBay." Jess's lips twisted. "They stuck around for three days, which was about two and a half more than they'd spent with me since I'd graduated from culinary school.

"After they left I apologized and promised it wouldn't happen again. Gwyneth was very gracious about it and I admired her even more." Jess looked away. "Fast-forward four years. One of the guests grabs me in the kitchen during the Fourth of July party. Gwyneth and the man's wife—who also happens to be Gwyneth's younger sister—walk in. Ian tells them I said I would do anything to work in his restaurant.

"Gwyneth didn't even ask for my side of the story. I never missed a day of work in five years. I planned the menus for every dinner party and brunch and gave my recipes to her friends when they asked for them. Do you know what she said when she handed me my last paycheck? Gwyneth said she should have known *someone like me* would take a shortcut to success. That the only people who make it to the top are the ones who deserve to be there. And we both knew I didn't."

Elaine had misread what she'd seen in Jess's eyes. It wasn't anger or bitterness over the way she'd been treated. It was shame.

Oh, how Elaine could relate.

"While I was growing up, people either avoided me or felt sorry for me," Jess said. "After culinary school I started to believe the past didn't matter. That I could be someone else."

"Gwyneth was wrong to judge you because of your parents' actions." Elaine measured out each word slowly. "That's on her, not you. And it doesn't matter—"

"It *always* matters." Jess pushed away from the island. "Look at Libby Tucker."

Shock rocketed through Elaine, stripping the air from her lungs. "Libby?"

"She didn't choose where she was born or how she grew up. She wanted to be someone who people admired. Respected. She wanted recognition for her accomplishments. Libby worked hard...did everything right...but she knew if people found out about her past, they would judge her anyway. And they did.

"No one asked Bryan why he'd kept those photos," Jess

continued. "Even if Libby *had* given them to him, he should have destroyed them. But he lied and destroyed her life instead."

"Bryan may have tried...but he didn't succeed."

"How can you say that?" Jess's voice thinned. "You saw what Libby wrote on the hotel stationery. She was alone. Her career was over. Her reputation ruined. Who knows where she ended up?" Horror flashed in Jess's eyes. "Is she *dead*? Is that why you're writing a book about her?"

Elaine felt a lump forming in her throat. She was beginning to understand why Jess had reacted so strongly when she'd filled in some of the missing pieces of Libby's life the night before.

I just want to be someone else.

It was all Libby had ever wanted.

And another young girl had had the same dream.

"Libby is very much alive," Elaine said softly. "It took some time, but she stopped running and started living. Her story didn't end with her diaries. It's still being written." The words came out a little garbled. Elaine paused and drew in a steadying breath. "Here."

Jess frowned. "Here?"

"I'm Libby Tucker."

Chapter Forty-Two

"You?"

Jess stared at Elaine. Her voice sounded unsteady, too. "But...no one said anything."

"No one knows," Elaine said simply. "When I moved to Winsome, I was afraid that if people knew who I was, what I'd done, they would look at me differently, so I kept it a secret.

"Like you, all I wanted to do was put the past behind me. Reinvent myself. After the scandal I became Elaine Haviland, freelance writer. For over ten years I traveled in and out of the country, stayed under the radar, until people forgot about Libby Tucker.

"By the time I met Samantha O'Dell on a beach one Christmas morning, I was tired of running. Tired of being alone." Elaine smiled. "Still, I was ready to walk right past the strange woman who'd made a campfire out of driftwood. Sam invited me to have a cup of tea and told me about a town that sounded like the setting for one of those feel-good type of television shows.

"It turned out Sam was at a crossroads, too. She had an opportunity to move overseas, but she was reluctant to leave her friends behind.

"I'd never heard of Winsome Lake, Wisconsin, and I had no faces to put to the names, but I offered to buy Sam's house, right there on the spot." Elaine chuckled. "Sam didn't look at me like I'd been in the sun too long, though. She said she didn't believe in coincidences."

A memory flickered in Jess's eyes, as if she remembered Elaine saying the same thing to her.

"I was ready to let you go when I realized you'd seen the diary," Elaine admitted. "I'd kept my secrets for so long, I still wasn't sure I was ready to put them in a book. But then I remembered that I didn't believe in coincidences, either. I asked God to take care of Sienna and my friends while I was in rehab, and you saw an ad in a newspaper that shouldn't even have been in that hotel."

Elaine saw the conflict in Jess's red-rimmed eyes, a mixture of fear and longing, and knew it didn't have anything to do with the restaurant. This one had started long before she'd arrived in Winsome Lake.

"He answered *your* prayer," Jess whispered. "I don't know Him like that."

"You can," Elaine said. "Jesus calls Himself the bread of life for a reason. When you invite Him into your life, into your heart, He satisfies and nourishes and strengthens you because He gives you Himself. Taste and see that Lord is good, Jess."

Jess reached out blindly and gripped the edge of the counter. "What did you say?"

Elaine hesitated for a moment and realized that God had

answered another prayer. He'd blessed her with words that would speak directly to Jess's heart.

"Taste and see that the Lord is good," she repeated. "It's a verse in the Psalms. God *is* good, and no matter what happened in your past or what's ahead of you in the future, nothing can separate you from His love. You aren't an orphan or an outcast. You're a beloved daughter. When you surrender your heart to the One who promises to give you a new one, there will *always* be a place at the table for you, Jess."

For the second time that day Jess fled, but Elaine didn't follow her upstairs.

This was between Jess and her Creator now and His words never came back empty.

Sometimes, depending on the listener, though, it took twenty-five years for them to sink in.

All this time Elaine had thought that telling the truth about who she was would leave her feeling vulnerable. Open to judgment and criticism. Instead, it felt as if a burden had been lifted. Shame had no place in her life, either. Not anymore.

The phone pinged at the same moment Elaine collapsed into the closest chair.

Okay?

She shook her head. How had he known?

Do you remember when you said that Libby Tucker's story might have the power to change someone else's?

Yes.

You were right.

Jess?

Elaine's finger shook a little as she typed the answer.

Mine.

No matter what happened in your past or what's ahead of you in the future, nothing can separate you from God's love.

The words had been true for Elaine... *Libby...* Jess was still having a hard time wrapping her head around the fact they were the same person.

She wanted them to be true for her, too.

Jess sank to the floor and closed her eyes. Knotted her hands in her lap.

I believe You're there, God. I believe You love me and that You're good. I want to know You like Elaine does, but I'm not sure how to start...

She remembered what Elaine had said about Jesus being the bread of life.

Taste and see...

What did she do when someone offered her a piece of bread?

She accepted it.

Slowly, Jess opened her hands.

And it was just like Elaine had said. When she let go of the shame and the guilt and the anger, God gave her something else.

Himself.

What do you taste, Jessica?

Hope. Joy. Freedom.

And the sweetness of it only made her want more.

Jess wasn't sure how long she sat on the floor, retracing every step that had led her to Winsome Lake.

But did that mean she was supposed to stay here?

"Hello in the house!"

Jess lifted her head at the sound of Merri's voice downstairs and scrubbed away the trails of salt on her cheeks.

The murmur of voices told Jess that Merri wasn't alone. She heard a canine snort and the comforting squeak of Peg's shoes against the linoleum.

Familiar sounds that reached out to Jess.

When she got to the bottom of the stairs, she heard Elaine say, "Jess is in her room, but I don't want to disturb her right now."

"Then we'll wait." This from Nita.

Tears banked in Jess's eyes again. She stepped into the doorway. The Scrappy Ladies had surrounded the island.

Christopher had lifted the lid on the Nesco and was handing Sienna a spoon.

Jess's heart swelled at the sight.

"I'm here."

Six pairs of eyes, seven if Jess included Bosco, swung toward her.

"We came to check on you…" Peg stopped, broadsided by Nita's frown. "I meant the soup. We came to check on the soup."

"The soup is fine," Elaine said. "And so are we."

Peg sniffed. "We'll be the judge of that."

Jess wasn't sure if she was referring to the soup or her and Elaine.

"It's done." Sienna passed the spoon back to Christopher. "Your turn."

"We'll all try it," Nita announced.

Merri already stood on her tiptoes at the cupboard, humming "Ode to Joy" as she grabbed a stack of bowls.

Elaine caught Jess's eye. Her shoulders lifted and fell in a helpless shrug.

Nita took over, ladling soup into the bowls Merri lined up on the counter. She nudged one toward Jess. Sprinkled a handful of oyster crackers on top. "I want to use these up before they go stale."

Jess carried her bowl into the dining room and slipped into a chair at the table.

The others joined her and there was a long moment of silence as everyone admired the soup.

"Thank you, Lord," Merri whispered, "for the blessing of good food and good friends."

The chorus of amens found soft ground in Jess's heart. She swirled her spoon through the soup and took a tentative bite. The eclectic blend of vegetables and seasoning and random pantry items that Jess had thought were a bit risky had turned into something delicious. Something worth savoring.

Like this moment.

"All right." Peg cleared her throat. "Why don't we all just wave at the elephant in the room?"

Jess looked up midbite.

No one was waving. But why was everyone looking at *her*?

"I think you should call your restaurant The House of Frittata," Peg continued. "Breakfast is the most important meal of the day."

"That name would scare off every flannel-wearing, truck-driving male in the county," Nita said bluntly.

"Pancakes," Merri chimed in. "There has to be pancakes."

"Blueberry," Sienna added.

"There isn't a decent steak house for miles," Nita said. "Everyone likes steak."

"Not everyone can afford it, though." Peg fed Bosco a tomato. "People can afford eggs."

Merri pointed her spoon at Nita. "And pancakes."

Jess's eyes met Elaine's across the table. Elaine winced. "I told them."

"She had to," Nita said. "You looked upset when you left this morning and we were worried about you."

"I'm still not sure why you left, though," Peg muttered. "The best thing to do when you have a big decision to make is to talk it over with your friends."

Friends.

When it had happened, she didn't know. But the word warmed Jess's heart.

"It wasn't the restaurant," she said slowly. "I got a call from the woman I used to work for...asking me to come back."

She sent Elaine an apologetic glance. But for some reason Elaine didn't look as stunned as the rest of the people gathered around the table.

"So..." Nita's eyes narrowed as she connected the dots. "It was the job you *left* to come here."

"Actually...she fired me."

"What did you do?" Peg asked. "Bad shrimp puff?"

"Peg!"

"What?" Peg blinked. "Ask my cousin Susie. It happens!"

Jess stifled the laughter rising up in her throat. "I didn't do anything."

"Then it really doesn't make any sense," Peg huffed. "If she fired you, why does she want you back?"

"Because J-Jess is the b-best," Christopher said.

Jess didn't think she had any tears left, but the hum of agreement had her blinking them back again.

She was under no illusions that Gwyneth thought she was the best, but Jess was...useful.

Gwyneth hadn't expressed any remorse for firing her. To Gwyneth, life was a game of strategy. She saw people in terms of what they could do for her. If someone helped her get ahead, they were in. If they made a mistake, they were out.

It depends on your definition of success.

Nick's parting words cut through Jess again.

Gwyneth would look at Elaine Haviland and see a woman who wasn't living up to her potential. A woman who'd run away instead of fighting to keep her place at the top.

Jess saw a woman who knew what was important. Who knew what to let go of and what to keep.

"Whatever you decide, we'll support you," Nita said. "You know that, don't you?"

Jess knew. And the decision she'd thought would be so difficult suddenly wasn't difficult at all.

Her spoon rattled against the bowl as she rose to her feet. "I'll be back in a little while."

The chorus of dismay jolted Violet from her nap.

"You're leaving again?" Merri looked confused.

"Why?" Peg asked.

"Something is missing."

Nita looked down at her bowl. "I don't think anything else would have fit in that Nesco."

Christopher tipped his head. "What does it n-need, Chef?"

Jess felt another tear leak out of her eye. This time she didn't even try to wipe it away.

"Chocolate cake."

She made it to the threshold that divided the dining room and kitchen before Elaine called her name.

"Jess?"

Jess stopped, glanced over her shoulder and saw the grown-up version of Libby Tucker's million-dollar smile.

"Say hello to Nick for us."

Their laughter followed Jess out the door, into an evening ripe with promise.

Into the future.

Epilogue

Jess glanced at the clock and felt her stomach pitch.

Thirty minutes.

The restaurant's grand opening strategically coincided with Memorial Day weekend because she hoped that after a long winter, people were ready to get out of their houses and try something new.

Jess had spent a lot of sleepless nights staring up at the ceiling, asking God for direction, not sure if the lodge was meant to be a supper club again. So when the Scrappy Ladies had taken an informal poll and the people of Winsome Lake had made their wishes known, Jess considered it an answer to her prayer. The restaurant would be open for breakfast and lunch every day except Sunday, from six in the morning until two. The dining room or patio could be reserved for private parties in the evening or on weekends.

Tonight, though, was Jess's dress rehearsal. A special gathering of the people who'd encouraged, supported and sometimes lovingly scolded her over the past nine months.

In a nod to the lodge's history, Jess had decided to host the celebration the evening before the doors opened to the public, with a sampling of the specials she'd be offering during the week.

"Sorry we're late." The back door opened and Nita stumbled in, laden down with grocery bags. "Someone—" she tossed a look at Christopher over her shoulder "—took an awfully long time getting ready."

He tugged off his ball cap and tufts of rooster-red hair popped up. "I w-wanted to look nice."

Jess smiled at him. "And you do."

She'd taken a few extra minutes to French-braid her hair, but it cut down on travel time significantly when you lived in the apartment upstairs.

Jess had helped Nick paint the walls. The furnishings were an eclectic blend of items from the annual church rummage sale and a neighborhood purge of garages and attics.

Elaine had donated her living room couch for the cause because she'd been doing some updates of her own. The house on Woodwind Lane now reflected Elaine's personality but hadn't lost any of its warmth or charm.

Jess loved every inch of her new living quarters, too, but spent the majority of her time on the lower level, experimenting with recipes in the kitchen or staring out the window at the lake.

"Here are the marshmallows and graham crackers you asked for." Nita was already emptying the grocery bags. "I picked up some extra chocolate bars in case you run out."

"Thank you, Nita."

A breeze scented with freshly mown grass preceded Nick's arrival.

Jess's heart, as always, lifted at the sight of him.

Nick greeted Nita and Christopher before turning to Jess. "Do you have a minute?"

"She has two," Nita said. "I'm going to find a table before the crowd gets here." She was trying not to smile as she disappeared through the swinging doors that separated the kitchen from the dining room.

"Chris…you can grab the list on the fridge and start the prep work," Jess said. "I'll be right back."

Christopher bobbed his head. "Yes, Chef."

Nick's hand closed gently around Jess's wrist, and he tugged her into the closet he'd converted into an office. There was barely room to turn around, but when it was Nick, Jess welcomed the close quarters.

He leaned over and whispered in her ear, "Nervous?"

"Terrified." Jess smiled at him. "But it's the good kind."

He planted a quick kiss on her cheek. "You've got plenty of help today. All you have to do is own that dance space."

The reminder of that evening struck a sweet chord inside Jess.

"I have something to show you." She walked over to the narrow table that served double duty as her desk. "The menus came in yesterday."

Nick scanned the first page and then flipped it over. Jess knew the moment he saw it because he pulled in a sharp breath.

"Grandma Jenny's chocolate cake."

"She gets top billing, but I'll take her secret ingredient to the grave," Jess promised.

"You're something else, you know that?" Nick said softly. "Any other surprises I should know about?"

He wiggled his eyebrows and Jess laughed. Felt the tension drain away, which, knowing him, had been Nick's plan all along.

"Only one and it's for my sous-chef. You?"

"Now that you mention it...there is something. Close your eyes."

Jess didn't hesitate. She even tilted her head back in anticipation of his kiss and heard a husky laugh instead.

"We'll put that on hold for a bit, but can I just say that I love knowing there's a Wildcats T-shirt underneath your chef's coat?"

"I have to support my favorite team." Jess heard the sound of paper rustling and resisted the urge to peek.

"Okay."

She opened her eyes and saw the cast-iron bell cradled in Nick's hands.

"I never did find the original, but I hope this one works just as well," he said. "I'll put it up before you open tomorrow and I know you're going to need it, Jessica Keaton. Because people from miles around will be waiting for a table."

"Thank you," Jess whispered. "I love it."

She loved *him*. Like a small town and the Scrappy Ladies and two sweet, incredibly talented teenagers, Nick had claimed a permanent place in her heart.

"Chef?" Christopher called.

"That's your cue." Nick set the bell down and framed her face in his hands. "You and God...you've got this."

After years of feeling like an outsider, of having to take care of herself, it was a truth Jess was still getting used to.

Heather and Amanda, the waitresses Jess had hired and trained, were walking through the back door as she and Nick returned to the kitchen. Neither one of them had worked at a restaurant before, but they were enthusiastic and patient with Christopher, traits Jess considered more important than experience.

Heather, the younger of the two women, had been in Nick's PE class the year he started teaching, but she still giggled and turned pink every time she saw him.

Jess heard another car door slam and looked at Christopher. "You're in charge of the prep station, Chris. It's going to get kind of busy in here, but you know what to do, right?"

"Yes, Chef. Take a d-deep breath and smile." He demonstrated. "I'm g-going to pray, too."

Jess wrapped her arm around his shoulders and gave them a squeeze.

"So am I."

Lights glowed in the windows, and Elaine caught her breath even though she'd been inside the lodge dozens of times over the past few months.

This felt different, though.

"Nervous?"

She glanced at Matthew. "Not a bit. Jess is going to do great."

"You're great." Matthew leaned over and pressed a lingering kiss on Elaine's lips that had her toes curling inside her shoes. "This was a very generous thing you did, Jo."

Elaine couldn't remember exactly when Matthew had started to call her that, but it wasn't long after she'd freely given him access to Libby's diary and her heart. Everyone thought it was a teasing reference to Jo March, the character in *Little Women* who wanted to be a writer, but Elaine knew the truth.

It was short for Julie According to Matthew, the name meant *God will increase*.

And when she looked at her life in Winsome Lake and the people in it, she knew that He had. Oh, He really had.

Over a second bowl of stone soup that night, Elaine had finally told her friends her secret, only to discover they'd been keeping one, too. They already knew.

Merri's brothers, it turned out, had had a poster of Libby Tucker on their bedroom wall. And even though twelve years had gone by since the scandal by the time Elaine had arrived in town and Elaine's looks had matured, Merri claimed there'd been no mistaking those big brown eyes.

When Elaine asked why they hadn't said anything, Nita had shrugged. *It didn't matter. We all have things in our past, so you fit right in.*

Elaine hadn't known whether to laugh or cry, so she'd done both.

"No." Elaine responded to Matthew's comment, not willing to take the credit. "This is a very good thing *God* did. I was ready to let Jess go, remember? Under the guise of doing her a favor, of course, and not because of my fear."

The fact Elaine could find humor in the situation now was more proof of God's goodness. It was funny, how shining a light on something made it seem a lot less scary. Like a child finally gathering the courage to look under the bed only to discover there wasn't a monster there after all.

"Of course." Matthew slanted a look at her. "The opening of the restaurant isn't the only thing we're celebrating tonight, is it?"

"Hilary." Elaine groaned. "What did she tell you and when?"

"Everything. And this morning." Matthew's elbow nudged hers. "Preorder sales are off the charts. Apparently, people want to know the rest of Libby's story."

Elaine wasn't concerned about sales. She planned to step

aside and let God do what He was best at. New beginnings. If her story encouraged someone to trust Him, she was more than ready to share it.

"Tonight is about Jess," Elaine said firmly. "Everything else can wait."

Matthew didn't say anything, and she was surprised he'd given up so easily.

"What's wrong?"

"It means I have to adjust my plan, that's all."

"You had a plan?" Elaine teased. "When were you going to share it with me?"

"That's the part I have to adjust."

"Now you've got me curious. And a little worried," Elaine added. Because Matthew was frowning instead of teasing her back.

He turned in to the parking lot and chose an empty spot near the tree line, away from the cars already parked near the door.

"I'm not getting out of this car until I know what to apologize for," she told Matthew. "If you're not willing to tell me, at least give me a hint. Or a hypothetical situation."

"A hypothetical, hmm?" Matthew cut the engine and turned toward her, shrinking the distance between them so Elaine could see the flecks of gold dust in his whiskey-brown eyes. "Okay. We walk down to the lake and sit by the campfire Nick is going to start after the restaurant closes."

"I'm liking it so far."

"And while everyone is talking and eating dessert—"

"Dessert." Elaine sighed, saw Matthew's expression and chuckled. "Sorry. Keep going."

"I would tell them a story about a man who believed that other people fell in love but never thought it would happen to him. But then he met a woman who was strong and sweet and feisty. For fifty-six years he didn't know she was out there, but now he can't imagine a day without seeing her smile or hearing her laugh. When he's not with her, he thinks about her. And when they're together, it gets harder to leave and...he's been praying she feels the same way about him."

The lump forming in Elaine's throat made it impossible to say that yes, she did, so she reached for his hand instead.

Matthew traced the outline of her fingertips, sowing goose bumps down her arms.

"And then, before I totally lost my courage, I would tell her I love her and that I'm tired of goodbyes. I want mornings and nights and everything in between. And then I'd take out the ring in my pocket and ask her to marry me in front of the people who want her to be happy, because they've become my people, too."

The tears that flooded Elaine's eyes spilled over the breaker of her lashes, but she didn't even try to wipe them away.

"But," Matthew continued softly, "hypothetically speaking, of course, if the timing isn't right, I'd respect her wishes. Because one of the things I love most about this woman is her sensitivity toward other people. But I'd probably be so nervous I would end up blurting out a proposal in an unromantic setting like, I don't know, maybe a parking lot? Because I couldn't wait another minute to find out what her answer would be."

Elaine finally found her voice. "Hypothetically...most definitely...she would say yes."

Matthew lifted her hand and pressed a kiss against her ring finger. And then her lips.

By the time he released her, Elaine had a plan, too. A backyard garden wedding after a short, very short, engagement.

"Matthew...you're not the only one who thought a bonfire would be the perfect setting for a proposal."

His eyes went wide. "Nick?"

"He showed me the ring yesterday."

Matthew threw back his head and laughed. "That would definitely be one for the books."

It certainly would.

"Matt?"

"Yes."

"You don't know what I was going to say!"

"It doesn't matter."

Elaine's love for Matthew, which she'd tried to keep contained for months because she thought it was meant for young people like Nick and Jess, who had years and years ahead of them, overflowed its banks.

"Let Nick go first tonight."

He grinned. "Done."

Jess plated the last piece of chocolate cake and stepped back from the counter, hoping Nick's Grandma Jenny would have approved.

She'd shooed everyone out of the kitchen five minutes ago. Now there was only one more thing…

"Nick said you wanted to talk to me. Is everything all right?"

The knot in Jess's stomach unraveled a little as Elaine walked into the kitchen, the hitch in her step barely noticeable now.

She even looked a little red carpet tonight with her hair swept up in a loose topknot and wearing the chic, wraparound dress that Sienna had helped pick out when she was home on spring break. The spring air held a bit of a chill, but Jess guessed the glow in Elaine's cheeks had more to do with her escort for the evening than the temperature outside.

Matthew had become a fixture in Winsome Lake over

the past few months, helping with last-minute details and the occasional crisis and slowly winning Elaine's heart in the process.

In that way he reminded Jess of a certain football coach.

Elaine's gaze traveled around the kitchen before lighting on Jess again. "It looks to me like you've got everything under control," she said. "Did you need something?"

"I need *you*." Jess smiled. "Peg told me they're expecting some sort of speech."

Laughter danced in Elaine's eyes. "It's a good thing I'm the silent partner, then, isn't it?"

Jess's throat tightened. Elaine was more than the co-owner of the restaurant. In spite of the gap in their ages, she'd become Jess's closest friend.

Like love, it was a gift she hadn't expected.

You are good, God. You are so good.

"Oh no. Yesterday you said, and I quote, 'We're in this together.' That definitely includes speeches."

The double doors swung open, and Christopher appeared, the toque perched on his head almost quivering in anticipation. "Everyone is h-here, Chef."

"We'll be right out," Jess promised.

Elaine smiled when the doors snapped shut again. "Does he know yet?"

"I'm pretty good at keeping secrets, remember?"

"It's all right as long as they're the good kind." Elaine's smile moved to her eyes, hinting she had one of her own.

Jess tipped her head. "What's going on?"

"The opening of your restaurant." Elaine linked her arm through Jess's. "Dreams coming true."

Well, Elaine had been instrumental in making that happen for Jess. It seemed only right that Christopher would know what it felt like, too.

They walked into the dining room together and even though Jess saw the result of Nick's handiwork every day, it till took her breath away.

Candles flickered on tables dressed in crisp white linen. The lipstick-pink tulips that had been growing in wild abandon along Elaine's fence filled a row of glass jars on the fireplace mantel now.

Everyone had gathered around the old bar overlooking the lake. Merri and Nita and Peg sat shoulder to shoulder, a beautiful trio of mismatched pearls. Anthony Silva and Nick's parents were talking to Sienna. She'd moved into Nita's spare bedroom and become a surrogate big sister to Christopher while she was home for the summer.

For a moment Jess let their laughter flow over her. Basked in the warmth of the familiar and the new.

Elaine cleared her throat, and even though the sound barely registered over the classical music playing in the background, everyone stopped talking and turned toward them expectantly.

"I'm so glad you're all here tonight," Elaine said. "Jess will be serving tonight's meal family style because…" Her voice faltered a little. "I believe I speak for both of us when I say that's what you are. Family."

Elaine turned to Jess and nodded. A signal that it was her turn to say something now.

Except…she couldn't. Not with a lump the size of a grapefruit lodged in her throat. Jess had half a speech prepared, but the words scattered in a dozen different directions.

"Thank you…" It came out garbled, but it was the best Jess could do.

"We were glad to help," Peg piped up. She grinned at Jess. "Can we eat now?"

Laughter bubbled up inside Jess even as tears zigzagged down her cheeks. "Yes…"

She had to lift her voice above the cheering and applause and swept her arm toward the tables.

"Welcome to Christopher's."

★ ★ ★ ★ ★

LOVE INSPIRED

Stories to uplift and inspire

Fall in love with Love Inspired—
inspirational and uplifting stories of faith
and hope. Find strength and comfort in
the bonds of friendship and community.
Revel in the warmth of possibility and the
promise of new beginnings.

Sign up for the Love Inspired newsletter
at **LoveInspired.com** to be the first
to find out about upcoming titles,
special promotions and exclusive content.

CONNECT WITH US AT:

 Facebook.com/LoveInspiredBooks

Twitter.com/LoveInspiredBks

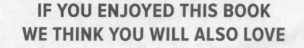
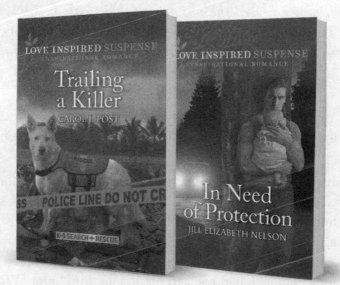

New guardian to her twin nieces, Hannah Antonicelli is determined to keep her last promise to her late sister—that she'll never reveal the identity of their father. But when Luke Hutchenson is hired as a handyman at her work and begins to bond with the little girls, hiding that he's their uncle isn't easy...

Read on for a sneak peek at
Finding a Christmas Home *by Lee Tobin McClain!*

On Wednesday after work, Hannah drove toward home, the twins in the back seat, and tried not to be nervous that Luke was in the front seat beside her.

"I really appreciate this," he said. His car hadn't started this morning, and he'd walked the three miles to Rescue Haven.

Of course, Hannah had insisted on driving him home. What else could she do? It was cold outside, spitting snow, and he was her next-door neighbor.

"I hate to ask another favor," he said, "but could you stop by Pasquale's Pizza on the way?"

"No problem." She took a left and drove the two blocks to the only nonchain pizza place in Bethlehem Springs.

He jumped out, and she turned back to check on the twins, trying not to watch Luke as he headed into the shop. He was good-looking, of course. Kind, appreciative and strong. And he had the slightest swagger in his walk that was masculine and appealing.

But he was also about to go visit his brother, Bobby, if he kept his promise to his ailing father. And when she'd heard about that visit, it had been a wake-up call: she shouldn't get too close with him. The fewer chances she had to spill the beans about Bobby being the twins' father, the better.

He came out of the pizza shop quickly—he must have called ahead—carrying a big flat box and a white bag. What would it be like if this was a family scenario, if they were Mom and Dad and kids, stopping for takeout on the way home from work?

She couldn't help it. Her chest filled with longing.

He climbed into her small car, juggling the large flat box to make it fit without encroaching on the gearshift.

She had to laugh at the size of his meal. "Hungry?"

"Are you?" He opened the box a little, and the rich, garlicky fragrance of Pasquale's special sauce filled the car.

Her stomach growled, loudly.

"Pee-zah!" Addie shouted from the back seat.

"Peez!" Emmy added, almost as loud.

"That's just cruel," she said as she pulled the car back onto the road and steered toward Luke's place. "You're tempting us. I may have to order some when I get these girls home."

"No, you won't," he said. "This is for all of us. The least I can do is feed you, after you drove me around."

Her stomach gave a little leap, and not just about the prospect of pizza. Why was he inviting her to have dinner with him? Was there an ulterior motive? And if there was, would she mind?

Don't miss
Finding a Christmas Home *by Lee Tobin McClain,*
available October 2021 wherever
Love Inspired books and ebooks are sold.

LoveInspired.com

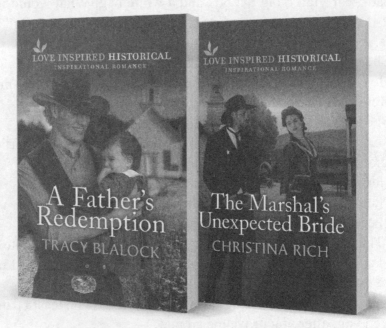